Letters from the Gods

D.C. BOND

D Bond & Associates, LLC

Published in the United States by D Bond & Associates, LLC.

Paperback edition ISBN: 979-8-9987597-1-0.

Hardback edition ISBN: 979-8-9987597-2-7.

E-book edition ISBN: 979-8-9987597-0-3.

1st edition 2025.

Contents

EGYPT
PYRAMIDS AND TEMPLES
ANCIENT CIVILIZATIONS MAP

King of Maps Original

Mediterranean Sea

Alexandria
Rosetta
Damietta

Tanis
Per-ramses

Heliopolis
Cairo
Per-hotep
Giza
Saqqara
Dashur
Memphis
Obelisc Heliopolis

Menkaure
Khafra
Khufu
Sphinx

Lower Egypt

Djoser (Saqqara)

Red (Dashur)
Bent (Dashur)

Meidum
Lahun
Herakleopolis

Meidum

Beni Hasan
Hermopolis
Amarna

Seti I Temple Cult of Osiris

Asyut
Badari
Qau
Akhmim

Karnak Temple

Thinis

Abydos

Dendera

Hatshepsut Temple

Thebes
Karnak Ipet-sut
Luxor waset
Esna
Tod
Hieronkonpolis
Edfu

Luxor Temple Ipet-resyt

Red Sea

Temple of Ramses III

Upper Egypt

Kom Ombo

Temple of Horus

Aswan
Philae

Temple of Kom Ombo

Ramses II

Abu Simbel

Philae Temple

King

Prologue

Pharaoh Khufu was not known as the most charitable of pharaohs. He knew his reign had been a disaster filled with lost battles and corruption. He knew the people hated him and his family. Khufu didn't care. The population existed for his pleasure. He often conscripted an entire town's population for labor building his vanity projects. Khufu felt that Egypt was nothing but a sinking swamp surrounded by desert. The people were lazy and were in constant revolt. The Upper Kingdom was already in open rebellion, and there was talk that a new pharaoh, blessed by the gods, would soon rise up.

Khufu had reigned for over twenty years, and now was his time. He had been ordered to meet Osiris in person. Pharaoh knew the secrets of the gods that had been passed down from his father and their fathers for thousands of years. Osiris and his people were not from Egypt, but from a place far away in the night sky. Now he was to meet one of these gods for the first time. Only priests had been allowed to attend and gaze upon the countenance of the gods for hundreds of years. In the past, when there were more gods in Egypt, they were often seen among the people. Their numbers had been dwindling for a thousand years.

Osiris's priests told Khufu that Osiris would be traveling to the Great Pyramid and stopping at Khufu's palace for an audience. Khufu spared no expense. He decorated the streets and prepared for a festival. It seemed the gods had once again decided to reveal themselves to the people.

Khufu spent a week barking orders at everyone in sight. This festival had to be the biggest and best. Dancers and musicians were brought in from all over the kingdom. The fattest cows and goats were slaughtered in sacrifice and would be served to Osiris and his retinue.

Khufu was told to expect Osiris in the afternoon, and he thought he was prepared until the six Osiris priests entered the palace, two of them blowing trumpets.

One priest garbed in shiny gold sequins stepped forward.

"I am Hem-netjer Osiris, High Priest of the Almighty. Attendees of Khufu, our Netjer Osiris has come and wishes an audience with the pharaoh. You will leave now."

Everyone looked at one another, then at the pharaoh, who had a confused look on his face.

"But, esteemed Hem-netjer, I was expecting the mighty Osiris to attend these festivities. They are in his honor," said Khufu.

"Osiris requires none of this. He will meet you in your apartments."

The priest stood there momentarily, then, seeing that people were confused, he loudly clapped his hands. This caused a number of the attendees to jump and begin scurrying out of the room. Khufu, realizing all of his hard work was in vain, started complaining.

"Does the great and powerful Osiris need anything else? Or should I go sit in the study and wait for him?"

"That will be acceptable," the priest said.

In a huff, Khufu dismissed his guards and staff and retired to his rooms. Two hours later, the Hem-netjer entered and announced Osiris.

"Pharaoh Khufu, I present Osiris, Netjer of Resurrection and the Afterlife, to you."

The god bent over to walk through the door as he entered the room. Khufu stood, his legs shaking in fear, as he watched the giant creature casually stroll into his home and sit on his couches. The god then motioned for Khufu to sit. Osiris looked in many ways like any other Egyptian, other than the fact that he was nearly eight feet tall, had pale-green skin, and had eyes more like a cat than anything resembling a human. He wore an elaborate golden headdress that gave him an extra two feet of height, and it was impossible to determine his age.

"Pharaoh Khufu, the netjeru that you and your people know will no longer inhabit Egypt."

The voice seemed to appear in Khufu's mind. Osiris hadn't even opened his mouth.

"Great Osiris, how is it that I can hear your voice when you do not speak?"

"You can understand me because I am directing my thoughts into your mind."

"Please, great Osiris. I cannot face my people and tell them the netjeru have abandoned Egypt," said Khufu.

"We have been in this place shaping your people and this kingdom to become one of the mightiest to ever exist in this world. We have been guiding all of mankind for nearly eight thousand years. Our time here is at an end. We made a covenant with your forefathers, Khufu. The pact states that in exchange for the labor of your people to help us build the gateway, we agreed to accept your pharaohs into the afterlife and resurrect them to live with us as they lived here. I am the last of us. Our pact ends with me."

Khufu's eyes grew large as he listened. "Osiris, does this mean I am not to be accepted into the afterlife with my ancestors?"

"Pharaoh Khufu, I will be departing through the hidden chamber in four days. When I activate the pyramid, everything in the pyramid's chambers will be sent along with me to the time and place of my choosing. In that time, if you have prepared the chamber in the portal, as you have been instructed, you may be the last pharaoh to travel to the afterlife from the Great Pyramid. A thunderstorm will be the harbinger of our departure. Once I am gone, the entrance to the main chamber will be sealed and forgotten in time. The Osiris Cult will destroy all the records that speak of us and how we came to build the pyramids. Your people will live on without us."

Abruptly, Osiris stood and walked away. Khufu was distraught with fear and doubt. As soon as the Osiris priests had all left, he began yelling at his servants.

"Bring my Hem-netjer, the Tjaty, and the Imi-r Mesha at once. We must prepare for my funeral."

Chapter One

Awakening

James's eyes slowly opened. Everything was pitch-black and silent. A metallic scent mixed with moisture, dust, and an ozone tang was sharp like the air after a lightning strike. A wave of panic hit.

"Where in the hell am I?" he rasped, voice echoing off unseen walls. His hands fumbled for his satchel, fingers trembling as they closed around his trusted Zippo. *Snap, flick*, the flame sputtered to life, a frail yellow glow in the void.

"That's right, the chamber," James muttered, steadying his breath.

The walls sloped inward toward the ceiling, pressing closer with every flicker of the Zippo's light. The room was barely wider than his out-stretched arms and felt like it was closing in, its surfaces shimmering. His throat tightened. The air was stale and heavy, as if the tomb itself was breathing down his neck. Claustrophobia, his old nemesis, sank its teeth in. He could almost hear the stone groaning, ready to crush him. He staggered to his feet, the walls seeming to tilt, shrinking the space to a coffin's width. Thoughts of a crowded Egyptian prison cell were at the forefront of his mind.

"Not now," he growled, slamming a palm against the cool gold to anchor himself, his pulse fluttering like a trapped bird's wings.

The small flicker of the Zippo's yellow and red flame reflected on the richly adorned walls. James reached for the LED lamp he'd left on the sarcophagus. It was dead, not even a flicker. A shake and a few frantic toggles of the switch confirmed either the batteries were done or the wiring was fried. The sarcophagus gleamed under the Zippo's flame, its gold sheen absurdly lavish.

No way it's solid, he reasoned, *just wood with gold sheets, has to be. If it were pure gold, it'd be worth hundreds of millions.* The symbols etched in relief on the walls and sarcophagus tugged at his memory—familiar, yet alien, and definitely not New Kingdom script.

James found himself a little disoriented, kneeling next to the sarcophagus.

"Holy shit, Khalid, what the hell was that? Khalid... Kal, did you feel that?" he called, voice cracking.

Silence answered. The tunnel entrance, which had been wide open moments ago, with Khalid monitoring air quality, was now a seamless wall of stone. No light came through, not a sound from the crew. His gut twisted. The space felt wrong, too still, like a void swallowing him whole.

"This isn't right," he whispered, the Zippo trembling in his grip as he stumbled toward the sealed door, its edges becoming more defined with his every step.

The claustrophobia hit harder now, a vise around his chest. Once a marvel, the room's gilded walls loomed like a predator's jaws. The sloping ceiling felt inches from his head.

"Too tight," he gasped, sweat beading on his brow despite the chill.

He'd faced tombs before, snakes, spiders, and dust but always with an exit in sight. Now trapped like a rat in a cage, his breath came in shallow bursts. He pressed his back to the sarcophagus, its cold bulk a lifeline, and squeezed his eyes shut, fighting the urge to claw at the walls.

"Get it together, Jim," he hissed, but the air felt thinner, the silence louder, every creak of his boots amplifying the tomb's suffocating grip.

"Ah, damn, my head's swimming," he muttered, sinking to the floor as dizziness overtook him. He collapsed again, the Zippo slipping from his hand, flame snuffing out. Darkness swallowed him again, a black tide pulling him under. When he woke, disoriented, he groped blindly for the lighter with his heart pounding. His fingers brushed the smooth steel, and with a *snap, flick*, light flared.

"Thank God," he breathed, though the relief was fleeting. The tomb's confines still loomed.

James rose unsteadily and shuffled to the sealed door, checking his Rolex Explorer II at 3:45 p.m. The union laborers had been eating lunch at noon when he entered, their ritual as predictable as the sunrise.

"Ten minutes down the ramps, fifteen to find the lever...a few moments before the noise," he calculated. "Three and a half hours out cold?"

But as he stared at the sealed stone, a wild thought gnawed at him. The air was too crisp, the silence too absolute—no hum of generators, no clatter of tools. He pressed his ear to the door and heard nothing.

"Khalid wouldn't ditch me," he murmured, confusion blooming into something sharper. The glyphs gleamed brightly under the Zippo, their precision uncanny. They were not hand drawn but machined, like something from a lost age or a future he could fathom. A chill raced up his spine, not only from the tomb's grip but also from a dawning awe.

"No way," he whispered, tracing a symbol that wasn't 20th Dynasty, too angular, too perfect. His mind reeled, piecing together the impossible: the chamber's hum, the flash before he blacked out, the sealed door.

"Did I ..." he laughed, a shaky, half-mad cackle. "Holy shit, am I in Ancient Egypt? Did it work?"

The idea was insane: time travel, straight out of his wildest theories, the ones colleagues had mocked for decades. But the strange air, the pristine glyphs, the missing crew... It all clicked with a terrifying thrill. He staggered back, awestruck, the tomb's walls no longer a prison but a portal, his heart pounding with dread and wonder at the reality he'd stumbled into.

He thought back to what had happened before everything went dark. He had reached over and touched the symbol on the sarcophagus, and it had come alive in his head. He had been thinking about his mom and how amazing it had been to visit the tomb of Ramesses IV when he was a child. James reached to touch the same symbol, but this time there was nothing. It was as if whatever had sent him to this place simply went dead.

This project was funded by a US-based firm that liked to keep all construction in-house, even flying the entire crew in from out of the country after completing another secret project. A few locals were hired for cooking and housekeeping to keep the nearby population happy.

How Black Sands Corp. was able to get the Egyptian government to allow this exploration was a mystery, and James was convinced that Black Sands "owned" most of the bureaucracy that would have objected to most US firms exploring ancient Egyptian sites. Regardless of how this dig was allowed, it was happening, and James had to be a part of it.

They had come to his house without even a phone call, in two large black SUVs loaded with six big operator types. To James, it seemed like something out of a Tom Clancy book. After the massive, muscly dudes climbed out of the vehicles, a small, thin man with glasses slid out of the back seat. He was blond and blue-eyed, and after exiting, he gazed at James as if trying to size up the man. He wore black slacks with a black blazer and a white button-up dress shirt. The top three buttons were undone, exposing a large medallion on a gold chain that he was obviously very proud of.

"James!" It was a statement, not a question. "I am thrilled to have found you."

James recognized the CEO of Black Sands Corp., who had him thrown in prison just a few years before.

With a slightly tilted head and confused expression, James said, "What in the world could you possibly be doing here?"

"That, my friend, is an excellent question. I know we have had our differences in the past, but do you perhaps have a place to sit and discuss a few things?"

James collected himself. Being locked in a small space was exactly the kind of thing he feared most. It was ironic that James, an Ancient Egypt historian and tomb explorer, was claustrophobic. Dealing with snakes and spiders was part of the job. Tight spaces were also not a dealbreaker. Being locked in a tight space with no means or understanding of how to get out was definitely a dealbreaker.

Luckily, the Zippo had fluid and was still working, and the small head-lamp was lying on the floor near where James had passed out. He collected his headlamp to begin inspecting the door. He worked to find the on button, which would not have been a problem with his regular headlamp. This was one of the fancy gadgets that Black Sands had issued and was way too technical for something that was supposed to simply light up. He toggled the switch back and forth a few times, but nothing happened.

First, the lamp isn't working, and now my headlamp. Could I have been exposed to an electromagnetic pulse? James had theorized in a published paper that the pyramids had been designed to harvest and store electromagnetism collected from the stars. An EMP (electromagnetic pulse) would have likely destroyed the circuitry of any electrical appliance in the pyramid.

The door itself, like all the walls in the room, was covered in gold. The symbols looked much less like pictures and more like a style of letter, laid out similarly to normal Egyptian hieroglyphics. There was an exactness and precision you wouldn't see in a normal hand-drawn glyph.

James stuck his nose up to the edges of the door and detected a faint scent of fresh air. The claustrophobia was beginning to kick in again. He didn't panic outwardly, but the fight-or-flight sense started working him up.

"Hello, can anyone hear me?" No sound came back.

It was beginning to get serious. No lights, no sound, limited fresh air.

Okay, think. This is not only a burial chamber. There is much more going on here. A burial chamber would not have a way for the mummy to get out, would it?

James knew tombs would never have a two-way door to the sarcophagus room. Some side rooms might have false doors or even small windows or openings so that the faithful could send offerings, but never an actual exit.

If this isn't a burial chamber, then maybe there is a lever or something like there was on the outside, James thought.

Groping his way around the reliefs and glyphs on the wall, he found a familiar symbol. Yes, this was the same symbol that was on the exterior. It was the glyph that James had recognized as "door" or "portal." He pressed carefully on the glyph, which seemed to depress for a second, then popped out. With a slow twist, he manipulated the lever until it stopped and gave a slight pull. Air and dust swirled around. It reminded him of some sci-fi shows he had watched where people opened an airlock on a spacecraft. *Swoosh*, the sudden movement of stale air put out the flame on his Zippo. Suddenly, darkness enveloped James. *Snap, flick*, again the Zippo came to life.

How long does a Zippo's fuel last?

He needed to figure out how to get out of this newly illuminated tunnel. The tunnel was long, and the chamber was near the pyramid's center. It also had a very steep incline and at least two areas that required ladders to descend when they were entering earlier that day. The first section of the tunnel was level until he reached his first obstacle. There was a ten-foot wall ahead of him. On the way down this morning, an aluminum ladder was waiting for him. This time, there was nothing.

He stepped back a few feet to examine the situation. The tunnel was narrow at this point, around four feet wide.

How the hell am I going to climb that?

The walls in this area were very smooth sandstone. Even a bit chalky, as sandstone can get. His thoughts brought him back to when he was a child, maybe ten years old. There had been a hallway in his parents' apartment about the same width as the tunnel that he and his friends used to sort of "spider climb" by bracing their hands and feet against the opposing walls and using that friction to work their way to the top. *That could work here.*

He got into position. This was going to be a bit harder than he remembered. Somehow, a flexible and limber ten-year-old had a leg up, so to speak, on a six-foot-three thirty-year-old with a beer gut. James wasn't in bad shape, actually, he was pretty athletic. The years of working with his hands had developed the kind of strength that comes from real work.

"Here goes nothing," he said out loud as he moved into position.

He tried to hold the lighter in his teeth and realized it was an incredibly stupid idea, singeing his eyebrows. The only plan he could come up with was to put out the Zippo, stick it in his pocket, and climb up blind. The thought freaked him out a bit, but what else could he do? *Snap!* The Zippo was off. The darkness moved in. Instantly, James's heart started beating rapidly, and sweat started dripping from his brow. He felt for the walls and, with a little jump, wedged his feet in and was able to climb his way up the first two or three feet.

I can do this, he thought, as he moved one hand and then the next up.

One foot, then the other. Little by little, he was making some progress. He figured he was nearing the top and reached for the ledge. It was almost within his grasp but didn't really allow for a better handhold than the friction the walls were already affording.

He flipped his canvas satchel onto the ledge and ended up climbing several feet over the ledge before moving forward until he felt he was no longer over the abyss below. He then slowly started to lower himself onto the floor. He felt he must have climbed a bit higher than he thought and tried to dangle his foot down to find the floor. To his satisfaction, the floor was right there, and he was able to let go and drop the three or four inches to the ground.

Snap, flick, the Zippo ignited. James was at the bottom of a steep ramp. This time, it wasn't a chore to brace against the wall and walk up the incline. He remembered from his original descent that there was only one more wall to climb and then a steep ramp to the outer wall of the pyramid. The next wall was a breeze after dealing with the first one. This wall was only about seven feet high, and he could set the Zippo on the ledge above him, then climb both walls to get to the top.

After ascending the last ramp, James found himself still in pitch black, with an enormous block of stone blocking his path. Strangely enough, this stone differed from what he remembered from the original expedition. This was a much smoother stone, like the smooth Tura limestone, in which the Great Pyramid had been originally clad. Nothing like that had been seen for a thousand years. Over the past three thousand years, people had pilfered these beautiful, white, smooth stones to build temples, palaces, and later mosques.

James held the Zippo up to inspect the stone. The flame began to flicker and was blown out an instant later. Darkness again enveloped him, but something caught his eye. There was light coming from near the base of the stone. He got on all fours and peered out of a rectangular-shaped hole, maybe eight inches wide and four inches high. With another quick *snap, flick,* the Zippo came to life again. He looked around the immediate area near the little window to see many small statues strewn about. There were also bundles of what must have been flowers, dried up, near the small opening.

When I found this space a couple of years ago, there was no place where light could have reached this spot. Someone must have hidden it in the past, the future, or... He was having a hard time wrapping his head around the situation. *This is a tomb. Perhaps this is one of the false doors that were often installed in order for the Ka or Ba, the spirit or soul of the deceased, to travel in and out of its tomb. People would have left offerings.*

James peered out again, and what he saw was hopeful. It was night, and there were no generators or worksite trailers, but some campfires were burning in the distance.

Campfires mean people are cooking and being warmed nearby.

James lowered his mouth to the little window.

"Hello!" he cried out at the top of his lungs. "Hello, is anyone out there?" Nothing.

He struggled to push against the stone, which wouldn't budge. He wedged his back against a nearby wall and pressed his feet against the stone with everything he had. It still wouldn't budge. He was going to need some help if he was going to get out of this damn tomb.

James sat in near darkness. The flame of the wonderful Zippo flickered, creating eerie shadows on the walls of the tunnel. He sat there wondering what he could do and what it would take to get out of this mess. But as the shadows danced, a deeper wonder crept in, overtaking his fear. The impossible beauty of the moment began to sink into his bones.

He leaned closer to the window, the Zippo's light trembling in his grip, and stared at the campfires flickering in the distance, like stars fallen to Earth.

"This can't be real," he breathed, as if speaking too loudly might shatter the spell.

The air carried a scent, not of diesel fumes or modern dust but of wood smoke, baked earth, and something ancient, even alive. His mind spun, grappling with the absurdity: those lights in the distance, the pristine Tura limestone, the glyphs sharper than any he'd studied in ruins.

"I've really gone back...haven't I?" he murmured, awe swelling in his chest.

He pressed a hand to the cool stone, sensing a time he'd only dreamed of, New Kingdom Egypt, the reign of Ramesses IV, alive and breathing beyond this wall. The realization hit him like a thunderclap, and he laughed.

"Twelve years of BS, and here I am," he said, shaking his head in disbelief.

He'd spent years chasing theories of pyramid portals, enduring jibes and sneers on the forums, yet now he sat in the belly of history itself. The campfires weren't Black Sands's—they were ancient hearths, tended by hands that carved the glyphs he'd spent his life decoding.

"This is Egypt," he marveled, voice cracking with reverence, "not some dusty relic, but the real damn thing, alive and untouched."

The weight of it pressed against his ribs, experiencing the sheer magnitude of standing at civilization's cradle, a witness to a world he'd only known through faded texts.

He traced a glyph near the window—Khufu's cartouche, vivid as if inked yesterday.

"I'm here," he whispered in awe. "I'm actually here three thousand years before my time."

The thought was dizzying, a cascade of wonder drowning his earlier panic. He imagined the Nile flowing beyond, unmarred by modern dams, its banks teeming with reed boats and priests chanting to Amun-Ra. The stars outside were brighter and sharper than he'd ever seen, the same stars that guided Khufu's builders and that lit the nights of a living pharaoh.

"What the hell do I do with this?" he asked the silence, half-laughing, half-reeling, his Zippo's flame a tiny beacon in a reality too vast, too miraculous, to fully grasp.

CHAPTER TWO

Growing Up

1999 AD

James was born in the mid-80s, right in the midst of hair bands and acid-washed jeans. He was from a small town near Cairo, the son of an American expatriate and an Egyptian mother. His father, Hank, was an engineering contractor who worked on local infrastructure projects, while his mother, Sara, came from a long line of Egyptian historians. Even as a child, James was fascinated by his mom's stories of pharaohs, pyramids, mummies, and ancient mysteries.

James's mom was well known in the archaeological community. She would occasionally go to dig sites to add insight into finds and sometimes even help with excavations. She was always sure to pull James from classes and bring him along. She knew the information he would learn on a dig site would be far more impactful than anything he could learn in a classroom.

James was twelve when his mom decided it was time for the family to visit some Egyptian historical ruins. She hoped to further James's love of her own passion. James had often been around the Egyptian countryside while visiting job sites with his father or dig sites and museums with his mother. This trip would be different. He was excited to see the temples, tombs, and ruins of which his mother often spoke. They rode in Hank's work truck, a white Ford F150 with his company's logo on the side. It wasn't brand new, but it seemed that way compared to the other vehicles on the road to Luxor. It was a long trip from their apartment in Cairo. They drove all day, stopping only for gas, food, and the occasional bathroom break.

They passed countless irrigation canals along the way, ferrying the Nile's riches through the land. The road was lined with concrete homes, all in some nearly complete construction phase. Hank looked in his rearview mirror and noticed the confusion on James's face.

"You have a question, son?" he said.

"Yeah, Dad. Why are all the homes here unfinished? It looks like they built up three or four stories high and have rebar sticking out of the roof like they are building higher."

Hank snickered. "There are two main reasons they look like that. Many of these families live together, with generations living in the same building. Whenever they need more room, they add to the top. Also, at some point, they adjusted the tax code to say that if a building is not one hundred percent complete, they do not have to pay as much property tax as if it were finished."

"So, everyone in Egypt is cheating on their taxes?" James said.

Hank laughed, "No, it is a clever way that local politicians can fleece rich hotels and corporations that would never leave a building unfinished. Those people will pay their full taxes, and the locals only need to pay a part. The politicians sort of wink at the residents, and they all know the drill."

"Isn't that unfair to the people who want to do the right thing?"

"You are twelve, James." He looked at Sara, and she nodded as if to confirm his age. "You are going to learn that rarely in life will you find that things are fair and never, ever expect them to be."

They drove on in silence for another few hours. James sat quietly in the back seat. He was used to American TV and the bustle of downtown Cairo. It always amazed him that stepping out of the city felt like traveling back in time by one hundred years. Dirty children of his age were in the fields behind their family homes, gathering crops and tilling. Donkeys and carts were the primary mode of transportation in these rural areas. You would see many old cars and trucks, but gas was expensive. Grass for donkeys was everywhere.

James couldn't help but feel wonder at the whole thing. Entering the ancient city of Luxor was awe-inspiring. As the Nile gently meandered to the coast, it bore witness to the rhythmic dance of seasonal floods that sculpted a vast, fertile delta and the ebb and flow of one of the world's greatest civilizations. Luxor was sort of the summer home for some pharaohs, and others would visit during festivals or to celebrate victories in battle.

His head was on a swivel, taking in the vistas. As they drove through the city, they saw an awesome mix of the ancient and modern. They passed massive obelisks and avenues lined with hundreds of sphinxes right next to contemporary high-rise hotels.

"Tomorrow, we will visit Karnak first and then go to the Valley of the Kings," said his mother.

"Can't we go now?" James said, wide-eyed and sitting up at attention in his seat.

"No, dear, we have to let your father have some sleep. He's getting old."

"Humph, old my ass!" Hank said as he waved away the bellhop and grabbed all three large suitcases himself.

The bellhop looked a bit shocked, as if he would surely lose his job.

"Don't worry, son. I'm in the prime of my life," he said as he struggled toward the stairs.

James didn't know if he was talking to him or the bellboy. "What floor are we on?" Hank asked Sara.

"Three."

Hank had been walking toward the stairs and, in one smooth move, changed course and beelined to the elevator. Sara glanced at James and gave him a sly wink.

The next morning, James was up at first light. He jumped into his clothes, ignoring any personal hygiene, and walked straight to the door that divided the two rooms.

"Mom, Dad, are you up? We need to get going." If they were going to fit both Karnak and the Valley of the Kings into one day, he knew they had better get started.

"Go away, pest," a grouchy voice muttered.

James barged in. He knew that was his invitation to cannonball into his parents' bed. Luckily, Hank and Sara expected this.

"Fine, let's get moving," said Hank.

The first stop was Karnak. James had read all about the great holy city. Built over thousands of years, the pharaohs of the ancient era built onto this vast, sprawling temple city. James was speechless, looking up at the hundreds of pillars, each covered with hieroglyphics. He stopped to read a few, but only for a moment. There was so much more to see.

The Tiberius family had forgone the usual tour guides and opted for Sara's detailed stories of wars, lives, and loves past. There was so much to take in. James closed his eyes and listened to the noise surrounding him. He imagined he was back in Ancient Egypt with people and priests going about their daily business. It felt so real.

The tour ended in a small chamber. Sara called it the Holy of Holies—the most sacred place in Karnak. Only the highest priests and the pharaoh could enter. In ancient times, it was thought to house a statue of Amun-Ra, the God of Gods. It was believed that the gods would manifest most fully in this temple, making it the focal point for its spiritual energy.

Sara finished her lectures and said, "Next stop, the Valley of the Kings."

It was only midday, and James was not happy about leaving Karnak, but he was too excited about visiting the tombs, so he didn't complain. They climbed back into the Ford and headed across the great Nile River. James looked out as they passed an armada of fishing boats and a few small river cruise ships. James imagined the cruise ships were Pharaoh's mighty oceangoing fleet, armed with catapults and bowmen with flaming arrows. The ride to the valley continued to be amazing. They passed massive statues of two seated men in beautiful headdresses.

"Wow, Mom, look at that."

"Those are the Colossi of Memnon, the guards protecting the temples and tombs," said Sara. They drove a little longer through ancient ruins on the left and right until they came to a gate and a visitor center. They hopped aboard an open tram and headed further to the tombs.

Sara planned to walk Hank and James through each and every tomb. A couple were chained shut, but these were not an obstacle for Sara, who walked right up to a guard and pointed at the tomb. They were immediately let in.

James thought, *Mom's important here. She's a boss.*

Even Hank was impressed and followed a few steps behind her in awe of her knowledge. Sara walked at a steady pace and read and explained the drawings. James tried to do the same but hadn't quite made it that far in his studies.

After a couple of tombs, she began collecting a following. Tourists were bleeding off from their guides and were quietly listening to Sara's vast knowledge of the history they saw in real-time. The stairs down to the ramps to the tombs were far steeper and longer than either James or Hank had expected. The final tomb of the day was Ramesses IV. Sara had saved it for last because she knew it was the one James was the most eager to see. It was getting near evening, and the park would be closing soon.

James and Hank were visibly getting tired, but when Sara mentioned the tomb of Ramesses IV, James sprang to attention. Upon entering, he walked down the first flight of stairs and a long ramp. James noticed that there were entire books of knowledge painted onto the walls and ceiling of the structure. At the bottom, upon entering the burial chamber, he read symbols that said things like "*The Book of the Dead*" on one wall, "*The Book of the Night*" on the ceiling, and "*The Book of the Caverns*" on yet another wall. He thought about asking his mother what it all meant, but he would have to wait. He saw an enormous stone coffin. This would have held Ramesses IV's sarcophagus and mummified body, but it had been pilfered, maybe one thousand years ago or more, by tomb raiders.

James pointed to a glyph on the coffin that he didn't recognize. "Mom, what is that symbol?"

Sara paused and knelt to look. Her fingers traced a faint, angular glyph that was out of place and didn't match the others.

"This one's strange," she quietly murmured almost to herself, with a furrowed brow. "It's not New Kingdom. It looks modern. I have been finding these symbols often lately. The older the tomb, the more likely we are to find some of these strange symbols. Dr. Geist and our corporate sponsors don't want me to talk about them, but between you and me, I think they are old, very old, in fact."

She glanced over her shoulder as if expecting someone to be listening in.

"But that's not something you need to worry about, Jimmy. That's my puzzle to work out." She changed the subject and said, "In fact, the only tomb in the valley that had not been robbed was that of Tutankhamen. His tomb had been covered by a landslide and forgotten over time. It hadn't been rediscovered until the 1920s by an English archaeologist named Howard Carter."

James was speechless, and in awe of all he had taken in that day. The elaborate hieroglyphics and beautiful, colorful drawings were still vibrant after three thousand years or more. He left the day's adventure behind. James and his father were beat, but Sara wanted to stop at every ruin on the way back to the hotel to tell the stories. James was asleep fifteen minutes into the drive.

At the hotel that evening, James woke to use the restroom and noticed his mom hunched over her notebook. She had a stern look on her face in the faint glow of a reading light. James walked up to see what she was looking at and noticed symbols that appeared very similar to the unknown script in the tomb. These had words next to them like "energy" and "stars."

The instant she realized what he was doing, she closed the notebook and said in a tight voice, "James, the work I am doing could change everything. Promise me that you'll keep asking the questions if I can't finish my work on these."

He nodded, confused and trusting. He could tell she was speaking of something important but couldn't grasp why she was so fearful, almost as if eyes were watching her even then.

CHAPTER THREE

A Dark Place

1153 BC

James was on the floor and leaned against the wall next to the little opening. It was a bit awkward, but if he hunched over, he could rest and still peer out. In the distance, the campfires went out one by one until the only visible light was from the stars. Assuming it was late evening, even though his watch showed 4:30 p.m., he sat back and tried to sleep. He decided that wasting the Zippo's fluid for no reason would be pointless.

He sat there for hours thinking, *What could I possibly do to get someone's attention? There has to be a way.*

The campfires looked to be as much as a quarter mile away. He realized there was no way they could hear him scream through the little hole. He was fully exhausted from the stress of the day and must have drifted off because the next time he opened his eyes, the light of sunrise began creeping into the little window. He checked his Rolex, 2:30 a.m. James tweaked his sitting position to get the maximum view. He noticed a series of small brick huts in the distance and could make out figures working in the fields. These were exactly like the structures he had seen excavated from ancient Egyptian work camps.

"Toto, I don't think we are in Kansas anymore," James said out loud. Somehow, his crazy theories were true. "Well, holy shit. Now what?"

He took in his surroundings. The room was not very big, about eight by six. What he took for offerings were strewn about in various levels of decay. Some looked perhaps months old, whereas others had been here many years, maybe hundreds. His eyes were adjusted enough to see clearly at this point. He looked back down the corridor he had come through last night. There were no side tunnels he had missed. It was a direct shot down into the tomb, as he had remembered while exploring yesterday. The exception was that the hieroglyphics were much more vibrant.

Positioning himself in front of the hole, he yelled again, "Hello! Anyone! Hello!"

There were no people anywhere near his little prison. Searching through his canvas satchel, he brought out his only sustenance. One Kind bar and a bottle of water. He had been holding out on partaking of either, realizing he may have to ration his treasures. After consuming half of each, James gathered all of the offering items. They were degraded beyond recognition. It appeared it had been a long while since anyone had visited this shrine, perhaps less than a year by the look of one of the bundles.

James had an idea and carefully undid all the bundles of sticks. He broke up the smaller ones, then reached through the window with both hands and placed them outside. James was an excellent outdoorsman and was very familiar with making a campfire. He decided a small teepee fire would be best, with the fuel available. Once he had it all set up, he considered lighting it. Given the very limited number of offerings here, he decided it might have the best effect at dusk or night. At this distance, people should be able to see a small fire. The only thing left to do was sit and contemplate what had happened to him.

James thought back to his mom and her research. His hand absently went to the satchel and grasped his mom's notebook. He kept it with him as much as he could. James was a very knowledgeable archaeologist, but he knew in his heart that he owed everything he was to his mom and the research she had done that sparked his imagination. She had called the creators of the script Anunnaki, a name given by the ancient Sumerians to visiting gods.

What did the future hold? With a chuckle, he thought he should know precisely what the future held. With a bit of a start, he realized he was in a position unlike any modern human. He would have to figure out whether he would be a quiet bystander in this new reality or try to shape the future to help humanity, and himself in the process.

He pondered two completely different theories. First, could he even change the future? Was it possible? If he were to say, kill the king, would that mean whatever the king had done in his lifetime would never have taken place?

The butterfly effect suggested that anything he did in this time would have a ripple effect that would change the future, perhaps creating a future where his parents never met, and he was never born. If that were to happen, would he cease to exist in this time, whatever this time was?

Perhaps an alternate theory may prove true. Any decision he made now could result in the future splitting off into branches. Parallel realities, each reality existing at the same time with completely different outcomes. If that were the case, could he ever travel back to the future he knew? Perhaps the two timelines were entangled so that travel could still be possible as long as the connection between the times existed. If that was the case, whatever he did now would have no effect on the future, and the two separate realities could coexist. With no clear answer, he sat back again to wait for night-fall. Hopefully, his signal fire would attract someone, and his future wouldn't end here in this dark prison.

James's back hurt, his ass hurt, and his shoulder was numb from leaning on it all night. He considered finishing his bar and water but thought he should hold off a bit. His lips were cracking, and the dry, hot air was sucking whatever water was left in his body out into the breeze.

I've made it out of worse jams than this, he thought.

"Maybe not worse than this, but pretty bad anyway," he said with a chuckle.

He wasn't exactly sure who he was talking to. His head started getting a bit light, and he figured it wouldn't hurt to take a little nap. He woke again with a jolt. It was pitch-black.

"Crap!" he said with a raspy, dry throat. "How long has it been?"

He looked at his watch, which, luckily, had glow-in-the-dark indicators. It read 2:00 p.m. The watch, which had a perpetual self-winding mechanism, was dead. He hadn't been moving around enough to keep it wound up. In a panic, he looked out the small window to see a sky full of stars and only two small campfires in the distance. His mind raced. *Am I too late?*

"Damn!" he said.

He quickly pulled out his Zippo. *Snap! Flick!* The flame once again began dancing. He slowly reached out through the window with the flickering flame.

That's it, he thought. *That should do it.*

The flames began climbing up the broken sticks. It was lighting. James quickly and gently set two of the idols onto the now-growing flame. He stacked more sticks and more idols onto the flame. It was definitely large enough now for someone to see. He tweaked his head and began to blow on the pile. The flames reacted with a whoosh and grew at an even faster pace.

James put every bit of the offerings onto the pyre. It had to be big. He considered saving some of the combustibles but decided it had to be now or never. The fire outside shone through the window, and the beautiful orange light danced on the wall. The colorful hieroglyphics were dancing and coming to life.

This is it. This has to work.

James could hear the weather picking up a bit outside. Some wind was swirling around, causing his bonfire to waver. A strong gust picked up the fire and blew half of it through the small window. It was like a maelstrom in his prison. Fire and sticks were blowing and swirling around. Fire licked at his clothes, igniting his pants. He quickly took off his leather jacket and hat. The fire was smoldering right through his shirt as well.

Damn, probably should have kept my jacket on, he thought.

The smoke thickened, and James laid down as flat as he could to suck the last bit of fresh air off the floor. He noticed that the lower he got, the better the air, so he grabbed his satchel and rolled down the steep ramp in an effort to extinguish the fire and reach breathable air. He tried to brace himself against the wall but was too weak. Sliding down and grabbing at whatever he could find to slow his pace, he made it to the bottom of the ramp, falling unconscious and rolled limply off the ledge.

When he came to, he didn't have any idea how long he had been at the bottom of the ledge, but he seemed to be in good shape. Good, considering his foot was pointed in the wrong direction. The pain came in waves as soon as he noticed. His stomach let go of whatever was left in it, and he began to swoon again. Reaching into his satchel, he pulled out the remaining sustenance. He decided to go ahead and finish both, as he didn't see how he could possibly navigate back up to the top of the ledge and couldn't find a way out of this situation.

With a little laugh, he thought, *I didn't find any skeletons sitting at the bottom of this ledge when we first explored it, so I guess we're going with the parallel universe theory.*

He passed out. His Zippo flickered wildly, once again revealing the colorful dancing figures on the walls.

CHAPTER FOUR

A Fresh Start

2000 AD

They moved to America soon after the Karnak trip. James felt like he really never fit in with the natural-born American kids, but he enjoyed pop culture, video games, movies, and TV shows. Heck, his dad had named him after a certain Starfleet captain.

He spent much of his time as a young student in America exploring museums and studying Egyptology. James's dad was a little put off by that and wanted his son to get out there and get into football or hockey or something. His mom watched her son with love, admiration, and pride. James was an excellent student.

He had no problem acing all his classes through high school. James made the hockey team at his dad's request and loved it, but was never really good. He ended his high school career with a solid 4.0 GPA, even with AP Physics and History, and many top universities invited him to see their campuses. James enrolled at Harvard with a partial scholarship.

The university would cover half of his tuition, but room and board would be up to him. They were enamored that James had presented and nearly won the International Science and Engineering Fair. His theories and presentation about how pyramids could focus electromagnetic energy were considered scientifically astute. Still, many of the judges thought it to be more science fiction than plausible, even if the science was sound.

James was expected to enroll in the university's engineering program, but to his father's dismay, he enrolled in the School of Archaeology. James had chosen Harvard, as it was considered one of the very best schools in the US for studying archaeology. He hadn't mentioned that to his father.

He had been mostly alone in the dorms for all of freshman year after his roommate contracted some staph infection from who knows where and had to drop out of school. James took that solitary time to immerse himself in his studies. To appease his father, he loaded up on high-level math and physics classes and dove head-on into history, specifically Ancient Egyptian history. That first year was an eye-opener. The physics taught was so basic and elementary that he didn't feel like he was learning anything.

Several of his professors asked if he could TA some of their classes. They didn't realize he was only a freshman. In that first year, it got to the point that James couldn't justify going into debt for half the tuition and room and board expenses, bringing the yearly total to nearly forty-five thousand dollars. He thought that by the time he got his doctorate, he would be in debt for hundreds of thousands of dollars. What could he do with that amount of money in the real world?

A friend of his father was a construction lead with an engineering company tasked with completing some pipelines in the oilfield on the North Slope of Alaska. Khalid knew James as the bright young kid who would follow his father around on construction sites, learning and helping out wherever he could. James's father had met Khalid on a construction project, upgrading roads leading from the refineries to population centers in Egypt. He worked for Hank on several projects worldwide over the next decade. In time, Khalid was considered part of the Tiberius family and was always invited to holidays at the ranch.

Hank hadn't been feeling great and had turned down a few projects, including the pipeline project at the Alpine Field. An oilfield service company sent Khalid to oversee the project that Hank had engineered.

After the spring semester had finished, James received a call from Khalid suggesting he come work in northern Alaska.

"Yer pop told me that ya were stressed 'bout finances and school. Come up ta the slope, and I'll get ya on a crew workin' four weeks on, two weeks off. With overtime, ya should be able ta clear enough ta pay fer school." He booked his flight the same day.

James had been to interesting places all over the world, but Alaska had been on his bucket list since he was a child. James packed up his dorm and stuffed everything into a tiny storage compartment off campus. The rest of his meager belongings and cold-weather gear fit in a single bag.

It took three very long flights to get to Deadhorse, Alaska, the point where Khalid would send a truck to pick him up. As instructed, he scheduled a twelve-hour layover in Anchorage to pick up the necessary fire retardant Carhartt bibs, jacket, and other PPE. The flight from Anchorage to Deadhorse was something for the books. It was a clear sky, and majestic Mount Denali rose conspicuously out of the Alaska Range in all of its snowy brilliance. The airport in Deadhorse was as tiny as you would expect for a town constructed solely to support operations on the Prudhoe Bay oil field.

Khalid was standing near the single baggage claim.

"Hello, my boy," Khalid bellowed.

James had an embarrassed look on his face. "Will you keep it down? I don't want people thinking I'm only here because you're my uncle or something." James's smirk turned into a smile and a huge hug. "Oh hell, I've missed you, Kal."

They walked together out the door to find Khalid's truck idling at the curb.

"You leave your truck running here?" James asked. "Aren't you afraid it will get stolen?"

With a huge belly laugh, Khalid said, "Where do ya think a thief is gonna go? Fairbanks is five hundred miles away, and there's only one road. I usually don't leave the truck runnin' all the time in the summer, but it's sort of a habit. All the diesel trucks run 24/7 in the winter, so they don't freeze up."

The truck was a white, three-quarter-ton Ford with a ladder rack on top, and "Black Sands Corp." was stenciled on the door.

"Are we working directly for Black Sands on this one?"

"Yeah, yer dad sent me here on a contract with 'em to oversee the new pipeline construction. Let's hit the road. It's a bit of a haul ta the man camp from here."

James noticed a lack of local pubs on the drive out of town. Most places like this that James had been to had numerous bars. A way for the workers to let off some steam after putting in twelve hours of hard work. These were not to be found in Deadhorse. James had heard that the North Slope was "dry"; no alcohol was allowed by law, as per the local native government.

"So if there is no booze, what do people do around here for fun?" James said.

"There really isn't a whole lotta fun ta be had up here. We've gotta pool table and ping-pong set up at the man camp, and the food's amazing. They spare no expense on that."

The man camp was not the pinnacle of opulence. It consisted of several temporary modular buildings that were connected together.

"Don't worry 'bout the looks. Everything's clean, and you've got at least one hot shower per section. Way better than what we get in Egypt, anyway. When ya get up in the mornin', we'll get ya over ta the safety officer, who'll go over the area's safety procedures, and if I'm not mistaken, ya still need yer confined space class."

James grabbed his gear and started walking toward the buildings.

"Which room is mine?"

"That's the thing. Each room is fer two people, and I already have a roommate, so looks like yer the lucky one who gets ta bunk with a stranger," Khalid said with a smirk.

"Great, that sounds lovely."

"Anyway, I know ya missed out on the joy of a roommate this year in school, so I'm sure it'll be awesome ta have a new friend," Khalid wailed like a donkey, startling James.

"You need to warn me the next time you laugh like that. I thought we were being attacked by a polar bear or something."

"Okay, get settled. Go talk ta the lady at the desk, and she'll get ya sorted."

With a little wave, James walked inside. The main lobby was where they had the entertainment. Along with pool and ping-pong, there was a PS3 with an extensive catalog of games and a few couches set up in front of a large screen.

"The DVDs are all over here."

James looked around and saw a big guy with a bigger smile standing behind him.

"Ah, okay, thanks," James said.

"I'm Tom. Are you here working for Black Sands?"

Tom was large in a few directions. He was about six feet three, nearly three hundred pounds, and had very short brown hair with a scruffy goatee. You could tell by looking at him that he wasn't a threat, more of a gentle giant type.

Reaching out his hand. "Hi, I'm Jim. No, not exactly. Technically, I'm working for the engineering contractor."

"Wow, that sounds nice. How do you get a gig like that?"

"Right place, right time, I guess," said James.

"Hey, are you looking for a room?"

"I guess I am. I was supposed to go over and talk to that lady at the desk."

"Sandy?" said Tom. "Oh, she's harmless. Come with me."

Tom sucked in his gut and started to sort of swagger toward the desk.

"Hey, Sandy, wassup?"

"Hey, Tom. Who's the cute new guy?"

"This is...uh. Oh, dude, what's your name again?"

James looked at the young woman. Sandy was pretty, not a model by any means, but the curly blonde hair and very little makeup suited her. She wore a white tank top and baggy Levi's ripped at the knees. Something told James that a seven down south was a nine or ten on the slope.

"Jim... Uh... James is what the reservation should say."

"Last name?"

"Tiberius," James said with a slight cringe. He already knew what was coming. This happened nearly every time he gave his full name.

"No freakin' way! Are you telling me your name is James freakin' Tiberius?" Tom said.

"The one and only. OK, maybe not one and only, but that's my name."

"Don't you get it, Sandy?"

"Yeah, I get it, Tom," said Sandy.

"His name is like Captain Kirk on Star Trek. Captain James Tiberius Kirk, here in the flesh."

"Yeah, Tom, I get it," Sandy replied, shaking her head and turning to James with a sly grin. "Have a roommate yet?"

"Uh, no, I haven..."

"Yes, he does have a roommate," said Tom. "He's sleeping with me."

"Uhm, sleeping with you, is he?" Sandy said while trying to hold back a laugh.

"Hold on a sec. I'm not sleeping with anyone."

"Listen, James, you should sleep with me. Everyone bunks up here."

"Okay, Tom, I will take you up on your offer, but I'm going to have to deny your sexual advances."

Sandy couldn't hold back. She started laughing so hard she nearly fell backward in her chair.

"You are going to fit in fine here, Jimmy," she said after collecting herself.

CHAPTER FIVE

A Knock at the Window

1153 BC

Neferu was always looking for something to get into. Many wondered why she couldn't be quiet and mind her own business like the other women. Considered tall at around five feet four, she was as thin as a rail. This was not a health or beauty choice but more a result of life's struggles and hardships.

She had been married young. Her father had provided a sizable dowry, attracting suitors of a very high caliber. Her father selected a somewhat wealthy merchant for her, who owned a brick manufacturing venture. Since she was thirteen, he was thirty years her senior—a very acceptable age difference at the time. Neferu's father was old-school. Who better to care for a young woman than a wealthy old man? Love and romance were not something the working class could afford. Neferu was young and naïve, having lost her mother in an accident soon after she was born. Her father did his best to do what his wife would have wanted for Neferu.

After fifteen years of marriage, Neferu's husband became ill. He was found in the privy, passed out. His face was gray, and his skin was cold and sweaty. Neferu convinced her neighbors to help carry him to their bed. This was not an idle request, as most people would turn and run after spotting any unknown illness. He died that night. Neferu's father had passed away a few years before. Being childless, she found herself alone in the world. Neferu took on her husband's duties, running his small enterprise.

After a few months, production was up, and the business was thriving.

Meret and Horemheb were both older, prominent businessmen and considered themselves to be the best possible suitors in their small town. They would usually try to trap her in a conversation when she was around.

"How were you able to get so few workers to do so much work?" remarked Meret.

"I call only upon free men to knead the clay and shape the bricks. When a man's heart is light, and his hands are rewarded with grain and copper, his strength flows like the river in flood. More bricks are brought forth from his hand."

"And does this not diminish the wealth that fills your storehouse, Neferu? Fewer bound laborers mean more must be given away," Meret said.

"A little, maybe, but we are able to produce so many more bricks that it all evens out."

With a little laugh, Horemheb said, "Pshh! Let her toil with her silly ideas. Bricks or not, a firm hand beats a woman's tricks any day. Let's go, Meret. Real work's waiting."

Neferu would have all hands making the bricks during the day, and then at night, they would stack them in the kiln and stoke the fire to cure them. One night, while walking along the edge of the kiln, double-checking that the temperature was correct, she happened to glance over toward the Great Pyramid.

Akhet Khufu, as they called it, was about a quarter mile away. She noticed a flicker of light. A small fire had been built only a short distance from the bottom of the structure. The fire was obvious against the white background of the casing stones. Neferu grabbed Bibi, her foreman, and pointed to the pyramid.

"Look! There! That is near the offering window? It is forbidden to go there, except during the Opet Festival! Could it be tomb raiders?"

"If that is true, best we do not get involved," said Bibi.

A moment later, the fire went from small and orderly to a swirl of wind and flames. It was almost as if a dust devil had grabbed and sucked it up until it was all gone. No light, no noise, nothing.

"You know the penalty for violating a shrine outside of festival. If they catch you there, they are likely to give you a whipping for your trouble. If those tomb raiders get caught, their entire families will be held responsible and put to death."

"Yes, I am sure you are right. It is better not to get involved," Neferu said.

That night, Neferu tossed in bed, unable to sleep.

What in the world could that fire have meant? Who would have dared to steal from the great pharaohs?

Neferu's curiosity got the better of her. Ignoring the advice of her foreman, she decided to investigate the flames for herself. Neferu dressed for the cool early morning. She wore her linen kalisaris and warm wool cape. The kalisaris was tight-fitting, ending above her ankles. It would be less likely to trip her while ascending the pyramid.

The path to the pyramid was not obvious. Years ago, there were streets all around this area and up to the pyramid, but access had been limited by Ramesses II many years before. He was terrified that people might disturb the tombs. Neferu wasn't troubled by this, having made several trips to the offering door over the years to appease her father. She had been instructed to give an offering and pray for his prosperity. Her father thought the prayers would be more powerful coming from someone with as beautiful a spirit as Neferu rather than a slave-beating taskmaster like himself.

As Neferu approached the pyramid, she couldn't distinguish much of the structure and had to navigate by Lah.

Lah, the moon, wouldn't be hidden in the sky by Ra's brilliance for another hour or so. She slowly approached the spirit door and found the charred remains of the small fire strewn about. While inspecting the mess, she noticed a few idols mixed in with the sticks, and her heart sank.

Surely someone has not burned the offerings that were carefully slid into the tomb, she thought, but one of the charred idols at her feet looked very familiar. *Yes, that is the idol I placed in the tomb last Opet Festival.*

Neferu's first instinct was to run. She should run back to her warm bed and forget all of this. The horror! These thieves would not only be caught and beheaded, but their souls would surely burn for eternity. The priest made the punishment for this type of offense very clear.

Maybe the fire I saw earlier was the netjeru burning away the thieves to nothing, she thought.

Neferu steadied herself. Her curious nature took over, and she knew she couldn't possibly run away until she had some answers. She decided, against her better judgment, to peek through the tiny opening, only big enough for the spirit's ka or ba to escape the tomb. It was nowhere near large enough for a person and barely large enough to shove in a bundle of flowers or an idol once a year.

Immediately, something caught her attention. There was some sort of light in there. Not right next to the door, but it was there. It looked like it might be coming from about twenty or thirty steps down a long corridor. Neferu had always looked through the door when she sent her offering, hoping that she might see the ka or ba floating around as her father had told her. Never in all those years did she see anything happen inside the tomb.

Her heart skipped a beat. *That light must be coming from the ka.*

Without thinking, she said out loud, "Hello, Ka, can you hear me?" She didn't know what had gotten into her. Who was she to disturb and try to speak to a great pharaoh's ka?

To her surprise, the ka answered back, "Hello! Hello! Is someone there?"

The words were halting and strange, possibly gibberish, not at all what she would have expected, and she was unable to understand.

The ka is not used to speaking to humans. Obviously, spirits speak in different languages in the afterlife, she reasoned.

The ka spoke again, and she listened closely. "Door small, want out, need help." She could only understand a little, but at least this was her language.

"Yes, Great Ka, I will find people to help you."

With that, Neferu ran as fast as she could. She ran past her home and through town to the local Imi-r niwt's home.

The sun was beginning to come up as she reached the villa.

The late-night to early-morning shift was always manned by the lowest-ranked guard on the list. This morning was no exception. The man couldn't have been over sixteen and looked terrified at the sight of Neferu running toward his shack. "Run quickly and fetch the Imi-r niwt at once," she said. He recognized Neferu as a high-ranking local businesswoman and decided that there must be an imminent threat of violence looming.

"Wait here. I will fetch Ptahhote."

The young guard ran past the barracks and straight into the Imi-r niwt's apartments.

"There is an emergency. Ptahhote, you must come now. There is a merchant out front who is terrified. It must be an attack."

Ptahhote was a tall man of about forty, with brown eyes and dark skin. He was known in the village as being fair and usually very helpful. Without hesitation, Ptahhote, who had already dressed for the day, ran the one hundred yards to the guard shack.

"Neferu, what is it? Who's attacking?"

Neferu cocked her head and furrowed her eyebrows. "Attack? Is someone attacking?" she questioned.

"No, wait, are you here to notify of an attack?" said Ptahhote.

"No, I am here to get help. A pharaoh's ka is trying to leave through the offering door of the tomb, but it is too small."

With a groan, Ptahhote looked at the guard. "You had me run through the courtyard as fast as I could, thinking we were under attack? And this is what I come to, a crazy drunk woman!"

"I am not crazy, and I am not drunk. I noticed a fire in front of the tomb, and I went to make sure it was not being robbed," she said.

Ptahhote gasped, dismayed. "You went to the tombs? In the dark? And it's not even Opet Festival. I should throw you in prison for this blasphemy."

"Listen, you idiot," Neferu said. "It talked to me. It asked for help to get out."

"You must be joking. You are telling me you spoke with a pharaoh's ka inside the tomb?"

"Yes, that's exactly what I am saying. We need some workers up there to open the tomb right now."

Ptahhote rolled his eyes. "You cannot be serious."

"I am serious. If you don't believe me, come and see for yourself."

Ptahhote decided the best course of action in this situation was to humor her, as she was obviously deranged. He couldn't imprison a person of her rank for investigating a fire.

"If I go with you now to the tomb and show you there are no ka or ba escaping, will that keep you quiet?"

With a curt nod, Neferu led Ptahhote to the altar of offerings and small doorway of the soul. Once they reached the small ledge outside the tomb, Neferu motioned to the charred idols and twigs.

"This is where the ka was angry that he couldn't get out. Those idols were all inside the tomb."

"Very interesting," said Ptahhote. "How did all of that get out here?"

"I told you. It was the ka. He must have been angry and blew out the offerings in a fiery wind."

Ptahhote knelt to look through the door. "Hello, Great Pharaoh, are you listening?" He turned to the nearest guard, and they both bent over laughing.

"Hello, here, tomb, help," a voice from within called.

The color left the faces of Ptahhote and his two men. "It's true," both guards said in unison.

"Yes, it must be true," said Ptahhote.

He looked at Neferu, back at the door, then to the guards.

"Quick, go to the village and bring back a workgroup. Have them bring their rock tools. Also, tell the tomb priests they are needed here with all haste to do Wepet-Ur," he said to the nearest guard, calling for an Opening of the Mouth Ritual.

CHAPTER SIX

Life on the Slope

2006 AD

James hadn't been sleeping well, thanks to the twenty-four hours of daylight. It was easy to wake up early though, because Tom had a habit of removing his CPAP mask while he was sleeping, and the early-morning snoring sounded something like a bear snugged up in its winter den. It had been nearly a month, and he hadn't minded being woken since he was too cheap to invest in a proper alarm clock.

Most of the workers in the camp preferred to get up, throw on their work clothes, and grab a coffee, a bagel, and a pre-made lunch bag from the kitchen. Others liked to sit down and gorge themselves on the massive piles of eggs, bacon, and pancakes that the kitchen put out every morning, Tom being one of the latter. James liked to wake up early, take a nice hot shower, and then sit down to read the paper while waiting for Khalid to get ready so they could head out. Tom finally made it out of the room and sat next to James.

"Wassup, Jimbo?" Tom said with a huge smile.

"Happy to see that you finally dragged yer ass outta bed," James said with a low five and fist bump.

"What? I'm hurt. I always show up on time to make the corporate overlords happy."

"Of course you do," James said with a chuckle.

"What's on the docket for you and Khalid today?" asked Tom.

"Oh, um, Kal said I'm supposed to get my scaffold training today."

"Sweet, bro, that's what I have too. Looks like we'll be in the same class. I'll let you cheat off my test like you did in the confined space training."

James chuckled and said, "Yeah, that happened."

"No, really, James, thanks. I don't read well. If you hadn't read the questions to me, I wouldn't have passed."

"It's cool. So why don't you know how to read, anyway? How did you graduate?"

"I played football at Colony High School in Palmer. They didn't want me to fail my classes, so they had the cheerleaders do my homework."

"Damn, that sounds good on one hand, but they screwed you in the long run, huh?"

"That's why I'm destined to be a grunt for eternity. At least I like hard work."

Tom could carry nearly double what anyone else on the crew could.

James overheard Jerry, the crew lead, say, "That kid's tough. Point him in the right direction and give him a nudge, and he'll move a mountain."

Later in the scaffold training class, James and Tom sat together through all the OSHA regulations and training videos. The last part was the one-hundred-question test, which pretty much followed line for line the OSHA CFR code.

James approached the instructor and said, "Hey, I have a favor to ask. Would you mind if I read the questions out loud for Tom? I promise I won't cheat. He doesn't read well."

The instructor responded, "Oh, that's fine. The test is just a way for us to prove you have been exposed to all the necessary information. It's open book, so you can work together."

James and Tom were the first to finish, and both came out with perfect scores. After everyone else finished, there was a competition to see who could tighten a scaffold clamp as close to the forty-foot pounds of torque that OSHA required. They were to use a scaffold wrench, which looked like a regular socket with a mallet on the back, to tighten the clamp. The instructor would then check them with a torque wrench to see how close they came. James went first and hit the forty pounds on the dot. Tom was surprised to find out he had wrenched his to seventy pounds.

"You're going to have to work on that, Tom," the instructor commented.

The next morning started like the last, with James sitting at the table reading the paper.

"Greetings, Captain!" Tom said while doing his best to perform the Vulcan hand sign, followed by the customary low five and fist bump.

"Are you guys heading out to the pump station today? That's where we will be."

"I think that's where the superintendent told Khalid to go today. We're supposed to inspect the underground access tunnels and sections of the pipeline."

Two young men walked up behind Tom. Jerry and Samuel were a few years older than James. The brothers were nice enough during the pool and table tennis tournaments but tended to bully Tom a bit more than James liked.

"What's up, guys?" said James.

"Not much. Tom, move your ass! The foreman is going to be pissed if we are late to the site again."

"I guess I'll see you there, Jimbo. I'm running a bit late." Tom was always running a bit late.

"Hasta," said James.

Khalid strolled out of his room and looked like he always did. He didn't bother with the Carhartt bibs and such. He wore a black specially-made, fire-retardant jacket with James's father's company logo on it and pressed jeans. James had no idea how Khalid could get his clothes laundered so well every day while he still had grease from last week's project on his chest.

Khalid wore a white hard hat. That alone was a signal that he was not merely a grunt. It was not the rule per se, but white hard hats would be worn by the brass—the guys who made decisions. James was given a blue hard hat when he arrived. This usually meant the person was in training, not necessarily a peon, but perhaps a future foreman in training who still had to get his hands dirty and probably didn't really know anything. Tom and his ilk would wear yellow or maybe green. Those were the guys who would do most of the actual work.

James had been hired as an informal apprentice. Growing up, James was always the lowest man on the totem pole and would get the worst jobs. Now that he was a college boy, he was being groomed to eventually run things. He missed the mind-clearing manual labor he grew up with, but he didn't miss the sore muscles, sweat, and dirt.

Khalid figured that one day, after graduation, James would take over his dad's engineering company, and he made it his mission to show James all the ropes, whether he wanted to learn or not. All James wanted was to make enough scratch to fund his schooling so he could one day be Indiana Jones. Schooling always felt like a waste of time. There was nothing as boring as working on a long math exam. James always wanted to solve real-life problems and questions that could mean something and make a difference. Busy work, sure. That repetition probably helped the equations sink into other people, but learning and remembering were never an issue for James. He could pick up most math concepts immediately and had no problem using them in the future.

"Let's hit the road. It's 'bout half an hour's drive ta the pump station."

"Right behind you," James said while taking the last sip of coffee and grabbing his lunch bag off the counter.

"Grab me one too. I'm not sure if we'll be done in time ta get lunch."

The trip out was as usual. The gravel road wasn't smooth by any means, but at least they did a great job dealing with the frost heaves. In Egypt, they had to build and repair roads to deal with the sinkholes. Here in Alaska, there was a different enemy. Throughout the summer, the tundra would occasionally melt and freeze and melt again. The constant expansion and shrinking would wreak havoc on the roads. Luckily, the maintenance was constant and thorough. You would rarely find dangerous frost heaves.

As they pulled up to the site, they noticed Tom, Jerry, and Samuel looking down an open manhole. Jerry began climbing down the ladder into the hole.

"Those boys are here ta help us if we need ta do any heavy liftin'," Khalid said.

"Oh, come on! Kal, we don't need any help. They will probably get in the way."

"There's more ta the story, though, Jim. They've trainin' in confined space entry and have special tools ta make sure the air's safe."

"We have had the same training, Kal. They should give us the sniffer, and then we could send these guys to do something more important."

"I get it, Jim, but everyone here's gotta job, and there needs ta be all the proper paperwork, includin' 'lockout tag-out' on the entrance ta that underground tunnel ta show it's been inspected and is safe ta work. There's a history of gas leaks 'round here. Sometimes a pipe or valve'll get damaged from the frost heaves and leak."

Khalid and James got out of the truck and walked toward the group.

"What's going on, guys?" said James.

Tom looked away from the hole as Khalid and James approached.

"Jerry just went down to turn off the water valve so we can get to work. The boss said to hold off, but we need to get this project going," said Tom.

Tom looked down as Jerry collapsed into a heap at the bottom of the maintenance hole. Samuel saw his brother collapse, too, and started down to help. Khalid quickly grabbed Samuel to hold him back, but Samuel struggled to escape.

"What the hell, dude? Let me go."

"What are you doing?" Tom said. "We have to help him."

"Don't go down there. Can't ya smell that? It smells like rotten eggs. Somethin's wrong," Khalid said.

"I can go. I'll hold my breath," James yelled.

Khalid lunged forward, tackling both Samuel and James to the ground.

"Screw it. I'm going," yelled Tom, sliding down the ladder.

"I don't smell it down here," Tom yelled as he collected Jerry. "Throw me a rope."

Predictably, Tom fell unconscious.

"We have to save them. Please ... let's get down there," screamed James, tears streaming from his eyes.

"Stop! Stop it, Jim. They're already dead." Samuel sat there in shock, seemingly emotionless. James sat next to him, sobbing.

Ten minutes later, the site safety officer was there and dropped his multi-gas detector to check the space.

"Damn," he said, "look at this. The hydrogen sulfide is at nearly 150 ppm. These boys had no chance of surviving that."

"I told Tom I smelled rotten eggs 'fore he went down, but he didn't wanna hear it. When he got ta the bottom, he said he didn't smell nothin'," Khalid said.

"That makes sense, actually," said the safety officer. "The first sign of H2S is a sulfur smell. Once the H2S is at lethal concentrations, it causes paralysis of the olfactory nerve, and you can't smell it any longer. Didn't you all have a sniffer with you to make sure it was safe?"

Emotionless, Samuel looked directly ahead and said, "Jerry took it down with him. He said it looked safe."

CHAPTER SEVEN

Into the Light

1153 BC

James awoke to a distant voice. The language was strange, but it sounded similar to what he theorized the Ancient Egyptian language sounded like. It was an angelic voice, straight out of heaven.

Is this how I am going to end? Taken up by an angel? Or perhaps down by a demon? What had the voice said? There was a greeting, then some reference to a soul.

With great effort, James worked the syllables through his head.

How should I respond?

"Hello! Hello! Is someone there?" he yelled in English.

There was no response. James's mind was fuzzy, but that voice was not speaking English or any other local language. James thought back to the thousands of hours he had spent studying the Ancient Egyptian language, one that had not been natively spoken for thousands of years. All the clues were there, though.

Many of the nouns carried through to modern Egyptian Arabic. James and his mom had meticulously pieced together an excellent idea of what the language had sounded like. They used Egyptian glyphs, which described certain phonetic tendencies, then cross-referenced ancient Greek and Roman texts that described the language. He tried to piece together a suitable response.

"Door small, want out, need help," James said in his best interpretation.

The response came immediately: "Yes, great, Ka. I will find people to help you."

And then there was nothing but silence. James was exhausted and decided he must be hearing things, so he leaned back and passed out.

He was awakened again by a new voice, male this time.

"Hello, Great Pharaoh, are you listening?"

James was delirious from a lack of food and water.

Am I hearing things? Was that Ancient Egyptian?

"Hello, here, tomb, help," he muttered before collapsing into the fetal position and, once again, lost consciousness.

By the time the work crew arrived, Ptahhote was nearly hyperventilating.

What have I done? What am I doing? I should leave it be, walk away, and pretend that the great spirit had never spoken. That would be the smart thing. Sekhmet is going to think I'm an idiot.

He wasn't crazy and had heard the ka. Neferu and the guards had also heard it. He was doing the right thing. Ptahhote stuck his head to the door.

"Be still, Ka. Ptahhote, Imi-r niwt of Khemenu-Ka, is here to help you."

There was no response. Khemenu-Ka, aptly named, was the village worksite nearest Khufu and was loosely translated as "Soul City".

Why was it not responding? Has the ka gone to rest? Did it even need to get out now? These questions would have to be asked later. Ptahhote had set this course in motion and would see it through.

Ptahhote pointed to the entrance. "You soldiers, start working to pry the casing stone away from the entrance."

"Stop this instant!" Three priests in full ceremonial garb, one wearing the distinct headdress of Anubis, began climbing and making their way up to the ledge. "This work is blasphemous without performing the Wepet-Ur."

Ptahhote stammered, "Of course, I would never. I mean, I was getting things all prepared for the ritual."

"Please stand aside. The Opening of the Mouth ceremony is extremely important. When dealing with the Akh, rituals are the only thing protecting us from the wrath of an unrestful spirit."

"Of course, Sebekhotep, I have always valued your station," said Ptahhote.

The Sem priest was not nearly as powerful as some other priest hierarchies, but a good word from any priest could make a difference when one wanted to petition for greater positions. Sebekhotep knelt down, lit a small bundle of wheat using his flint, and said a few words under his breath.

"You may begin," he said when he was finished.

"Is that all?" said Neferu.

"That is all for now."

With great effort, the stone began to move. They were able to slide it back about twelve inches, wide enough to send a couple of men into the tomb to search for the ka.

Ptahhote looked at the priests as if to say, "Are you not going?"

Sebekhotep shrugged and said, "We are done for now. You go ahead and tell us what you find."

Ptahhote smirked and went first. He decided that if he was going to send his men into the mouth of an evil akh, he should probably brandish his bronze and lead the way.

Once inside the first chamber, Ptahhote, with shaking knees, said in barely over a whisper, "Ka, are you there?"

There was no response. The chamber was a mess. What looked like charred cloth and twigs were strewn about. He decided to walk a bit farther down the steep ramp. The soldier behind Ptahhote sparked his flint, igniting a torch, and handed it to him. Ptahhote peered down the first ledge at the bottom of the ramp. What he saw startled him. He slipped to the ground and would have fallen off the ledge if one of his men hadn't grabbed him by the neck of his robe.

"It looks like a man," said Ptahhote. "He looks dead or maybe asleep. I can't tell. Get some ropes and a ladder. Tell Sebekhotep to get in here. We need to get down to him."

James was mostly asleep. He heard some noises, whispers, the thump of something soft like wood against stone. There was a moment of searing pain in his ankle as it was twisted straight. The pain was a reminder that he was still alive. He couldn't bring himself to open his eyes. They were dry, crusted shut from the soot and dehydration.

But he could feel hands on him. It was not comfortable. There were ropes around his chest, and he was being dragged up to the top of the ledge. More whispers.

What is the word for water? Think, you idiot, think. James's head cleared a bit, probably some adrenaline kicking in. "M'u," he groaned.

Moments later, water poured over his face and into his parched mouth. He opened his eyes to see a jackal staring back at him. James closed his eyes.

Did I just see a jackal? No, clear your head. That was a Sem, a ceremonial funeral priest. Of course, I'm in a tomb. They would perform the Opening of the Mouth ceremony, he thought.

They put him on a stretcher, carried him to the top of the ramp, and placed him on the ground. The jackal knelt over him and whispered something he couldn't understand while touching first his eyes, then his mouth. The priest reached down and touched his...

"Uhm, okay, thanks, that's good. I'm fine," he said in English.

The priests looked at each other in bewilderment.

"Thankful, I be good," James said in slow, broken Egyptian syllables.

James couldn't take his eyes off the jackal-faced Sem priest. The headdress was a marvel of craftsmanship. Its sleek, elongated snout was crafted from polished wood painted a deep, glossy black. The jackal's predatory muzzle jutted forward, and the two pointed ears rose upright and were edged in gold leaf, which shimmered in the light of the torches. The most haunting feature was the eyes, twin orbs of inlaid amber set deep within shadowy sockets. The unblinking stare was unnerving.

The priests looked amazed, and all started to talk at once. James could catch only bits of words and phrases from the conversation. He heard words he had memorized, like "burnt offering," "soul," "pharaoh," and "god." James slowly rose to his feet. The pain in his ankle nearly had him back on the ground, but the two guards grabbed and steadied him.

James was eager to leave the tomb, which he had earlier resigned to become his own. With the entire group watching, he stumbled toward the opening and daylight. James stepped into a world he had only dreamed of. In fact, he had dreamed of it for as long as he could remember. What would it have been like to share this moment with his mom? Standing outside the entrance, James stood tall, stretched his arms in the air, then twisted side to side.

He took a moment to get his bearings. He was standing on a small ledge of the Great Pyramid of Egypt, looking out over a vast empty space. Cairo was not there as he remembered. Brick and mud huts, tents, and a few buildings, none over two stories, were all he could see. In front of him stood a man dressed in what he assumed was priestly garb and one woman. She was around five feet four with huge haunting brown eyes rimmed in kohl, black as the richest earth, with a faint dusting of malachite green shimmering on her eyelids. Her honey-brown face, kissed by the sun, was framed by beautiful high cheekbones, and her full-painted red lips curved into a shy smile. She was slender and very muscular but soft in all the right places. James stood there staring. A moment later, the woman's face turned red, and she looked down and then turned away.

James tried to think of something profound to say and pieced something together. "I come in peace. I am not a ka or a netjer."

What everyone heard was, "I am here for peace. I am not a spirit but a god."

Everyone around him threw themselves down and put their faces to the ground.

"No, wait! I don't think you understand."

Neferu listened carefully to what the priests were saying in the tomb. She couldn't make it out exactly, but it became apparent that they did find the Pharaoh's Ka, and they were going to try to lead it out of the tomb. What seemed like hours later, a man walked out from behind the smooth white casing stone. This man was unlike anything that Neferu had ever seen. He was easily the tallest man she knew of, standing at well over three cubits, four and a half palms tall. He had strange blue eyes and very light olive skin, lighter than the skin of most Egyptians. His chest and arms were enormous and hairy. She could see the health and strength in this man. He was obviously a man of great wealth.

That was when she fully realized what she was seeing and had difficulty looking away. The man was fully and completely naked apart from a pair of very sturdy-looking sandals, but they weren't sandals. They were something else. There was soot and ash all over his body as if he had been in the midst of the maelstrom she had seen earlier that night.

The man stood for a moment, then raised his hands to the sky, likely to Ra himself, and said, "I am here for future peace. I am not a ka but a netjer."

Neferu instantly knew what to do. She threw herself to the ground, prostrated, hoping that this god would see fit to spare her life for seeing his nakedness. The others around her did the same. He then said something else that didn't make any sense and was obviously the language of the gods.

CHAPTER EIGHT

Going On

2006 AD

After the accident, the rest of the summer was mostly uneventful. The entire Prudhoe Bay Oil Field was in shock. "Accidents happen," they would say. "These men had the necessary training and should have known better." That was the official position. While that all was true, it didn't make his room in the man camp feel any less lonely. They came to remove Tom's belongings the next day. James's eyes filled with tears as he watched them box up Tom's CPAP.

James spent his two weeks off in Anchorage. The company was happy to stick their employees on their charter plane during their off time, so they didn't have to feed and house them. James explored the many hiking trails and learned the nuances of combat fishing on the Russian River. Khalid wanted to come along on his journey, but James wanted some alone time. He was perfectly happy throwing on a backpack and heading out into the wilderness for a multi-day hike with no company but his own head. Tom's death was the first time he had faced mortality.

Someday, that will be me. Someday, Mom and Dad will be dead. How am I supposed to deal with something like that? How do I want to spend my life? Thoughts ran through his head as he tried to sleep in his one-person tent, the midnight sun blazing behind his closed eyelids and preventing actual deep sleep.

Once back to work, things returned to business as usual. Sandy had been his one constant on the Slope. Every morning, she greeted him with a shy smile and brought him that extra cup of coffee when he looked down. She even giggled at his terrible jokes. Soon after James returned, Sandy knocked on his door.

"Oh! Hey, Sandy, what's up?" said James.

"After Tom and Jerry died, I got very lonely. I was thinking about cutting my hitch short and heading back to Texas, but I need the money," she said as she sat on his bed. Her red eyes mirrored James's sadness.

"I get it. It's not the same around here. It's almost like there is no reason to stay here and work."

Sandy looked at James and took off her shirt.

"I am lonely and bored," she said with a flirtatious grin.

James was not very experienced in this area, but even he was able to get this hint. Suddenly, this North Slope nine was a ten to James. They spent the next week with each other trying to cure each other's loneliness and boredom, and it worked. That week, they clung to each other, nights of whispered stories about her Texas childhood, days of stealing moments between shifts.

She told him about her dream to open a bakery and how she'd sketch recipes on napkins during breaks. He confessed to his Indiana Jones fantasy, and she didn't laugh. She sketched a fedora on a napkin and tucked it in his pocket. Sandy did her best to direct any new arrivals to other rooms, but eventually, a new roommate showed up. James didn't bother to get to know him and kept to himself. He felt if he were to like this new guy, it would somehow betray the memory of his friendship with Tom.

The weeks went by, and Sandy's hitch was coming to an end. James met her at the front door of the man camp as she stood waiting for her ride.

"Promise you'll write," she said, kissing him, her arms tight around him. "I'll send you a napkin sketch when I get home."

"Promise," he said, hugging her back. The warmth of her embrace faded as her ride pulled up.

The new semester started, so after fulfilling his employment contract for the summer, James returned to the joy of his sophomore year. Once at school, he was able to enroll in some advanced physics—tougher stuff that might actually challenge him.

Maybe Dad's right. I should get my degree in engineering and take over for him when he retires. That would be the logical thing. Then, find a girl, maybe Sandy, and start a family. How am I going to pay off all of these loans with a history degree, anyway?

Deep down, something gnawed at him. A whisper that this wasn't his path, that something bigger waited out of reach.

Weeks later, a letter arrived at school, a napkin sketch of a cupcake. "Miss you, Slope boy," it read in Sandy's loopy feminine handwriting.

He smiled and tucked it in his satchel, but the warmth faded fast. Life at Harvard was difficult. The classes were simple, but the loneliness he felt in Alaska had begun to settle into him. He didn't enjoy being away from his friends and family. He missed the rough camaraderie of the Slope, the stakes that felt real. Here, it was all lectures and the shallow chattering of fellow students. He had left behind Tom's snores and Sandy's shy smiles for a cold, concrete dorm room that echoed silence.

He tried to fit in and joined a study group, but the irrelevance of it all had him sit and stare out the window at a manhole cover, and his thoughts went back to Tom and a dark place. The summer had changed him. Jerry collapsing and Tom sliding down the ladder as a hero, only to suffocate and die in front of him. Those things were real. This mindless prattle about whose frat party was the best or how the football game went was ridiculous to James. The busy work at school was a far cry from the hands-on problems he craved. He'd ace a physics exam in twenty minutes, then spend the rest of the day wondering why any of it even mattered.

Winter break was a few days away. If he could make it a little longer, he would be able to pack it all up for the semester and head back home. The Tiberius Ranch was about one hundred acres, which had been handed down to Hank by his father and had been in the family since the '20s. It wasn't a sprawling Texas ranch, as you read about, but rather a humble homestead with plenty of room for hunting and a bit of fishing. James knew if he could get through the semester and head home, things would start looking up.

Hmm, I wonder what Sandy's doing for Christmas? She lives only *about sixty miles away.*

He was getting ready to pick up the phone and dial Sandy when it rang in his hand, startling him. The screen showed his mom's number.

"Hey, Mom, what's up?"

"How would you like to spend Christmas in Egypt on a dig?"

James's heart skipped a beat as he said, "You're serious? Heck yeah, what's the deal?"

"The Ministry of Antiquities has located some interesting tunnels under Giza that we have never seen before. They have hired your dad's company to do some excavating and shoring to make the site safe, and they want me to lead the dig."

"Mom, wow, that's amazing. I can't wait."

"Your dad wants to put you on his crew as a foreman. How does that sound?"

"You know I'd rather be working with you and the archaeologists, but I would jump at any opportunity to get my hands dirty. You made my day! I love you. Can't wait to get there."

James whizzed through the rest of his finals. Things were looking up. He packed his clothes in his duffel, jammed his laptop and books in his satchel, and headed to Egypt. He didn't even bother trying to sell his mini-fridge and desk.

I'll leave that for the next guy. He had no intention of returning.

CHAPTER NINE

Uninvited Guest

1153 BC

The great unknown god gestured for everyone to stand. The priests, the guards, and Ptahhote slowly stood with bowed heads. Neferu was wary of standing. Surely, the god was not content to have one as lowly as herself stand in his presence.

Ptahhote removed his white linen robe and helped the now red-faced god into his new clothes. He looked a bit confused and didn't say much. He started to walk forward but stumbled and was aided by a nearby priest. Ptahhote relayed that he had injured his ankle and would need support.

Neferu said, "Netjeru can hurt their ankles?"

"Silence! Do not spew your blasphemy here, Neferu. Everyone knows that when a netjer takes the form of a human, they can be hurt like anyone," said Sebekhotep.

"So you have seen this before? A netjer in the form of a human?" said Neferu.

"Keep your mouth shut, Neferu. Can't you see that you are disturbing Netjer?" said the priest. "You must learn to control yourself, as it will be your responsibility to care for him until his ankle heals, and we can bring him before Pharaoh."

"What? Me? Why?" said Neferu with a look of shock and fear.

"You were the one he chose to speak with. We are priests. Our temple in this small town is not suited to care for the needs of one as special as this. We cannot nurture him and tend to his whims. You have a large home and many servants to aid you in his care."

"Yes, it must be you," Ptahhote said, relieved that it wouldn't be his responsibility.

Somehow, he didn't feel that Sekhmet, his wife, would be excited about housing and caring for a netjer either.

"His needs! What do you mean by tending to his needs?" she asked.

The priest glared at her and motioned for the two guards to aid the god down to the pyramid's base.

"Run now and fetch a ke-nee-oo."

It was what modern English-speaking people would call a palanquin.

Sebekhotep sent the other priest running toward the village. Not knowing the proper etiquette for attending a god, Neferu meekly touched the god's arm.

"What shall we call you, oh great pharaoh of the pyramid?"

James was able to understand most of the question. "Call me James," he said, using the ancient dialect as he understood it.

"Thank you, Netjer James," Neferu said.

"No, not Netjer James, only James," he said.

"This way, Netjer, who calls himself James," she said as she led him down.

James sat at the base of Khufu, the Great Pyramid of Egypt, on the Giza Plateau. He had been here many times during his life. The awe and beauty of this vista stunned him. All three of the pyramids were covered in polished white casing stones. Looking up, he noticed that the very top of the pyramid was pure gold.

In the back of his mind, he thought, *Of course, gold. What a great conductor!*

The giant sphinx stood majestically in the distance, looking out to the horizon as if standing watch over the entire area. The morning fog had dissipated, and the intense sun was beaming down on the small group who were waiting for the ke-nee-oo. James sat in awe as his mind drifted back to all of the amazing expeditions that he had accompanied his mom on as a kid. She knew everything there was to know about this place.

I wish she could be here now.

She would have given anything to see what he was witnessing. After about half an hour of sitting in quiet contemplation, as five Ancient Egyptians pretended not to stare at him, the ke-nee-oo came bouncing up. It was a small gold box with purple curtains, and it couldn't have been more than six feet long and three feet wide. It was probably only about five feet tall. It sat atop two long, thick poles that were carried by sturdy-looking fellows wearing wen-khu, a sort of diaper-looking shorts.

Ptahhote took one look at the procession and chastised the eight slaves for looking directly at James and not lowering their gaze. The ke-nee-oo was followed by what looked like the rest of the village priesthood, who were eager to catch a glimpse of the god. Ptahhote walked right up to one of the two now-returning priests and slapped him directly in the face.

"Were these slaves not instructed how to approach Netjer, you fool?"

"Uh. No, sir, we were in a hurry to reach you," he said.

"Think next time, you imbecile, or you could get us all killed," Ptahhote said as he glanced side-eyed at James.

All James understood was something about slaves and death. He wasn't exactly sure what was going on, but apparently, these slaves were expected to carry him, literally, on their shoulders. That was un-American. Steaming, but not knowing exactly what he should do, he looked toward the men who had set the ke-nee-oo down on the ground.

James pointed toward the slaves. He thought he said, "It is not right for these men to be forced to carry me."

The Egyptians understood something different. "These men are not worthy to carry me."

Upon hearing this, Sebekhotep threw himself to the ground, prompting the entire procession of officials, guards, priests, and slaves to do the same. James burst out laughing. The whole thing reminded him of a bunch of prairie dogs barking and disappearing into their dens when a predator was approaching.

"No, no. Relax! It's okay," James said in English. Realizing his mistake, he tried to say it again in Egyptian.

What the procession understood was some gibberish in the god tongue, followed by, "No, it is agreeable."

Everyone looked at each other. Ptahhote, who understood exactly what needed to happen, walked over to the ke-nee-oo and motioned for everyone but the slaves to grab a pole. James decided this was a preferable outcome. He walked up and climbed into the compartment. Once inside, he noticed two seats facing each other. It looked a little tight, but what the hell? With a grin, realizing he was taking advantage of the situation, he motioned for Neferu to join him.

She was instantly shocked and horrified, understanding the implications of a man and a woman riding together, even if a god didn't.

The Sem priest assessed the situation and said, "Silence, woman. Netjer has taken an interest in you, and you must obey."

With a groan and a glare directed at James, Neferu climbed into the carriage and sat down.

The trip back to town was mostly uneventful. James sat with a silly smile, looking out of the window, taking it all in. Men and women tended small gardens. It was very dry here, so any water needed to grow these gardens would need to be carried in. Carpenters were busy building fences and scaffolding for the few structures that were under construction.

Neferu sat back and studied this new god. She had never seen a man like this.

Those eyes, she thought. *This man is undoubtedly a netjer to have haunting eyes like this, as blue as the deep ocean. Did they not say the netjeru were giants? Those shoulders and arms could surely crush the guards, whose scrawny, hairless bodies seemed half his size. A woman could feel safe with a man like this at her side.*

Neferu hadn't felt safe in years. She always felt like the other merchants and businessmen watched her. It was as if they wanted and would take everything she had worked so hard for. She wanted nothing to do with those suitors who eyed her small empire with lust and greed. She knew that if she let one of them into her bed, she would lose everything, including herself. She would be forced to be subservient to a new husband. She had been there before, and while her late husband wasn't abusive, she'd had a taste of freedom and power, and she was not about to let it go.

Loneliness was a small price to pay to be able to control her own destiny. Looking at this god before her, though, she thought he was something different. For some strange reason, as big and powerful as he seemed, she was not fearful of him. This was a god in front of her, and she was intimidated, but he didn't seem to want to force his will on anyone. This was not what gods were supposed to be like. They were giants who would intimidate and even kill subjects for any reason that they saw fit.

James could barely take his eyes off the landscape as they passed. The people, the beasts of burden, and the ancient tools for plowing and cultivating were straight out of a textbook. These were the same tools and clothing he had seen in the museums his mother had always taken him to. He happened to glance at the beautiful young woman across from him.

As he looked over, he noticed her staring at him intensely. As soon as she realized what she was doing, she quickly looked down, and her face turned bright red. He reached over and put his hand on her arm. She trembled slightly as he gently grasped her.

"It is good. Do not fear," he said with a big smile in perfect Egyptian.

She looked up into his eyes and began to tremble more, and her eyes began to well up. James couldn't tell if she was angry with him or terrified, so he released her arm, smiled, and looked back out the window. Neferu thought she was strong, having survived her husband and all of the other forces that tried to beat her down as a woman in her delicate social position.

Something about this god told her all was well. She hadn't felt that since her father hugged her as a child. She trembled and wept from the strange emotions. It was all too much to take in. She was riding in a ke-nee-oo with a god and was supposed to take care of him, whatever that meant.

Upon arriving in Khemenu-Ka, people lined the sides of the streets. Word had gotten out that a god was visiting the normally quiet work village. There were so many that James figured it must be the whole town. They stood there either completely quiet or mumbling and murmuring. James spread open the curtains to get a better look. At once, all who saw his face dropped to the ground in a sort of worship.

"This has gotten completely out of hand," he said in English.

Neferu watched the god intently, even while not exactly staring at him any longer. He had a commanding presence. At one point along the ride, he spread open the curtains to show the masses his glory, and after the people prostrated themselves in piety, he offered a prayer to them in the god tongue. What a fantastic creature this was. They entered the town through the main avenue. Once there, the small temple was at the end of the way, but the procession didn't head toward the temple. They made a right turn. Neferu called out to the priests carrying the litter.

"Why are we not going to the temple?"

"I have decided not to go directly to the temple," said Sebekhotep.

"Oh, fine; where are we going then?" she said.

"We are going to your villa," said the priest.

Neferu was mortified. "Stop, what? Now? I haven't prepared. There is cleaning and decorating that must be done. We must have palm branches at the foot of the door to welcome him, and olive branches must be set out around the house to give him peace."

"I am sorry, Neferu, but we have no other option. The temple is not prepared to receive a netjer."

"Of course it is not, you idiot, and neither is my house. You know what that means."

The Sem priest scowled at Neferu. "You need to know your place, woman. Keep your mouth shut and do as instructed."

There was little she could do. She would have to suffer this humiliation, and there was no reprieve. This would surely be the most embarrassing thing ever to happen to a household. They had no right to force her into this relationship, and they knew they could get away with it because she was a woman. She must suffer in silence.

James saw the interaction between Neferu and the Sem priest and could tell she was distraught and that he was likely the cause of this confrontation. He looked toward her and gave her a sheepish grin, not understanding exactly what was happening.

She scowled at first, then a few moments later gave him a bit of an embarrassed shrug and grinned back. That caused James's heart to skip a beat. Something about this woman felt familiar, as if he had found a compatriot in this mad new truth.

Without realizing it, James let out a sigh of relief as if reality had started to settle in. This was no dream. He was no longer in the dark tomb without food, drink, or hope.

CHAPTER TEN

Is This Real?

2006 AD

Hank and Sara were waiting at the baggage claim for their boy. It had been nearly a year since they were all together. James picked his mom up off the ground and squeezed her like he did when he was six. That familiar feeling that everything was going to be okay washed over him. He turned to Hank, and James tried to get away with the classic bro hug, but Hank wasn't having that and instead pulled him in for a bear hug.

"You ready to get to work, squirt?"

"Squirt? I'm taller than you, Pop."

"Doesn't matter how big you are. You're still a squirt."

James smiled and shook his head.

"Yeah, I'm ready. I'm so sick of school. I need to get some work done."

"You need to hang in there. You'll be done in a couple of years and can start at the firm."

James didn't comment further, not wanting to start another lecture, and changed the subject. "Are you guys hungry? The meal on the plane was horrible."

They stopped at James's favorite restaurant when he was a child.

"So, Mom, tell me what we are doing here."

"Oh, James, you will be floored when you see this place. We just got started, and I have a feeling we are on to something big. It may be a new tomb."

"You're kidding. A new tomb? That's huge, Mom."

"Don't get your hopes up too much, though. It could turn out to be nothing."

To Hank's frustration, James started in with Sara on their old game of speaking in Ancient Egyptian. Hank had no idea what they were saying.

After a few minutes of this back and forth and their laughing in front of Hank, he said, "matlhoblaH'a' DaH." Satisfied, he sat back with a smug smile.

"Dad, we don't speak Klingon," James said with a chuckle.

"Yeah, and I don't speak Ancient Egyptian. Can we order?"

James and Sara burst out laughing.

On the way to the hotel, James hounded his parents with questions about what he could expect.

"Dad, are you sure I'm up to lead the crews? They are going to look at me like a kid."

"Jim, you are the most capable 'kid' I have ever seen, and you're six feet three and have a scruffy beard. You don't look like a kid. I wouldn't worry about it. I was thinking that what we should do, so you can get a fair shot, is not to tell anyone you are our son. You're a capable foreman with experience working the oilfields in Alaska. That'll give you some street cred."

"Dang, Pop, that's a great idea. Yeah, let's do that."

"Hey, people know you as James Jones from the forums. Let's use that," said Sara.

"That sounds like a great idea, Mom. James Jones, it is."

James showed up at the job site the next day wearing his sparkling new white hard hat. He had pulled out the hard hat's adjustable headband and flipped everything around so the bill was on the back. James had always seen the seasoned, cool guys do that. That served two purposes. It gave him a bit of a gangster look, like a reversed ball cap, and also an unobstructed view when looking up. When you had to crane your neck to supervise a crew working up high all day, you might have a sore neck when the hard hat's bill was in the way.

Hank and James arrived in different trucks to start the day. As the job site foreman, James was given a work truck to use while he was in Egypt. It was nothing fancy—a plain white F250 with the company logo on the side. They pulled up to the job shack, where the small crew had assembled for the daily briefing. When they walked in, everyone was already seated around the table.

James noticed that it was a mix of Egyptian and American workers. Officially, they would be using Masri, but nearly everyone spoke English, so they would always give instructions in each language. This was no problem for James since he could speak both fluently.

Hank said, "I want to introduce everyone to our job site foreman. This is James, uh, James Jones." Hank looked over at James with a wink. "He will be filling in the crew leads on their daily projects. Crew leads will also need to get with him to have their work inspected after each shift. I don't want to hear any of the whining and bitching, either. As of right now, all problems will be directed to James."

"Great!" James said in a low, sarcastic groan.

Hank reviewed the daily project schedule and planned work for the next week. This included work for the scaffold crew to build shoring that would support the tunnel system and make it safe for the archaeologists. There would also be some extensive above-ground dirt work with heavy machinery to remove the sand that covered the entrance for hundreds, maybe thousands, of years.

Sara entered the job shack, followed by a short, pudgy man with very thick glasses.

"Ah, Sara, Howard, perfect timing. I want to introduce Dr. Tiberious and Dr. Geist. They are the real bosses around here. We all do what they say, got it?" Hank turned to the two professors. "Is there anything you want to add before we start?"

Sara chimed in, "First, I want to thank everyone for the hard work that you will be doing. We trust you all to keep us safe so we can focus on our work. The main thing I want to drill into you is this- we are not here to make money. That's not what we are about. We are here to further science. It's imperative that you do not disturb or harm anything inside the tunnel system. If you see something that could be an issue or damage anything, speak up! You will be paid regardless, even if we shut down work, so don't worry about your job."

Sara looked at Dr. Geist. "Is there anything you would like to add?"

"Only that you have all signed nondisclosure agreements. If you don't know what that means, here it is. You don't tell anyone anything about what you do or see here. Understand?" Geist said with furrowed eyebrows and a slight downward curving of his mouth.

Sara patted him on the shoulder and continued, "I think they got the idea, Doctor. Thank you all. Let's get this show on the road."

Everyone stood and headed to their work area.

The work was slow going. James was used to the fast-paced work on normal for-profit construction sites, where time was money. It was strange to him to slow down and work methodically. He knew he would have to learn this if he was ever going to be an archaeologist.

After a week, the dirt work removing the sand overburden was progressing well. James hadn't seen Hank much during the project. He was usually away from the site, working on engineering. Every aspect of the project had to be meticulously planned with drawings, as required by the Egyptian Ministry of Tourism and Antiquities.

James had decided that if they couldn't work quickly, they could at least work efficiently, and he did everything he could think of to remove any wasted time or effort. The scaffold crew had been working all week to shore up the entrance to the tunnel system and were able to get the archaeologists access to the first fifty feet of the tunnel system.

James noticed his mom and Geist standing in the distance, watching the progress and walked to them.

"Dr. Geist, Dr. Tiberius, it's nice to see you. I think we can get you into the tunnels this afternoon."

Sara's eyes lit up. "So soon? I didn't expect that for another week."

"We are ahead of schedule. I had the scaffold crew work on the shoring as soon as we uncovered the entrance enough to get them in."

Geist had a shocked look on his face. "We told you to work slowly and methodically. If you have disturbed anything, you will never work here again."

Sara was about to speak up when James winked at her with an unspoken "I got this" look.

"Oh, Dr. Geist, you don't have to worry about that one bit. I have been on archaeological sites my entire life. You know me from the forums as James Jones. I have been holding these guys' hands to ensure they do it right. I can assure you the shoring's safe, and the structure is completely unharmed."

"Oh, James Jones, of course! I'd pictured you older. It's nice to put a face to the name, finally. I read your paper on Khufu. Brilliant stuff."

James motioned for Dr. Geist and Dr. Mom to follow him to the entrance.

Once there, James called to the work crew, "Alright, guys, let's take a few. The brass is here to make sure you haven't screwed up too bad." The workers finished what they had been working on and sat on the tailgates of the work trucks for a smoke.

James motioned for the two doctors to follow. "See, any place the shoring comes in contact with the stone, we have used this non-marking rubber and soft lumber to keep the steel plates from hitting the surface."

"That's brilliant, Mr. Jones. Who came up with it?" asked Geist.

"I did, but I cleared it with Hank and the other engineers before starting."

"This shoring system is perfect," said Geist as he looked at Sara. "I will be using this system from now on."

Sara beamed with pride. "Impressive, Mr. Jones. I guess that Harvard education is paying off."

James's face flushed a bit, embarrassed by the attention.

"Oh my! A Harvard-educated construction worker. That is impressive."

"Thanks for the compliments," James said, "but look here at the end of the tunnel where we had to stop. I noticed some strange symbols I have never seen before. See here and here. From what I can tell, these are too perfect, not Ancient Egyptian."

"Yes! Yes, I see, very interesting," said Geist.

"Jim, that's incredible! I have seen symbols like this before." She let their little facade slip for a moment.

Geist looked at Sara. "Dr. Tiberius, you know that information is not to be shared! Mr. Jones, I want to remind you that what you see here is confidential. You must forget what she said."

James looked at his mom, who was becoming uncharacteristically angry.

"Dr. Geist, you know as well as I that this information is too big to keep hidden. This is for the science community, not for some corporation to exploit."

"Sara, that's not your decision. McDermott and I have been working on this for years."

Sara spun around and stormed off.

"Don't worry about her. She won't make trouble. You seem like a smart kid."

James cringed. "Um, thanks, I guess."

"Listen, I need someone like you to help with some other projects after this. Are you interested?"

"Yeah, sure. Thanks."

"I would like your crew to take the day off tomorrow. Dr. Tiberius and I will need to spend the day assessing the site. Remind your men about the NDAs they signed. I wouldn't want to sue anyone if they open their mouths."

Geist walked away as his cell phone rang. He flipped it open, mumbling about Sara. James didn't know what to think of the whole exchange. It was nearing the end of the workday, so James had the crew finish up what they were doing. He would have to find a new project for them in the morning. After everyone left, James walked through the work area, double-checking that all the clamps were tightened to specs and that the proper safety gear was in place for the archaeologists in the morning.

The next morning, James instructed the scaffold crew to build some temporary structures that would eventually be used as a staging area for any artifacts brought out of the site. Once he had them all set up and arranged the project for the crew lead, James met with Hank in the job shack to review the latest engineering drawings for the remaining shoring. He hoped the archaeologists could complete their work so the scaffold crew could return to work in the tunnels.

"Dad, I didn't get a chance to talk to Mom after that strange meeting at the tunnel with Dr. Geist. They both seemed pissed. Any idea what that was all about?"

"Your mom was upset last night but didn't want to bother me with the details. I don't think she trusts Dr. Geist. She said he had some important business and asked your mom to do the evaluation without him today."

There was a loud rumble, and the ground began shaking. James looked out the window and watched as a D8 tractor and a front-end loader were moving a large pile of dirt and sand that had been removed for the excavation.

"That seems strange. He was all about getting in that tunnel yesterday. Dad, are you concerned about the heavy equipment shaking the ground so much with the shoring?"

"Not at all. I designed it so they could drive the equipment right over the top without disturbing the dig. As long as it was installed properly, we will be fine. I personally went out there to inspect it last night. They did a fine job."

"Yeah, that crew does great work, and I checked the clamps myself," said James.

"See, nothing to be concerned about. It's all in the excavation plan."

Something was troubling James, and he couldn't get it out of his head. He decided to double-check everything one last time. As he approached the entrance, everything seemed fine. The shoring wasn't affected at all by the vibrations. Sara was deep inside the tunnel on her knees with a camera, taking photos of the strange glyphs they had found the day before.

James glanced to the side and noticed that one of the braces had slipped a bit. The two-inch steel scaffold tube had been scraped as if the clamp was failing. It wouldn't be a problem for one brace to fail. James looked at another, and it, too, had slipped. His heart began to race as he pulled out his scaffold wrench to see if they were loose. As he tightened the clamp, there was almost no resistance. It couldn't have been more than three foot-pounds of torque.

"Mo... Dr. Tiberius, can you please come out of the tunnel? Something is wrong with the shoring."

"Oh, Jim, that's ridiculous. Your dad designed this. It's bulletproof."

"Humor me for a sec, Mom. Please, drop what you're doing and come outside so I can double-check a few things."

"Fine, Jim, if you insist."

The ground began to rumble and shake, and the scaffold shifted, causing debris to rain down, creating a dust cloud.

"Yikes, I see what you mean, Jim," Sara said as she quickened her pace.

Then, all hell broke loose. The large timbers above their heads began to fall, striking James on the shoulder and knocking him to the ground. The dust was so thick he couldn't see Sara.

"Mom, can you hear me?"

James didn't hear a response.

"Mom! Mom, answer me," James screamed out. Nothing.

The ground was still shaking, and debris was falling. James stood, trying to feel his way deeper into the tunnel as he reached for the radio transmitter on his lapel, but he couldn't lift his right arm, so he used his left hand.

"We have an emergency. Cease all operations. Cease all operations now. I need help in the tunnels."

Moments later, the rumbling stopped. The shoring was a jumbled mess all over the ground. The dust settled as James began to feel his way toward his mom. She had been thirty feet farther in. He had to belly crawl underneath some debris, then climb over some more, all while yelling, "Mom, can you hear me?"

James blindly felt his way forward as the dust choked his lungs. He pulled his shirt up over his mouth as an ad hoc mask. Finally, James's fingers brushed cold, soft skin, her arm limp and unmoving. Fearing the worst, his heart hammered as he felt his way up her arm and touched her lovely face. She wasn't responding to his call or touch.

The dust had begun to settle enough to reveal her lower half, crushed and pinned beneath steel I-beams and wood cribbing.

"Mom, please," he whispered. His stomach lurched.

This can't be real.

Part of the ceiling structure had collapsed, and stones held everything down. James struggled frantically to pull the debris from his mother with the only arm that would function, sweat beading on his brow as he screamed and struggled to remove the stones. They wouldn't budge.

Sara's eyes fluttered open, glazed with pain.

"Jimmy? You're all covered in dirt, and there's blood on your face. You okay?" Sara spoke in a weak voice.

"Thank God, Mom, you were passed out. How are you? Hold on. They're coming to help us," James said, tears welling in his eyes with renewed hope.

"You're gonna make it out of this, Mom. I'm gonna get you out."

Sara's eyes grew wide in understanding as she moaned, coughing blood on James's shirt.

"I don't know, Jimmy. I can't feel my arms," Sara rasped out, blood now spilling from her nose before she passed out again.

The shoring shifted, and more dust and debris fell around them.

James could hear people yelling and pulling rocks and broken shoring from the tunnel near the entrance. He was frantically doing everything he could to move the debris, which was pinning his mom to the ground. He was able to pull out one of the scaffold tubes and try to use it as a lever to lift the stone.

"Come on. Move, damn it. Mom, hold on."

Sara woke with flickering eyes. "Jimmy, stop. Listen to me."

Tears were pouring down James's face. "Mom, I can't. I have to…"

"Jimmy, stop."

He stopped and looked at her.

Sara whispered to him in her frail voice. "Jimmy, my sweet boy, I am not going to make it."

"No, absolutely not, Mom, stop! They are coming for us."

"Don't let this sadness bury you. You're my adventurer, my pyramid chaser. Promise me you'll keep seeking when I'm gone. Study those symbols. Don't let them hide them from the world."

Tears streaked down James's face as he gently held her hand.

"I promise, Mom, but I don't know how to do it without you," he choked out.

"You will find a way. I love you, sweetie."

Her limp hand tried to slide out of James's, but he refused to let go. He cradled her hand against his chest. Tears fell on her lifeless fingers.

Rough hands grabbed him from behind, dragging him away.

"No! Stop, we can still save her," James screamed as the rest of the shoring came crashing down.

I'm sorry, Mom, so very sorry. *It's my fault.*

CHAPTER ELEVEN

Neferu's Home

1153 BC

Neferu had selected some of her late husband's garments for James. She had a few others hastily made due to his size. The servants dressed him in a pleated fine linen shendyt, reaching mid-calf, with a tunic and a beaded wesekh collar. He agreed to set aside his leather jacket and Keene boots, as the short-sleeved linen tunic and papyrus sandals were better suited for the hot, dry environment. When they began to apply the black kohl to his eyes, he waved them away.

James spent the next few days absorbing everything he was experiencing. He would sit with Neferu, and anyone else he could find, to practice speaking the new language. He realized that he and Sara thought they had mastered the language when, in fact, they had barely scratched the surface.

It was time for him to get out and see this new, old world he had imagined his entire life. James hadn't fully decided what his role in his new reality would be. Should he be a bystander and watch the history he was familiar with happening around him, or perhaps this was a chance to change things and make the world a better place?

James took every opportunity to hobble outdoors. To Neferu's dismay, he refused to let the servants help him get around. The house was next to the brick factory, and as soon as he walked out, everyone stopped what they were doing and lowered their heads. James was embarrassed and didn't know how to react. He noticed a bundle of tools leaning against the wall nearby, grabbed one, and looked around to see if it was okay for him to use, but everyone refused to return his gaze. The tool was about four feet long and had a T at the top. It looked like it might have been used to maneuver hot bricks in the kiln, but it would suit his purposes nicely. He grabbed a nearby rag and wrapped it around the top.

Have I invented the very first crutch? he thought with a laugh.

The look on everyone's face, as he used his new crutch, led him to believe that he may, in fact, have invented the first crutch, but he knew that was stupid. People had been using crutches forever. He would have to find a better way to affect his new reality.

He walked out of the villa, hoping to find some sort of transportation with which he could see the village. The landscape was much different from what he had expected. In his time, civilization had encroached on the area, and all the bogs had been filled and leveled for construction. In this time, there were few structures around. The area flooded by the Nile every year was as wild and untouched as he had hoped. He started hobbling down the street toward the edge of town.

Neferu came running out, followed by the two guards who had helped him out of the tomb.

"You must not leave, Netjer James. It is not proper for you to walk unaccompanied."

James was disappointed and struggled to say, "I wish to see this village. Am I not allowed?"

Neferu cocked her head. "Allowed? Oh yes, Great James, these men have been ordered to go with you wherever you go to keep you safe. They are here to serve you."

"Yes, they can come," he said with a smile. "I have need to look around."

"In that case, Lord James, may I accompany you as well? It is expected," she said.

It took him a moment to translate in his head. "Yes, good, come along."

They walked together, the two guards about ten paces behind. His ankle hurt, but he didn't let that slow him down. He had to see some of what this new world had to offer. They walked along a couple of streets until they came to a market, which was exactly what James had hoped for. Open tents lined the avenue with the sounds of people milling about doing their daily shopping. Besides the clothing, nearly everything was the same as he had experienced in modern Cairo. You would see the fruits and vegetables right next to a butcher carving a lamb. Many of the textiles, blankets, rugs, and the like were virtually identical. It was amazing to James how little these things had changed, or more appropriately, would change, in three thousand years.

James approached one of the fruit vendors. The woman bowed and held out a few different varieties of dried figs. He grabbed a couple and ate one.

"These are delicious," he said in English with wide eyes.

The grocer shook her head. She obviously didn't understand.

"What is cost?" James said.

The woman answered, "One copper kite per bunch."

James blushed and looked back at Neferu, now realizing that he didn't have any type of currency.

"Neferu, what used for trade here?" said James.

Neferu, realizing why James was embarrassed, quickly took a small bit of metal out of her purse and handed it to the woman.

James looked regretful. "I have no currency," he said as he handed a fig to her and the two guards, who all eagerly chomped down on their snack.

"Netjer James, you have no need for currency here. All of this is yours," she said as she bowed her head and took two steps back in respect.

James wasn't sure how all of that was supposed to work. He kept telling them he wasn't a god, but they insisted he play the role. Was he to take from people as he saw fit? That didn't work with his convictions. He would have to figure something else out.

They came across a small girl, probably around ten. She had dirty clothes and tangled brown hair, with the biggest brown eyes. She was sitting cross-legged on a blanket, and four small jars were in front of her. She was holding a bowl, crushing some reddish-orange rocks into a powder. James watched as she added olive oil and wax to the powder and mixed it together. James looked at Neferu with a question in his eyes.

Neferu leaned over and whispered to James so that the small girl couldn't hear.

"She is an orphan. The temple houses and feeds the orphans who are in need, but often some of the wilder children prefer to take care of themselves. This girl is one of the children on the streets who refuse any help from the temple. The people watch over her, and we often leave food out for her to steal."

"I do not understand. Steal food?" replied James.

"Yes," Neferu said with a pained face, "this one refuses help from anyone. It is the only way we can make sure she gets enough to eat."

"Why not force her to go to temple?" said James.

"That is not our way. She will have to make her own decisions."

James approached the young girl. She saw that she had captured his attention and said, "You look like a great merchant. Would your wife like to have some of my colors on her beautiful face?"

At the word "wife," Neferu squinted and glared at the girl.

"No, thank you, dear. I would not like that put on my face. Thank you very much."

Neferu looked over at James, who had a very disappointed look. Neferu's heart sank a little. She didn't realize how much this man's opinion of her mattered. James leaned down to take a look at the small rocks that she was crushing to make the mixture.

"Where did you get rocks?" he said.

The young street urchin squirmed, her ragged clothes barely hanging on, and quickly said, "I did not steal them. I found them."

"Where did you find them?" James asked.

"These were along the edges of the swamp," she said.

"How much for you to paint lady and give me rocks?" James said.

Neferu grabbed James's arm with huge, wide eyes. "James, no, that paint will probably burn my face or something worse," she said.

"It is iron oxide with olive oil and wax. It can't hurt you," James said, mixing English into his Egyptian.

She eyed him and then the young girl and said, "Fine. Go ahead. Let us get this over with."

The young girl had a huge smile. "Really, wow, no one has ever let me paint their face before."

James grinned while Neferu looked utterly fearful. She was already wearing the customary copper-based, green-blue eye makeup with black kohl eyeliner. Neferu sat on a stool while the young girl worked with her red paints and brushes. Each jar held a different shade of red. With a brush, she applied the powders to Neferu's cheeks. Then, with her finger, she delicately painted Neferu's lips with the waxy mixture. The whole process took only a few minutes.

"Okay, finished," she said.

Neferu had a very concerned look on her face. "Oh, uh, thank you very much."

The young girl had a sly look on her face as she got off her knees. She collected her jars and bolted down the street, leaving the few red rocks she had been crushing.

"Do you not want your payment?" Neferu called as the girl disappeared around a corner.

"Okay, James, you have had your fun humiliating me. Can we please go back home so I can clean this off? I'll put my scarf around my face until we get there."

"What? Why?" James said. "Hold, look first."

James walked over to the next shop, grabbed a polished copper mirror, and held it up for Neferu to see.

"By the netjeru, it is beautiful," she said. "She has colored me as if I still had the glow of youth. My cheeks look vibrant and healthy, and my lips ... so shiny and red. It is wonderful."

James and Neferu left the market while all of the women's eyes were on Neferu. They stared at her with jealousy.

"I am going to have to get some more of this paint," she said with a big smile.

When he left the market, James was on a mission, but it would be too time-consuming to try to explain. They walked toward a swampy area on the outskirts of the village. James began to run his hands through the thick mud. Neferu glanced back at the two guards and shrugged as if to say she had no idea what this was about. James started to tread through the mud, feeling around.

"Here is one," he said as he climbed out of the mud. "See this. It is bog iron."

James held out his hand to show what looked like a small piece of orange-colored stone.

"You two." He pointed at the two guards. "Find this. We need more."

James wasn't exactly sure if he was saying the correct words, but the two men got the hint quickly. Both climbed into the swamp and began to feel around. Neferu looked at James and then, with a shrug, pulled up her dress and waded into the mud. Within a few minutes, each of them had a handful of the strange, heavy stones.

"This is good," James said. "We go back."

On the way back, he instinctively looked at his wristwatch.

"Neferu, my watch is gone. I had it when we left. It must be in the bog," James said, using the word for bracelet.

"More likely that street waif stole it," she said.

"Do you think girl who painted face could steal watch?"

Neferu looked at James and shrugged.

"Did you see how fast she jumped up and left the market?" she said.

People came out of their houses to watch the four of them, now covered in mud, walk down the brick-laden avenue and back to Neferu's home.

James was up early. After spending a few hours with the priests practicing his Egyptian, he walked out of the house and into the courtyard. All the workers stopped what they were doing and knelt down. He couldn't have everyone flailing around on the ground and stopping work every time he walked by. He resigned himself to figuring out how to resolve the situation soon, or he was sure he would wear out his welcome with Neferu. He knew that time was money.

He looked at these people and could tell there was something different about them compared to the other workers he had seen along the streets. They seemed happier and healthier.

James waved to the workers. "Continue!" he said, which came out as much more of a command than he had intended.

The workers looked at each other, then a large man nearby waved at them all and said, "Everyone, get back to work. Quickly now!"

In almost frantic haste, the entire host of workers returned to their daily routine. James sat back and watched the work. It was about what he expected, and he was sure they had been doing it this way for maybe a thousand years or more. He could only see the glaring waste of time, energy, and manpower, and he estimated that nearly half of their effort was wasted.

They had eight separate stations, all manned by six men. There was a pile of straw and clay next to each workstation. Men would walk along and add to the pile when needed. One man would mix the clay and straw together. Another would scoop up that mixture and press it into the forms. They would wait about thirty minutes for the bricks to set up, at which time the last two men would collect them on a spatula-like tool and slide them to their designated place in the kiln. When each kiln was filled by the end of the day, they would seal the opening, and then stoke the fire. Any bricks that would not fit into the kilns would be set aside to air-dry. They were much less valuable when air-dried.

James realized he was sticking his nose into an area he had no right or obligation to, but what was it worth being a god if you couldn't help people? He felt he had no choice but to streamline the operation, as he had done so many times when taking over a dig site. James approached the person he figured was in charge. Bibi was a proud man and had been in charge of this factory for a dozen years, but when a god walked up and instructed you, you did not question or disobey.

James stopped all work, gathered the men around, and organized them into groups according to the skills they had demonstrated. There were sixteen clay mixers, sixteen brick packers, sixteen kiln loaders, and a few men milling about restocking the mix at each station. James had them pull all the tables together in a line. He then chose five men, one for each duty. He directed the clay mixer to follow along with the packer, scooping directly from the wheelbarrow. He could barely load the forms fast enough before the packer pushed them along to pack the forms all down the row.

By the time they made it halfway down the row of tables, James motioned for the kiln loader to check the forms. They were cured enough to be transported to the kiln. The workers who had not been involved in this process began milling around and looking nervous. Soon, all eight kilns were filled to the brim, packed tightly and closed. Four men had carried out, in several hours, what usually took as many as fifty men to accomplish in the same amount of time.

James looked up and saw Neferu peeking through the window opening on the second floor. This was her regular perch while inspecting the goings-on in the factory. She looked astonished and walked away from the window. She had been watching the entire time.

James walked up to Bibi and said, in perfect Egyptian, "You are going to need more kilns." Then he hobbled back toward the house to fetch the basket of rocks he had collected the day before.

Did I revolutionize the brick-making process by introducing an assembly line? "Yes, yes, I did," he snickered to himself.

"Bibi," James said, "I have another project for you." He held out his small basket of rocks. "I need you to melt these down in a kiln like you do with copper, but I will need to show you how to heat the kiln beyond anything you have needed before."

James walked with Bibi and described to him exactly how they would produce the very first bog iron ever to exist.

After watching the new brick-making process, Neferu couldn't believe what she had seen. At first, she wanted to run down and stop the farce. She had been sure there was nothing new to learn about making bricks. They had been doing it this way for as long as anyone could remember. Now she knew that what man knew about making bricks was a thimbleful of information compared to what the gods knew. She realized that if she were going to be able to keep her entire crew busy, she would need many more kilns. That would be expensive, but at that rate of production, her business would surely become the premier brick producer for the empire.

James hobbled into the house as Neferu was walking down the stairs. Their eyes met, and Neferu quickly looked away and blushed. Who was this strange giant who had invaded the sanctum of her home? She knew she had no say in the matter, which angered her. She didn't enjoy the priests exerting their power over her as if she were no one. She had fought for her place in this society with all that she had.

"They had no right at all," she said to herself in a whisper.

But this man, as strange and unsophisticated as he was, embodied something special. He was not fully versed in their language or customs, but somehow observed the problems with the long-standing process for making bricks and miraculously changed it for the better in every way. She knew her workers would soon begin to become wealthy, and she could be one of the wealthiest women in Egypt, apart from the royals. All because this giant, light-skinned, hairy man had walked into her life. He was amazing, wonderful even.

I wonder what holy, spiritual thoughts are going through his head right now? Surely this netjer is here to transform our nation.

James sat down at the table near the kitchen. *Mmm, something smells good. I wonder what's for lunch?* he thought as he reached down to scratch the ant bite on his butt.

CHAPTER TWELVE

Home Isn't Home

2007 AD

The air reeked of diesel and dust as the crew hauled out tons of twisted steel and wood. James and Hank stood motionless. Tears, dirt on his face, and dried blood on James's shirt were a testament to the carnage. Finally, the broken body of the woman whom these men loved and protected was carefully brought out on a stretcher, already covered in a bag.

James didn't remember the ambulance ride to the hospital. The shock of his loss and the pain from his shoulder clouded his mind. Hank arrived later after answering questions from the investigators. He slumped in his chair at James's bedside, both men deeply ashamed, and neither spoke a word. James suffered a dislocated shoulder and damage to the cartilage that surrounded the socket. It was painful, but the shoulder would heal with time, unlike his heart.

They brought his mom home in an ornately decorated hardwood coffin. She wouldn't have wanted a fuss, as she hated being the center of attention. There was a very small, quiet funeral. To the surprise of Hank and James,

Dr. Geist, Sara's partner for the last six years, was absent. Khalid was there, of course. Neither Hank nor Sara had any relatives, and both their parents had passed. Sara was laid to rest in the small graveyard at the ranch. It had been there before the Tiberius family had purchased the property, and they had adopted it as their own. Hank's mom and dad were there, as were his grandparents.

After the funeral was over and the guests had gone, real life began to set in. The silence in the house was deafening. James longed for the joking and playful laughter that had followed Sara.

The Tiberius boys sat down to a hearty Kraft Mac & Cheese meal with peas. Defeated, Hank slumped down into his chair.

"Dad, I don't understand what happened," James said, trying to calm his shaky voice. "The clamps on the vertical diagonals were loose. I checked them myself the day before. How did they get loose? It doesn't make sense. I should've seen it, Pop."

Hank's hands went to the armrests of his chair, and he held them there, white fists murderously gripping the wood.

"Don't you dare take this on yourself, Jim. I designed the shoring. Me. It was supposed to be foolproof. I checked it the evening before she went in." His voice came in a low growl, thick with self-loathing. "She trusted me to keep her safe."

"Trusted us, she trusted both of us, and it killed her. I knew something was off. I was the foreman. I should have pulled her out the second things seemed wrong."

James slammed his fist down, smashing the empty bowl before him. Beautiful pain crawled up his arm. The dripping crimson blood finally shattered the black and white of this new reality.

Hank stood in fury, unsteady. His bright-red face pulsed with bulging veins on his forehead. James had never seen his father like this and was afraid.

"You think you could have stopped her? You know as well as I do that she was stubborn as hell. She wouldn't have come out unless she had wanted to. If my engineering was sound, none of this ..."

Hank suddenly grabbed his head with a moan and fell back in his seat. His eyes widened in a moment of realization. James threw himself across the table to protect his father's head as he slumped to the floor.

"No, no, no, Dad. Stay with me." James lifted Hank's head to see the right side of his face slumping.

In a flurry, James reached for his phone and dialed 911. The nearest hospital was not nearby.

The ambulance ride was a blur of sirens and the smell of antiseptic. Hank's eyes were open, and he looked pleadingly into James's eyes as he held his father's limp right hand. At the hospital, the doctor declared, "Massive stroke ... Right side paralyzed ... Emergency brain surgery ... Round-the-clock care, if he pulls through." The danger to his brain was far from over.

Later, the doctor entered the waiting room with news that they had stopped the bleeding in the brain, and only time would tell how Hank would fare in the long run. A nurse came to the waiting room and waved to James. He looked at her name tag, Grace Shepherd.

Grace was a sturdy black woman whose energy immediately calmed James. She had sorrowful eyes and a kind, knowing smile. With a hug, she led him through two massive doors to the intensive care unit. James had never been in a hospital ward like this. Nurses in their colorful scrubs walked every which way. Unfamiliar smells assailed his nose as the beeps of machines and sensors rang from every room. There wasn't much privacy here. Every room had large glass doors that faced out in a sort of courtyard with the enormous nursing station in the middle.

Hank looked bad. His face was pale, and his usually well-kept hair was flat and askew from bedhead. Wires came from all points on his body, and a breathing tube was in his mouth. Grace walked up behind James and put a hand on his shoulder. With a little shiver, he stepped back and turned to the nurse.

"Your dad is stable," she said. "The stroke was severe, but thanks to your quick action, they were able to get him to the hospital in time. You gave your dad a fighting chance."

Tears welled up in his eyes.

"I didn't expect him to be this bad off," he said. "Has he woken up or talked or anything?"

The nurse responded, "When he came in, he was responsive. We had to induce a coma in order to prep him for the surgery and let his body recover."

"So he'll live and wake up?" asked James.

"That's what we are hoping for," said Grace.

A quick glance at her told James the staff did not expect a happy ending. James knew his mother well enough to know she would have expected him not to give up hope.

He sat with Hank for several days, using the bench next to the window to get some sleep. The kind nurses continued to bring him blankets and would sneak him food when they felt he should eat. He took breaks occasionally to run home and grab a shower. Various doctors and specialists would come, who would speak of Hank using unfamiliar terms and diagnoses. After they would leave, the lovely nurses would come in and explain what the doctors had said. James was smart, brilliant even, but had never once studied medicine.

After returning from a trip home, he noticed a doctor and several nurses in his father's room.

James grabbed Grace's arm and quietly said, "What's going on?"

"Hank responded to some stimulus on his cheek a few minutes ago. They are going to bring him out of the coma. When he wakes up, we will have to evaluate his mental and physical condition. You can sit next to the bed if you'd like."

James walked past the doctor and sat in his usual place. He watched as they unplugged the medicine hooked to the saline bag, which had the sleeping drugs in it.

"It shouldn't be long before we see some consciousness," the doctor said, walking out of the room.

James and Grace looked at each other with hope and anxiety on their faces. Grace had to continue her rounds, but James sat quietly and watched Hank for the next thirty minutes or so.

Hank began to move, dragging his arm to his chest, bending his knee, and flexing his hand. All were good signs, according to the nurses who would come in periodically. With a slight groan, Hank slowly opened his eyes to narrow slits. A second later, his eyes got bigger, then with a look of terror, Hank struggled to reach for his breathing tube and, doing his best with a sleepy hand, tried to pull the tube from his mouth.

With panic in his voice, James yelled for the nurse and grabbed his father's one working hand to keep him from hurting himself. Hank's eyes were like saucers, pleading with James to let him pull the foreign object out of his throat. He started to squirm and move in fright. Hank frantically motioned for him to help pull the tube out.

"I can't, Dad. Hold on," James insisted. He hated to think his father might consider his refusal to help to be disloyalty, even if he wasn't entirely in control of his faculties. "Nurse! Nurse! Help us."

Grace walked in calmly, displaying none of the panic James and his dad felt.

"Oh! Hello there, Mr. Tiberius. How are we feeling today? Oh, that tube? Don't worry about that one-bit hun. We needed to leave it in to make sure you were breathing on your own. It looks like you are breathing fine, so let's see about getting that tube out." Hank closed his eyes as the nurse gently removed the tube. "There, is that better?"

Hank tried to speak, but his throat was dry and scratched, and the stroke had numbed half of his face. That afternoon, and through most of the night, various specialists would come in to assess his progress. There was a breathing specialist, an eating and drinking specialist, and so on.

They all had a great laugh when the eating specialist had Hank sit up to try to drink some water. According to the doctor, stroke victims often had a difficult or impossible time eating and drinking. While trying to swallow, food and drink could enter the lungs, causing pneumonia, if proper precautions were not taken. The doctor held a cup of ice water with a straw up to his mouth. As he sipped, the water came out of the opposite side of his mouth and down his shirt. James laughed, causing Grace and Hank to laugh too.

The days went by slowly. Hank's right side was partially paralyzed, but he was able to breathe, eat, and drink on his own. He could use the bathroom, but getting him in and out was difficult. James often helped, even when the nurses were available. A few weeks in, Hank decided he had had enough and wanted to go home. James thought it would be better for Hank to stay in the hospital for a few more weeks for rehab. The doctors thought he might be able to walk again with a physical therapy regimen. Against James's better judgment, the nurses loaded Hank into a wheelchair and sent him on his way.

The stroke had changed the man James knew growing up. That larger-than-life figure, who had men admiring his business skills and outside-the-box brilliant engineering schemes, was now reduced to a shell of that man. This broke James's heart. He refused to see his dad in the new "brain-damaged" existence and treated him with the respect he deserved and had earned his entire life.

Hank had taken Sara's death hard, and it seemed he was giving up. Sara had been his compass, her laughter a map through life's chaos, and now she was gone. The nights grew heavier as summer waned. Each tick of the clock was a hammer against James's chest as he realized his time with his dad was slipping away. The sadness clawed at him. It was a hollow ache that swallowed every hope he'd clung to since his mom's death.

The air in the Tiberius family's home hung heavy that autumn after-noon, the kind of stillness that followed a storm's departure. James sat on the porch rocking in his dad's chair. He remembered the days past, when Hank and Sara would sit together. Hank rocking and reading his novels, Sara fully engrossed in her knitting. James held the framed photo of his mom that had been on the mantle, her eyes bright with the same passion she'd poured into every dig, every story she'd shared with him. It had been almost a year since the swift and merciless accident had left a void that James couldn't navigate.

Later, James was sitting on the couch debating internal pyramid archi-tecture with a group of archaeologists on the forums when the doorbell jolted him from his conversation. He shuffled over to find Khalid standing in the doorway, his familiar white cap tilted, a paper sack of Whataburger clutched in his hand.

"Figured ya hadn't eaten today, kid," Khalid said, stepping inside with-out waiting for an invite, his voice a steady anchor in the quiet.

James slumped back onto the couch as Khalid set the burgers on the coffee table, the greasy scent a faint comfort against the ache in his chest. "Dad's not doing well, Kal," James muttered. "Says he doesn't know how much longer he's going to be around. He blames himself for Mom, Kal. I think he has given up."

Khalid unwrapped a burger, sliding it toward James with a nod.

"He's grievin' his way, Jim. You're grievin' yers. Ain't no right or wrong, it feels like hell either way."

James picked at the burger, his throat tight. "She was supposed to be here, Kal. Teach me the glyphs. Drag me to ruins. I keep thinking I'll hear her voice telling me to quit moping."

Khalid's eyes softened, crinkling at the edges as he leaned forward. "She's still with ya, son. Every time ya read those glyphs, every dig ya chase, that's her livin' through you. You're her legacy, not some kid feelin' lost."

Khalid took a bite, chewing thoughtfully before wiping his hands on his jeans.

"Listen, I've seen men crumble under less. Hank's tough, but ya got her fire, Jim. Don't let this break ya. You're gonna hurt, and that's okay. It means ya loved her fiercely. But ya gotta spark of adventure, same as Sara, and it's gonna burn for somethin'. Dig in those books, chase those crazy pyramid ideas she loved. Hell, prove 'em all wrong, me included. And when it gets heavy, ya call me. I ain't yer dad, but I've got yer back, always will."

James managed a slight nod, the weight lifting just enough to breathe. "Thanks, Kal. I'll try."

Khalid clapped his shoulder, firm and warm. "You'll do more than try, kid. You'll be great. Give it time."

Hank spent the next few weeks preparing James for what he felt would be coming soon and walked him through their bank accounts, where to find the deed to the house, and where all of their investments were recorded. Hank spent days talking about all the players in his engineering firm and how he hoped James would one day take his place as CEO. James wasn't interested in any of this, but Hank insisted.

"You need to prepare, son," Hank said with a struggle.

James sat with his father by his bedside for a few days, as Hank had contracted a cold and was stuck in bed. Hank told James stories about his mother and their life together before James was born. Stories that James would never forget. They were little Band-Aids that he could use to cover the pain in his soul temporarily.

Hank looked at James and reached out his good hand to grasp his arm. "Don't need... to worry 'bout school, son. Your mom and I ... plenty of money."

"You're kidding," James said. "Why didn't you tell me? I could have skipped the whole Alaska work summer."

James could tell his dad had something he needed to express, and he listened patiently as he struggled for words.

"That's why, son. You need to work ... learn things for yourself. If Mom and I ... gave you everything you wanted, you'd never have grown into the man ... I know you are. Love you, son. I want you to live ... how you want. If you don't run the company, that's fine. They'll find someone ... it will go on without us. Chase your dreams, son. That's what Mom wanted ... for you."

Hank raised his left arm.

"Take this off my wrist," he said, holding up his beloved watch. "This is for you. My dad ... gave it to me after college ... I wanted you to graduate from Harvard ... I don't think we have time. I want to ... give it to you now."

"Dad, there is plenty of time. I don't need to take your watch."

"I know, but I want you to take it ... Don't need it. You need a watch like this more."

"Sure, Dad, okay, I'll take it," James said as he looked at the floor.

The next morning, Hank didn't wake up. James went into the room to see if he was ready for breakfast, but Hank was not responsive. The doctor later said he had a stroke in his sleep, but James knew his dad hadn't recovered from the passing of his first and only love.

CHAPTER THIRTEEN

Dirty Water

1153 BC

James watched from the second-story window as the factory created brick after brick. It had been only a handful of days, but in that time, the crews were able to construct several more very large kilns and four more assembly lines. Bricks were pulled out of the kiln each morning. There was a massive surplus of bricks now, and Neferu had to rent an empty lot next door to store all of the product. Carts and wagons would come and transport them all over Egypt.

James stood with a sly grin, feeling like maybe he was a sort of god. At that thought, he looked down while remembering his father. His dad was never cocky when he would revolutionize an engineering system. Hank had made innovations in his day that saved millions of dollars in production and had a lifetime of experience. James decided any modern person would have done the same thing, and he wasn't special.

As he watched the process, James noticed the foreman was not working. At this time in history, missing a day of work was missing a day of food. There must be something wrong.

"Where is Bibi?" James asked a nearby worker.

The worker bowed and said, "Master Bibi is home with his family. His three children are very ill."

James was no medical doctor by any stretch of the imagination, but perhaps he could help with what little he knew.

"Can you take me to his home?" James asked.

"Of course, My Lord," the man replied. "His apartment is down the street a few blocks."

Neferu's main house consisted of a small open courtyard surrounded by the kitchen, dining area, and some sitting rooms. Most of the living quarters were on the second floor. The factory was set up similarly. It had a large open courtyard, surrounded by brick walls and some apartments. As the foreman, Bibi was afforded a monthly wage that also provided for his accommodations. James and the worker walked to his front door, and the worker knocked quietly. Bibi threw open the door in disgust.

"Quiet, my daughters are sleeping."

Then he looked past the worker and saw James. He quickly threw himself down and begged, "Oh Lord, please forgive my outburst. My only explanation is that I am driven nearly mad with fear and sadness for my daughters."

"Please explain," James said.

"Of course, Lord." Bibi brought James to each child. They all looked so small and malnourished. James wanted to cry, but realized it wouldn't help anything.

"These children look as if they haven't been properly fed. Is your wage not enough to feed your family?" James asked, with a disapproving look.

"No, My Lord, I am paid well and the children are well-fed. They have been unable to keep any food down for many days. This is a known sickness here that we call 'the wasting'."

James walked up to each child. Each one had dry lips and a fever.

"Have they been complaining of a stomachache?" he said.

"Yes, of course. That is one of the first signs of the wasting."

James was not sure what he could do. He had no antibiotics or antiviral medication. He looked at Bibi with a sad smile.

"Bibi, you must do your best to ensure they have clean water and whatever food they will take. Let me think about this," James said.

"Yes, Great James, your will be done. You need to know this sickness is spreading. It starts with the very young and then the old."

"I understand. I will see if there is anything to be done."

On the walk back, James heard a strange noise. It sounded like a dog whimpering. Behind a pile of refuse, a little tent made from blankets was set up.

"Hello in there," he called out, but there was no response. "Hello, is anyone inside the tent?"

James heard the pitiful sounds again, but they sounded more human this time. He pulled back the blanket to see a young child lying face down, using the trash as a mattress. The smell took James aback. He knelt down and touched the back of the girl's neck. She was burning up. The child rolled over, and her eyes became the size of saucers.

"It is you," she said before passing out in delirium.

James began to pick her up when the worker stepped up.

"If you plan to carry this child to the temple, please let me. It would not be seemly for you to," said the worker.

"Nonsense," said James. "I will be carrying her. We are not taking her to the temple. We are taking her home. Go now and prepare a bed."

"But... Lord, I... Are you sure she must go to the villa?"

"Yes, now go and tell the cooks I want a meal ready for her and some fresh water."

The worker bowed and ran off as fast as he could. James swept the tiny body into his arms and carried her, filth and all, to Neferu's home. About three-quarters of the way, Neferu came running toward them with a frantic look on her face and a lady's maid in tow.

"Is she alive?"

"She is, barely. I need to get her out of these clothes and cleaned up." He looked at the maid. "Can you do that?"

"Oh, yes, Great James. It will be done."

"Afterward, I want her in a bed with clean sheets. Do you understand?"

"Yes, Lord James, I understand."

Excited and eager to be of service, the maid took the waif from James and ran her to the bath.

Neferu gave him a curious look. "It is good you brought her here, James. They would have likely let the inevitable happen if they had received her like this at the temple. At least here we can make her last hours comfortable."

"I don't accept that. I believe we can do something."

The condition of the children reminded James of dysentery, a sickness virtually never seen in the US but very prevalent in most of the places that James had explored.

He walked across both courtyards to the main floor and kitchen area. Two cooks and several women served food to the workers when the midday meal came. Neferu wasn't like other business owners. The prevailing thought was that eating should be done on your own time. When you were at work, you worked. On the contrary, Neferu believed that a fed workforce could do more work in a day. She was the only local business owner to feed her entire retinue once a day. Often, that would be the only meal these men would receive.

Other owners would send the workers home with their agreed pay, and the families would either feast or face famine, depending on how well the worker or business performed. Neferu's men were never hungry, and she allowed any leftovers to be brought home to the families along with a generous wage. The men worked longer and harder for her, knowing their families would be cared for.

James stood at the prep table and watched the cooks. He had instructed them on several occasions not to prostrate themselves before him. They watched him out of the side of their eyes, not fully trusting that he wouldn't devour them at any second.

He quietly asked for a glass of water. The women looked at each other with a spark of fear, then one walked to a carafe and poured the liquid into a clay mug. She walked over and handed it to him with a bowed head. James took a huge mouthful. He had been getting used to drinking tepid water. He furrowed his brows at the women, then, with a look of disgust, spat the liquid onto the floor. Immediately, they knew they had done something wrong and would surely be killed. They all, once again, dropped to the floor. James realized his reaction was a bit over the top, but he had been served a weak beer and had expected fresh water.

"Everyone, stand. I was not correct in my anger," he said.

He had been working tirelessly on his Egyptian, and the women slowly rose to their feet.

"I did not ask for beer. I asked for water."

He was fairly sure they could understand him at this point.

A tiny maid, around fourteen and probably not more than eighty pounds, rose and said, "Please, Lord, forgive me. I thought you would want beer, as all of the water in town was found to be tainted." She wore the traditional white servants' kalisaris trimmed in brown with small white handprints all over from helping the kitchen staff bake bread.

"Oh, I see," he said. "Worry not. What you did was right. What is your name, young lady?"

"Meryt, Lord," she said.

"Please bring me a mug of water so that I may see, Meryt."

Meryt gave a slight bow, then ran to a cupboard to fetch a mug and poured the contents of a jug into it. When she handed the mug to him, he first looked at the contents, then smelled it. Had he been drinking this the whole time he was there? He seemed to remember the strange smell and flavor of the water, but didn't think about where it came from. He poured some of the contents into his hand. It was light gray, almost soapy looking, and a few particulates were floating. Realizing he had been drinking this for days, James started to feel a little sick. No wonder he had that horrible diarrhea, though he had figured his stomach was adjusting to the mutton diet. He didn't want to complain because he knew it was the very best they had to offer.

"We have been serving only beer today," said Meryt. "Some of the workers have taken sick, and we believe it is from the water."

James hadn't noticed Neferu standing at the base of the stairs, watching. When James turned and saw her, her face flushed, and she looked down.

"Please forgive us, Great James," she said. "All of the water coming out of the cisterns is like this. The Nile's waters have grown murky from bloom."

James assumed she was referring to an algae bloom. "We have cisterns filled with water around the city, but these too are tainted. Many have become sick, and some children have perished. Ptahhote has sent carts to Men-nefer to fetch fresh water, but it will take several days to return. We fear the beer will soon run out; if that happens, people will begin drinking the water again. Please do not worry. You will always have the best beer and will not suffer from our misfortune."

James was taken aback. How many people, children even, would die in the next few days simply because they couldn't drink clean water?

"Neferu," he said, "I need you to do a few things for me. First, I need a large papyrus. Next, I will need one full crew of brick makers to stop what they are doing and work directly under my instruction."

"Yes, Great James, it will be done now." With a look from Neferu, everyone began to scurry.

"Put the papyrus on one of the worktables and we can begin."

James went to his room and grabbed something out of his satchel. The entire household was abuzz. It seemed like people were coming out of nowhere, running past.

Within minutes, Neferu said, "Come with me, My Lord."

The papyrus was on the worktable, and eight workers stood there watching expectantly. They were already aware of James's abilities and were eager to see a new miracle. James hovered over the table, pulled out his pencils, and then began drawing up plans for a crude water filtration system. He had seen one built on a reality TV survival show, and things like that stuck in James's mind like glue. The entire household stood and watched as he drew four connected cisterns, all stepping down like stairs. The top had an opening coming out from the bottom, leading to the next cistern, and so on. He labelled the bottom cistern with the symbol for clean water.

James had drawn his diagram using a three-dimensional isometric perspective and symbols to represent the different materials. No one had ever seen anything like it before. The growing crowd looked at each other in disbelief.

"It looks so real," they whispered to each other.

He labeled the top cistern with the symbol for small river rocks. On the second, sand from the desert. The third was for layers of charcoal and sand, though he didn't know the symbol for that.

The entire group looked at Neferu. She slapped her hands together once, and they began to work quickly.

James watched the progress from Neferu's favorite perch. They stood there together, side by side, watching his drawing come to life. It took two days to build and another for the mortar and clay to dry to where it would hold water.

James couldn't get excited like everyone else. There was one thing he had to figure out. The charcoal that had been scooped from the bottom of the nearest kiln gnawed at his mind. Regular charcoal would help, but he remembered enough from his studies to know it could be far more effective if activated, transforming it into a porous powerhouse for trapping toxins.

He turned to Bibi, a spark of determination in his eyes. "We need to make this charcoal better. I'll show you how."

The entire household buzzed with curiosity as James gathered a small crew of workers, including Bibi, still shaken but eager to save his daughters. In broken Egyptian hand gestures, he explained that they'd use the kiln to "wake up" the charcoal, remembering a book he had once read about steam activation. They sealed the kiln with mud and sand, packing it tight to limit oxygen, then piled in the burnt wood and charcoal from last night's firing. James instructed them to heat it fiercely with acacia wood, aiming for the intense heat of 800–1000°C, a temperature he knew Egyptian metalworkers sometimes reached for copper.

After hours of stoking, he had them pour water from Nile jugs onto hot stones inside the kiln, releasing clouds of steam that hissed and swirled, penetrating the charcoal. The process took half a day, the workers murmuring in awe as James checked the glowing embers, ensuring the steam opened tiny pores without burning away the carbon. When it cooled, the charcoal emerged blacker, lighter, and more crumbly. It was now activated and ready to absorb far more toxins than before.

James walked around and inspected the system. They had done a phenomenal job of building what he had drawn. He walked up the stairs he had designed beside the stepped cisterns, which ended at a platform where the dirty water would be poured into the top, and looked into the container. The small rocks and sand were exactly what he was expecting.

James pointed to the cisterns and said, "These will need to be removed and replaced once every ten days, or more often, if it starts to clog. We must layer our new charcoal with sand in the third cistern."

They hesitated for only a second before two men grabbed some shovels and worked to fill the third cistern with the charcoal, then sand, then charcoal. It was ready. James motioned for the workers to pour the tainted water into the top of the device. They poured slowly at first, but after noticing the water entering the second vessel, they began to pour faster.

Everyone watched in anticipation, and James stood on the platform to try to explain what was happening using a combination of hand gestures and broken Egyptian.

"This first vessel holds small rocks that will catch and stop large particles from going through," James said. "Next, the small particles will be trapped in the sand, and the water will drain into the third vessel. When the water gets to this point, it should be free from debris, and it falls into the charcoal, which removes any poisons that will make you sick. Once it is through, it will be safe for everyone."

Meryt had been feeling a bit guilty about shirking her work to watch the process, but she didn't worry too much about it since the entire factory was there.

They had emptied six great jugs into the top before water slowly started running out of the bottom of the charcoal layer. A moment later, clean water began to stream out of the last layer and into the largest container at the bottom. The entire group raised their arms to the sky, and many fell to their knees. Meryt passed out cold at James's feet, and Neferu began to cry. Everyone who saw it knew this was a miracle and that the great and powerful James had saved their village from the ever-present scourge, the wasting.

The people began drinking their fill directly from the bottom cistern, and James waved for their attention.

"You must still boil this water before it is given to the very sick," he said.

James looked at Bibi and said, "Now, I need you to build one of these at every cistern in the town."

CHAPTER FOURTEEN

Becoming a Legend

2009 AD

A few weeks passed. James could feel himself falling into the same funk he had experienced on the slope.

I'm bored and lonely, he thought.

He remembered when Sandy had said that, and a grin appeared on his face, the first since his father died. The food in the refrigerator was all but gone, and the pantry was getting sparse. James had even resorted to eating some of the emergency dried rations that his parents had stashed in a closet in case of an emergency. Most of it was not great, but the beef stroganoff was like manna from heaven. How they could pack so much deliciousness into a freeze-dried package, he did not know.

James didn't know what he was supposed to do. He was virtually alone in the world, didn't have a degree, which would be required for most jobs that would pay the bills. He wanted to chase his dreams, as his father had suggested. He knew his mother would have wanted that. Could he do that and take care of the ranch simultaneously?

He thought of selling the ranch and using the money to fund his adventures. He pushed that thought out of his mind. This house, this ranch, would always be here and *could* never be sold. This was his family's home. He had been raised here since he was a child. This place is where he buried his parents. No, this place *would* never be sold.

Hank had mentioned that he had squirreled away some money. He said it was maybe enough to pay off his college debt. College debt was not going to be a thing, so how much was there? Could it be enough to ensure the future of the ranch at least? It was time to start re-engaging with the world. His mom and dad would never have wanted him to sit around depressed and lonely. James sat in Hank's oversized leather recliner and popped open his laptop. Hank's laptop was enormous. He had been born at the cusp of what was to be called Gen X and had grown up using computers and playing video games.

James laughed a little, thinking about how Hank would show disgust whenever Sara pulled out her Mac. No, Hank had to have the biggest, heaviest, fastest gaming laptop he could find. He claimed it was so he could run AutoCAD properly, but Sara and James knew the truth. Sara, on the other hand, loved her sleek MacBook. It was quiet, simple, and easy to use. No wimpy flat Mac for Hank. It didn't matter that he would curse half the time at the little lit-up alien on the back of his monitor because it had blue-screened in the middle of a game again.

James remembered how he and Hank often sparred in a multiplayer game called *Civilization*. James always chose Hatshepsut of Egypt as his leader, and Hank always stuck with Washington. Every time they would start, Hank would yell, "Murica!" Even when James took a break at Harvard to log in and fight his dad, he could hear Hank in his head saying, "Murica!" They often played, and much to his frustration, Hank rarely won. He would usually go for his total world domination win, while James quietly built his civilization up and would build the first colony ship to Alpha Centauri.

The laptop took a moment to boot. The screen asking for his password came up. He looked over at the model of the Starship Enterprise on his dad's shelf, typed 1701, and brought up the home screen. There were many files. James was curious about the "Black Sands Corp." file, but opened the financial folder. It held various spreadsheets, the most interesting one labeled "Assets and Liabilities", and James clicked it. He scanned the numbers. There was a section showing assets. Things like 401k, Texas ranch, vehicles, jewelry, guns, and collectibles were listed.

This was all as James expected, but looking further, he noticed things he wasn't familiar with. One line that read "Misc. Stock Portfolio" showed a balance that had James doing a double-take: $232,568,250.24, and it was growing, constantly clicking higher. James saw that the stocks listed were actually connected to the stock market in real time. He looked through the list of company stocks. Most were very familiar, but some were a surprise.

Is this real? James thought.

Right next to the growing numbers was a red box that read, "Click Here, James."

The note from Hank was short and to the point. A tear welled in James's eye, anyway.

James,

As you can see, there is enough here to last you a while. My hope is that you will use this to follow your dreams. Your mom and I never really needed any money from this account. We had all that we needed and enjoyed a simple life together. I've always wanted you to take over my company, but that is not who you are. I realized I spent most of my time working and getting through life, and not really living it. Your mom always knew better. Make her proud.

Our assets are already in your name. The CPA will take care of everything, including estate expenses. You shouldn't have to fight the government for the inheritance your mom and I worked to build. We did that so you wouldn't have to worry like we did when we were young.

We love you, son.

Dad

James sat back in his father's chair, sobbing. He really didn't care about the money. What he wanted was his parents back. He realized it was time to get his legs underneath himself again. He called his parents' financial advisor and had them set up a monthly money transfer into his checking account. It would be enough for him to live his life, but it would not really affect the portfolio balance. If he could keep these assets intact, he could pass them on to his children, if that would ever be in the cards. With his finances secured and knowing the ranch would be safe, he opened his laptop. It was time to engage again.

He logged into one of the forums using the handle he and his mom had chosen when she had created it. He was one of the original moderators and went by JamesJones, using the last name of his favorite movie character. One forum that had recent traffic mostly concerned Central American civilizations. The most popular thread was about some anomalies found in a pyramid that had only recently been uncovered in Belize. This thread was asking for graduate students to help with the dig. He figured he could pass for a graduate student and get his hands into some old dirt. Mom would be proud.

Doctor Geist had called for graduate students to apply under the handle Geyser1966. Hearing the name made James's stomach turn.

James sent a private message to Geyser1966 asking if he had room for another hand.

Geyser1966 responded, "JamesJones, it has been crazy here since the new structures at Caracol were discovered, but I need a break from this project. My wife has become annoyed at my absence for the last three months, and her sister is getting married. We would be honored if you would come and take over for me here until I can return. You don't need to worry about that mess in Egypt. Everyone knows it wasn't your fault, and your work has always impressed me."

James was taken aback. He had been planning on joining a group of kids digging with small garden spades, not taking over an entire archaeological site, and it seemed Geist was unaware that Sara was his mother.

I'm not capable of that, am I? This is way out of my skill set, isn't it? he thought.

He knew he understood ancient pyramid construction better than anyone, including his mother. Perhaps he was the man for the job.

James's mom popped into his head. "Fake it until you make it," she would say. "That's how everyone feels when starting a new project."

"Okay, Mom, here goes nothing," he said to himself before writing, "Dr. Geist, I am currently between projects and am in a position to take you up on your offer. Send me whatever information I need. I will review it while I travel. I should be able to arrive within a few days."

The response was instant.

"Oh, thank heavens. My wife will kiss you. I will be leaving at once. I will email you everything you need to know."

That night, James packed his bags, donned his leather jacket and hat, and took an Uber to the airport.

CHAPTER FIFTEEN

How to Please a God

1152 BC

I t had been several days since James had seen any priests. At first, they would come to him once a day. They would all sit on the mats around a table in the reception area. The priests would sometimes bring gifts and always ask questions about the afterlife.

James didn't fully understand that they thought he was talking about the afterlife. What he thought was that they understood he was talking about the future. He tried to make it clear many times, but the concept that a civilization could grow and change over time because of the advent of new technologies seemed lost on them. All of the knowledge they knew had been passed down for generations. The way things were done hadn't changed much for thousands of years, so they couldn't wrap their heads around what he was saying.

James knew that Neferu was always sitting at the top of the stairs, listening to the conversations, but he was afraid that if he let her know that he had seen her, she would be embarrassed. This was how James perfected his understanding of the language. Whenever he heard a word or phrase he didn't understand, he would stop and ask for an explanation of the word. He only had to hear it once and could commit it to memory. During these conversations, James learned he would eventually be brought in front of the living God, Ramesses IV.

He couldn't help but think that his arrival in Egypt could be the harbinger of the total collapse of their civilization, if he couldn't find a way to keep others from accessing what he knew as the Chamber of Time. It was imperative that he meet with Pharaoh. James had to show him there was impending danger from Black Sands if they accessed the chamber like he did. It could only be a matter of time before they tried a full-scale invasion of Egypt.

Ramesses currently lived in Waset, which James knew as the modern city of Luxor, and stayed in Lpet-sut, the Karnak temple, to oversee new construction. The priest would soon organize an expedition to bring James before their god-king later in the year. James knew the Egyptian calendar well. It was similar to the calendar that modern Western civilization used and was based on the moon's cycle with ten days (heru) per week (deken), thirty days in a month (abed), and twelve months in the year (renpet).

When James heard he would be traveling to Karnak, butterflies sprang up in his stomach. Karnak was in Waset, next to the Valley of the Kings. He had been there many times, but the very first time was what he thought of. That was the last vacation before leaving Egypt for a new life in the US. He thought of his mom and dad, and all the emotions he had felt during that first expedition came flooding back. James looked at that trip as a turning point for him, where he had decided what he was and who he wanted to be. At the time, he had to keep it to himself, as his dad wasn't keen on the idea of James becoming some Indiana Jones-type explorer, but that was precisely what James envisioned for himself. It was up to him to do what he could to protect the people of this time.

"When can we leave?" he said.

His excitement surprised the priests, who were happy to tend to Pharaoh as rarely as possible. Best not to tempt fate, as he could have you put to death with a glance. It was an uncomfortable position to be in for a priest. They were eager to visit the afterlife, but not today.

"It will be a while. The Nile has flooded most of the safe routes, and bandits plague the others," they explained.

"That is fine, but we should go as soon as possible," James said.

James left the group of priests and figured he would inspect the filtration system to make sure it was functioning efficiently. He walked through the sitting room and noticed Neferu sitting by a small window, looking out. She seemed a bit sad, and when she saw him walking up, she turned to hide the fact that she had tears in her eyes.

"What is wrong?" James said.

With a sniffle, Neferu said, "So much has happened these last decans. I am not sure I can go back to how it was before. So many wondrous things have happened because you came to us. I am afraid for you to leave."

He stepped closer with a sad smile. "Neferu, it has been wonderful staying here and enjoying your home, but there are so many more things I need to do in this world. I enjoy your company, and if I had my choice, I would want to stay with you, but I don't think I can."

"Yes, Lord, I understand," she said as tears streamed from her eyes. "When Ptahhote ordered me to house you under my roof, I was shocked and afraid. I have not had a husband for many years, and for them to force one on me ... I was afraid I would lose everything I had worked so hard for. Please do not be angry that I was tempted to reject you."

"Hold on. You said something about your husband. I understood that he died many renpet ago. I am confused."

"No, My Lord, I am speaking of you," Neferu said with a confused look on her face.

"I am not sure I understand. I may not be translating what you are saying properly," James said.

Neferu cocked her head to the side with a perplexed look on her face.

"James, you know I am your wife, do you not?"

James fell back into the seat behind him. His mind was whirling.

"Um, Neferu, can you please explain?" James said.

"Do not tell me you are refusing me. After all of this! After everything. I have accepted all of this, which was out of my control, and you reject me?"

Neferu's face was beet-red, and tears ran down her cheeks.

"I thought you were here for the good of the people. Now I see you just came to do as you please," she said as she stormed out of the room and up the stairs.

James chased after her through the kitchen but stopped for an instant to see the entire staff glaring at him. He knew he had done something terribly wrong, but what?

Then the waif, running at full speed, barreled into James, who grabbed her as he nearly fell backward on his butt.

"It looks like you are feeling better," he said.

The girl's eyes grew wide in fear. Hapi, the cook, ran out from the kitchen. "Stop that thief! She has stolen the honey cakes."

James looked down into her arms to see the plunder nearly falling out of her tiny hands. She pushed past James and ran from the house.

The guard at the door gave James a look as if to say, "Am I supposed to try to catch this street rat?"

James waved him off and turned to the cook.

"Let her be. We can make more cakes," James said.

"*We* are making more cakes, are *we*? I am so glad *we* will have to return to the kitchen and start all over again so *you* and my lady can have cakes for dinner." She stomped off.

James didn't think she had much respect for the gods. He glanced down and noticed the girl had placed something in his hand as she ran off. It was his Rolex.

"That little brat had stolen it after all," he said out loud, to no one in particular.

Then he remembered Neferu was mad about something.

James tried to talk to the cooks, but they bowed and scurried away. Even Meryt eyed him, then lowered her eyes and walked away. Yes, he had done something very wrong. James wasn't sure what to do. This predicament threatened everything he was planning, not to mention the fact that his greatest ally and supporter in this crazy place hated him. It must have been something he said.

Is she just upset that I'm leaving?

It seemed like she was, but there was something else he was not understanding. James walked to the courtyard, trying to figure out his transgression. Bibi was standing in his usual place, watching the massive brick operation. Bricks were produced in quantities that no one had thought possible before. Bibi noticed James approaching and knelt.

"Thank you, Great Lord, you have saved my children, and I am forever in your debt. I will burn incense at your tomb for the rest of my days," he said.

"Please stand, Bibi. Your daughters are doing better?" James said.

"Yes, Lord, all of them, and most of the townsfolk who had taken sick have fully recovered."

"That's great. I figured they would recover fast once they had good, clean water. Their immune systems are probably used to whatever was affecting them, and they needed food and clean water to get everything working again."

This came out in a mixture of English and Egyptian, as some of the words that James had used did not have an Egyptian counterpart.

Bibi laughed and said, "I don't know of this 'immune' you are talking about, but what you did was surely a miracle. Please tell me your favorite incense, and I will worship you by burning it daily."

"Please, I don't want that, but there is something you can help me with."

"Yes, Lord, name it."

"You could help me understand why Neferu and all of the kitchen staff are angry with me."

"I see," Bibi said. "And what did you do to cause this?"

"That is what I am saying. I don't know. We talked about how I must leave for Lpet-sut to be brought before Pharaoh soon. She was sad to hear that, then she said something about... Wait, she said she is my wife. What did she mean by that?"

Bibi laughed until tears ran down his face. After a few seconds, this began to irritate James.

"Bibi, stop! What is so funny?"

"Oh, I am so sorry, My Lord. I realize now you are not knowledgeable in all things. You understand the world far beyond that of any man I have ever known, but you do not understand a basic custom in the land you protect. The moment the Mer, Ptahhote, and the priests required Neferu to house you under her roof, she became your wife. When two unmarried free adults of high station live together, they are by all rights married and are recognized as such by the community. You, my friend, are married."

James's legs became shaky, and he sat down on the edge of the clean water cistern. He thought back to what he understood about Egyptian marriage. Yes, he could see that. They didn't have traditional marriage that modern society understood. Here, marriages were more of a social contract that was often started by cohabitation or declaring in public that a couple was together.

James didn't remember agreeing to any of this, but he had offered her a ride in the carriage on that first day, after Neferu was ordered to take him in. Perhaps that was enough to seal the deal in this culture. James was at a loss as to what he should do. He had never been one to shirk responsibility. On the contrary, he was always the one running toward it.

He went to the sitting room to contemplate the ramifications of what had happened. How would this affect his plans to bring forth a techno-logical revolution in Egypt? He felt he had two options. The first was to disavow the marriage and move out, perhaps to the nearby temple. This choice would alienate all the people he had grown to admire, and even love, in this household. They were all somehow bound together after his latest clean water miracle. He had saved lives. Many had been near death and had recovered. He felt a sense of responsibility toward these people.

The people here looked at him as a god, sure, but also as their protec-tor.

The second choice was even harder. He thought about Neferu. He knew he wasn't in love with her. She was beautiful, intelligent, kind, and friendly, exactly what he wanted in a wife, but they barely knew each other, and she thought of him as a god. It was crazy. If he were to take on the role of husband to this naïve woman, it would take advantage of her innocence. Wouldn't it?

Ah, but she is so beautiful, he thought. *Maybe I do love her, or at least could love her.*

It was time to decide. James weighed everything that was going on in his head. He decided then that he did not want to take the first option. He would miss everyone ... especially her.

He tried to decide how to move forward. Perhaps he should ignore all that had transpired today and go on, as if it had never happened. He realized the time for that was past. He would have to go to her now and have a conversation. James's heart began to beat out of his chest, and he started to feel a bit light-headed. He was afraid, not of the entire Egyptian Empire that he would face, but of the 110-pound woman who seemed to have found her way into his soul.

James walked toward the stairs, noticing the kitchen workers' glares had turned into grins. They looked at one another and whispered, then giggled. Somehow, they had all figured out that James wasn't purposely causing pain to their mistress but was just another stupid man. Stupid men were something these women knew much about.

That jerk Bibi must be out there telling everyone what an idiot I am.

There was complete silence as James walked up the stairs. All of the bustling in the kitchen had stopped. He was embarrassed as he listened to the sound of his own feet clipping and clopping up the stairs. He could feel the entire room staring at his back. When he reached the top, he heard all of the women in the kitchen begin to whisper and laugh again. They knew he heard them, but didn't care. Insufferable gossips, all of them.

His room was there on the right. Neferu's room was at the end of the hall. The hall, about twenty feet long, seemed to go on forever, but the walk toward Neferu's door seemed to take only a step or two. Neferu's villa didn't have doors on the interior rooms. Instead, it had heavy curtains. This allowed better airflow that would keep the rooms cooler in the summer and warmer in the winter.

James wasn't quite sure how one should announce himself in this time and opted for the modern-day method of knocking on the wall and saying, "Hello, Neferu. Are you there?"

He could hear Neferu shuffle around inside, but she refused to answer.

"Neferu, please let me come in and talk. I need to explain some things."

"Oh, I see," she yelled back. "You need to explain to me." James stepped through the curtain and into the lioness's den.

"You need to set me straight. Did you not tell me that I was nothing to you? No, I understand. I'm just an old widow. How foolish I was to think that a god, like the great and powerful James, would accept me? Accept my home and order around my workers as if they were his. I agree. You should reject the old widow. You can find a dozen new virgins whose families are more than happy to give them to you."

Neferu wouldn't even look at him. Seeing her this distraught broke his heart. Neferu was steaming and looking out her window away from him. He wasn't really sure what to do or say. He hadn't ever been in a situation like this. What would Indiana Jones do? James walked right up behind Neferu and quickly spun her around. He didn't see anger or hatred in her eyes. What he saw was sadness and fear.

Neferu began to speak, "I don't know who you think you are, to come in here and..."

He stared at her momentarily while she was talking, then kissed her.

CHAPTER SIXTEEN

Fake It Until You Make It

2009 AD

The flight from George Bush Intercontinental Airport to Belize City was quick. James spent the three hours in flight reviewing all of Dr. Geist's emailed notes. He was very thorough and even listed all the current site workers and their bios.

He was to function as a temporary project director until Dr. Geist returned, at which time he would continue as a field archaeologist. James wasn't exactly keen on taking over the day-to-day hassle of overseeing the entire project. He wanted to get his hands dirty, covered in the black soil his mother loved so much.

The on-site crew was small. Their work permit was very specific and wouldn't likely require any heavy machinery. Manuel, the other field archaeologist, would handle much of the site's management. Manuel was from the University of Texas at Austin and part of the Agenda for Belize Archaeology Mission, as were half of the workers doing the digging. AFBAM was known for providing student volunteers with hands-on experience in archaeological methods and usually focused on the Mayan civilization.

The other half had followed the professor from Oxford. A contractor was also hired to survey the site. They would map the finds and have the ground-penetrating radar gear that could allow them to survey deep underground. Things like caves or voids underground would be revealed. An unnamed corporate entity had sponsored the project itself.

After processing through immigration, James grabbed his gear and headed for the taxi row outside the airport. It would be an expensive cab ride from Belize City to San Ignacio, the closest city to the dig. Walking toward the taxi, he noticed a young American kid holding a sign that read, "Doctor Professor James Jones." James cringed for an instant when he realized that Dr. Geist thought he was both a doctor and a university professor, and he didn't even realize that his screen name was not his real name. James was nervous, but could hear his mom whisper, "Fake it until you make it."

"I'm James," he said. "You don't need to call me doctor or professor. James will suffice."

"Yes, Mr. Jones."

James cringed again. "No, just James."

"Really? Oh, I've never had a professor ask me not to use his prefix before," he said with a little laugh. "Matt, UT Austin. I'm supposed to take you straight to the dig site, according to Dr. Geist. He had already boarded his plane for home."

Matt had the usual Texas boy firm handshake and led James to the waiting vehicle.

"I expected you to be older," said Matt.

"I've heard that before," James said as he climbed into the white Ford F-150.

The truck had a familiar logo on the door.

"Black Sands?" he said.

"Excuse me?" said Matt.

"The truck is from Black Sands?"

"They gave us four pickups and a van to use for the dig. I guess Black Sands has an oil exploration project going on nearby and had the extra trucks to loan. We are all staying in San Ignacio, but we have a base set up near the dig site. It takes two to three hours to get to the site from the city on some rough roads."

"Wow," said James. "That could be what, like a four-and-a-half to six-hour daily commute? How do you get any work done?"

"And that doesn't even include the stop at the military checkpoint. They love to give us crap and make us wait around every day."

"Military checkpoint?" said James.

"Yeah, we pass right next to the Guatemala border. There have been some guerrilla attacks, and people are scared."

James was beginning to think he may have stepped in front of a bullet by taking on this project. They drove straight through San Ignacio and headed south toward the dig site.

"Are you sure you don't want to stop and drop your gear off at the hotel?" asked Matt.

"No, I want to get eyes on the site before it gets late," James said.

They stopped at the Douglas D'Silva Forest Station, about half the distance to Caracol. The two guards waved them over for inspection.

"They always pull us over. I think they know we are easy to harass. "Usually, a twenty-dollar donation to the guard's donut fund speeds things up a bit," said Matt.

"Do you always give them money?" James asked.

"Uh, yeah. That's what the prof wanted us to do," said Matt.

"Ever stop to think that maybe they are always pulling over your vehicles because you happily pay for their meals?" said James.

"Uh, when you put it like that, I think that makes sense," he laughed.

James rolled his eyes and said, "Great, let's get rolling. I want to get there before it's time to pack up and leave."

"Don't worry about that. They are probably only getting started."

"Wait, a second. It's almost 2 p.m., and they are getting started?"

"Yeah, we wait for everyone to finish lunch before we start, and some of us take our time, if you know what I mean. We get paid some for the travel time, but once we are here, the clock starts ticking, and we get paid regardless."

James shook his head and chuckled. His dad would have had a field day with all this nonsense. James and Matt rolled in as the last workers finished their siesta-style lunch.

"Matt, will you gather everyone up? I want to say a word or two, and where is Manuel?"

"Right here," said a gentleman standing directly behind James.

That startled James, and he jumped a bit, making Manuel grin.

"I am not sure what you are doing here, but the prof said I should expect you. I can use you over at Site One on Caana. They're short one excavator, who is back in San Ignacio sick."

James, ignoring Manuel, knew Caana was their primary worksite. It was a recently uncovered pyramid that had the archaeology community very excited.

James looked at the gathered crowd.

"Hello, everyone. You probably know me as James Jones from Dr. Geist's forum."

The workers looked at each other, and one said, "You are the famous James Jones? I thought you would be older."

Everyone laughed.

James snickered and said, "I get that a lot. You can call me James. Not doctor, not professor, just James. Dr. Geist asked me to come here and take over the project in his absence. I'll make some changes, but the work will proceed as the professor wants."

"Hold on, kid. I don't know what this is about, but I'm in charge here," said Manuel.

James looked at Manuel. *Will he be a problem?* In his haste to leave, it appeared the professor neglected to fill his right-hand man in about the changes. James frowned a bit and handed his notes from Geist to Manuel.

"Looks like you didn't get the memo," he said with a smile in a manner that he had hoped would ease the tension.

"This is BS!" exclaimed Manuel. "He thinks I can't run things for a few weeks while he's gone? What? Is this kid supposed to be here to take over? Screw it. I'm done," Manuel said as he walked toward the nearest pickup.

"Manuel, go ahead and take the rest of the day if you need to, but be ready to start in the morning. We've got a ton of work to do," James said.

Manuel jumped in the truck and sped away.

"He's always like that," said Matt with a chuckle. "He'll be back. He needs this on his résumé."

"OK, everyone, let's get back to work," James said, and the group began to break up and head for their respective dig areas.

"Matt, hold up a sec. Can you show me around?"

"Yeah, sure, let's head over to Caana and start at dig site one. That's where things have started to get interesting."

They spent the rest of the day visiting each dig site. There were three sites that were currently being excavated. It was a very slow process. They would start by setting up a grid using string and red tape. Inside this grid, they would dig through soft soils to uncover existing man-made structures buried for over a thousand years. Every scoop of dirt would be sifted through a screen in the hopes of finding smaller artifacts.

The dig itself was expected to reveal the main pyramid structure. As James walked around the sites, all he wanted to do was stop, stick his hands in the dirt, and get busy, but he couldn't help but see what his father saw every time he visited one of his worksites. Everything was done so inefficiently. They were wasting hours each day, not only with travel, but inefficiencies plagued the digging process. James knew where he had to start.

"Matt, is there any reason we can't stay on-site to do the work?"

"Well, we need a place to sleep and prepare meals. We can't do that here on-site."

"I have worked on dozens of sites like this. Something this remote shouldn't require that commute time. Are there any regulations or rules that say we can't stay on site?"

"No, the ground radar crew stays here in tents. They were tired of forking over the donut money and driving all the time. I hear they only get paid for the actual time working on-site."

It was already starting to get dark. They all put away their tools and piled into the three trucks and the van to head back to San Ignacio. It was late when they piled out of the vehicles and headed straight for the restaurant to catch dinner and head to their rooms. All the workers were completely exhausted, more from the dirt road commute than their actual work at the site. Matt led James to his room.

They had pretty much taken over the small inn on the outskirts of the town. The meal was delicious—fresh, authentic Central American cuisine. Enchiladas de pollo con mole was the entrée of the night and was the best James had ever had. After dinner, James left the group to do their own thing and went to his room to plan his next steps.

James noticed the crew spent only three or four hours digging. The rest of the day was spent commuting to the site, uncovering the digs, preparing the tools, and after working for those few hours, they needed to put away all their tools and gear, cover the site with tarps, and then commute back to San Ignacio. This would never fly in a for-profit venture. Only a project that had no accountability for expenses could exist like this. James decided the entire project needed a new way of doing things.

Is this why Dr. Geist wanted me on the project?

Maybe, maybe not, but in James's mind, it had to happen. James called an old friend to see what could be done.

The next morning, everyone was prepared and ready to head out.

"One thing," James said, "I need everyone to go ahead and pack enough gear and clothes for at least a week."

The group began to mill around and look at each other.

"Trust me. I'll fill you in soon."

They slowly began to head back to their rooms and prepare their gear. Manuel walked up to James.

"What's this all about? This is a waste of time. Let's get them loaded and head out."

"Bear with me a while, Manuel. You decided to stay after all, huh?"

Manuel scoffed and walked off to his room. James was glad that only he and Matt would make the trek in the first pickup. Everyone else had piled into the other vehicles, which were loaded with everyone's gear. James was also glad he wouldn't have to play twenty questions with a truck full of workers all the way to the dig site.

Matt was driving as they pulled up to the guard station. The men motioned for them to pull aside while the rest of the caravan sat and waited. The officer approached James's window, recognizing him as the one in charge.

"Buenos días, amigo," he said. James was fluent in Spanish but decided to answer in English.

"Morning. What can I do for you?" he said.

The officer had a strange look on his face. "Isn't there something you want to give me?" he said with a sly grin.

"No, we will not pay you to pass here anymore," James said.

The man had a confused look on his face and looked toward the other trucks.

"Neither will they," James added.

James told Matt to continue down the road and leaned out of his window to wave at all the other trucks to follow. They all drove by, with the two guards looking at each other.

James turned to Matt and said, "They have no authority to do anything other than search our vehicles for stowaways or contraband. Something tells me they won't bother us anymore."

"Wow, that was easy," Matt said with a smile as they drove off.

They reached Caracol at their usual time, before lunch. Everyone sat down to eat the bagged lunch prepared by the inn from San Ignacio. They were finishing and heading to their allotted worksites when two large trucks pulled up. James walked to meet them and waved to show them where to set up.

"We are going to postpone starting today for a bit. I need you all to follow me."

"What the hell is going on here, kid? You've got some nerve," said Manuel with a puffed chest.

"Chill for a sec, and I'll explain." James walked toward the smaller box truck as the occupant stepped down.

"Jimmy!" said Khalid while grabbing him in a full bear hug.

"It's great ta see ya."

"You too, Kal, and thanks so much for setting this up so fast."

"Don't worry 'bout it. The crew that we'd all this gear prepped for ain't due fer a while yet. By then, y'all will've a more permanent solution figured out," said Khalid.

James addressed the expanding group of college students.

"What we have here is a box truck full of everything we will need to move our entire operation to this site. I need everyone to grab themselves a tent and a sleeping bag. We should get them set up over by the courtyard. There are also a couple of large pavilions that we need to erect with tables and chairs for dining."

James waved to the second truck.

"This trailer over here has the shower and bathroom facilities we need. Manuel, would you please head over there and tell the driver the best place to drop that trailer?"

With a barely noticeable grin, Manuel walked toward the trailer.

"Let's spend the rest of the day setting up our tents and getting used to our new digs. I have already instructed El Hotel de la Selva folks to cater our meals here instead of in San Ignacio."

The group stood quietly for a few moments, then Matt said, "Oh hell yeah, this is going to save so much time." They were all nodding and smiling as they walked to pick out a tent.

"So how'd ya know ta call me 'bout all this gear?" said Khalid.

"I noticed that Black Sands had loaned the group these trucks, and since you weren't up in Alaska, I figured you'd be the one to call."

"It's lucky ya happened ta be the one outfittin' the Black Sands project. What exactly are ya all doin' here anyway? Are there oil deposits nearby?"

"Sorry, sport, can't tell you. Signed an NDA about the whole thing. It's all hush-hush. At any rate, I am sure lucky to have gotten hold of you. I was about to start calling around Mexico to find what we needed. I couldn't find anything in Belize that would work."

"Yeah, some coincidence," Khalid said with a shrug. "Somehow, when the boss mentioned we'd be workin' near pyramid ruins, I thought I might see ya. I'm glad ta see ya back at it. Oh, hey, I forgot. There's someone who wants to see ya."

Khalid grabbed James by the arm and led him over to the semi-truck that had finished dropping off the bath facilities trailer. James walked up as the driver stowed the last tie-down straps.

"Jimmy!" Sandy said as she turned to the two men walking up.

"Sandy? What the hell are you doing here?" James said with a huge grin.

Sandy replied, "Got tired of sitting at a desk in the land of the midnight sun, so I figured driving trucks would pay better. Black Sands has projects going on all over the place. I got here a few days ago. Manuel said James Jones is in charge. Who's that?"

"It's a long story that I'd love to tell you over dinner tonight. Will you be around?"

"No, Jim, Kal and I need to get moving back to the base camp. There's supposed to be a storm coming, so we need to get back before the roads get bad."

She leaned over and gave him one of those kisses that he remembered so well, which made his heart skip a beat.

"So when will I see you again?" he said.

"Maybe soon, maybe not at all," she said with a sly grin and a wink. "Why? Do you wanna see me? I barely heard a word from you after Deadhorse, so I figured you had your fill of me." She feigned a broken heart.

"I'm so sorry, Sandy. I've missed you. I was so messed up after what happened, and then my parents passed away. That whole trip is still a bit of a blur," he said.

"Oh, Jimmy, I am so sorry. Khalid told me about your parents earlier today."

James let out a sigh as Sandy wrapped her arms around him.

"I hope you didn't forget everything about the Alaska trip, though," she said with a wink as she hopped into the cab of the truck. "See ya soon, babe."

James ran up to the window as she started pulling away. He reached into his satchel and pulled out the napkin with the drawing of a cupcake she had sent him at school.

"Hold a sec, Sandy. I thought you might like to see this." He waved the napkin.

"Ah, isn't that cute? He's sentimental," she said with a wink while blowing a kiss.

"We'll be back in a few days," Khalid said while driving off.

Matt and Manuel saw the whole exchange. "Look at this guy finding a chick out in the middle of who knows where. That must be some sort of superpower," Matt said. Manuel nodded and laughed.

They all spent the rest of the day unloading the trucks and preparing their new camp. They had everything they needed. Khalid had been prepared to house about twice the number of workers James had, so there was plenty of gear. A pickup loaded with the night's fare arrived from El Hotel de la Selva. Everything was warm and delicious.

Afterward, they congregated in the dining tent to play games and watch a little TV. The generator and satellite dish were a welcome addition. Thanks to the long commute, this was the first time they had any real time to themselves. James noticed Manuel laughing and enjoying a game of poker. Manuel looked at James with a quick nod and a smile.

James took that as an apology for being such an ass when he first arrived. Likely the only apology he would get, but it worked. Everything was going according to James's big plan, and everyone seemed to be on board. Then it began to rain.

CHAPTER SEVENTEEN

Journey to Luxor

1152 BC

James was beginning to settle into his new life. Neferu understood he was not fully prepared and didn't exactly understand her culture's norms, so she was fine with what James called "taking it slow." She hadn't ever really heard of a husband and wife "taking it slow" before, but was willing to give it a shot. James didn't think she understood what he was talking about since she was constantly calling him in to help her with things in her room, but when he would come in, she was usually getting out of the bath and was barely wrapped in a towel. She seemed to take a lot of baths, and for some reason, a candle was always on the shelf. This continued for a few days until James decided it was no longer time to "take it slow."

When they walked down for breakfast the next morning, the maids and kitchen help kept looking at each other and giggled. He had had his fill of that and grabbed his food to eat in the sitting room.

Why is my private life everyone's business? he thought.

For the next several days, they took their meals in their room. Neferu had decided it was time for James to take his place in the master bedroom, and he had no objections.

Around four months after James had first arrived in Egypt, Ptahhote, the Imy-r niwt of their town, came to visit along with Ptomak, a chief lector priest whose job was to preside over ceremonies and rituals. He had come from Men-nefer, the city James knew as Memphis, in response to the letters sent to Ramesses regarding the reconstitution of the Ka into the god James, who emerged from Khufu and was now residing in Khemenu-Ka. The priest had been ordered to bring Ptahhote, his guards, the two priests who had witnessed the resurrection, and the god James himself to Karnak to be received by the God incarnate Pharaoh Ramesses IV. James could barely contain his excitement.

The priest told them they would leave at first light. They were to make all haste back to Men-nefer and then requisition a boat for the two-week journey up the Nile to Waset (Luxor) and the Ipet-sut (Karnak Temple). James couldn't believe his luck. This would be the journey of a lifetime. He would be able to see many temples and tombs along the way, most of which he would have toured as a boy with his mom.

The guests left and asked James to be prepared to leave in the morning when they would have the entire caravan ready. He ran to the top of the stairs and grabbed Neferu, who sat in her usual spying position.

"The journey is on. We are to leave at first light," he said with a huge smile.

Neferu was anything but happy. She had a few tears in her eyes and had been crying.

"I knew the time was coming, husband. I had hoped for more time with you."

"What?" James said, "I don't understand."

She replied, "You have told me, husband. This is why you came to our people. To help all of Egypt. I am happy for you."

"You don't look happy. What's wrong, Nef?"

It wasn't common for pet names to be used in Neferu's culture, but she loved to hear him call her Nef.

"I will miss you, my James," she said.

"Miss me? Wait, you are coming too, right?" he said.

Neferu furrowed her brow and had a confused look.

"You mean for me to go?"

"Of course, you are my wife. You are going."

Tears burst from her eyes. "I thought, since we would no longer be sharing a roof, that you would move on without me," she said.

"I may not completely understand how you do things around here, but where I am from, you don't leave your wife to fend for herself while you go chase your own interests. I want you... No, I need you to come with me. Will you?"

He kissed her, and when they hugged, he sank into her and realized he was home again. Home was not a place but a state of contentment and love.

James packed light. He didn't actually own anything but his boots, satchel, and hat. Neferu, on the other hand, did not pack light. She brought extra warm clothes for both of them, a sewing kit, a fire kit, and a whole host of other necessities. She instructed Meryt, her lady's maid, to prepare her own things. When Neferu asked the cook to prepare her cooking pots and enough food for two weeks, James thought she might be going too far.

"Are you absolutely sure we need extra food and a cook?" he said.

She smiled and nodded. No explanation needed, apparently. James shook his head.

When James woke up the next morning, Neferu was already up, and everything was ready when Ptahhote arrived with his retinue.

"We will meet the rest of the caravan outside the city. I brought these extra camels for your people," he said.

James looked at him questioningly.

"How did you know to bring so many?" he said.

"You are married, are you not? It is your wife's responsibility to ensure you are prepared for the journey, unless you have rejected her."

"Oh, I knew that. We will load up and be on our way."

The servants loaded the luggage and strapped it down in a few minutes. Neferu came out of the house dressed in her best clothes and was fully made up. James had not seen her like this and couldn't keep his eyes off her. She was gorgeous, easily the most beautiful woman James had known. She walked up to the camel chosen for her and James, then turned to him with that coy smile, holding out her hand to him. The camel was already kneeling and ready to be mounted.

"James, husband, it is customary for you to help me mount."

James stood there gaping for a moment, then realized everyone around him was also gawking at Neferu. They were sure they were watching the wife of a god. James helped Neferu, then climbed up behind her. He wrapped his arms around her and held her as the huge beast swayed back and forth, and with effort, it rose to its feet.

Neferu leaned back and whispered, "You must snap the reins and lead the group away. This will let everyone know you are in charge of this journey."

"You are so beautiful. Why did you spend the time dressing in all your best clothes and jewelry to travel on a dusty road?" James asked.

"You are a wonderful Netjer, James, but you know nothing. This is the only way the wife of a netjer would travel. The people must see the trappings of power if they are to respect it."

"I have told you I am not a netjer," James said with a smile.

"Yes, I know," she said.

James smiled, and with a quick snap of the reins, they were moving.

"Go left here," she said. "No, not right, I said left. Slow down." James realized exactly who would be in charge of this expedition.

The journey to Men-nefer took most of the day, but they made it before dark. They would spend the night at the royal estates, which housed the local Haty-a (governor). James and Neferu were given a large suite with connecting rooms to house Meyrt and Hapi, the cook. James often laughed when Hapi's name was mentioned, as she was usually moody and rarely happy. Once they were settled, a servant came to them with bowed head.

"You are requested to join our master for the evening meal and conversation," the servant said.

"Please inform your master that we thank him, but we have plans to eat here and stay in our rooms tonight."

The servant seemed fearful.

"Please," he said, "my master is not patient and made his wish for you to accompany me very clear."

"If that is the case, then maybe we—" Neferu grasped James's arm, looked at him, and then at the servant.

"Please tell your master thank you, but the netjer incarnate James will have to decline his gracious invitation."

The servant was aghast, but realizing it would not happen, he retired.

"What was all that about?" said James. "I would have enjoyed talking to the Haty-a."

"Oh, James, you are sweet. You need not worry. You are of great interest to the nobility. He was trying to order you as if you were his subordinate. You are a netjer to us, James. He must show you proper respect," she said.

James shrugged and went back to his work. He had been working on a new project and was not ready to share it with everyone. Minutes later, Ptahmose, the High Priest of Ptah, who governed Men-nefer, was outside James's suite. When Neferu came to the door, Ptahmose knelt down.

"I am Ptahmose, and I ask your forgiveness, Great James. I was informed that my incompetent servant requested your presence at the evening meal. This was obviously a grave error. I plead with you to grace us with your presence. Most of the nobility and priesthood will attend, and if you cannot, I will endure great shame."

James looked at Neferu, who smiled with a wink and nodded.

"Please rise, Ptahmose. Under these circumstances, I will forgo my own comfort and attend. We are ready. Please lead the way."

As they entered the open-air banquet hall, the sun dipped low over the Nile, gilding the river's surface. James stopped, and his breath caught as he took in a sight that the modern world couldn't possibly recreate, even in movies. Neferu, her glistening green, kohl-lined eyes glinting with subdued pride, dragged him forward. Off to one side, massive date palms loomed over a reflection pool that mirrored the blue sky. James's gaze drifted upward and followed the towering columns that were painted with vibrantly colored scenes of gods in triumphant war campaigns. Hanging between each column were linen banners dyed crimson and lined with gold.

The servants moved between guests with practiced grace, twirling their trays in a skillful dance to the rhythm of a harpist accompanied by a flute and delivering honeyed figs, roast duck with pomegranate sauce, and seasoned flatbreads.

Neferu led James to a low table of ornately carved cedar, and they sat together on cushions at the head of the table. Neferu picked a grape from a golden bowl and hand-fed it to James.

"You stare as if you have never seen a palace like this before," she said with a coy smile. "Are there not palaces where you are from?"

The voices around the table seemed quiet as each guest pretended not to listen to their private conversation. James fumbled for a response and, speechless, shook his head. A servant poured water from a blue glass pitcher into a golden basin, offering it to rinse his hands as another stood over him and fanned. The wealth of the empire was shown in every opulent aspect.

Ptahhote, Ptomak, and two other priests attended with most of the highest nobility and priesthood from Men-nefer. Sebekhotep sat at the far end of the table and conversed with a smaller group, occasionally sneaking a glance in James's direction.

For the second course, they were served fish baked with onions, garlic, and dates. This was a meal that was comforting and reminded him of his childhood. The wine had a familiar flavor but was sweet and not exactly what he expected.

Once everyone was done with the meal, the questions began. James's head spun back and forth, trying to attend to each person asking a question, but he couldn't respond before someone else would chime in. He became a bit frustrated and said, in a stern voice, "Enough!" The room became silent.

"I am here to answer your questions, but I will only answer one at a time. You will all listen, so I do not have to repeat myself."

Neferu eyed him and smiled.

"Please proceed," he said.

They spent the next two hours listening to James talk about what he knew was the future, and what the attendees thought was the afterlife. Everyone was quiet and captivated by the stories.

One of the priests asked, "You say you are from a world that is more than three thousand years from now. I do not understand those words."

James realized that when he spoke, he was using the words and terms for the number system that he and the rest of the modern world had adopted, not the system these ancient people would understand.

James picked that moment to broach another subject.

"I am glad you asked about that," he said, and the questioning priest beamed with delight at the praise.

"I have been working on a papyrus that will explain a new way of working with numbers. You will be adopting this new system through-out the empire."

The priests looked at each other, confused. James unrolled the papyrus he had been working on. In the next hour, he did his best to describe the concept of zero and base-ten numbers. The Egyptians had a sophisticated system of hieroglyphics and hieratic scripts for numbers, but their system was cumbersome without the concept of zero.

"Imagine you have nothing," he said, holding up an empty hand. "How does your system of numbers represent this?"

The priests looked at each other, confused.

Ptomak said, "Why would we need a symbol for nothing?"

James pointed to the number zero on the papyrus.

"This is zero. It represents the absence of a quantity, but it is also a number."

The Egyptians were confused. Their system started with one, so they had to wrap their minds around a number for nothing. James pointed to the papyrus and showed how numbers could be lined up and that zero could be used as a placeholder.

"See here," he said. "We have 10, which is ten, but when we want to show many of tens, like 100, we can use the zero to show the difference between 0, 10, 100, and even 1000.

He was pointing at the representations on the papyrus.

"Your numbers are beautiful and rich with history, but with this new system, arithmetic will be much easier."

He then spent the next hour reviewing how the numbers could be manipulated and how to add, subtract, multiply, and divide using the new system.

Many of the priests were speechless. Others were in small groups discussing the implications of this revelation. One group at the other end of the table, which included Sebekhotep, did not look happy.

One of the older priests, Ptahmose, stood up and said, "We thank you, Great James. This way of manipulating numbers is very interesting. We will have our acolytes look into it."

Two of the younger priests looked at the elder and said, "I don't think you understand, Great Hem netjer." He referred to the elder priest's title. "This will change everything. Surely this is the wisdom of Amun-Ra himself."

James thought of a way to make the elder priest understand.

"Let us consider the collection of tax," James said, and the older priest began to pay close attention.

"I believe that the recognized tax is one goat in ten, which would be taken at the time of slaughter. Let me show you how to calculate the number of sheep one would need to collect from a citizen who was to slaughter two thousand two hundred sheep." James wrote the numbers in their script and then in the new system. "Here we have 2,200 sheep. We divide that by 10, and the new tax will be 220 sheep."

The older priest's eyes went wide.

"That was so quick and simple," he said.

"That is only the beginning," James said. "I have described many ways of manipulating numbers using this system, and you will all come to learn them and others."

Everyone in attendance looked at each other and agreed that this was a gift from God, and they would treat it as such.

CHAPTER EIGHTEEN

When It Rains, It Pours

2009 AD

The rain came that first night. James could hardly sleep thinking about what this meant. He hadn't really accounted for the approaching rainy season, which could very well turn his plans to revolutionize the archaeological process here at the site into a literal quagmire.

The next morning, the sun came out as they were preparing for work. Everything dried quickly, and James thought he was in the clear. That was until the truck arrived with the day's meals from San Ignacio. They told him the roads were barely passable and were temporarily closed. No more traveling in the mornings until the afternoon sun dried the roads from the nightly rains.

When the workers heard this, a few cheered. James was surprised, figuring they would be upset about being unable to travel back and forth. Manuel approached with a frown.

James prepared for another confrontation, but Manuel leaned over and said, "Looks like we dodged a bullet here, huh?"

"I don't get it. What do you mean?" said James.

"How did you know to move us all here before the rains? If we had been one day later, we would probably have been stuck in San Ignacio and would've had to call off the dig for the rest of the year. Brilliant! I'm sorry forever for doubting you," he said.

James leaned back in his chair and said, "Uh, yeah, no problem."

He recalled his mom's phrase, "Fake it until you make it."

The workers broke into their normal groups. James had decided to let them continue digging the way they had been up to this point. He had a few ideas about simplifying the processes, but he knew that if he started changing everything right from the start, people would get upset. He knew it would be necessary, but people reacted better to change at a slow pace. Big, earth-shattering changes were often met with resistance and a tight-fisted hold on the techniques they were used to.

The first order of business was to get the ground-penetrating radar crew set up in the location that James believed held the most promise for discovery. James had noticed that the stones from the pyramid at the Caana site seemed newer and were installed less precisely than many of the others in the area. He felt something strange was going on there, and he intended to figure out what it was.

Once the radar crew got their orders and understood what James was looking for, they headed off to the first in a series of ten locations that James wanted to be surveyed. James started at dig site one, the same as he had the first day, which seemed like a week ago. The team had already removed the tarps protecting the dig from the rain. They had dug channels around to ensure any residual water would run out of and not into the site.

The grid had already been marked off, and several students had begun digging. James realized this was a slow, meticulous process and decided it was best to leave the work of removing soil and revealing structures using small spades and paint brushes alone. One area that he knew he could fix was the sifting of tailings. At this point, each worker would collect a five-gallon bucket of dirt via spade or brush. They would then walk up and stand in line to sift the dirt to look for small artifacts.

There was often a line of two or three people waiting for one person to use the sifting device. To remove this bottleneck, James had two people constantly man the sifter, one to load and the other to shake the box. Any small artifact would be bagged and labeled appropriately for further study. The workers who had excavated the soil would set down their five-gallon bucket for the sifter crew and grab one of the empty buckets.

At the end of the day, this site had not only been able to excavate the ruins for twice as long as they had previously, but were able to move and sift as much as fifty percent more material per hour due to forgoing the waiting line at the sifter. Once word got out of this process, James didn't have to go around and micromanage each site. They all adopted the new way without being told after recognizing the benefits. This was exactly what James had hoped for. They would be happier workers if they felt they had a say in their use. James realized most of these workers had no real-world practical knowledge and had probably never held a real shovel at a construction site in their lives, but they were eager to learn.

After a week of this, James decided to check on the survey crew. He noticed they were all bunched together in the main tent.

"How is it going, ladies and gents?" he said.

They looked at each other and one said, "Um, it's going well, but we are confused by some of the findings."

James was not an expert on the subject, but he had done extensive research on the capabilities of GPR. They would use a transmitter and receiver to emit electromagnetic waves that could penetrate the ground. Some of these waves would bounce back when they encountered a boundary between different substances or structures, which was picked up by the antennae. They used a data logger to record the returning signals, which could then be used to translate the information into a three-dimensional representation of what was underground. Things like changes in construction material and voids were noted and graphed.

"See here," the crew foreman said. "This is where the type of construction material changes."

James tried to understand exactly what he saw, but it was not as obvious as he had hoped.

"These readings are consistent with the others you had us take from halfway up and all around the Caana structure. It's almost as if there are two distinct pyramids here."

James cocked his head. "What does that mean?"

"See this area." He pointed to the graph. "There is definitely an older structure underneath this pyramid, and it is constructed using completely different stone."

James leaned back on his heels and scratched his head.

"OK, wow, that's something," he said, realizing his understatement. "This could seriously upset the current thinking on who built these and why."

"That's exactly what we were thinking, but that's not all. Look at this."

"What am I seeing?" he said.

"Right there, see? It's a void, perhaps a tunnel, and it starts below the surface of the inner pyramid."

James's heart began to beat in his chest. He hadn't been this excited in years.

"It looks like we have a direction to continue our excavation."

"Does the charter that Belize issued allow for that type of excavation?" said Nicole, the foreman.

"Uh, sure it does," James said, having no idea if it really did.

The next morning at breakfast, he shared the news with the rest of the crew. No one seemed at all surprised. The word had already gotten out the night before and was discussed at length around the bonfire. James decided that he should join the evening bonfire in the future.

"I need volunteers to abandon your current dig. Work with me to uncover the pyramid underneath and investigate the void." Every hand went up to volunteer.

"Okay, let's see, Site 1, I am going to pull you all off to work the new site."

The rest of the group booed while those picked gave each other high-fives.

"I want to get started right away. The GPR crew is already there, marking the probable location. I want you to mark off the area and set up a grid pattern. We will be working to remove the top layer of stones to uncover the structure below, and with some luck, we will locate the tunnel that they believe could exist."

The new excavation went on for another week. James watched as the old stones were carefully removed, and their original positions mapped and logged. The original plan didn't call for logging and moving any pyramid structure, so they were unprepared to move the huge stones. A flatbed truck showed up two days later with a reaching forklift on its slide. It was not rated to lift the largest ones, but it would work for everything he intended to move. Manuel was impressed by how quickly the items they needed were showing up.

"The prof always said it wouldn't be worth it to bring in any machinery due to the site's remoteness and the limited time they had to work. How did you get this here so quickly?" he said.

"The sat phone finally connected for once, and it's amazing what a little extra cash incentive will accomplish," replied James.

He was going to make this dig work, and he now had the means to ensure that happened. He wanted to do everything as carefully as possible, not to disturb anything yet to be discovered, so the going was slow.

After an added week of work, they had removed the outer pyramid's stones, revealing the inner pyramid's exterior. The stones were remarkably well-preserved, having not been pounded by the local weather for millennia. James called over the foreman of the GPR crew.

"Nicky, can you give me the exact location and depth of the initial void you found?"

"Sure, Jim, but it will take a few hours, and we can't have the workers or the forklift here. They could throw off interference and give us anomalous readings."

James had been spending time at the GPR contractors' camp lately. He was fascinated with GPR technology and wanted to know everything about it. Manuel was inspecting the site and motioned for James to come over.

"Do you see this? Look over here at this as well," he said, pointing to the cover stone.

"Yeah, I see. There are no cutting marks whatsoever on the inner stones. How in the world could they have cut this stone out of solid marble? I don't think we could get anything to fit this perfectly unless they were laser measured and finely honed and polished," James said.

"That is exactly what I was thinking. What are we looking at here?" said Manuel.

James replied, "I don't know, but let's pull everyone off so that the GPR crew can give us an idea of where to go next."

With that, the crew was sent to lunch early and would be directed to help at another location for the rest of the day.

"Don't let me slow you guys down. I'll get out of your way. I have a couple of emails to send anyway," he said.

James had decided it was time to fill Dr. Geist in on what they had uncovered. The sat phone left here for him rarely worked properly, and there was no Internet on-site. Dr. Geist had obviously contacted him from the hotel in San Ignacio. James had no desire to leave the site at this exciting time. He opted to type the emails, send his laptop back with the caterers, and have them sent from the hotel. James wrote two emails. The first was to Dr. Geist.

Professor,

I wanted to be the first to relay some exciting developments at the site. We were able to see, with GPR, that there was an older structure underneath the newer Caana pyramid. I know this will be a bit of a shock, but it has been confirmed. We removed the top layer of stones to reveal the older structure. And there is more. We are locating and excavating a void in the older structure. GPR shows a likely tunnel into the older pyramid. Within the next few days, we should have more information. I suggest returning with haste, so that you may be present for the reveal.

Regards,

James

The second email was of a more personal nature.

Sandy,

The sat phone doesn't work, and I don't have internet on-site, so it may be a while before I can send another email. It was great seeing you a couple of weeks ago. I would love to see you again. Don't be a stranger. You know where to find me.

Love,

James

James decided to join the GPR crew at their nightly campfire that evening. The talk was all about their findings. They had indeed pinpointed a void, and it was a few feet below the surface. Nicole was convinced it was a tunnel likely built into the original structure. This was exciting news, and James asked that the GPR crew keep it to themselves until morning.

The next morning after breakfast, James gathered the entire retinue together. He stood up on a chair and asked for everyone's attention.

"I believe today is the day we'll finally get some answers to the many questions that have been on our minds since we discovered the older structure. Who built it, when, and why? I expect we will be through the first layer of older marble stone and into the unknown void today."

A cheer rose through the camp, and everyone looked excited.

"I think it would be best for everyone to share in this discovery, which is why I am calling off all excavations this morning, except for the void dig."

Again, everyone cheered.

"I need everyone from dig site one to head over now and prepare to remove what looks like a casing stone. Let's see what's beneath all that dirt we have shoveled for weeks!"

With a couple of hoots and whistles, everyone began to get to work.

The entire company of people stood watching as the marble casing stone was completely dusted and cleaned. They could tell no mortar held the piece. It was so perfectly smooth that you could hardly notice the edges.

"How are we going to get this off?" one student protested. "It's way too smooth, and I don't want to damage it."

"I have an idea," James said as he handed a box to the crew. "Try these suction cups. I think it is smooth enough for them to stick."

The suction cups were traditionally used for moving things like windows, but James had seen a crew use them to aid in laying down a marble countertop and figured they would work here. They were put into place, and two of the larger male students stood on each side to grasp the handles.

"Let's go ahead and see if we can ease it up on three. Okay? One, two, three."

A puff of dust blew out, and the square stone was pulled up and out onto a pile of foam pads to prevent chipping.

The entire group was silent. They all stared at an opening into a dark hole approximately three feet by three feet. James stared in awe into the hole.

"It looks like this is a tunnel."

The entire crowd erupted in applause.

"I think we can safely remove this upper stone as well to get a better look."

The same men replaced the suction cups on the upper slab and, without a prompt, pulled it up and out. They laid it beside the other, and James pulled out his flashlight.

"I can see about forty feet into the tunnel," he said. "It is level, but it looks like there's a stairway going down inside the pyramid."

There were a few gasps. "Oh my God, this is incredible," someone said.

A small breeze kicked up, and for an instant, James thought he smelled something familiar.

"Everyone back," he yelled, "at least twenty feet." The crowd looked confused and slowly began to back away.

James pulled out his phone and clicked a few photos before stepping back himself.

"It looks like we have found something significant, but more exploration will have to wait for the morning. I smell sulfur, likely from hydrogen sulfide, lingering in the tunnel. We must get some fans and ventilation going if we want to explore more." Reluctantly, everyone began to walk away from the site. "We should be able to get that specialized equipment here by afternoon tomorrow," he said.

The group was dejected but understood the caution.

James pulled Manuel and Nicole aside.

"Come here and take a look at this," he said. "What do you make of them?"

The two peered at James's phone and the picture of the inside of the tunnel.

"My God," said Manuel. "I have never seen markings like these. They are not like any hieroglyphics that I know."

"I agree," said James. "This is incredible. I have seen glyphs like this before. We may have uncovered writings from a new, previously undiscovered civilization. This could be old, very old."

They taped off the area and decided not to cover the opening so the H2S would dissipate faster, knowing no rain was in the forecast for the next two days.

The next morning, James had everyone go back to their original digs. There was a bit of hesitation, as everyone wanted to concentrate on the new discovery, but nothing could be done until the tunnel was cleared of danger.

James spent most of the day standing near the tunnel's entrance. He felt like he was guarding it and wanted to be the first to enter. He thought back to the times he had been ridiculed for his theories about older civilizations building the original Giza pyramids for a purpose, and that theory included all of these Mesoamerican structures. He was itching to find some evidence that would support his theories.

Mom, I think we may have found something, he thought, remembering her last words.

Installing the ventilation and fans would take a couple of days. They had to be sent all the way from Cancun. James tried to charter a helicopter to bring the gear sooner, but getting the permit for the aircraft to cross the Belize border was an issue.

The next morning, James woke up to the noise of a large caravan of trucks pulling up to the site. He expected to see perhaps a box truck or a van. What he saw approaching gave him a sick feeling in his stomach. Three military deuce and a halfs were pulling up, sandwiched by armored Humvees in front and behind the column. James noticed a familiar logo, "Black Sands Corp.," plastered on each door.

Nearly twenty soldiers filed out of the trucks, and three men jumped out of the first Humvee. James recognized one as Khalid.

James walked toward Khalid with his hand out. "Kal, what brings you all the way back here?"

Khalid replied, "Listen, Jim, there's somethin' you need to know. These guys..."

"That will be enough, Mr. Khalid," said one of the other men in a business suit. "Mr. James Jones, we appreciate the work you have done here on our worksite, but we'll be relieving your group. We are taking charge of this site."

"Oh, the hell you will," James said. "Who the hell do you think you are? You have no right or business here."

"On the contrary, Mr. Jones, this is our dig site. We obtained the license to work here and hired Dr. Geist to bring the archaeologists here to work.

We weren't expecting things to go quite this well, and we owe you a debt, sir. We are very excited to see this tunnel. You have our site weeks ahead of schedule."

That damn email I sent, James thought. *They were monitoring the prof's emails.*

CHAPTER NINETEEN

Meeting a God

1152 BC

The sun cast its first golden rays over the Nile as the small group boarded their barge bound for Waset, known by James as Luxor. Leaving the beautiful villa, on the banks of the Nile, was bittersweet. They had been there only the one night, and the entire priesthood begged James to stay longer, but they all knew it would not be in anyone's best interest to delay one who was meant to stand before Pharaoh.

They set out the next morning on a flat barge, captained by a large, surly fellow who went by Amani. The barge, its hull built from cedar planks caulked with pitch and resin, was curved gently upward on each end with a single square sail spun from striped blue and yellow linen.

James guessed the sail probably rarely helped, as the wind was usually sporadic. In the center of the barge was a small altar to Hapi, the Nile god, for the rich yearly flooding that brought fertility to the entire delta. Not to be confused with Hapi, the testy cook. The Egyptians often named their children after one god or another.

There were fifteen slaves lining each side of the barge with long poles to fight the current and push it up the river. This was an exhausting, labor-intensive task. This barge would typically have been loaded with many passengers and trade goods, which would be sold or traded along the route.

Amani didn't mind displaying annoyance at being sequestered by this group of bureaucrats and priests. He wouldn't be able to trade along the way, but he would be compensated for his time once they docked in Waset. James watched the grand temples of Ptah in Men-nefer (Memphis) fade into the distance as they slowly progressed to the south, traveling against the current.

Neferu grabbed James by the arm and led him to the only cabin on board. The captain generally used this small reed-lined cabin with a linen, tent-like roof. He didn't mind sleeping on the deck once he heard he had a god aboard who wanted to use his bed, and the bag full of silver sweetened the deal further.

The second day, they passed Sakkara, where the Step Pyramid of Djoser stood majestically against the horizon. James had visited this pyramid as a child, but seeing it now blew his mind. He was in awe of the temples and villages, many of which had crumbled to nothing and, in modern times, had been devoured by the desert or built over by cities. James hated watching the slaves laboring. He realized this was how their society worked, but he decided this was one aspect of Egypt he had to change. James had grown up with his American father, who taught him that all men were created equal.

The priests were all lounging while the few government officials sat together near the bow in deep discussion, often glancing over in his direction. James didn't feel comfortable with either of these cliques and had servants set up a bench near the rear for Neferu and himself.

They would sit together while James told Neferu his plans for Egypt. There were a lot, and Neferu only understood a fraction of what James was talking about, since much of what he said was in English, having no counterpart in Ancient Egyptian. James went through his satchel and showed Neferu all the wonders he had brought from the future. There were several full days of discussions with the priests about the new number system. He sometimes felt like a second-grade teacher, explaining how to add and subtract. Then, when they were comfortable with that, he threw in some multiplication and division. By day four, they were going over long division, and James was running out of papyrus.

By day five, James was completely bored. The only stops they made were to anchor at night, and an occasional stop at a village harbor to load up on food and fresh water. James wanted off the boat. He was watching the stuff of his dreams slowly pass by, and he was a passenger, not a driver of this experience. James preferred to be in charge.

James was anxious and decided to relieve one of the slaves of his oar duty. At first, Neferu didn't understand what he was doing, and the entire contingency sat and watched as he took the oar, shook his hand, and motioned for him to have a seat. James had a huge smile and was aiding the other slaves in their effort to push the massive barge ahead. For a moment, they sat there with their mouths hanging open.

Neferu ran up to James and said, "James, My Lord, what are you doing?" She looked horrified.

"What, this? I figured I could use a workout and wanted to try rowing a barge," he said with a huge grin.

"Can you not do the work of slaves, please, husband?" she said while looking over her shoulder at the gaping priests.

"Because of them? Those priests are harmless. What are they going to do?"

"Yes, my husband, that is true, but this is unseemly and a bit embarrassing," she said.

"Fine. Great," he said as he handed the oar back to the confused slave.

"You know I am unhappy watching all of these men work and not lending a hand."

"Yes, I know. Now come back and sit with me. Tell me more about the afterlife," she said.

"Now you are teasing me," he said. "You know I am talking about the future, not some afterlife."

"Of course," she said with a wink. James didn't know exactly what she believed.

Two more days passed. At one point, the captain motioned for the crew to begin moving the barge to the opposite side of the Nile. James questioned the captain about the purpose of the change.

"We are coming to the holy city of Abydos," he said. "The Holy Cult of Osiris controls this area. The farther away from their port we are, the less chance they will require offerings and tributes to their netjer."

"Not your favorite netjer, I presume?" James said.

"The captain's face turned beet red. "No, that is not it at all. I love and honor the great Osiris."

"Sure, you do," James said with a wink, and they were on their way.

James watched, and after they were at least a quarter mile past Abydos, a boat was placed in the water, and men began to gather on the docks while pointing at them. The barge must have already been far enough away to dissuade the cult followers from pursuing.

"Is this how you pass Abydos every time?" James asked the captain.

"No, your priests requested that I attempt to pass without notice."

"The priests requested that?" James said, and the captain nodded.

James walked to the group of priests, who had been intently watching the shoreline but were now returning to recline on their cushions.

"Why did we bypass Abydos and the Temple of Osiris?" James asked.

The priests were not ready for such a blunt question.

Ptomak answered, "It is not well known that the Cult of Osiris has openly defied Pharaoh. They have rejected calls to disarm and disband but defied those orders. We do not know their motivations and would rather ignore them and pass by unmolested. Pharaoh would not be pleased if Netjer James could not attend to him."

James returned to his bench and sat with Neferu. He thought this Osiris information might be important for her to hear. She was the only person he felt he could fully trust.

The captain told James that this would be the last night of the voyage. They wouldn't be able to make it to the port at Waset today, so they would stay overnight on the barge so they could make it to the harbor early in the morning. Two priests took a small raft to the banks and began walking.

Ptomak walked up to James. "We sent those two ahead to prepare for your arrival, great James. We will be at the port in the morning, and hopefully you will be brought before Pharaoh in the afternoon. It will be a great day," he said.

"I am here to instruct you in approaching Heqamaatre-Setepenamun Ramesses IV, Pharaoh of Upper and Lower Egypt," said Ptomak.

"Wow, that is a large bit of chewy mutton to spit out," James said with a chuckle.

"My Lord, you must take this with all seriousness. We will all be held responsible if you do not approach Pharaoh properly."

"Okay," James said, waving for Ptomak to calm down. "I understand. Proceed."

They spent the next twenty minutes going over the protocols for an audience with Pharaoh.

James let him know he was grateful they went with him this far and that he hoped to see them again once they were all settled.

"You don't understand, Lord. We are to attend to and advise you on state matters. We are all at your service."

James was caught off guard by this. He didn't relish the fact that everywhere he went, this entire group would follow him around. That didn't sound like something he would enjoy, but that would be a conversation for later. It was time to get his game face on and prepare to meet Pharaoh Ramesses IV of Upper and Lower Egypt, a person James had grown up studying and admiring. What would it be like to meet him in the flesh?

When exiting the boat, there was a stark contrast: the breeze swirling from the cool Nile to the hot stones of the harbor and the avenue beyond. James wore his thick-soled boots and looked to Neferu to make sure her thin papyrus sandals were adequate. A roar erupted from a mass of people hundreds strong, their voices a chorus of awe and delight.

"Netjer James! The divine one comes!" they called through the streets. The people were pushed back and cordoned off the main avenue by dozens of spearmen clad in leather kilts with their bronze-tipped spears held menacingly aloft. In front stood Sebekhotep, who led the procession with his imposing jackal headdress and announced the new netjer's arrival.

The procession veered north, past the sprawling Temple of Luxor, known to them as Ipet-resyt, a marvel of towering sandstone pylons carved with colossal reliefs of Ramesses IV vanquishing his foes. Twin obelisks flanked the entrance, their granite tips sheathed in electrum pointed ominously to the azure sky. Ramesses II had finished the temple in its current state and dedicated it to the god Amun-Ra, his consort Mut, and their son Khonsu. The temple also played a role in the Cult of the Royal Ka, the spirit of the dead pharaohs. To James's dismay, they skirted around the temple as they reached the Avenue of the Sphynxes.

Their path stretched ahead, a sacred avenue nearly two miles long, lined with hundreds of sandstone sphynxes, human-headed lions. Each statue, placed a few feet apart, rested on a platform with eyes inlaid with obsidian that gave the impression that you were being watched.

James's procession proceeded down the avenue while the crowd swelled, standing with the sphynxes. Farmers in rough tunics, nobles in pleated kilts and broad, brightly beaded collars, and women waving palm fronds chanted, "Netjer James! Lord of the two lands!" Children tossed lotus petals, which swirled in and around the procession in a surreal pink flurry.

The celebration continued along the entire route. Dancers spun and twirled while tambourines rattled to ancient rhythms, foreshadowing the promise of Karnak. Lpet-sut in this day loomed in the distance. He had made this same journey as a child with his mother and father, more than three thousand years in the future. When he was young, he thought it was opulent and grandiose. Now it seemed simply massive. He walked toward the towering gateway.

The tower on the left was covered in scaffolding and seemed to be under construction. Priests, officials, and workers were all milling about, but when they noticed the approaching procession, they all stopped to stand at the side of the great hypostyle hall and bow their heads. The temple was so much more than James remembered. The hieroglyphics that adorned the hundreds of massive columns were beautiful and in rich, vibrant colors from top to bottom. Even the underside of beams, probably sixty or more feet in the air, were decorated with ornate carvings.

What James remembered from the other visits was incredible, but these drawings were on the next level. He had truly never seen anything as vibrant in his life. The old dead temple of his youth was fully alive and thriving in this age.

A new priest walked out and motioned for everyone else to stay where they were, but James was to be taken alone to attend Pharaoh. They walked toward an area that James was not familiar with. He assumed he might be taken to the sanctuary, but that was the holy of holies, and the statue of Amun-Ra was housed there. Only the pharaoh and his high priests would be allowed there.

They came to a foyer that was lined with soldiers. These were not guards of the same caliber as those he had met in Khemenu-Ka. These soldiers were completely decked out in boiled leather armor that had been worked in a way to accentuate abdominal and pectoral muscles. Each wore a striped head cloth with a cobra at the front. Shiny brass scales polished to look like gold were attached to the leather pauldrons and chest cuirass. They also wore brass arm guards and a kilt covered with brass scales.

Each soldier held a spear and stood partially behind a tall shield that looked like it was constructed from wood, covered with leather, and painted in Pharaoh's colors. It was all too much for James to take in, and the entire production did exactly what was intended. James was utterly and completely terrified and intimidated.

The priest bowed and led James farther into the throne room. The soldiers still lined the way. There must have been nearly one hundred in all standing there. James knew they were not there for a practical purpose. No one could threaten the safety of Pharaoh here; they were here to demonstrate his absolute power. Near the back of the room, James saw him—Ramesses IV in the flesh.

Ramesses was very tall compared to the general population. At six feet, he would definitely stand out among his people. The torchlight caught the pschent crowning his head, which seemed to radiate authority. The double crown was a blend of two distinct headdresses, crafted to proclaim his dominion over the Two Lands.

He had lighter skin, similar to James', brown eyes, a dark curly beard, a chiseled jawline, and abs that a bodybuilder would be envious of.

He knew he had to control himself. The last thing he should do is run up like some sort of fanboy. The priest leading James lay face down twenty feet from the throne and said, "Great Heqamaatre-Setepenamun, King of Upper and Lower Egypt, Pharaoh Ramesses IV, before you stands the Netjer James, recently resurrected from the Ka of an unknown pharaoh."

The priest glanced at James with a look of horror. He didn't seem to remember proper etiquette.

"Is this true?" he said. "Did you reincarnate from a Ka and exit your tomb?"

"It is true, Great Pharaoh, that I did wake in the tomb at Khufu."

"And you were resurrected from a ka?" Ramesses said.

"I was hoping to talk to you and clear some of that up, your honor," James replied, then cringed about adding "your honor", an English word.

Ramesses doesn't know English. What was I thinking, approaching Pharaoh like this? Am I some sort of imbecile? Why did I have to say something stupid like that?

Pharaoh had a confused look on his face. His voice was low, edged in disbelief. "You address the living Netjer Horus, as if he were some common herdsman? You proclaim yourself a netjer and stand in defiance to mock the divine order in my presence? Blasphemy! Begone!"

CHAPTER TWENTY

Bad Decisions

2009 AD

"We are taking over this dig. I need anyone not directly associated with the Agenda for Belize Archaeology Mission to head to your tents and pack your things. We appreciate your hard work, but your services are no longer needed at this site. All students and faculty, please line up outside the mess tent. We will interview you all individually to assess your position here."

The suit spoke through a bullhorn. James just stood there, looking at the documentation and permits. Everything seemed legit, but he knew this was BS. How could the professor have agreed to any of this?

A small group walked up to James. "How can they do this? Is there anything we can do?" they asked.

James replied, "All of their documentation looks legit. There's nothing I can do. If the prof were here, maybe he could do something, but I don't have the authority."

Manuel asked, "How did they know about the find? We have all been stuck here with no communication for days."

"I think that's my fault. I sent Geist an email asking him to return a couple of days ago," James said.

"This is crazy anyway. What would this paramilitary group want with an archaeological dig?" Manuel said.

James replied, "I really don't know. I have worked with this company before, and back then, they didn't have Hummers and armed security guards. Something is going on with this pyramid and tunnel, something these people will do anything to take. Matt, I want you to take your phone to the tunnel and take as many pictures of the interior as you can. Don't let them see you."

"On it, boss," said Matt as he casually walked away.

The rest of the morning had all but a handful of the workers packed and ready to head to San Ignacio to prepare for the journey back to their respective schools. James was packed as well, but noticed Khalid standing behind a tent, motioning for him to join him.

"What's all this about, Kal? What in God's name does Black Sands want with a tunnel I discovered a few days ago?"

"I can't say much, and I'm goin' against my NDA just sayin' this, but yer tunnel ain't the first ta be found. There've been several o'er the last decade, all o'er the world. Nobody can talk 'bout it due ta state secrets and corporate NDA's. If ya talk 'bout this online, they'll come fer ya."

"Who gave them the authority to do any of this?" James said.

"Cash. They buy off any officials they need ta. Anyone who gives 'em trouble either disappears or 'ventually plays ball."

"What could be so important about these archaeological finds?"

"Believe it or not, it goes all the way back ta yer high school science project. It's lucky fer ya they've no idea who ya really are and who yer parents were. They'd have ya locked away somewhere ta get information if they knew. They're convinced there's somethin' not of our world goin' on at these sites."

James was shocked. "This is a lot to take in. What are you still doing working with them?"

"After the project in Alaska, I was kept on as a consultant. I've been watchin' this all go on fer a few years now. I figured if I stuck 'round, maybe I could do some good, keep people from gettin' hurt and such. I also wanted ta see what the hell this is all 'bout. I can't be seen talkin' to ya, or they might think we know each other. That could end bad. I need ya ta pack up and leave."

"You want me to leave?" James said, aghast. "After all that I've accomplished here, I am supposed to abandon the dig and run away?"

"Jim, there's nothin' ya can do here. If ya stay, it could go bad fer all of us. I'll be in touch, and we can work together 'hind the scenes ta try and make all this worth it."

Khalid looked over James's shoulder.

"What the hell? James, what'd ya do?"

James turned to see Matt being escorted toward the mess hall in handcuffs.

"Crap, I told him to go take some pictures before we're kicked off the site," James said.

"Ah, okay, I can fix this, but ya gotta stand down. I need ya ta go home and start yer research. We'll be ready ta change all this in a few years. If anyone can figure out what these symbols are 'bout, it's you."

With a note of resentment, James settled down and said, "Fine, Kal, I'll do it, but you've gotta keep me up to speed. Screw that NDA. I need to know."

An hour or so later, a bus pulled into the parking area. The door opened, and out jumped Dr. Geist. The professor approached the Black Sands suit and said, "McDermott, what's the meaning of all of this? Why are my workers lined up to get on this bus? I was told I had complete authority on this site."

"Simmer down, Geist, that was true before the recent discovery. If you read your contract, it clearly grants us permission to take over any dig site that we consider significant for our purposes."

"What is that supposed to mean? That makes absolutely no sense."

"Listen, you and most of the academic crew will continue working for us. We expect you all to honor your contracts and adhere to your NDAs. Things could go badly for you if you don't comply," he said.

The professor stood there looking lost, then stomped off shouting, "This was not our deal, McDermott."

James caught up to the professor and grabbed him by the shoulder.

"Professor, can you tell me what's going on?"

"Oh, James, I'm happy to see you. You've done exemplary work. Can you explain what Black Sands is doing here?" he said.

"All I know is that we found that tunnel. I messaged you, and two days later, we were swarmed by mercenaries in Humvees. There is something about this tunnel that these people will do anything to discover. If you are staying around, please be careful."

"Staying around? Of course, I'm staying, and so are you," Dr. Geist said.

"The suit made it perfectly clear that I would not be staying. In fact, I am supposed to be getting on that bus right now," James said.

"This is preposterous. They don't have the right," he said.

"No, they don't have the right to do this, but they have the authority, which you gave them."

That took the wind out of the professor's sails.

"I guess you are right. McDermott and I had a deal, but it looks like he's trying to cut me out. I don't know what can be done, but thank you for getting us this far."

The professor offered his hand to James, who took it.

James then noticed Nicole, the GPR foreman, in line to get on the bus.

"I am surprised they are getting rid of you. It seems like they might need some more surveys."

"We don't like what is going on here. They told us that if we were to stay, we would have to sign new contracts and NDA's. That all sounds a little Gestapo to me," she said.

"Same here," James replied.

They all loaded the bus with their personal belongings and gear and headed home.

The bus ride was rough. The ruts from the wet roads jostled them back and forth. It hadn't rained in several days, so the road was dry, but the ruts were a different thing altogether. The driver seemed to be used to this sort of thing and wasn't concerned. About halfway back to San Ignacio, three miles before the guard shack, they drove up to an accident on the side of the road.

A tractor-trailer was on its side. The truck had been carrying a small excavator, which had also broken free from its straps and was down in the ditch. James noticed the familiar logo on the truck's door: Black Sands Corp. James grew concerned as the bus pulled to a stop. He and the bus driver exited to assess the situation with a few other men. James immediately noticed several bullet holes in the door.

"Everyone, be careful. This was not an accident," he said as he walked to the front and peered into the cab through the front windshield.

The cab was empty, but there was some blood. The windshield had been broken through and was hanging loosely. James's heart began to race.

"Spread out and look around," he said to the remaining group exiting the bus. "Keep a lookout for blood. Someone has been injured."

A young woman yelled, "Over here. Someone's hurt."

James grabbed the first aid kit, then ran to where the young woman stood. There, propped against a tree, was a man James recognized as one of the drivers who had delivered their gear a few weeks back. He was in bad shape with cuts all over his face and a bullet wound in his shoulder. There was blood everywhere. James knelt next to the man.

"I'm here to help. Let's see if we can't get you fixed up enough to catch a ride on the bus to the hospital."

The man shook his head and said, "They took her. Those bastards kidnapped her."

"What? Who's been taken?" James said.

"The guerrillas, they had AKs and started shooting as we drove up. They took her for ransom. Would've taken me too, but they said I was too injured and wouldn't make it."

"Who did they take?" James asked in a much louder, cold, calm voice.

"Sandy, they have her, and I think she's hurt. It's been about an hour, and they're long gone. I can't believe they took her," he said.

Blood ran to James' face, and the veins in his forehead pulsed.

"Everyone, spread out. They have taken a woman for ransom. We need to find where they went."

"We can't wait, Mr. Jones. We have to get this man to a hospital now," Nicole said, and James knew this was true.

"OK, you all get him loaded and head to the guard station to let them know what happened. I'll stay here and see if I can find out anything."

"You can't stay here, boss. It's not safe. You don't have any protection," Matt said.

"Jim, let's all load up and get out of here. There is nothing that we can do but tell the authorities. They can handle it," Manuel said.

James didn't like leaving, but he understood the logic.

"OK, let's get moving," he said.

The bus ripped down the road at dangerous speeds. They stopped at the guard post and told them what had happened, then went to San Ignacio and the hospital. The bus pulled up to the emergency room at the small hospital, and James went directly to the police station across the street. When he entered, it didn't seem like anything was happening, and he walked up to the front desk.

"I assume that you have been informed about the kidnapping and shooting on the road earlier. What is being done to find Sandy?" he said.

"Sandy?" The man looked at James questioningly.

"Yeah, Sandy Thomas. She's the one the guerrillas kidnapped on the road to Caracol," James said.

"Oh, we don't normally get involved in these corporate ransom situations. It's best to leave that up to them," the clerk said.

"Are you shitting me? Leave a kidnapping up to a corporation?"

"We don't have the resources to find her, nor do we have the funds to pay a ransom," he said.

James was at a loss for words. He turned around and walked back to the bus, which was preparing to bring all the workers back to their hotel before the long trip to Belize City and the airport. James wasn't about to leave.

James caught a cab to a local car rental company and leased a Jeep. He loaded up the jeep with all his gear and headed to Caracol. He made it back before dark and walked right into the new command tent. Seated around the table were Dr. Geist, Khalid, and McDermott. A security guard at the door tried to grab him as he entered, but James pulled his hand away and walked past.

"It's okay. Let him come in," said McDermott.

"What exactly is being done to get Sandy?" he said.

McDermott replied, "I am not exactly sure what business it is of yours. She is an employee of Black Sands Corp."

"Fine," said James, "but what is being done? Can I help?"

"There is nothing for you to do. We're experienced in these matters. I have sent for a mercenary group to go in and extract her. They will be here in a few days, and she will be back before you know it. You don't need to think of us as the bad guys, James," said the suit.

"Days! It's going to take days for them to get her? Why don't you pay the ransom and get her back now?" James said.

"If we went around paying these ransoms all the time, it would encourage more of these kidnappings."

Khalid and the professor looked at James and shrugged, as if they had no idea what else to do.

"We know she's injured. She could be in bad shape. What if I pay the ransom?" James said. The entire room stopped and looked at him.

"How are you going to come up with half a million American dollars?" Dr. Geist asked.

"Don't worry about that," he said. "You just tell me where I need to take it to get Sandy back."

McDermott thought for a moment. "I guess there's no rule against someone other than Black Sands paying the ransom. I don't see how we can legally stop you, but you must know this is a bad decision. She's probably dead already. I don't expect the extraction team to be successful. Even if they have her alive, what is to stop them from killing her, then you, and taking the money?"

"So this is how you treat your employees? You write them off? What the hell happened to this company? I'll be doing your job and getting her back," James said.

The plan was for Black Sands to contact the guerrillas to let them know the ransom would be paid. Black Sands would relay to James when and where he would need to take it. James would be back in San Ignacio collecting the money. Khalid handed James a new sat phone.

"This phone should work. I'll let ya' know what ta do when we hear somethin'. Are ya' sure ya' wanna do this, Jim? It's much more dangerous than ya' think."

"I have to, Kal. I have to save her," he said as he ran out to the jeep.

It was going to be difficult to put that much cash together quickly. James rushed back to San Ignacio; by this time, it was evening. He knew no banks would be open at this hour, and with nothing else to do but wait for morning, he sat at the hotel bar with Nicole, Manuel, and Matt. He filled them in on what was going to happen.

"Listen, this is some dangerous stuff. I'm going to come along," said Manuel.

"Me too," Matt and Nicole both chimed in.

"I think that's a bad idea, guys. We don't have any weapons. I'm afraid it will piss them off to see a whole crowd there."

The call came through at midnight. Khalid said the meeting would take place at three in the afternoon. James was to drive down a dirt trail to a dead end at the same location where the truck had been rolled. The truck had already been salvaged at this point, but James figured he could locate the spot. The next morning, he went to every bank in San Ignacio. He put together the cash that was asked for, and that had basically drained the cash supply for the entire town. He loaded the money into a black duffel bag and headed to the location.

According to his calculations, he should arrive ten minutes early. Thanks to his lead foot, he arrived twenty minutes early. The guards at the checkpoint knew what was going on and waved him through.

He slowly pulled into a small lot surrounded by jungle at the end of the trail.

This has to be the place, he thought.

He jumped out of the truck and resigned himself to waiting. About thirty minutes later, a group appeared from the trees. They were all decked out in clothes with various camo patterns, and they had AK-47s leveled at him. James could see a couple of people holding back a bit, and they had Sandy cuffed with zip ties and a hood over her head.

Thank God, she's alive.

There was one huge man in front with a large gash across his face and part of his nose missing.

"Bring the money," he said in broken English.

"Let the girl go, and I'll bring you the money," James said.

"I don't think you get it," said the big, ugly guy with a smirk. "I'm not asking. Bring it now."

James hesitated long enough to hear Sandy cry out in pain.

"It's going to be okay, Sandy. I'm here to get you," James yelled.

"Yeah, it will be okay. Move forward and drop those bags here," the leader said with a scrape-clank, charging his AK.

"Relax," James said as he walked forward with the bag.

"Bring the girl." The two people holding Sandy brought her forward and pushed her to the ground at James's feet. James tossed the bag and knelt down to her.

He pulled the hood from her head. "You okay, Sandy?"

"No, not really, they shot me in the leg."

James tenderly put his hand on her face. She looked up at him, pleading with those big blue eyes. The filth on her face was streaked with tears, and her leg was caked with blood. There was a bandana tied around her upper leg. All he could see was her fear and pain.

"You have your money. We'll be going now." James glared at the leader.

The leader looked James directly in the eyes, turned toward Sandy, and shot her in the back of the head. James screamed in terror. Her brain matter was caked all over his shirt.

"Why? Why the hell would you do that?" James screamed out in pain, grabbing her limp body as it slumped to the ground.

"We don't need her anymore. We have you, and something tells me you're worth quite a bit more than that bitch."

James looked away for an instant, then, with everything he had, he charged the big guy and tackled him to the ground. They struggled and rolled around until the big guy was able to pull out his knife and hold it at James's neck.

"You better calm down, or you are going to see your little bitch girlfriend again sooner than you expect."

Two others stood over James with their AKs poised to shoot.

Two shots rang out. James was sure he was a dead man, but both of the AK-wielding guys dropped dead, like a bag of rocks. There was an instant of chaos, and more shots rang out. James took that opportunity to grab the knife from the distracted guerrilla and plunge it up through his lower chin, into his brain. The man had a shocked expression and sort of fell over. There were more shots, and the remaining guerrillas took off into the jungle. James looked around as Khalid, Matt, Nicole, and Manuel cautiously walked out of the jungle carrying rifles. Khalid knelt next to James.

"Damn, kid, I'm so sorry. I was 'fraid somethin' might happen, so we followed ya' out here."

"They killed her, Kal, right in front of me. She was looking at me, begging me to help her, and I let her down, Kal." James could barely speak through his tears.

"Ya' did everything ya' could. They never planned on lettin' her go."

Khalid sat on the ground next to James and Sandy. He put his arm around James.

"Ya' did everything right."

"I should have waited," he said, "I should have waited for the extraction team."

"Ya' see her leg? She wouldn't have lasted that long. There was nothin' more ya' could've done," said Khalil, but James wondered if that was true.

CHAPTER TWENTY-ONE

Good Decisions

1152 BC

James was led away by guards with none of the ceremony of his arrival.

"Where are you taking me? Can I speak with Ptomak? Where is Neferu?"

The guards were tight-lipped as they hurried him to some apartments. The next few days were a bit of a blur.

As he entered the apartments, he was accosted by Ptomak, Ptahmose, and Ptahhote.

"What have you done? Ramesses is furious," said Ptahhote.

"Did you not heed my instructions, Lord James? I was very specific," said Ptomak.

"Where's Neferu? Is she safe?" said James.

"She is residing in your apartment. While Ramesses was angered and offended, he must still be interested in you, or you would have been put to death immediately."

"Wait, put to death for not bowing down and lying on the floor?"

"Yes, Lord James, as I have told you, it is a great offense to the incarnate Netjer Horus," said Ptomak.

"We may have been executed beside you if he had not changed his mind. A priest came before you requesting that you demonstrate your netjer power to Ramesses in one decan," said Ptahhote.

"Please do not worry. I will make sure you are all protected. We will have to make a demonstration he can't ignore."

James and Neferu would walk hand in hand all through Karnak, taking in its majesty. There was so much more to see now than when he had spent time here before. James delighted in seeking out areas where the hieroglyphs had been destroyed in his time to see the original scenes. There was so much to see, but James came to realize he was wasting his time studying what he saw as the past, when he could begin to look toward his future, and in truth, the very future of mankind was dangling in front of him, daring him to meddle. He was here in Ancient Egypt now and didn't see any way to return to the future. It was time to make a difference in the world.

James had a couple of ideas on how he could impress Ramesses, but finding all the specialized materials he needed would take some legwork. He enlisted his entourage to search for all of the necessary components for his first device.

"What I need is a yellow powder that smells of rotten eggs. I think you may call it desher."

Ptomak chimed in, "Yes, desher, that is a yellow powder that is used in making dyes and embalming."

"I need you to get a jar full of it."

"Ptahhote, I need you to find some resin they use for sealing ships. A jar full of that as well. Bring them to my apartments this evening, as I will need to do some testing."

Later that evening, with Neferu looking on, James began experimenting with the compounds needed to make his device work. He started with two tablespoons of sulfur, one tablespoon of powdered charcoal, and around a tablespoon of the resin. He mixed all of them together, making a sticky paste. Grabbing a long candle, he told everyone to stand back while touching the flame to the concoction. *Pssst*, a tiny flame began to burn the sticky mess.

Neferu laughed out loud as Ptahhote and Ptomak looked at each other.

"My Great James, you will need something a bit more exciting to impress Pharaoh."

James looked at her with a glare. "Thank you, Nef. That is very helpful. You all can go now, and I will send for you when I have something."

James spent the next few hours trying different proportions of the ingredients, settling on the most promising mixture of five parts charcoal, three parts sulfur, and two parts resin. He called for a servant to fetch Neferu, Ptomak, and Ptahhote. A few minutes later, they slowly strolled in.

"I need all of you to stand back and watch."

James lowered the candle to the mixture. *Whooshes*, sparks, bright white light, and thick smoke erupted from the table. The three Egyptians staggered back, covering their eyes, and gasped as James clapped his hands together. "Perfect," James said with a snicker. The group stood quietly with their mouths open.

He then took some small, very thin-walled clay jars that he had purchased in the market and filled them three-quarters of the way with the mixture. Then, after carefully placing a resin-soaked strip of linen in the jars, he sealed them all in with wax that he had melted in a different room to keep the flames away.

With the first project complete, James knew that if he were going to impress Pharaoh truly, he had to pull off something huge. A project had been on James's mind ever since he found the young girl in the market with the bog iron. James had taught Bibi how to get the furnace hot enough to melt the iron in order to combine it and draw it out into rods. To achieve his end goal, James had to find a glassmaker in Waset who was skilled enough to create a bulb. The challenge would be achieving the vacuum required inside the bulb. For a filament, he would use hair-thin gold wire. James realized that using gold like this was way too expensive to be a long-term solution, but it would work for the demonstration.

He found a glassmaker in the market who was excited to work with him on this project. Rhemi was young and had only recently been released from his apprenticeship. James felt he wouldn't be too stuck in his ways and might be able to bring some insight into the project that James hadn't already considered.

The plan was to heat the glass to a very high temperature and form it into a thin-walled bulb in the shape of a vase. Rehmi didn't know how to make the clear glass that James described, so they settled on a bright blue, opaque glass that would have to do. These bulbs would be much larger than their contemporary counterparts. James had Rhemi craft a small glass disk as a lid to the vase, pushed two copper rods through to seal them to the lid, and then attached the curled gold wire between them.

He knew modern bulbs would have a vacuum inside, making the filament last longer than a few seconds. Realizing it wasn't a perfect vacuum that was required, but rather a lack of oxygen, an idea popped into his head. James pulled his Zippo from his satchel, and with a *snap, flick*, the flame ignited, to Rhemi's delight. He lit a small waxy wick and dropped it into the bulb as he placed the copper rods through the top and sealed the lid with resin. The wick burned for a few moments, consuming the oxygen inside. It wasn't a vacuum, but it should be good enough.

Ten days later, the demonstration loomed in James's mind.

Neferu stared into his eyes. "This could either lead to your execution or your ascendence into the netjeru. I know you will prove yourself, James, but please do as the priests have instructed."

James gave Neferu a kiss and a wink as he left. She was still not sure he would take it seriously.

James had spent hours in the last few days creating his demonstration, which would be performed in the throne room before Pharaoh and the entire court. As Ramesses sat on his throne, James entered and, without a word, lay flat on the floor until he was addressed by the god king himself.

"Proceed."

He stood and arranged six copper jugs on the table. The entire room watched as he had servants pour vinegar just below the brim. James pulled a roll of copper wire out of his satchel and set it on the table. It had taken him minutes to explain to a craftsman that he needed a spool of wire. The metalworker already had a process for drawing copper out into wire, as it was a recent fashion trend to wear as a bracelet.

James attached a wire to the handle of the jug. He then pulled from his satchel something no one had seen before. Six twelve-inch-long thin iron rods had been driven through circular wood disks. These were the rods Bibi had created for James from the bog material in those first few weeks in Egypt.

He attached a wire to each and plunged them into the center of the pots. The disks were fashioned to sit on the jugs and hold the iron rod away from the sides. By the time James had all the pots, cylinders, and wires in place, many attending had lost interest. Not so with Ramesses and Neferu. They grew more curious with every addition. James finally connected it all.

He attached the copper jug from the first jar to the rod in the second jar and so on, leaving him with two unattached wires on either end of the assembly.

James began to explain. "What I have made is what we will call a battery. When they are connected together, as you see, I have made a tiny bit of lightning."

That last statement got everyone's attention. Ramesses was unable to stay seated and stood next to James.

"Please continue, James," he said.

He hadn't completely planned the end of this demonstration, so he looked around for inspiration and noticed that Tentopet, Queen and first wife to Ramesses, had one of the new fashionable bracelets on. Her bracelet was constructed with the thinnest coil of wire that he had seen in this time, no thicker than a human hair. James asked Tentopet if he could use it. She had a strange look as she handed the bracelet to James. Neferu looked at Tentopet and sat up in her chair with a worried look on her face.

Tentopet gasped as James used a small hatchet to chop off a few inches of the wire. Realizing the improperness of his actions, he looked over to her apologetically. Neferu patted her, shaking her head. James then wrapped one end of the wire from the chain of jugs to one side of the coiled copper wire and then attached the other wire to the opposite side. James laid it all down on the table as the coil began to glow red and smoke.

To James's dismay, burn lines started appearing on the table. James got a little panicked as a small fire started in the wood, and he pushed the burning wire away to save the table. The wire came into contact with a bit of papyrus, which was instantly set aflame.

"Oh shit, sorry," James said in English as he yanked the wires from his makeshift battery. "I didn't mean for it to catch fire."

The entire room was silent. James looked around, worried he had ruined a perfectly good table.

"Is it magic? Some sort of sorcery?" Ramesses said.

"No, not at all, it's technology," James said, using the English word.

The priests looked at each other, and there were whispers all around.

James looked at Ptahmose and asked, "Is everything okay? Why are all the priests so concerned?"

"What you have done here today is surely of the netjeru. They are concerned that your power comes from the foreign Netjer Baal. He is said to be able to control lightning and storms. Baal is an enemy to our priesthood."

James understood this and tried to think of a good way to ease the tension in a way they could understand.

"Now that I have shown you where the power comes from. I want to show you a way to use this fire to better your life."

He reached underneath the table and set his new bulb on top of it. James motioned to his two guards, who went around and systematically snuffed the flame on the oil lamps in the room, causing complete darkness. James attached the wires from the crude battery to the two copper rods on the bulb.

Instantly, light emanated from the bulb, bathing the chamber in sky-blue brilliance.

"By Amun-Ra, it is beautiful. It is as if we are in the sky," exclaimed Tentopet.

There were gasps throughout the room.

"This is truly a miracle," said Ramesses.

A few priests, including Sebekhotep and Khety, the High Priest of the Osiris Cult, stood. "Or is it a tool of Baal himself?" Khety hissed. "We have seen enough." He stormed out.

"What I have shown you here today is not the power of a netjer. It is a tool created by man and is meant for all to share. In time, we will learn to harness this power to better our civilization."

Ten minutes into the demonstration, the lightbulb made a popping noise and went out.

The soldiers sparked and relit the lamps in the room.

"These are my crude first attempts. In time, bulbs like these will be used all over the kingdom," James said.

Ramesses stood and in his commanding voice said, "What you have shown today is nothing less than a miracle. It is natural for the priesthood to be skeptical of new ideas. Fear them not, they answer to us."

James understood the implications of what Pharaoh had said. He used the term "us" to describe their relationship. Ramesses was looking at James as an equal or at least a compatriot. The demonstration may not have gone over exactly as James had hoped, but the desired effect had been reached.

"Tomorrow will be a good day," said Ramesses. "It is the first day of the Opet Festival. There is much to celebrate, and I want you to understand who we are."

James knew from his studies that this was the largest festival of the year and had always imagined what it had been like.

"It would be my honor to attend your festival, Great Pharaoh," James said.

James had noticed that the tension only eased a bit as the room dispersed. He had expected more enthusiasm, but could understand how science could challenge the very fabric of their civilization. He would have to tread lightly and manage the subject with more care.

When James woke the next morning, Neferu was already dressed for the day and had ordered a light breakfast that they could share in their apartment.

"I hope you are not concerned about things at home, Nef. I believe Bibi is honest and capable of running things while we are here," James said.

Neferu replied, "You must not concern yourself with these trivial matters. You are too important to the kingdom to worry about our brick factory."

"I am not sure that I agree, love. I have time to concern myself with matters that are important to you, as well."

She walked up and kissed him on the forehead.

"Yes, I know you do. I want you to get dressed and prepared. I am very excited to attend the festivities with the queen while you are at Ramesses's side."

The festival was considered a rejuvenation of the royal Ka of Pharaoh and served as a link between the earthly ruler and Amun-Ra, chief of all deities. It was an annual ritual that reminded the masses that Pharaoh was, in fact, a god. Ptahmose described what would happen and how James would participate in the festivities. Ramesses would travel along the Avenue of Sphinxes between Karnak and Luxor Temple, accompanied by statues of Amun-Ra, Mut, and Khonsu. Upon arrival, Ramesses would enter the temple and have a symbolic marriage with the god Amun-Ra, representing divine right and renewal of the Ka of Pharaoh. A few other ceremonies would take place, at which time James would join Ramesses on his balcony to be revealed to the people of Egypt.

James decided to watch the entire procession from the balcony. It was a sight to behold. The whole procession was nothing short of a grand spectacle. Every citizen in Waset attended, and everyone who mattered traveled to the city to join in the festivities. The festival lasted as long as two or three dekans, twenty or thirty days, and there would be music, singing, and dancing. Ramesses had made a gift to the people of his best wine for the festivities.

The ceremony on the first day was to take about four hours, so James leaned against the balcony railing and took in the spectacle. He was witnessing something that had played out only in his imagination since he was a child. Once Ramesses had entered the temple for his various rituals, the crowd outside sat and waited, presumably for his grand reappearance on the balcony.

Without warning, twenty armed soldiers marched onto the balcony and lined up on each side. James was not exactly sure what the protocol was and stepped back and to the side to ensure Pharaoh had a clear path to the front. Ramesses stoically walked between the soldiers, as each one saluted, right up to the railing. The crowd roared and cheered, shouting his name. James could feel the excitement in his chest. Ramesses motioned for James to come forward and stand at his side. These people loved their pharaoh.

As James stood on the balcony with Ramesses, gripping the pharaoh's hand amidst the roaring crowd, a darker scene unfolded below in the shadowed alleys of Waset. Neferu and Tentopet, adorned in festival finery, had slipped away from the main procession earlier that morning to join the women's festivities near the Nile's edge. The air buzzed with laughter, the clinking of wine cups, and the rhythmic chants honoring Amun-Ra.

Neferu, ever vigilant, kept Tentopet close, her sharp eyes scanning the crowd, not out of fear but from a habit honed by years of managing her factory and protecting her people. Tentopet, less attuned to danger, sipped Ramesses's gifted wine, her regal poise softened by the festival's revelry.

Unknown to them, Khety, High Priest of the Osiris Cult, had been seething since James's demonstration the previous day. He whispered to others that James was "a tool of Baal himself," which masked his conspiracy to undermine Ramesses's growing trust in this foreign "netjer" and reassert the priesthood's dominance. Khety saw James's new light as a blasphemy against Osiris, a threat to the sacred order he upheld.

With Ramesses distracted by the festival and James's prominence, Khety seized his chance. He rallied a cadre of loyal acolytes, cloaked in dark linen, their faces obscured by hoods, and devised a plan to strike at the heart of their power by killing Ramesses and capturing the wives of the pharaoh and his new ally.

The trap sprang as Neferu and Tentopet paused near a merchant stall displaying glazed pottery. A sudden hush fell over the nearby crowd, replaced by the rustle of cloaks as six figures emerged from the mass, surrounding them in a tight semicircle. Neferu's hand instinctively dropped to the small dagger she kept strapped beneath her linen skirt, a precaution James had insisted upon after hearing caravans often came under bandit attacks.

"Stay behind me," she hissed to Tentopet, who froze, her wine cup clattering to the ground.

The acolytes parted, and Khety stepped forward. His gaunt face was framed by a golden headdress, and his eyes glinted with malice.

"The consorts of false netjeru have no place in Amun-Ra's festival," he spoke, his voice low and venomous.

Neferu squared her shoulders, her courage flaring despite the odds.

"You dare defy Ramesses in his city?" she challenged, gripping her dagger's hilt.

Khety sneered, raising a hand to signal his men. "Ramesses bows to a heretic, and Osiris demands retribution."

The acolytes lunged, but Neferu was faster. She slashed at the nearest one, her blade slicing through his arm, sending him staggering back with a cry. She pivoted, shoving Tentopet toward the stall for cover, and struck again, her dagger grazing another attacker's thigh. The crowd scattered, screams piercing the air, but no one dared intervene for fear of Khety's sacred authority.

Tentopet, trembling but spurred by Neferu's defiance, grabbed a clay pot and hurled it at an acolyte, shattering it against his chest. Their resistance faltered as Khety barked an order, and two more men flanked them, pinning Tentopet's arms. Neferu fought like a lioness, kicking and twisting, her dagger drawing blood from a third assailant's hand before a heavy blow to her temple from a staff dazed her.

She stumbled, her vision blurring, but she still swung wildly, her voice a defiant roar: "You'll answer to my James for this!"

Khety, unruffled, seized her wrist, wrenching the dagger free as his men bound her with coarse rope. Tentopet, sobbing, was similarly restrained, her royal dignity shattered.

Khety loomed over Neferu, his breath hot against her ear.

"Your husband's 'technology' will not save you from Osiris's judgment," he spat, dragging her upright.

The acolytes hustled the women through a side alley, away from the festival's chaos. They were hastily brought to the Temple of Osiris to face judgment.

Neferu's blood trickled from her temple. She glared at her captor, her resolve unbroken even as the ropes bit into her wrists. She whispered to Tentopet, "Stay strong. They will come for us." Her bravery somehow warmed Tentopet, like a flickering torch in the gathering dark.

Meanwhile, on the balcony, something strange caught James's eye. One of the soldiers had relaxed from attention and was moving toward them. In an instant, the man pulled out his sword and was mid-swing toward Pharaoh's head when James tackled him hard to the ground. James rolled on top of him and quickly put him in an armlock. Either the assassin would submit or his arm would be broken in half. The assassin cried out for mercy, and as three other soldiers grabbed him, James rolled away and stood up.

Most of the crowd below had seen the attack. A few women had screamed, and most of the mass became silent for a few moments. Ramesses grabbed James's hand and thrust it into the air, and the crowd went wild, screaming out the name of Ramesses, all while wondering who this giant stranger was who had the hand of Pharaoh.

This lasted for only a few moments before a priest quickly and silently walked up and whispered something into Ramesses's ear.

Ramesses's face turned pale, and he looked over to James. "It is not over," he said with a grim look.

"What is it, Ramesses?" James said.

Ramesses replied, "They have taken our wives."

CHAPTER TWENTY-TWO

The Gang's All Here

2009 AD

There was nothing left in Belize for James. He, Matt, Manuel, and Nicole stopped at the police station to give their testimonies. The police had arrived at the site of Sandy's murder about two hours after Khalid had called them. James and Khalid agreed it would be best for Khalid to return to the Black Sands dig site, where he could keep an eye on things.

"I need to thank you guys. I'd be dead if you'd listened to me," James said to the group.

"Honestly, we were planning to stay put until Khalid called. He was able to grab some rifles from some of Black Sand's goons for us," said Manuel.

James decided he had had enough of Black Sands and didn't want to return to the site. James bought Manuel a ticket and upgraded Matt and Nicole's tickets to first class for the trip back to Houston.

On the plane, James leaned over and said to his friends, "I was thinking it might be a good time to start a company. I've been studying GPR tech and think it would be a great way to have access to dig sites all over the world," said James.

Nicole said, "That sounds great, but I'm not sure if it'd be smart to jump ship; however, my boss, the owner, has been talking about selling this company for nearly a year. If we could find someone to buy it, maybe it would give us an advantage. We would already have all the gear and personnel needed to operate at dig sites."

"That's a very interesting idea. I might know someone with the funds to make something like that happen," James said.

The sale of the business took nearly six months. GRT, Global Radar Technologies, was called Grit by the employees. The offices and warehouse were in Conroe, Texas, about an hour from the ranch. James appointed Nicole CEO, and Manuel and Matt would head up the field units.

This idea had worked out better than James had imagined. With Grit, he would be able to access not only any site that he wanted to work on, but also hire out teams with GPR gear to other sites. It was extremely rare for anyone working a dig to keep their own GPR gear, since it was highly specialized and expensive. Nicole could send out a crew to any number of highly classified dig sites all over the globe without raising any attention.

He left his name off the company paperwork to maintain some anonymity, holding the stocks in a shell corporation. Manuel, Nicole, and Matt were the only people who knew James had anything to do with it. This would allow James to continue accessing the forums and chat rooms without unwanted attention. That was where the authorities in their field, he and Dr. Geist included, discussed the nitty-gritty of the dig sites.

James was obsessed with the pictures he and Matt had taken before they were kicked off the Caracol site. It was interesting that the new glyphs had not come up as a topic and were never discussed in the forums. Apparently, the signed NDAs were enough of a threat to keep people's mouths closed.

To James, it was a travesty. He felt that information should be shared with the scientific community so that anyone who wanted to view it could. James tried to post his pictures anonymously a few times, but they would disappear minutes after they went up on the Internet. Someone was actively suppressing the information, and James needed to find out why.

It had been six years, and everything was clicking with Grit. Nicole had crews on every significant site around the globe. James noticed in the forums that there was a new group exploring the areas associated with the Library of Alexandria. It was believed to have been created around 300 BC and was said to house as many as 700,000 scrolls. It was founded by Ptolemy I, one of Alexander the Great's generals.

The library was intended to house a collection of all the world's knowledge, and its curators' mission was to collect at least one copy of all the books in the world. It attracted many scholars, including famous figures like Euclid, Archimedes, and Eratosthenes. However, the library was lost to time.

The original location was said to have either been swallowed by the sea or the sand. No one was exactly sure where to look, but Sara, James's mother, had been a party to one of the excavations back in 2004 with the Egyptian Ministry of Tourism and Antiquities. They believed they had found the original site, but it was never confirmed. When Sara had returned from that expedition, she and James sat around for hours discussing the possibility that *if* the library could be discovered *and* some of the scrolls were still intact, then maybe some ancient mysteries could be solved. These discussions were what prompted James to send his science fair project about the pyramids to ISEF all those years ago.

James decided it was time to go through his mom's things to see if he could locate any of her old notes about her experience with Alexandria. They had been boxed up and were sitting in a closet in Hank's old office. There were stacks of notebooks and folders to go through, but one in particular caught his eye. It was the same notebook she had been writing in when he was a child in Egypt.

He did a quick search, looking for anything he could find about Alexandria. This was not the notebook for that dig, but some concerning notes caught his attention. James's eyes widened as he realized these notes were from the project at Giza, where she had died.

"Black Sands reps threatened me today. I must tell Hank he can't trust this McDermott guy."

"These people are obsessed with keeping the new glyphs to themselves. What do they hope to accomplish by keeping them secret?"

"There is more going on here. I need to warn Hank and James to be careful."

"Visited the tunnel with Geist. James has done a marvelous job preparing the area."

"Overheard Geist and McDermott talking in whispers. Geist is going to be off-site tomorrow. It makes no sense. Why doesn't he want to work with me in the tunnels? This is what we have been waiting for."

"Geist isn't around this morning. As soon as these Black Sands goons finish their inspection of the shoring, they'll let me in. It's silly, really. I trust Hank's design and James's building expertise more than these idiots. I'm going to ignore Geist, take pictures of the Anunnaki Glyphs, and post them online for the world to see. This is way too big to keep secret."

James's head was spinning as the notebook fell to the ground. The pain of his mom's death returned in a flood.

Is this what I think it is? Black Sands sent their people into the tunnels before Mom went in. We assumed Dad was the last person to inspect the shoring the night before it collapsed. It wasn't Dad's fault. It wasn't my fault. Those bastards murdered my mother!

His fist smashed down on the desk as a murderous rage blazed from within James's soul. A furnace roared to life in his chest, searing away all the guilt since her death.

I'm going to finish what Mom started, and they will pay.

James sent a message to the Ministry of Tourism and Antiquities offering Grit's services at a highly discounted rate. Grit's reputation was stellar, and they had been working on a new system for mapping using drones. They would fly a grid pattern while emitting the ground-penetrating radar. Their revolutionary software generated a high-definition 3D model that you could display and manipulate on a screen, showing any small anomaly or hidden void underground.

He decided to attend this dig personally under his assumed name of James Jones. He had hoped that if the library could be found with some intact scrolls, then perhaps the foreign hieroglyphs could be explained and translated. He asked Matt to run the crew so he could focus on his own agenda.

James's primary crew arrived two weeks later. They were not there to do any groundwork. Grit was brought in to survey the area that Dr. Muhammed Abdel, Director of the Egyptian Ministry of Tourism and Antiquities, believed to be the best candidate for the ancient library site. Dr. Abdel was a long-time member of James's forum and was very excited to meet him.

The advanced team had been there for over a week and worked with Dr. Abdel to obtain living accommodations for the rest of the crew's arrival. They had sequestered a small hotel about two miles from the area to be surveyed. Outside the hotel was a small pub that would be perfect for gathering after a day's work and reviewing the findings with his crew. James sat at a table with Nicole, Matt, and Manuel. Normally, James's trusted leaders would all be running separate sites, but James wanted all hands on deck for this dig.

Dr. Abdel walked up with a big smile and offered a handshake.

James stood. "You must be Dr. Abdel. It is very nice to finally meet you in person. I feel like I've known you for years."

"Likewise, Mr. Jones. I have been following your work for years. The advances you have brought to GPR in the last five years are nothing less than incredible."

"Wait until you see my new toy, which was developed for this type of project." James spent the next half hour explaining the benefits and uses of the drone technology he had recently perfected. Dr. Abdel was very impressed.

"I knew we were hiring the right people. I'm excited to see your findings," he said.

"We should have a pretty good idea of what we are looking at within a week," James replied.

"Oh, that's amazing. I can't wait."

With a handshake, Dr. Abdel walked away.

James turned to his crew. "Well, it seems like we are not going to have to worry about having anyone looking over our shoulders with every step we take. That will be a welcome change."

With the clinking of glasses, they finished their drinks and headed to their rooms. "Big day tomorrow," said Manuel.

It took a few days to survey the area from the ground, to find the best possible targets to investigate later with their drones. A few promising regions were found, and Nicole took it upon herself to pilot the drone over target area one. The data would be collected, then collated on a computer later that day. Once the area had been fully surveyed, they moved to target area two. This time, James wanted a go at the drone controls.

The survey continued as planned, but James felt uneasy when he noticed a couple of men standing behind a brick wall nearby watching them work. They were not the half-starved, skinny locals he had seen for the last few days. These guys were big and paying way too much attention to the work going on. A few Egyptian groups were not excited about letting outsiders work on one of their cultural sites and were known to try to sabotage digs.

"Manuel, we need to keep an eye on those two standing on the other side of the fence. They are acting like they're not watching us, but they clearly are," said James.

"Will do, boss. I'll spread the word to keep an eye out."

That afternoon, while the rest of the crew was still working, James, Nicole, and Manuel returned to the room at the hotel that they had set up as a field office.

"It'll take about an hour to collate the data. Do y'all want to meet at the pub to review the findings?" said Nicole.

"That would be great, Nicky. Let's meet at the pub in two hours. That will give us enough time to get a meal."

"Will do, boss," said Nicole, who would only call James "boss" when they were in private company.

James was eager to see the results and was sitting at the table with Manuel and Matt when Nicole sat down with her laptop.

Nicole opened the laptop and said, "I've only glanced at these results before coming here."

Suddenly, James felt cold metal pressing against his spine.

"OK, relax, people. I suggest you sit there and be quiet for a second," a voice came from behind him.

A man walked up behind Nicole and held a pistol to her as well. They were trying not to make a scene, so James figured they may not be there to outright murder them.

"We want the laptop!" said the man behind James. James noticed that the man standing behind Nicole looked familiar. These were the guys from that morning who had been watching them.

"What are you guys, like Al-Qaeda or something?" Manuel said.

"What, are you stupid? Keep your mouth shut and hand over the laptop."

The two men looked Middle Eastern but had typical American accents.

"Listen, we can't give you that laptop. There is nothing valuable on it, only some scientific graphs," said Nicole.

"You let me decide what's valuable. Hand it over, and you can go about your day," the man standing behind James said.

"Fine, easy, take the laptop and leave us in peace."

The man behind Nicole holstered his gun to reach down and take the laptop. James eyed his two companions, and each understood what was about to happen. James swooned over a bit, acting like he was fearful, then spun around, pinning the pistol between his elbow and his side. He delivered a blow to the assailant's face. At the same time, Nicole smashed the laptop into the face of the man next to her, while Manuel tackled him.

James wrestled away the pistol, and it went sailing underneath some tables. Manuel's tackle didn't work exactly as planned. The man was staggered from the laptop hit to his face, but easily directed Manuel past him, knocking his head into the nearby bench. He then slammed his fist into Nicole's solar plexus and knocked her out cold. James took another swing at his attacker's jaw. The man ducked the swing and grabbed James's wrist, spinning him face-first into the table and holding him there.

"It would have gone easier for you if you had just given us the laptop. We will be back in a few days. We are going to want any information you have collected. Do you understand?" He slammed James's face into the table.

All three regained consciousness a few seconds later, and the attackers were already gone. He looked at his two bruised friends and said, "I think we need to hire some security."

CHAPTER TWENTY-THREE

The Osiris Conflict

1152 BC

The honor guard quickly took Pharaoh away, leaving James alone on the balcony. The crowd was still cheering, and James took that opportunity to quiet the crowd.

"People of Egypt, I stand before you as a friend of Egypt and Pharaoh. Please know that Pharaoh is unharmed, but enemies have taken your queen."

Gasps rang out from the crowd, and then yells of anger.

"Who did this?"

"We must get her back."

"Please know we will do everything possible to return your beloved queen. There are people in this very crowd who know who took her. I charge all citizens to come forward with any information. You will be rewarded," he said, and with that, he trailed after the soldiers who had already gone.

The palace was buzzing with people walking back and forth. It seemed that no one had any clue what to do. James approached a priest he recognized as one of Pharaoh's top aides. James didn't know his name, but grabbed him and pulled him aside.

"Where is Pharaoh? You must take me to him," James said.

"I ... I am not sure, Great James," said the priest.

"Don't play stupid. I know you know where they took him. You don't want to anger me. They have taken my wife as well. Now lead."

With a nod, the priest led James through a corridor and down some stairs.

"He would have been taken to his rooms in this temple, through those doors."

He pointed ahead, where three guards were standing. James walked up to the door and reached for the handle when one of the guards shoved him back with his spear.

"Pharaoh is being attended by his priests and will not be disturbed," said the guard.

James stepped back. "Your orders do not include keeping me from him."

The guard who shoved James had a look of disgust on his face.

"You should not have been there," he said. "We have other plans for you and your bitch wife."

The other two guards looked at each other, not understanding, as the first guard turned and lunged toward James with a well-aimed spear thrust at James's heart. James had seen the anger in the man's eyes and was prepared for the attack. With a simple sidestep, the tip barely grazed his left shoulder. James grabbed the shaft with his left hand as the spear passed while swinging with his right, hitting him square in the jaw. The man fell to the ground like a sack of rocks.

"You two, bind this man and follow me. We will be presenting this traitor to Pharaoh," James said.

"The two quickly looked at each other and said, "Yes, My Lord.""

The guards grabbed the limp assailant and followed James as he opened the door. Four more guards were inside the room, all instantly holding their spears towards him.

"Stop! Pharaoh is not to be disturbed," said the captain of the palace guard.

"Stand aside, Intohep. My business is above your orders," replied James.

Intohep knelt and said, "Great James, I regret that I must deny you access to Pharaoh, by his direct order."

James put his hand on Intohep, "Rise. I have no desire for you to go against Pharaoh's direct orders. Please go to him now and tell him I am here and that I have a prisoner."

Intohep quickly walked away and returned a moment later.

"Please forgive me, Great James. I was wrong to have stopped you. Pharaoh wants no interruptions apart from his closest advisers. I have been made aware that you are now included in that company. Please follow me."

James entered a small room with a large table in the middle. At the head of the table sat Ramesses, and around it were the tjaty, Nebamun, and Djehuty, the Imi-r Mesha, the highest-ranking general in Pharaoh's army. Two others were also in attendance whom James did not recognize. The space directly to the right of Ramesses was open.

"Please, James, come. I was wondering where you were after the attack. Are you well?"

"Yes, Pharaoh, I am well. I have brought you a gift."

James grabbed the traitorous guard by the hair and threw him to the ground at the feet of Pharaoh.

"Another assassin in your guard, My Lord," James said.

Ramesses glared at the captain of the guard.

"Intohep, how can this be? Two traitors among my personal guard?"

Intohep looked mortified.

"I do not understand it, My Pharaoh. These men, who have betrayed you, were brought in today from Abydos. We had two guards disappear last week, and they were to replace them. They were highly regarded by Amenemhet the Haty-a."

"This is very strange," Ramesses said. "What is the purpose of attempting to kill me and take my wife?" He looked at James. "My apologies, our wives. James, please sit here at my right hand. I need your counsel."

"I will, Lord, but first we must see that this traitor is secured. Intohep, make sure both prisoners are bound and gagged with hoods over their heads and place them in separate rooms. I will be interrogating them when we are finished here."

Intohep looked at Pharaoh, who nodded, then unceremoniously dragged the captive away.

James walked over to Pharaoh as the others watched with envy. He sat at Pharaoh's right hand and said, "Great Pharaoh, we believe these traitors came from Abydos and were highly regarded by Amenemhet. Do you know any reason why he would want to put assassins in your honor guard?"

"No, I cannot understand why my half-brother would want me dead."

"Amenemhet is your brother? Does he have any claim to the throne?"

"I know what you are thinking, but he is my brother. We were together often as children, and he has always been a loyal friend. He fought alongside me when I ascended the throne."

"How long has he been away from the palace as the Haty-a of Abydos?" James inquired.

"My father appointed him nearly ten renpet ago. He has always attended the Opet ceremonies for my father, as was his duty."

"It is curious, Great Pharaoh, that he has not attended ceremonies for the last two years, nor did he attend this season. In fact, he has not been seen in Waset since your coronation," said Nebamun.

"I cannot believe my brother, my friend, means for me to be slain," Ramesses said.

"It is true, Pharaoh, that he would perhaps have a claim to the throne if you were assassinated," said Djehuty.

James said, "On my journey to Waset from Men-nefer, we passed by Abydos on the other side of the river. The priests seemed to believe our barge might be in peril if it were discovered that we were aboard. They said the Cult of Osiris is in rebellion against you."

"Lies! I am not aware of any rebellion. Bring Ptomak to me at once," shouted Ramesses.

Nebamun held out his hand. "Great Pharaoh, please forgive me. The Cult of Osiris has indeed been speaking out against you. Their rhetoric has only gotten worse now that Netjer James is in a position to advise you."

"That priest at the demonstration... I think he was called Khety. Was he not the high priest of the Osiris Cult? Could he have something to do with this?" said James.

Ptomak entered the room and was likely on the other side of the door, waiting in case James needed him.

"It is true, Pharaoh. The attendants of Lord James have been accosted by the Cult of Osiris the entire time we have been in Waset. They are convinced that James is of Baal and that he has bewitched you. There are rumors they have corrupted Amenemhet and fed lies to him so that they may place him on the throne to gain power over all of Egypt."

Ramesses sat in shock.

"I thought my people loved me. I have been Pharaoh for only three renpet, and this is only my third Opet Festival. What did I do that would make them want my throne?"

"Before we condemn Amenemhet and all of the Cult of Osiris, we need proof. I agree that they are the most likely to carry this out, but why did they take our wives? What is the purpose? Would they take them for ransom?" James said.

"No, that would not make sense," said Nebamun. "They would know Pharaoh would hold them responsible, and even if they were returned safely, they would never be forgiven."

"They never meant for either Ramesses or me to live. They expected their assassin would hit his mark and then come for me," James said.

Pharaoh nodded. "But what is the purpose of taking our wives?" he said. "What would they have hoped to accomplish if not a ransom?"

Ptomak had a disgusted look on his face. "Great Pharaoh, something has occurred to me, and I fear to say it out loud. I ask for your patience in hearing me."

Pharaoh nodded and motioned for him to continue.

"There are rumors, Lord."

"Go on," said Ramesses.

"There are rumors the Cult of Osiris has returned to practices that have not been used in generations. They may believe that if they were to sacrifice Queen Tentopet and Neferu, the wife of our Lord James, on the altar of Osiris, Osiris would be set to judge Pharaoh and James as unworthy to enter the afterlife."

James stood in anger and disgust. "Let us be clear here. You are saying these scum have decided to assassinate Pharaoh and myself and make human sacrifices of our wives in order to take the throne?"

"That may be true," said Ptomak.

"So now that they know they did not kill us, there will be no point in the sacrifice," Pharaoh said.

"That very well could be true," said Nebamun.

"Djehuty, I want you to send a messenger to Abydos. Tell them I am displeased and require Tentopet and Neferu to be returned within three heru. A sufficient ransom will be paid for their return."

"It will be done at once." Djehuty stood and began to walk out of the room.

A sinking feeling began to well inside James's stomach. This was too familiar, and he knew what must be done.

"Stop, Djehuty, just a moment," James said. "I do not like this, Great Pharaoh. I believe they have made a grave error in leaving us alive. Their only option is outright rebellion in the name of Osiris. They will not stop until our wives are sacrificed and we are dead. I do not see any motivation for them to send them back to us alive, even for ransom. They are not doing this for wealth. They believe Osiris has ordained our death and that of our wives. If we give them a few heru to prepare, they will send more assassins to ambush us when we are not expecting it, and they will sacrifice Tentopet and Neferu."

Pharaoh looked at him shrewdly. "James, I do not believe they would do that. I am beloved by my people, and we have lived peacefully for many renpet. They would not resort to this."

"Great Pharaoh, it is time that we talk to our captives. They can shine a light on the situation, and perhaps we can find motivation for all of this," replied James.

As James had asked, the traitors had been placed in separate cells with bags over their heads.

When James approached the first prisoner, he removed the hood to see cold, dead eyes staring back at him with a bruised, blood-streaked face.

"What happened here? These prisoners were only to be questioned," said James.

"My apologies, Lord, it seems he didn't live through the first round of questioning."

"Djehuty, do you understand what you have done? This is one of the only men who might know where your queen has been taken."

"Please forgive me, Great Pharaoh and Great James. Sebekhotep was here earlier, and it seems he was overzealous in his questioning. When this man did not survive, we put a stop to it. The second prisoner is alive."

"Sebekhotep? He has no business here," said Ramesses.

James looked at Ramesses and said, "Please, Great Pharaoh, give me leave to interrogate the second prisoner. I believe I can get the information we need while keeping him alive so he can be punished."

"You may proceed, James," Ramesses said sternly.

"Djehuty, I need your men to do exactly as I ask with no questions. Ramesses, would you be interested in aiding me with this?"

Djehuty gasped, "No, you cannot ask this of Great Pharaoh, for it is beneath him."

"That may be true, Djehuty, but I am intrigued. What is it that you need me to do?"

After a few minutes of explaining the concept of 'good cop', 'bad cop', they began.

"Remove his hood," James said. Then he walked up to the man and slapped him.

"Where is my wife?"

Pharaoh stood in the back of the room and watched the man say, "I don't know where your wife is. I would not tell you if I did know."

James grabbed the man by the hair and pulled back his face to look into his eyes.

"You will tell me. It is only a matter of time. I have your friend in the room down the corridor. One of you will tell me what I want to know. You have taken my wife. Your life as you know it is over, but you may be able to keep your family alive. Do you know who I am?"

The traitor looked directly in James's eyes and defiantly said, "Yes, you are an imposter, the false netjer who has bewitched Pharaoh."

"No, you do not understand. I am the netjer of death and pain. You are less than an insect to me. I may leave your soul intact if you tell me exactly what I want to know. Now sit there and think hard about your next answer," James said as he walked away.

Once out of earshot, James said, "He thinks he is going to die. He is not. Djehuty, I need you to bring me the offal from a sacrificed lamb."

Djehuty looked at Pharaoh, who shrugged and then went on his way.

Ramesses walked towards the prisoner with pleading eyes. "How is it that a subject of mine, one who follows the netjeru such as you, could come to harm your Pharaoh and his wife? Have I not been a just pharaoh?"

"Please, Great Pharaoh, forgive me, Osiris instructs me to carry out my mission. This false netjer has bewitched you."

"That is not true, young man; I make my own decisions, ruling this kingdom. Do you not understand what is at stake here? This Netjer, James, has the power to steal your very soul. You will no longer be able to join your ancestors in the afterlife if you do not submit."

"Please, no, Great Pharaoh."

"I want to help you, but my hands are tied. As a netjer, he has a right to this information." Ramesses sadly shook his head and walked away.

James then approached, pulled the man's hair back, and stared into his eyes.

"I am the Netjer of Death and Pain. Say it. Who am I? Say it."

The prisoner stared defiantly.

"I will die a thousand deaths before I will forsake Osiris, you fool."

James looked over as Djehuty returned with a bowl of entrails, then put a linen over the man's chest.

"You have so much faith in Osiris. Will your netjer save you here today? If your soul is condemned, is he here to ensure your ancestors are allowed into the afterlife? I am here to tell you that I am the Netjer of Death and Pain."

James held up the sheet to block the view of the traitor.

"Guards, hold his head. I want him to see his very soul removed," James said.

James reached under the sheet with his knife and dragged it along the man's abdomen, causing a painful but shallow gouge. The man screamed out, believing his belly was being opened up. James reached over into the bowl and grabbed the heart of the lamb. He dragged it over the gouge, pulled it up, and presented it to the man.

"Behold your heart. I will sup on your very soul. Now, tell me, am I going to have to do this to your children? Your wife? Who am I?"

"Enough, Netjer James, you may have a right to take his very soul, but I will fight to protect his innocent children," Ramesses said, feigning disgust.

The prisoner wept openly. "Oh, praise you, Pharaoh, for you are surely Netjer and Pharaoh of this land. Oh, Netjer, I will tell you anything. Yes, we are the Cult of Osiris. We have your wife, and we have his wife as well."

"I want you to tell me exactly where they are keeping the women and how many guards there are. If you are lying to me, I will not be able to stop him."

The traitor paled and let the floodgates open, talking in detail about how the women were to be held at the palace in the guard's quarters. They were to be allowed to have their way with them as soon as the death of Pharaoh was confirmed.

"What was the purpose of attempting to assassinate Pharaoh?" said James.

"High Priest Khety knows you have bewitched Pharaoh. He believes you are an evil netjer from Baal who has been sent to subvert the true netjeru of Egypt."

James plopped the heart back into the bowl.

"I think we have gotten everything we need from this man," James said smugly.

Djehuty walked up to inspect James's work.

"Well done, Netjer James. Your methods are very interesting and effective," Djehuty said, as he reached over and slit the traitor's throat.

"You do realize that these men were both traitors to Pharaoh, and therefore, must be executed."

James was shocked and began to protest, but realized this was what justice looked like in Ancient Egypt. A death sentence would have been given to the prisoner in James's time as well, but it would have taken much longer.

James shook his head and shrugged. Looking at Pharaoh, he said, "You know this is an excuse for this Khety to murder you and set up Amenemhet as his puppet."

"I see your wisdom in this. I am now sure that you speak the truth. What do we do?"

James knew it was time to act. "Ramesses, your kingdom is in peril. You need to understand that these people have taken the Queen, your wife, and you are now at war. I know you have been at peace for years and have no interest in killing, but times have changed. We must retaliate. We must rescue our wives. We must act now before they are sacrificed."

CHAPTER TWENTY-FOUR

Beefing Up Security

2015 AD

After a brief trip to emergency care, the three went back to their rooms to lick their wounds. Their bodies and egos were thoroughly bruised. Matt met them in the foyer.

"What the hell happened to you?"

"We were robbed. Two operator types jumped us at the pub when we were reviewing the survey data," said Manuel.

Nicole added, "They held us at gunpoint, and James had the bright idea to poke the bear."

"Hey, I'm sorry, guys. I didn't expect them to be so good at violence. They had to be Special Forces, right?"

"For sure, they didn't even see us as a threat," said Manuel.

"Who do you think sent them?" said Matt.

"They were definitely not your regular terrorists. They wanted the information about the site, and that's all," replied James. "They could have easily killed us and walked away."

"I think you're right, but who are they, and why do they want our data?" Nicole said.

"Nicky, did you get a chance to review the data before they took the laptop?" said James.

"I did. The funny thing is, the two targets that we surveyed came up empty. They got nothing, and I can tell you it will be next to impossible for them even to retrieve the information from the laptop. It is password-protected and encrypted. It will take weeks to get that data."

"We're going to need to be prepared for next time," said Manuel.

"Next time? You mean these guys are coming back?" Matt sounded intimidated.

"Yeah, a full shakedown, I guess. They said they would be back to get any new information we come up with," James replied.

"Should we call the police? Who'd have the balls to do this in a public area?" said Matt.

"I can give you one guess. Who has the influence, manpower, money, and motivation to move on us like this? Black Sands Corp. Their fingerprints are all over this. Screw them and their BS. We are going to be prepared next time," said James.

James went to his room and made a few calls. The first was to Khalid. He had kept in contact with James, filling him in on any project that had anything to do with archaeology. Black Sands had morphed from an oilfield service company to primarily a defense contractor with hands in more pots than anyone could manage. They owned more politicians and officials around the globe than any other company that James knew. On the surface, they were extremely legitimate and always used back-channel contractors for their more clandestine endeavors.

James had done enough bowing to the proverbial overlord. He was going to take them head-on.

"Kal, I need a favor, and I don't have any idea who else could help me with this. I need some security. I'm talking the best guys who are willing to get their hands dirty and are not afraid of Black Sands."

"That's funny, ya should ask, Jim. I happ'n ta know a group of mercs who were fired by Black Sands fer refusin' ta sign an NDA 'bout an illegal op they were involved in. The Black Sands handler they were assign'd mistook a group of hikers in Belize fer guerrillas and were killed. 'Parently, the men said he was careless and reckless. They said these guys tied up the boss and delivered him ta the cops, only ta have 'em released on orders from the feds. They were pissed and all bailed. I met the leader once in Belize, 'fore all the shit went down, and I think he's a decent guy."

"Perfect, Kal, can you put me in touch with him?"

"I've got his digits on a list of persona non grata that Black Sands hands out ta site managers. I'll send it over."

"Make sure not to email the info, Khalid. Remember what happened last time?"

"Yeah, Jim, I 'member. Sorry 'bout that. That whole thing was screwed, then with Sandy ..."

"Yeah, message me the info in the chat room. I have it very secure," James said in a shaky voice.

Chris Wiggins was at the top of the list and was considered the leader of the group. James called him and told him he had a job that might interest him. James didn't want to share more details on the phone, in case someone was listening, but wanted to meet face-to-face in Cairo. James agreed to pay for all of his expenses and would pick him up at the Cairo airport.

James spent the next day driving to Cairo. He instructed Nicole to have the crew find some more sites of interest while he took care of the security issue. It was obvious to James that it was Chris who was walking out of the arrivals door. He was white, about six feet tall, and built like you would expect a mercenary to be. James waved for him to get into the truck. He silently threw his gear in the back seat and slid into the pickup's passenger seat.

James began to speak, but Chris motioned for him to be quiet and to drive on. After a few minutes, Chris signaled for James to pull into a parking garage. Without a word, he jumped out of the truck and rummaged through his pack, pulling out what looked like an RF detector. James had one himself and often scanned his rooms and truck for bugs.

Once Chris was satisfied they were not being listened to, he began, "Nice to meet you, Mr. James ... Jones, is it?"

"Nice to meet you as well, Chris. I appreciate your checking for bugs and being thorough."

"That's what I'm here for, sir. So, can you please explain why I am here and why you are using a false last name?"

"Oh, wow, you noticed that, huh?"

"Yes, sir, I noticed. If I noticed, then others will notice too."

"For the time being, I would appreciate it if you would keep that to yourself."

"That's your business, sir, but I have a policy that I know what type of person is hiring me."

"Perfectly understandable, Chris. That is exactly why I need you. I understand we have a common enemy."

Chris looked at him and cocked his head.

"Black Sands has gone rogue and is out of control. They are threatening me and my crew. I am not interested in capitulating. Can you help?"

"I did some research on you, Mr. Tiberius. I have no reason to believe you are not telling the truth. I am familiar with the Caracol dig they took over from you after you did all the work, and then your friend Sandy ..."

"Yeah, they did that, and they will try it again. This time, they're bypassing local laws and robbing us of the information. They recently stole a laptop with sensitive information from us at gunpoint in broad daylight."

"Yes, I heard about that," replied Chris.

"How did you find out about that? It happened last night."

"I still have some assets around Black Sands, and it came up when I was investigating you."

"That proves it, then. I was assuming it was them."

"Yeah, it was them," said Chris.

"Can you help us?"

"I think we can figure something out," he said with a grin and a handshake. "We are not cheap, though."

"Yeah, no, I didn't think you would be."

James was to treat the security detail like any contractor. They would handle all their expenses and be outside any regular chain of command. They would answer only to James and Nicole.

James, Nicole, Manuel, and Matt were waiting to meet the whole crew at the pub a few days later. As they entered, it was obvious to all that these were not the type of guys you'd want to mess with. James introduced Chris to everyone, and after a round of greetings, James asked if Chris would introduce his team.

"This is my number two, Frank 'The Tank' West. He was a US SEAL for twelve years. This asshole beside me is Alexander Kristov. We call him Ivan.

He was a soldier in the old USSR and later Russian Spetsnaz. He has been living in the US for about ten years."

"Screw Russian commies," Ivan said in a thick accent.

Chris chuckled and said, "He doesn't speak English very well yet, but we are working on that. This is John Westing. He is some sort of English lord or something. I think it's all bullshit, but he insists."

"I am not an English lord, you twit. My uncle is. Nice to make your acquaintance, gentlemen. Former SAS." He shook each hand in turn.

"It's great to meet all of you, and I'm glad you're here. I'm guessing Chris filled you in on the details," said James.

"Yes, we're read in. I think I know the crew who accosted you. I am surprised you all decided to try to get the upper hand on them. That takes balls," said John.

"Yez, ballz," Ivan said.

"It was my bad idea. I'm used to being one of the larger guys in the room, and handling things like that is usually not a problem when the attackers aren't trained."

"Do any of you have any firearms or hand-to-hand combat training?" asked Chris.

"We are all efficient with firearms, but none of us has had any real hand-to-hand combat training," replied James.

Frank said, "I'd like to fix that, if you wouldn't mind, sir. If we are going to intimidate Black Sands to keep off your ass, you and your top guys will need to learn to fight. I don't doubt that you know your way around a rifle, but I need you to be able to defend yourself if they catch you alone or outside of our protection. Would that be acceptable?"

"Absolutely," they all said in unison.

"We've always thought hand-to-hand training would be important, but we didn't know how to get it done," James said.

"We will go one-on-one with each of you in the evening for at least the next month."

"Don't get excited. It is going to be hard work, and your asses will be thoroughly kicked every night," said Frank. "In fact, James, I'd like to work with you myself, if that would be okay."

Frank was about five foot eight, and while he was very built, he was small in stature compared to James.

"Are you sure you want a piece of this?" James said as he flexed his arm. "Think you can handle it?"

They all laughed.

"I'm sure I'll be fine, sir. Shall we start tonight?"

"You just got here. Don't you want to get settled?"

"We won't be settling tonight, sir. There are far too many security concerns at present, but I think it's a good idea for Frank to work with all four of you tonight while the rest of us address the issues," said Chris.

They spent the next few weeks working at the Alexandria site during the day and having their asses handed to them at night. They would show up to work in the morning with sore muscles and bruises, even the occasional black eye. They were getting the full "Neo" treatment from The Matrix. They were instructed in kung fu, krav maga, jiujitsu, and good ol' ultimate fighting. The SEALs decided everyone should be skilled in defending against a knife or dagger as well.

At the end of the second week, James felt that he had learned enough to make a much better accounting of himself if he were put in the same position against the Black Sands thugs. The thugs hadn't been seen again since the night of the robbery, but they all knew they were watching, waiting for a way to take advantage. It wasn't clear if they were aware of the security upgrade, but Chris said they would have already figured that out if they were worth their salt. It was the consensus of Chris's mercs that they would likely try a snatch and grab of one of Grit's leaders to use as leverage.

On the science side of things, they were coming up empty. They had recorded fifteen areas of interest, but so far none of them had amounted to anything. That was until about a month into the job. Matt came back after his three-man crew inspected a hot spot showing on the 3D diagram. He walked up behind James and put his hand on his shoulder to turn him around.

"We found something," he said.

"Great, Matt, what is it?" James responded.

"I think you need to see this, boss. It looks like the capstone to a vault."

James's cell phone rang—not his regular phone, but the one Chris had given him and said was secure. Chris was on the other end.

"James, we have spotted the Black Sands guys. They are in an apartment about a click from your location with a direct view of the operation. They're watching everything you do."

"What do you recommend?"

"There is nothing we can legally do with them, simply watching. I recommend you find a way to disguise anything important, so they won't notice it."

"Understood. Thanks," James replied.

James whistled for Manuel and Nicole to come over and told them about Chris's recommendation.

"What is our play, then, Jim?" asked Nicole.

"I have an idea. Have you seen *Raiders of the Lost Ark*?" They both nodded.

"I think we need a distraction."

About an hour later, Nicole and Manuel were jumping up and down and pointing at their site, and the whole crew followed suit.

Chris phoned James and said, "You're all set. They have left their position. I'm not sure what they plan, but they're not watching you now."

"Roger that. Proceeding with the plan," James said.

He and Matt were at another location with a backhoe, trying to remove the stone covering what they believed could be a small vault. They ran a cable all around the edges of the square stone and up to a D-ring attached to the backhoe. James motioned for Matt to start slowly lifting. The stone was very heavy, almost too much for the small backhoe, but with effort, they were able to pick it up enough to slide it aside.

There was a slight breeze, and a puff of dust blew past James from the hole. It wasn't a vault but some sort of tunnel. It was only about four feet wide, four feet long, and eight feet deep. At the bottom was an intersection of two side tunnels. James looked at Matt with raised eyebrows. His heart was pounding out of his chest.

Could this be part of the library? He was about to find out.

James dropped a ten-foot ladder down the hole. He started down as anxiety hit him like a ton of bricks. He had seen this before. Going down into an unknown pit. It didn't end well for Tom back then. He looked down at the multi-gas meter he had pinned to his lapel. It was quiet. No alarms, and the reading showed no dangerous gas and acceptable oxygen levels, so he continued to the bottom.

At the bottom, James turned on his headlamp. He could see a dozen feet down one tunnel and a small room about eight feet down the other. Neither of the tunnels had much in the way of hieroglyphics, so he doubted it was a tomb. James walked into the room, and his heart leaped.

There were two small wooden chests with bronze bands. These were not ornate chests like those found in Tutankhamen's tomb. They were old, likely from the time of Alexander the Great's reign. James looked closer. They had markings similar to Ptolemy I. This had to be something of enormous importance. He started to remove the lid but then stopped. If he removed the lid, he could cause damage to the chest as well as the contents. He would have to use proper care when handling any of this.

James was getting anxious. He had a piece of history in front of him. Who knew its story or why it was there? He felt for the size and construction of the chest. It seemed sturdy enough to pick up, but he didn't know if he could risk it.

A few moments later, Matt trotted up to him.

"James, you are not answering your phone. There is a problem at the other site. Black Sands has moved in with a contingency of police, and they are taking over the site."

"You're shitting me," James said.

"I'm not joking, boss. I have a feeling they will be heading our way shortly."

"Matt, this is important. Remember Caracol? We have to get these chests out of here and safe before those paramilitary bastards get their hands on them. Head up. I'm going to carry them out."

"Boss, are you sure you should handle those without the proper precautions?"

"There is no time to worry about that or argue. Get up there. When I hand you the first one, get the hell out of here and hide it. I'll work on getting the last one up and out."

"If you say so, boss."

James carried the first chest up the ladder and handed it off to Matt as he saw some people in a Jeep starting in their direction.

"Get that thing out of here, Matt. We are going to have to leave the last chest to them."

Matt quickly walked away, put the chest in the back seat of his pickup, got in, and drove away. A few moments later, a pair of Jeeps drove up. It was McDermott. Hot blood flooded James's face. The vein in his forehead began to throb. *This is the murderous asshole who killed my mom.* Dr. Muhammed Abdel and five Black Sands mercenaries accompanied him.

"In the name of God, Mr. Jones, what is this?" said Dr. Abdel.

James struggled to keep his cool. "This afternoon, we discovered a conspicuous void below a stone here. We removed the stone and voilà, a series of tunnels."

"Did you find anything?"

"I haven't had the opportunity to explore the tunnels, Dr. Abdel. I was about to call you and your people to come investigate them."

"There will be no need for that now. We're here to take over the dig," said McDermott.

"Bullshit you are. On whose authority?"

"It is true. Black Sands has a legal warrant to take over the site, not only from you, but from me as well. They have authority directly from the Ministry of Defense," said Dr. Abdel.

"You're kidding me. You bought off the Egyptian Ministry of Defense? How much are they going for these days?" James asked.

"That is cute. Now come with us for debriefing," said McDermott.

"Like hell, you have no authority to take me, and I owe you nothing. You can find shit all by yourself," James replied.

"Didn't you hear Dr. Abdel? We have the authority of the Ministry of Defense. Men, please escort this man to a holding area until we can question him," McDermott ordered.

"We'll take him from here," Chris Wiggin said as he stepped out of the growing crowd.

"No, he'll be going with us. Security take him," McDermott sternly said.

The guard reached for James's wrist, and out of instinct and muscle memory from the last month, James grabbed and twisted his arm, putting him on his knees. It was the same special forces operator who had man-handled him before. Two other guards raised their weapons. Chris swung his AR-15 rifle around so they all could see it.

"I think we all need to settle down," he said. "Now I know you people, and I know how you operate. You have no legal basis or authority to take anyone."

Chris raised his hand, and two red dots appeared on the chests of the two men with raised guns.

"I think y'all might want to lower your weapons and step back, or my team might feel like you are endangering our boss here. James, you alright?"

James was still holding the security guard's twisted arm. He then kicked the man to the ground.

"Grit employees, let's pack up all of our toys. We're going home," said James.

McDermott was furious. "Take them, you pussies. What am I paying you for?"

James walked up to McDermott. "I guess they're not as stupid as you are."

James shoved him, and he screamed as he fell to his knees.

"Do something!" he yelled.

It took James and his crew about an hour to collect all their gear. The Black Sands guards were helpless to intervene. James walked up to Dr. Abdel.

"Dr. Abdel, I am very sorry for your trouble here. As this has nothing to do with us, and we have completed our contract, can I assume our invoice will be paid in full?"

"Of course, Mr. Jones. I know you are not responsible for what these men have done. In fact, I have another project that may interest you." He leaned closer to James and whispered, "Khufu."

CHAPTER TWENTY-FIVE

A Time for Action

1152 BC

The arid wind buffeted the loose-fitting robes of the two riders galloping down the road toward Abydos. Two cloaked figures on horseback entering the city in the middle of the night would usually have gone unnoticed. This night was different. Word had come earlier that a plot to assassinate Pharaoh and the false god James had failed.

Amenemhet had ordered that all persons entering the city be questioned. He was concerned that spies might try to investigate the claims that he and the Osiris Cult had abducted the queen and James's wife. He had been raised with Ramesses and knew his temperament. If Ramesses suspected the truth, he would send an envoy to discuss the possible release of the queen long before he would try to mount any sort of attack.

The four soldiers at the city gates halted the two riders.

"Stop and submit to inspection," said the man in charge of the watch.

"We are simple messengers with word from the temple Lpet-sut. We must take news to High Priest Khety in all haste," said the smaller of the two riders.

"In that case, you will have been issued a password. Speak it and be on your way."

The larger of the two riders looked at the other and said, "I guess I should have asked about a password."

The other man frowned and said, "I have the password written down. Let me pull it out of my bag."

He dismounted his horse, reached into his satchel, and with a single motion slit one guard's throat. He then spun around and opened the stomach of the guard standing next to him, then stabbed him through the neck. The rider on the other horse reared back his mount. The horse kicked the guard in the face as he jumped down to pull the fallen man's spear from his hand. He turned and impaled the fourth man in the heart with a single thrust. The man who was kicked in the face moaned and rolled over. His face was a wreck, but he didn't have to suffer the pain long before he was pierced through the heart with his own spear.

"I am impressed," said the larger rider with a smile.

"When you said you wanted to come with me, and you could handle yourself, I was skeptical."

"I have been trained in war since childhood, James," Ramesses said. "I could not let you come here to save our wives alone, or with a half-competent soldier, for that matter. You were right. We must save our wives and do it now," he said.

"Let us pull these soldiers off the road so no one will raise an alarm."

They pulled the bodies and all of their gear to a nearby ditch.

The two men proceeded through the streets cautiously. Ramesses knew the city but hadn't been there in several years. Only a few things had changed, and he was sure he could find the palace and the guard's barracks. They knew there would be no more than ten men in the barracks at any time, and they would be sleeping at this hour. The rest would be out on patrol.

"I don't believe anyone, even a spy in my court, could have sent word of our plans to rescue the women. We should be able to sneak in and dispatch the few guards on duty easily."

"I hope you are right, Ramesses. I can take on two or three at once, but if they attack in numbers, we may have problems."

"Fear not, James. Amun-Ra has blessed this venture and wishes to punish Osiris and his followers."

"If that is true, Pharaoh, it is still wise to be cautious."

They rode up to the palace gates.

"Stand aside, soldier. I have a message for Amenemhet himself from Lpet-sut. I have already submitted to a search by the guards at the gate and have no time to wait."

"Let him pass. News from Lpet-sut is to be sent along," the guard said.

James and Ramesses rode through the gates and stopped short of the main entrance. The barracks were a few hundred feet before the palace entrance.

"Let us hope they do not question why we are entering the barracks and not going straight to Amenemhet."

Ramesses had never been inside these barracks, but he assumed it would be set up similarly to the one he inspected at his own palace. They entered a dining area surrounded by rooms occupied by sleeping soldiers. At the other end of the dining area was a hallway where the traitor had said the women would be held.

James and Ramesses cautiously approached and found the door to the cell unlocked and partially askew. They could hear men's voices, and a moment later, a woman whimpered in pain.

The cell door slammed open under James's shoulder, revealing a scene of horror. Tentopet was bound and gagged against the wall, her eyes wide with terror, and Neferu was pinned to a scarred wooden table by two priests and a soldier, her kalisaris torn, blood streaking her face. Khety, his robes hiked up and glowering, loomed over her, his dagger glinting as he pressed it to her throat.

James roared in a primal scream that echoed off the stone and tackled the soldier nearest the door, slamming him into the wall with a sickening crunch of bone. Ramesses was a blur of fury. He swung his blade at the second priest, shearing his neck in a spray of crimson, the man's scream gurgling into silence.

Neferu, battered but unbowed, seized the moment. Her hands, still bound, clawed at Khety's face, her nails raked bloody lines across his cheek.

"You will rot for this, snake!" she spat, wrenching the dagger from his grip as he recoiled. She slashed wildly, catching his arm, but Khety snarled and backhanded her, sending her sprawling into the table's edge with a crack that split her lip. James wrestled the soldier's sword free and plunged it through the man's chest, his blood fountaining as he twisted the blade.

He spun toward Khety, but the priest was already lunging, his dagger aimed at Neferu's back. Ramesses intercepted, his own blade parrying Khety's strike with a clash of metal, and shoved him against the wall.

The air thickened with the iron stench of blood as shouts echoed down the hall. Reinforcements were coming.

"We are not alone!" James yelled, yanking Neferu to her feet while slashing through the ropes on her hands. She swayed, clutching the stolen dagger, her eyes blazing with anger while bruises bloomed across her jaw.

"I'll gut them myself," she rasped as she staggered toward Tentopet to cut her bonds.

The queen whimpered, her wrists raw, and Neferu steadied her. "Hold strong. We are not dying here."

Khety, pinned by Ramesses, sneered, "Osiris will claim you yet!" James silenced him with a brutal thrust, the priest's head lolling as blood pooled beneath.

Footsteps thundered closer, and six soldiers burst in with drawn swords, their sergeant barking, "Submit or die!"

James shoved Neferu and Tentopet behind him, snatching a small clay jar from his satchel. *Snap, flick*! The Zippo's flame quickly ignited the resin-soaked linen wick. The soldiers paused for a moment at the door, just long enough for James to whisper, "Cover your eyes," as he hurled the jar against the door next to the incoming soldiers. Bright white light, with flames and a deafening crack, staggered the soldiers.

James and Ramesses took this opportunity, attacking the group of six blind soldiers. Ramesses opened the first from crotch to throat with an upward cut, then brought his sword down on the second man, cleaving his skull. James moved in closer, dropping his first opponent with a full-force punch to the throat, destroying his trachea, then stabbed the second through the neck, severing the man's brainstem, the blade sticking out of the back of his head. The first soldier fell to the ground, choking and grasping his throat.

Neferu sprang forward, her dagger sinking into one man's thigh with a savage twist, toppling him as she hissed, "Stay down, traitor!" and smashed the hilt of her blade into his temple.

Ramesses parried the last, his blade clanging against a spear, sweat and blood slicking his grip. The soldier, wild-eyed, hurled his spear. James ducked just enough to have the blade take a chunk of scalp, the shaft splintering against the wall inches from Neferu's head. She screamed and then lunged, her dagger slashing at his stomach as he kicked her ribs.

James tackled the man and flipped him into a chokehold.

The man soon went limp, his dead eyes staring into James's soul.

Breathing raggedly, James hauled Neferu up, his head throbbing as blood streaked his face from the spear wound, while Ramesses freed Tentopet fully.

"We are not out of danger yet!" Ramesses growled, peering down the hall as more shouts rang out.

Neferu, clutching her side, grinned through gritted teeth. "Let them come. I've got one good stab left!"

James snorted, "Save it, Nef. We do not need to kill them all tonight."

He pulled a second clay jar from his satchel and, with a *snap, flick,* threw the second flashbang out the door into an approaching group. An ear-splitting *crack* with light and fire erupted from the center of the new group as they all rolled to the ground. At this point, the only guard still alive came to.

James hauled up the cowering guard.

"Run along and tell your friends that the netjeru are here, bringing lightning and death. If they want to live, they should move along."

Urine splashed on the floor underneath his kilt as the man threw down his sword and ran away. Ramesses, Tentopet, and Neferu stood back, horrified, with their hands over their ears. Ramesses approached James.

"First, you tell me that you are no netjer, then you tell the prisoners and these priests that you are the Netjer of Death and Pain. Then you throw thunder and lightning from your hand. What are you, James?"

"I am a man, just like you, from the future who possesses technology and knowledge you don't understand."

"Thanks to Amun-Ra, you are on our side."

Neferu whispered in his ear, "I was afraid you might have forgotten your toys."

"You should know, Nef, I never miss an opportunity to show off."

After the soldier who escaped the massacre relayed his story to the soldiers outside, they were left alone. No one even bothered to approach the room. Several hours later, they heard the telltale noises of a battle going on outside.

"I believe we should go and assess the situation. It seems my host has arrived, and if they do not see us alive, they will slaughter everyone in the palace as well as the Osiris Temple."

"Lead the way, Great Pharaoh."

They cautiously walked down the hall holding their wives' hands. Exiting the barracks, they saw fighting in the streets, which had nearly reached the palace gates.

"Cease your resistance in the name of Ramesses IV, Pharaoh, Horus incarnate."

The soldiers defending the gate to the palace looked back. Ramesses had removed his hood and stood proud and defiant. The soldiers dropped their weapons and knelt. Upon seeing this, all the other soldiers of Abydos followed suit.

"You soldiers want to live and someday redeem yourselves? Go and bring Amenemhet to me alive."

They gathered around twenty soldiers and headed to the palace. Djehuty and Nebamun walked past Ramesses's soldiers and knelt in front of the Pharaoh.

"Thank the netjeru, you are safe, Pharaoh. We were afraid that we would be unable to gather enough soldiers to carry out your plan," said Djehuty.

"It looks like you were able to accomplish much, General. Netjer James and I slew High Priest Khety and rescued our wives. The palace is ours, or will be, as soon as they bring me Amenemhet. Send a force to the

Men-maat-re Hwt," which would eventually be called the Temple of Seti I after the pharaoh who built the temple for Osiris.

"We must bring the Osiris priesthood to heel."

"It will be done, Great Pharaoh," replied Djehuty.

A few soldiers sent to capture Amenemhet returned a few moments later.

"Great Pharaoh. Amenemhet has fled the palace with his family. Please spare our lives, and we will never disobey you," one man said, face down in the sand at Ramesses's feet.

"Fear not; you all were misled by my half-brother and the Osiris Cult. I grant you clemency to work the rest of your lives in my service."

"Praise Great Pharaoh! Praise merciful Ramesses," they cheered.

James leaned over to Ramesses and said, "I don't think we have seen the last of Amenemhet or the Osiris Cult."

"I think you are right, James. We will be more prepared next time."

CHAPTER TWENTY-SIX

Out of the Clutches

2016 AD

Butterflies and bumblebees were busy at work drinking in the myriad flowers covering the meadow. The Texas spring was beautiful, and James enjoyed sitting on his front porch with a tall glass of sweet tea, moving back and forth on his father's favorite rocking chair. Sara had bought Hank's chair a few years before they died. They were waiting for a table at Hank's favorite restaurant, Cracker Barrel, and Sara enjoyed watching Hank rock back and forth. He seemed so at peace that she walked into the store and bought it on the spot. Hank was a little annoyed at first because the chair seemed a bit overpriced, and he would have to come back in his pickup truck to get it. But when he set it on his porch and sat down, he was hooked. James had watched him for hours, sitting back and enjoying life. Now, rocking and thinking about his parents was about the only thing that could pull James away from his work.

James's cell rang. It was Nicole. "This is James."

"Hey, boss, I wanted to check in. We're starting a new dig this morning, and I was wondering if you might be interested in joining."

"Thanks, Nicky, but you know what I'm working on is too important for me to stop and jump into a new project."

She said, "You've been studying the scrolls in the chest for nearly a year without a break. Maybe you should take a few weeks and come back with a fresh perspective."

"You may be right, but I feel like I'm on the verge of cracking this. The language of these scrolls in the chest is exactly like what we found at B1 in Caracol. Luckily, we were able to sneak it away, or it would be another relic that Black Sands would have seized and hidden. How are Chris and his guys working out?"

"They're great, pitching in and helping work sometimes instead of walking around looking angry. I have at least one of Chris's guys on each site."

"That's perfect. Having them around may dissuade certain groups from pulling that shit at the bar in Egypt. That laptop they stole had some very sensitive information on it. Let's hope they never get into the hard drive."

"Okay, I'll let you get back to your work then. Please do me a favor and get out of the house. Go meet a girl or something. I don't like thinking of you there all alone week after week."

"Great, thanks for the life advice. I don't have any time to entertain a woman at this point in my life. I have way too much to do."

"Suit yourself, boss. Bye."

"Bye."

James walked into his office. He left it set up just as his father had it, with a large dark walnut desk and matching bookshelves. He sat in a well-used brown leather chair and stared at the chest full of ancient scrolls on the bookshelf. He thoughtfully pulled out the desk's middle drawer and removed a letter. The letter was from Dr. Muhammed Abdel.

James,

I am very sorry about everything that happened at the Alexandria site. I know you realize it was out of my hands, but I feel responsible because I contracted for you to work. Black Sands has since taken over a few other dig sites that looked promising, and I don't see an end to their meddling as long as the Ministry of Defense is giving them carte blanche to do as they please. I don't know exactly what they are up to, but I believe, like you, that these discoveries are for all mankind and not only these rich elite assholes, excuse my language. I considered posting this letter on the forums, but I don't want Black Sands to start thinking of me as an adversary. They can make my work here next to impossible if they want to.

The reason for this letter is to fill you in on some of the work that is being done at the Khufu site. It is top secret, but I'd be surprised if you haven't heard of the PyramidScan Project. I'll give you a brief synopsis of it, as it uses Muon Radiography. Muons are subatomic particles created when cosmic rays collide with Earth's atmosphere. They penetrate virtually any material - dirt, stone, water, etc.

We have placed detectors in key areas around and inside the pyramid. These detectors will show how dense a structure is due to how many muons can make it to the detector, like an X-ray. We have had these detectors in place for over a year now. You probably know all of that already, but what you don't know is that we have some results back. They are astonishing. We have detected a room behind the chevrons at the main entrance, as well as a very large void just above the Grand Gallery. Those are the locations that will soon be released to the public in a peer-reviewed study.

The interesting thing is what we left out of the material sent along to be reviewed. Only three of us know about what we believe to be an additional tunnel system that starts near the pyramid's base and travels to a room near the very center of the structure. None of us here has any idea what it could be, but we don't want to make it known. Otherwise, Black Sands is likely to find

a way to steal the information. I am sending you all of the data we collected,
including the graphs and charts showing everything we found.

If it is discovered that I have sent these things to you, it will be my job, and
I will likely be arrested. I want to send this to you in case something happens
to me. This information should be the scientific community's property, not
corrupt businessmen and politicians. I am sure you will know if and when to
use it. I'm leaving that up to you.

Sincerely,

Dr. Muhammed Abdel

Director of Archeology, Egyptian Ministry of

Antiquities and Tourism

James looked over the graphs and diagrams for the umpteenth time. He had to find a way to use this information.

In the first few weeks after he returned from Alexandria with the scrolls, he hermetically sealed the office space and had air recirculated in and filtered to create positive pressure. All UV lights were removed, and the relative humidity was regulated religiously. The temperature never fluctuated outside the range of sixty-four and sixty-eight degrees, the perfect environment to open and study Ancient Egyptian scrolls. Soon after, James pulled out each and every scroll to take high-definition digital photographs of them. He hoped to limit their exposure to possible damage after sitting for a couple of thousand years.

He had decided to unroll them only a single time to take the digital photos so he could study them at leisure. There were fifteen scrolls in all. About half of the scrolls were written in Greek and Ancient Egyptian, probably sometime after the Library of Alexandria was founded, around 250 BC. There were others that were much older, and after cross-referencing the pharaohs who were mentioned, he dated them to around 2200 BC.

Three scrolls did not fit with the rest. They looked to have been copied from some older scrolls and were similar in construction to those dated 2200 BC. These scrolls were not written in any language James was familiar with. They were very similar, if not the same, script that James had found in the tomb at Caracol. If he'd had time to study the actual ruins and not the few photos Matt had been able to get before they were kicked off the site, James was confident he would be able to decipher the new script.

Later that day, James was checking the forums when he noticed a post by Dr. Muhammed Abdel. The post had been put up minutes before, and a scroll found at the Alexandria site was outlined. Black Sands had not taken over this particular dig. He had included a picture of the scroll, and to James's amazement, it had some markings that were identical to the ones he had found on the three scrolls he had taken. James's heart began to pound.

Is this happening? Are we finally going to go public with this new ancient language?

He studied it briefly and then, out of nowhere, the screen flickered and an Error 404 popped up, file not found. James refreshed his screen, and Dr. Abdel's entire post had been removed. James tried doing a keyword search and then tried searching for all past posts from the doctor. It was all gone. He kicked himself for not instantly taking a screenshot as soon as he found it. James didn't know if it was the three-letter American spy agencies or Black Sands that were shutting down everything on the internet about the script. It was hard to believe that Black Sands alone would have the power to do that. Either they had some powerful friends, or the powerful friends were using Black Sands for their dirty work. Either way, James wasn't having it. He picked up the phone and dialed Dr. Abdel.

"This is Dr. Abdel."

"Dr. Abdel, this is James Jones from Grit."

"I was wondering if I would hear from you, Mr. Jones. I am sure you have seen the picture that I posted of the ancient script. It reminded me of how you described some of the scripts you have encountered."

"Yes, sir, do you still have the scroll in your possession?"

"I am sorry to say I do not. Soon after it was discovered, the same group that took over your Alexandria Library site came with official documents and a warrant from the Ministry of Defense to take the scroll. I'm not exactly sure how they knew about it, as I had only recently discovered it. I have told only a few people about it, and none have had an opportunity to inspect it. I did post a picture on your forum. Perhaps you could take a look and tell me what you think."

"Do you still have that picture, sir?"

"Uh, yes, I believe I do. They had me delete it from my computer, but I still have a copy on my phone. Why do you ask?"

"Your post about the picture was taken down."

"I don't understand," Dr. Abdel said. "I posted it a few hours ago. Surely, they haven't already found it and removed it."

"I am afraid they have, Doctor. Could you please check your phone to make sure it is still there?" James asked.

"Let me see if I can pull it up here while I am speaking to you. Yes, here it is."

"Dr. Muhammed, it is imperative that I have that photo. Could you please hold on to it without telling anyone else you have a copy? I am coming to you to get it."

"Coming all the way here to get a photo? Preposterous, I'll text it to you right now."

"Please don't, sir. I am convinced someone is monitoring your communications, and I hope to God they aren't listening to your calls."

"Well, I highly doubt they would go through all that trouble, but of course, Mr. Jones. I'll be waiting for you, and please call me Muhammed."

"I will be there as soon as I can. Please call me James, or Jim if you prefer."

James ended the call and immediately called Nicole.

"Hello?"

"Nicky, I need you to get Chris's crew together and have them meet me at the Cairo Airport asap."

"Cairo, boss?"

"Yeah, I need them to back me up while I visit our old friend, Dr. Muhammed Abdel. He has some information that could shed some light on my ancient script."

"Got it. I should be able to get them all there within, say, ten to fifteen hours. They are all over the globe."

"That's fine. It will probably take me about the same if I can get a flight out of Houston soon. I need you to set us up with rooms at the St. Regis."

"Can do, boss. I'll get my assistant to schedule their flights and the hotel."

"I'll call Chris myself and fill him in on the details," James said.

"You sure you don't want a few more of us with you? We've all been training."

"No, Nicky, I appreciate it, but hopefully I won't even need Chris and his guys. If they're not enough backup, I'll have to come up with a different plan."

Twenty-four hours later, they had a staging area set up in Chris's room. He had all their gear prepped and ready to go. James had no idea how Chris was able to get the firearms and tactical gear through customs in Egypt, but navigating local bureaucracy was one of his areas of expertise. They had several laptops with access to street cams and real-time satellite imagery.

"How much did all of this cost, Chris?"

"Do you really want to know? You can't put a price on this," he said.

"Maybe you can't, but something tells me I will. Just giving you shit. It looks like you've done a stellar job preparing. What's the next move?"

"It was as you thought. Dr. Abdel seems to be off the grid. I think he has been abducted."

"That's what I was afraid of. I will head to the museum to see if I can get some answers. That's where I talked to him last. Maybe some of his coworkers can give us some information," said James.

"That'll be the best place to start. I'll send John with you. I was able to track the doctor's phone, and it is definitely still at the Cairo Museum."

"That's good to know. Thanks," James said.

James and John Westing headed to the museum. James knew Muhammed had an office there, even though their main headquarters was where his primary office was. They approached the museum's entrance. It was guarded by multiple security positions with metal detectors. James quietly handed John the Glock Chris had given him.

"I think I'll have to go inside without you. Unless you know a way past those guards."

"Yes, sir, I'll stay here, but please call and check in."

"Will do, John. Thanks for looking out," James said as he bought an entry ticket.

James walked toward the administration offices and had difficulty not being distracted by all the displays. He hadn't been to this particular museum for many years. He walked up to the receptionist's window, and he could see that the lobby was all glass and chrome, with a high-tech security desk. Sitting at the desk was an attractive mid-twenties woman in a pantsuit. She had a confident, sharp smile and sat behind multiple monitors with security feeds.

"Morning, Amina," James said with a warm, engaging smile after reading the badge hanging around her neck on a lanyard.

"Good morning. How can I help you today, Mr..."

"James. Just James." He leaned in slightly, his demeanor playful. He presented the badge he had been given back when he worked on the Alexandria project.

"This badge is old and expired. We have new ones now," the receptionist said.

"Darn, I was really hoping to speak with Doctor Abdel."

"You need a new badge, then. We have strict protocols for these things," Amina said with a coy smile.

"I can only imagine the red tape you have to deal with. I'm sure someone as competent as you can navigate through those protocols. I bet you are the best one to fix this little...inconvenience."

"Flattery will get you... Oh well, we'll see. The new badges have RF chips in them. Alright, James, I'll make an exception for you this time, but don't make it a habit."

"Absolutely not. Thanks, Amina, you're amazing."

"Don't mention it. Now stand on that tape and I'll take a new photo. Your card will be ready in a minute or two."

"Do you mind if I pick it up on my way out? I have some urgent business."

"Yes, you said with Dr. Abdel. I am sorry to tell you, but he is not in right now."

"He's not in? I talked to him yesterday. Can you tell me when he might be back?"

"Well, he would normally be here, but some men who looked like police came for him earlier today. I'm not sure when he'll be back."

"That's really too bad. I was hoping to reach him. Did they show you any identification?"

"Yes, they had the standard government-issued access badges, but I never saw anything like a police badge or anything."

"Does he have a secretary here, or is there anyone who might know where he has gone?"

"I'm sorry, but his secretary is at his main office. Would you like the number or address?"

"No, thank you, I know where it is."

"It looks like your card is ready now. Here you are."

"Thanks, I'll make sure to keep this one up to date." As James stepped away, he looked back, catching her eye. She smiled and subtly waved. He grinned and gave her a wink and a curt nod as he walked away.

James rounded a corner and found a secured door labeled in both Arabic and English, "Administration." He swiped his new card, and the lock turned green. There were only a few offices that he would have to check out, and most of the offices were occupied. He noticed one with the lights off and the door cracked open. The stencil on the window told him he was in the right place. James peeked through the crack and didn't see anything unusual, so he entered. He was surprised to see the room didn't look like it had been searched yet. Perhaps he had beaten them to it.

The room was mostly bare, but James figured most of his files would be at the other office. He opened all the drawers on the desk but didn't find anything out of the ordinary. James realized he didn't really know what he was looking for—just something to give him a hint of where he had been taken. On a hunch, James decided to call Dr. Abdel's cell.

Immediately he heard ringing coming from the desk and noticed one of the desk drawers didn't pull out as far as the others. He depressed the glides on both sides and pulled it out. Behind the drawer was the phone.

This has to be it. The doctor must have been worried after our conversation. James replaced the drawer as if he hadn't been there at all and walked out.

As he was ready to exit the administration area, he noticed a couple of men dressed in black pants with black jackets with logos on the shoulders. They were Black Sands goons for sure. He watched as the two men entered Muhammed's office and shut the door. James walked up to the door and could hear them rustling through the office.

Looks like I was just in time.

James exited the administration office and was about to leave the museum when he had a thought. He returned to the receptionist, who greeted him with a coy smile.

"Back so soon?"

"I was curious if you might know if Dr. Abdel had a personal phone as well as his business phone."

"James, you must know I am not supposed to give out his personal phone number."

"No, of course, Amina, and I would never ask you for it unless it was an emergency. Dr. Abdel is missing. I'm worried about him and simply want to give him a call. He's an old friend."

"Oh, if they hadn't just pulled him out of the office, I probably wouldn't do this, but I'm worried about him, too. Here is his private number."

Amina wrote down Muhammed's number on her business card and slid it to James with a concerned smile.

"My number is on there as well, if you happen to need it," she said as she blushed and looked down.

"Thanks, Amina. You're the best."

James winked at her and left the building. As soon as he was out, he dialed Chris.

"Like we feared, Dr. Abdel was taken by Black Sands. I have his phone, but he may have a different phone on him now. I have a new number for you to trace. John and I are on our way back to you," he said as he gathered John and headed for the rental car.

CHAPTER TWENTY-SEVEN

When in Egypt...

1151 BC

By the time the Ramesses's entourage returned to Waset, the Opet Festival was nearly at an end. They spent a few days recuperating from their adventure and tending to the frayed nerves of their wives. The final day would normally have been a feast in honor of Ramesses, but he decided to celebrate something new. Ramesses stood on his balcony before the population in the avenue below.

"People of Egypt, you are all aware of the evil brought forth in our kingdom. I am pleased to share with you that the enemy we faced has been vanquished."

The population went wild in praise.

"The blasphemous priests of the Osiris Cult have been properly punished."

The crowd again erupted in applause.

"I am displeased to tell you that the traitorous Amenemhet has escaped with his retinue."

The crowd yelled out in anger, "Kill them! Traitors!"

"Rest assured, I will do everything in my power to bring these miscreants to justice. The last time I stood on this balcony and addressed you, I was interrupted by a murderous assailant right before introducing you to someone whom you have all heard rumors about. I stand here today and share with you the truth. This is the Netjer James. He has come to us from the Khufu pyramid, and I believe him to be the reincarnated ka of a great pharaoh. He has come to our people to usher in a time of great peace and wealth."

The crowd roared with excitement.

"You may have heard of a few of the miracles he has performed in service to the kingdom. Not least of which is the fact that he saved my life, and not only mine. He also saved the life of your queen and was instrumental in her rescue. Today, I want to formally introduce you to the Netjer James, who we will be known as Yemhotep, Netjer of Peace and Contentment."

The crowd was going wild. Ramesses leaned over to whisper to James, "I thought that might be better than the Netjer of Pain and Death."

Ramesses stepped back and motioned for James to address the crowd.

"Your Pharaoh believes me to be a netjer. I am not claiming to be one. I did not come to Egypt to be lord over you. I did not come here to be worshipped. I came to this place to bring peace and prosperity to the Kingdom of Egypt."

The crowd screamed, "Yemhotep, Yemhotep, Yemhotep!"

Ramesses moved to the center of the platform.

"From this day forward, all men of Egypt will consider James...Yemhotep, a Netjer of Egypt. Now, feast and be merry!" He raised his glass of wine, took a sip, then handed the golden goblet to James.

James took the goblet, and the hint, and took a drink himself. They both waved to the crowd and left the balcony.

Ramesses looked at James while walking through the halls toward the feast.

"Would you do me the honor of attending me tomorrow at noon? I would like to learn more about where you are from."

"I would be honored, Ramesses. I want you to understand that I keep no secrets from you. I will answer any questions you have."

"That is wonderful to hear. I may be able to answer some of your questions as well. Do you mind if I call you Jim? And you will call me Ramesses. I noticed that is what Neferu and your people often call you."

"Of course, that is what my friends call me, but you mentioned that you may be able to answer some of my questions. How so?" said James.

"There are some stories about the pyramids that have been passed down from pharaoh to pharaoh since they were created."

James stopped in his tracks and stared at Ramesses.

"It is true, James. I may be able to help you understand how you came to be here with us."

"Ramesses, you cannot say something like that and leave me wondering," James said.

Ramesses laughed, put his hand on James's shoulder, and said, "Patience, great Yemhotep, we can discuss it at length tomorrow. Tonight, we feast."

By the time Ramesses and James entered the banqueting hall, festivities were in full swing. James had not been in this room before, and he was wowed by what he saw. The room was spacious, with high ceilings and ornate columns. Every wall was adorned with reliefs or paintings depicting Pharaoh's achievements, historical battles, and divine mythology. The banquet tables groaned under the weight of their lavish offerings. Large platters of roasted meats, including goose, beef, and the finest cuts of lamb, were seasoned with spices from the farthest reaches of civilization. Baskets of fruits, figs, dates, and nuts abounded on a table packed with bread and cakes, some sweetened with honey.

They made their way to a series of cushions at the end of the room where Neferu and Tentopet sat. The women eyed their men mischievously as they approached, as if they shared a secret.

"It looks like you are enjoying the feast, Yemhotep," said Tentopet. "Have you had the opportunity to enjoy an Opet Festival feast before?"

"Yes, My Queen, I am enjoying this, but I have never been to one like this. I don't think I have seen anything like it."

"Come sit next to me, love," said Neferu with a sly grin.

The wine flowed freely while male and female dancers performed. They moved with the grace of a leaf falling in a breeze. They performed in groups as their bodies, adorned with gold and semi-precious stones, shimmered in the torchlight. The dances told stories of the gods, great victories in battle, and Yemhotep's divine connection to the celestial gods.

The rhythms of sistra, drums, and harps filled the air, guiding the dance that was both sacred and seductive.

Ramesses leaned over to James and whispered, "I had them create that new dance to honor you."

His attention was drawn to a particularly sultry dancer with barely anything on. She noticed his attention and began dancing for him personally.

James looked at Neferu and Tentopet as if to say, "Is this okay with you? Aren't you offended?"

They didn't notice James's concern and seemed to be enjoying watching the dancer give what James considered a lap dance to Pharaoh. Next, an equally attractive, scarcely clad dancer eyed James, who met her eyes for a moment, then looked away. That was enough of an invitation for her to approach him. Her beautiful body undulated in expressive sexual suggestions. As she approached, James's face turned beet red, and he turned to look at Neferu and Tentopet. The ladies were laughing hysterically.

"You act more like a fearful boy than a God of Egypt," Neferu said. "It is okay, my James. You are a god. It is expected of you to indulge and even perhaps take new wives. It is our way. I told Tentopet you would not, and she didn't believe me."

"I would apologize, but my mother would leave her grave to slap my face for doing that."

Ramesses turned to James with a huge grin. "You are Egyptian now, Yemhotep. You need to start embracing who you are."

"Baby steps, I will take baby steps," James said.

Tentopet fell back in laughter. "I understood that. Baby steps are very small. You want to be Egyptian, one tiny step at a time. That is funny, Yemhotep."

The festivities continued into the morning hours. Ramesses finally stood, bid good night to his guests, and was led out of the hall by his new dancer friend.

James leaned over to Tentopet and said, "So that does not bother you?"

Tentopet replied in a dry voice, "You must be joking. Did you see how much wine he was drinking tonight? If he can perform at all, that poor woman is in for about ten minutes of hard work and a restless night of a Netjer snoring in her ear."

Neferu and Tentopet began laughing again. Neferu then stood and reached out to James.

"My James, dear, should you not come and tuck me into bed?" she said with a coy wink and a smile.

James quickly hopped to his feet, maybe too quickly. Tentopet burst out laughing again.

"It looks like you are like other men after all."

CHAPTER TWENTY-EIGHT

Risky Business

2016 AD

The team met in Chris's hotel room to come up with a new plan.

"We have Dr. Abdel's cell phone, and he said the picture was on it. Frank, what are the chances you will be able to hack into his phone and retrieve it?" asked James.

"I think there isn't much chance with the tools I have here. It's an iPhone, and they are not easy to get into without passwords or...facial recognition. I can break into it if you bring me his head," Frank said.

Ivan leaned back in his chair and chuckled.

"Thanks, Frank, but we're talking about the life of an abducted friend. Can we maybe show a bit of decorum?" Chris said.

"Sorry, I'm in the habit of making light of difficult situations. It helps me cope."

"Okay, I didn't mean to get into a head-shrinking session. Let's stick to the script. How do we get the phone unlocked, and as a side note, can we rescue Dr. Abdel? Does anyone have a plan?" James asked.

John spoke up, "We don't have a location for him yet, but once we do, I say we surveil the location, see who is going in and out, and what kind of security assets they have."

"I agree, John. Frank, any luck with the second number?" said James.

"Not yet, I have been trying to hack into his cell phone provider's system, but it isn't one I have accessed before, so it could take some time. I have a few friends who may be able to help with that. I'll contact them and see if they can get me access. Once we have it, we'll get historical CSLI showing where the phone has been and which cell towers have connected with it. If I can get a little deeper into their system, I can get real-time GPS data. I'll get started on this. It could take a while."

"That's great, Frank. Fill us in on any progress. What're your thoughts, Chris?"

"I agree with John. Once we get the cell intel we need, we must start surveillance around the clock. You will want to go in guns blazing, James, but we need to play this smart. We don't know what we are walking into."

"Yeah, let's not sit on our asses while a good man is being held against his will. I don't trust them. They'll eliminate him like any other evidence about this pre-Egyptian civilization," James said.

"So, what you are calling is a pre-Egyptian civilization?" Ivan said in his broken English.

"Yes, I'm convinced whoever that script belongs to predates all recorded Egyptian civilizations. I believe they're the ones who either built the pyramids or taught the early Egyptians, who used stone tools and lived in grass huts, how to design and construct structures like the Great Pyramid of Khufu. I'm not saying these prehistoric people built every pyramid in the world, but I am saying the first ones were."

"Interesting," said Chris. "What was the purpose?"

"That, my friend, is why I am standing here today. I will find out."

Frank chimed in, "I think I have something, gents. I was able to access his phone's historical data. Everything looks normal. He spent some time in a building in Zamalek, Cairo, but most of his time was spent in a downtown apartment building down the road from the museum. We must assume that's his home."

"That checks out with my intel," James said.

"It looks like he spends most days at the Cairo Museum, but I have some very new tower pings that put him... Uh, it looks like it is outside the Khufu Pyramid. I'll pull it up on Google Earth. Here it is. Looks like a patch of desert to me. Does it mean anything to you?"

"A couple of years ago, when we were kicked off the Alexandria project, Dr. Abdel whispered to me that he might have a project coming up surveying Khufu itself. Perhaps this is related."

"Seems logical, but this location will be a nightmare to surveil. They will be in the open desert if they have a camp set up. It will be tough to get a couple of people close enough to watch them round the clock," said Chris.

"What about satellites? Can we get eyes on them from space?"

"We can, but it won't be enough. There are holes in the coverage. We will only be able to see them twice a day for about thirty minutes," said Frank.

"Well, that's not going to do. Any suggestions?" said Chris.

"Could we perhaps get an RV and rig it with some telescopic cameras?" John suggested.

"Great idea, but we'd stick out like a sore thumb. If they ever happened to come by to check us out, it would all be over."

"What if I get our camp right next to theirs? We could set up a couple of conexes and maybe an ATCO trailer," said James.

"What are you thinking?" Chris asked.

"We present them with some paperwork, signed by Dr. Abdel, noting that we have the authority to conduct GPR studies of Khufu," said James.

"You have to be joking. They are going to know there is no way the Egyptian Government is signing off on archaeological work on Khufu," said John.

"They will if we have a signed document directly from the head of the Ministry of Tourism and Antiquities," James replied.

"Won't they go to Dr. Abdel and show him the document?"

"That's exactly what I'm hoping for. Dr. Abdel must believe people are looking for him by now. If they bring him a document showing that Grit is contracted to work on Khufu, I am willing to bet he will read that and understand what we are doing. It'll give him a heads-up that we know he's there and are planning something."

"That plan is crazy," said Ivan.

"I don't like all the moving parts and questions, but damn, I think it's a great plan," exclaimed Chris.

James spent the next few hours organizing this new expedition. It was 7 p.m. local time, which put Texas at noon. James emailed Nicole, Matt, and Manuel to get together on a video conference call at 12:30.

"Nicky, guys, it's nice to see you. First off, I want to confirm you are all on a secure network and routing through a VPN?"

All three replied in the affirmative.

"I want to fill you in on what's been going on here in Egypt. I assume Nicky has told both of you about the situation here with Dr. Abdel?"

"That you contacted Dr. Abdel after noticing his post, only to see it disappear, and then him being kidnapped. That's all I know so far," said Nicole.

"That is the tip of the iceberg. I'll be short and sweet. I believe Dr. Abdel has a cipher on his phone that could translate the ancient language we found at Caracol, and later, Alexandria. To access his phone, we need him. He's been taken by Black Sands to a location east of Khufu."

"You're joking," said Matt.

"I shit you not. We will create documents, signed by Dr. Abdel, allowing Grit to conduct a GPR survey of Khufu."

"Boss, am I hearing you correctly? We're going to actually survey the big one?" asked Manuel.

"That's the plan. We're going to set up our normal camp southeast of the pyramid. We need to use the camp as a front to surveil Black Sands for the purpose of extracting Dr. Abdel."

"That is a crazy plan, Jim, but I gotta tell ya, if it gets us up on that pyramid, I'm in," said Nicole.

"Same here," said Manuel.

"I'm definitely in," said Matt.

"I thought so. Okay, the clock is ticking. We need to mobilize an entire crew with all the gear we will need, including several trailers for shelter and an ATCO trailer with a generator. On second thought, I want you to bring only the people who have been training with Chris's guys. I don't know what to expect if things go bad. We can have the crew here fitted with work gear, so they don't look so obvious."

"Do you think it will be odd to them that Grit is on the project? Don't you think they'll find that fishy?" said Chris in the background.

Matt heard him and replied, "Hell no, they won't. We are already on every archaeological dig of any importance. We'll be another subcontractor to them as long as we don't run into that one guy who always wears the suit. He seems to watch us too carefully."

A slight snarl crossed James's face as McDermott was mentioned.

"Good point, Matt. We'll be aware if that becomes an issue. OK, you have your marching orders. Keep me informed of your progress. Let's get to it."

CHAPTER TWENTY-NINE

The Gods Are Real

1151 BC

The next morning, James rose early. He had difficulty sleeping because he couldn't wait to speak with Ramesses about the pyramids. *Could he possibly have information about the original creators? Could it be as easy as that?*

The scrolls he had found near Alexandria pointed to a civilization thousands of years before any language was recorded. Could understanding be as simple as going to Karnak and rifling through the scrolls they had stashed there? That had been his goal and one of the main reasons he had wanted to travel to Waset in the first place. James thought if any mention of ancient builders were referenced in the scrolls, they would likely be hidden away. It couldn't be as easy as walking into the library and checking out manuscripts for ancient mystical beings.

Perhaps he could even find the three scrolls he had at his home in Texas here in this time. Maybe he could also find the scroll that Muhammed had uncovered. He knew the answers were here in this time, but where to find them in this great kingdom could take years, if not a lifetime, to uncover.

All this was going through his mind as he made his way to Pharaoh's sitting room. The sitting room was basically an open-air patio with a view of the Nile. It was hot this time of year, and James didn't look forward to sitting in the sun, slowly soaking his robes in sweat.

There were exotic plants, flowers, and even a small fig tree. Near the center were two chaises that were constructed of ornately carved gilded wood, which were upholstered with soft red cushions that looked like velvet. James hadn't seen furniture of this style during his time in Egypt. These were likely the type of keepsakes that a pharaoh would take with him to the afterlife.

James lounged in one of the couches as a beautiful woman in a white robe entered with a basket of grapes. She walked right up to the chaise and sat on the edge. With a smile, she began to hand-feed James one grape at a time. Another woman dressed in the normal servant's garb walked in with a large fan. She walked behind the chaise and began slowly fanning James.

A few minutes later, Ramesses entered the room. Both women knelt as he approached. James was about to stand, but Ramesses motioned for him to stay reclined and for the servants to rise and continue. Ramesses positioned himself in the second chaise and settled back in ease. Two more young women strolled in and began fanning and feeding him as well.

"I like what you have going on here, Ramesses," said James with a big grin.

"Yes, Jim, this is my respite from the stresses of being pharaoh," he said with a wink and a chuckle.

"So what were you talking about yesterday before the feast?"

"Slow down, Yemhotep. Given our position in this kingdom, it is important for us to sit back and relax occasionally." Ramesses clapped his hands and rolled over. "James, lie back and roll over. You need to relax after what we have been through."

James complied and seconds later two more young women dressed in servant's garb began a massage.

"I could definitely get used to this, Ramesses," James replied.

"Now that I have your ear, Jim. I want to warn you of some possible danger."

James cocked his head, showing concern.

"We thought that we had rooted out all of the Osiris Cult followers who were deemed treasonous. It seems that while we did kill High Priest Khety, most of his secondary priests escaped with Amenemhet. We have no idea where they are or what they are planning. Nebamun, my tjaty, believes they are being offered sanctuary at some of the other Osiris temples. I fear they have only begun to trouble us."

"Thank you for the warning. I will notify my entourage to be wary and to inform me if anything suspicious happens. We should keep guards on Neferu and Tentopet in case they try that tactic again."

"I agree and will arrange that when we are done here. Now be at peace and enjoy yourself," said Ramesses. "I wish you to speak truth now. How did you come to us?"

James looked directly into Ramesses eyes and said, "I did wake up in the tomb, and I was there for days trying to find a way out, nearly dying of thirst, but I am no netjer."

Ramesses closed his eyes, began to grin and then simply burst out laughing.

"Oh, thank the heavens. I thought from what everyone said that you were actually a god, or at least thought you were one."

James began to smile and chuckle.

"Yes, I have been telling them from the very beginning that I am not a god. They will not listen to me."

Ramesses continued laughing. "Oh, they have been doing that to me as well for years now."

This got James laughing.

"Well, now that we have that all cleared up, who are you, where do you come from, and why are you here in my kingdom?" Ramesses had a much sterner demeanor now.

"Great Ramesses, I am called James Tiberius. I will be born near Men-nefer in around three thousand years from now, and I am here to help transform your kingdom and bring forth a period of peace and knowledge."

Ramesses looked directly into James's eyes and again began to laugh hysterically, and James followed suit.

Ramesses collected himself, thought for a second, then said, "I have been told of how you can make good water out of bad. I have also been told of the new way of counting. Your wife's business is prospering beyond anything I have seen. I witnessed the magical light bathing my throne room in the color of the sky. Can you make me believe what you say is true?"

James thought for a moment, reached into his satchel, and pulled out two items. "This, Great Pharaoh, is an item I brought from my time." *Snap, flick*, the Zippo came to life. Ramesses's eyes grew wide.

"A flame from the air?" he questioned.

"No, it is called technology," James said, using the English word. He also held out his watch.

"This is a device that will tell us the position of the sun in the sky. It is like a sundial, but the sun's rays are not needed for it to work. I believe that in time, I can prove to you that I am truthful by my knowledge and deeds. In time, once you understand, I will tell you how we are going to make Egypt the center of the world."

Ramesses quietly soaked in the massage in contemplation. This went on for another twenty minutes. James was relaxed but couldn't keep quiet any longer.

"So, Ramesses, did you know that ta is round, and above the clouds is emptiness with no air that we call space, and people have built boats that can travel through that emptiness to walk on lah?"

James wasn't above pulling out some of the big guns to start the conversation rolling. Ramesses looked up, and his eyes became huge.

"In the afterlife, people travel to the seba?"

"No, Ramesses, we have not gotten that far, but we have sent boats to other ta that seem like seba. I have said it before, Great Pharaoh, but I am not speaking of the afterlife. I am speaking of the future."

"So this existence of which you speak is for anyone who is alive now and still alive in that time?"

"Uh, no, these people will be long dead."

He pursed his lips. "I guess if it is not the afterlife as the priests explain, it is something similar. What do you mean the ta is round?"

"This will take a few minutes to explain. The ta, our ground, is a giant ball floating in emptiness. The emptiness is nothing. There is no air and very little gravity."

"What is air and gravity? I do not know those words."

James's head began to swim a bit. There was so much Ramesses didn't understand and couldn't possibly grasp with his primitive understanding of the world.

"There is much to speak about both of those things and many more, but let me help you understand this one concept first." James held up a pomegranate. "Ra is a giant ball of burning fuel floating out in emptiness... Our ta, Earth, is a planet." In his other hand, he held a grape and moved it around the pomegranate. "A ball of rock, water, and air that spins around ra. There are other balls spinning around ra as well. You call them wandering seba. What you call seba duat is not a seba but another ball of rock, water, and air. There are eight or nine of these balls that are spinning around ra."

"What of lah? Is it another ball of rock, water, and air that we spin around, for we can see that it is nearly as large as ra?"

"That was a very astute question, Ramesses. I am impressed."

Ramesses beamed with pride.

James held a raisin and moved it around the grape. "Lah is much, much smaller than ra and much smaller even than ta. Lah circles ta, as ta circles around ra."

"So are seba that are not wandering also balls of rock?"

"No, all of the stars we see in the night sky are other ra."

James sat back and let that sink in, and Ramesses took that opportunity to have a few grapes. Something clicked inside his head.

"Are you saying that every single seba I see when I look into the night sky is ra, like ours? That would also mean they all have balls of rock spinning around them? Do those balls of rock have people on them? Are there people on the other rocks that are spinning around ra?"

"It is hard to grasp this. Yes, the other seba in the sky are as ra. Many of those ra do have balls of rock spinning around them. No, we do not know of other people who live on any balls of rock, other than ta. I like to believe some of them could have other people on them. I believe the people who built Khufu could be from one of these rocks."

James had decided it was time to steer the conversation in a direction where perhaps he could get some answers.

"That is a question that has never occurred to me, James, but before we get into that, I will want to dismiss our servants." Ramesses motioned for the servants to leave. "Tell the guards I do not want to be disturbed," he said as the women scurried from the room.

With a solemn expression, Ramesses began, "Jim, my friend, what I share now has been whispered from pharaoh to pharaoh, from father to son, through the sands of time. My forefathers were taught by the netjeru themselves, or so the ancient stories say, about the true purpose of the pyramids."

Ramesses spoke of legends where the gods, beings from the stars or perhaps beyond time, descended to Egypt.

"They came with knowledge beyond our understanding, wisdom that could bend the threads of creation itself. They taught us to capture the essence of life," explained Ramesses, "the invisible force that flows through the universe, even in the emptiness as you call it between the seba. We call it the Breath of the Netjeru."

Ramesses described a special area where this energy was stored, far below the Great Pyramid, hidden from common view.

"This place is where the world of men touches the realm of the divine."

He used simpler analogies to explain complex phenomena.

"You see, everything in the world is connected, like the strings of a harp. When you pluck one string, others vibrate in response. The pyramid resonates with these strings, pulling energy from where there seems to be none. When you stepped into the pyramid in your afterlife," Ramesses said, "you were not only entering a pyramid but a gateway where now and then can touch."

He drew a line in the dust on the floor, then another crossing it.

"Imagine that these lines are not only here but everywhere. When you entered the pyramid, you touched this line, connecting you here to me in this moment. The netjeru called this The Binding of Light. Our ancestors built the pyramid not only to house their remains but to serve as a beacon for these energies that could draw in wisdom from across the ages," Ramesses explained.

"The very reason we entomb our greatest citizens stems from the understanding that this energy keeps things as they are, untouched by decay, much like how the netjeru do not age."

Ramesses looked at James with a mix of curiosity and earnestness.

"You were brought here for a reason. Your presence and knowledge are part of this cycle, the dance of time and energy. I ask you, Yemhotep, to join in this guardianship of knowledge. To help us understand what was given to us and perhaps to guide us to new heights with what you know."

James was floored. Ramesses was obviously much more sophisticated in his knowledge than James understood. This information was everything he had imagined since he was a child. James felt like his paltry effort to shake Ramesses's worldview had backfired, and now he was the one who had to sit back and contemplate his own world and existence.

Always the skeptic, James began, "Ramesses, are you familiar with the term evidence?"

James used the English word, as he didn't know an Egyptian equivalent.

"Physical proof that what your ancestors passed along is true? With all that you have been taught, have you seen proof of these netjeru or who they were with your eyes?"

"Do you believe I am telling fanciful stories? We only have to look at the Great Pyramid Khufu itself to see the evidence. It is right before your eyes," Ramesses said in a bit of a huff.

"No, you do not understand. I am not questioning you, My Lord. You asked that I help in the guardianship and understanding of this knowledge. I would like to examine evidence in order to help my understanding. I came through the pyramid a year ago. If I came through, that means there may be people from my time who are wondering where I went and are trying to replicate my travel to your time."

"James, if you are saying more people who are like you, more netjeru, may be coming, we should prepare for their arrival with open arms."

He cringed. "I don't think you understand the place where I come from. In my time, we know much about our physical world, and we have technology that makes our lives easier. We have also become masters of war. We use technology to fight against those who have different beliefs than we do. In the same way, the Osiris Cult would like to remove you from power and will kill to reach those ends, my people would likely come here with powerful weapons. They would be able to use those weapons to remove you, take your throne, and subvert your people."

"They would do that?" Ramesses was appalled at the implications.

"I know they could and believe they would. We need to work together to find an understanding of these ancient netjeru, who they were, how their technology works, and lastly, where they went. With that understanding, we could perhaps prevent what I fear could already be in the process. An invasion from my time."

"Yes, of course, Yemhotep. You may use whatever resources Egypt has to aid in your mission."

CHAPTER THIRTY

A Shot at Khufu

2016 AD

It had been only two days, and already the camp was coming together. Matt found a location a few hundred yards from the Black Sands camp. They were going to set up the trailers in a fashion that would create a sort of private courtyard in which they could prepare unseen.

"It looks like we're basically all up and running here. We need to wait for Nicole and Manuel to begin the survey. Frank, anything new on the cell phone?" questioned James.

"As a matter of fact, I was about to come and get you. It looks like we're a go. I pinged the cell phone and was able to triangulate it. It's still in that camp in their main office," said Frank.

"We have to assume they've taken the cell from him, or he would've already checked in with his office. We're assuming because his cell's here that he's here. We can't be certain," said James.

Chris responded, "Yeah, but it's all we've got to go on, and I think I'd have noticed if they'd moved him in the last three days."

"That's good to know. We can't always expect certainty," said James.

Only James, Matt, and Chris's guys were currently on site when a black Humvee was seen leaving the Black Sands camp. It abruptly turned and seemed to be approaching.

"Chris, I want your guys to stay out of sight for this in case they recognize you. I am not sure who will be driving up, but I'd rather they didn't know we have security on-site."

"Will do. We will be geared up and on alert if they try anything."

"That sounds good. Matt, stick with me. I'm gonna give them something to chew on for a bit."

The Humvee pulled up to their makeshift gate. James saw the two men who exited, and his heart sank.

He turned and whispered to Matt, "These are the two assholes who jumped us in the bar in Alexandria. Be ready for anything."

They jumped out of their vehicle and, as if on cue, both men slung their rifles over their shoulders and approached. James and Matt decided that, in this particular instance, it would be best if they were not armed, so they would look less like a threat and more like a typical GPR crew. James was thankful that Chris and his guys were standing by.

"Follow my lead," James whispered to Matt before turning to the approaching men. "Good afternoon, gentlemen... Hey, aren't you the two assholes who jumped us at the bar in Alexandria? We don't want any trouble. You guys can turn your asses around and go."

The bigger of the two, the one who smashed James's face into the table, approached with his hands out in a gesture of peace.

"Oh, I remember you. You're one of the archaeologists that we scared away in Alexandria. Hey, listen, sorry about all of that. We were under orders."

"I know who you are as well. Tony, right? So you were under orders to attack us and steal our laptop?" James asked.

"We might have gotten a little overzealous back there, but that's not why we're here. My boss wants to know what you are up to," Tony said.

"And why should I tell you anything, asshole?" said James.

"Listen, I think we may have gotten off on the wrong foot. We're here because our boss is curious about your business. That's it. Fill us in on what you're doing, and we'll be out of your hair. No harm, no foul."

"It's really none of your business, but we are planning on GPR mapping the lower areas of Khufu," Matt said.

James looked over at Matt as if he had given away some secret.

"Really? I doubt that. I was told no one is allowed near Khufu," said the smaller of the two guards.

"We have the legal right to proceed from Dr. Muhammed Abdel, Director of the Ministry of Antiquities and Tourism. He contracted with my boss, Nicole, for this project weeks ago, so if you have a problem with us being here, take it up with him. Now, I suggest you hit the road. Nicole is due here any minute, and if she sees the two guys who assaulted her are in our camp, she will be calling the cops," James said.

"Okay, fine. We're leaving. You keep your people away from our camp and our work. You understand?"

The two men turned to leave. They jumped in their Humvees in time to see James and Matt flipping them off. They gave their own one-finger salute and left.

James and Matt met up with the team inside the command trailer.

"Good job, Matt. Nice touch jumping in and *accidentally* telling them what we are doing. I don't think they have a clue what we're up to. We didn't even have to produce the forged documents. Something tells me that once their boss hears about our project, they may try to jack this worksite from us, like they have done in the past. We'll have to be done before they get the chance. If some actual Egyptian officials get wind of any of this, our plan is cooked," said James.

All Grit personnel were on site by day three, and the camp was completely ready. James, Nicole, Matt, and Manuel had set up all the gear for the ground-penetrating radar, while Chris, John, Ivan, and Frank the tank were manning surveillance of the Black Sands operation. They had four long-distance night vision cameras recording, as well as individual scopes. Chris was confident they had enough eyes on the camp to thoroughly understand what they would be up against for a hostage retrieval.

"Okay, where do we start, Jim?" said Nicole.

"That's a great question. I'm going to need a private meeting with you, Matt, and Manuel before we get started. Chris, if you wouldn't mind?"

"Sure, we have plenty to do," said Chris as his team exited the main office.

"You all are aware of the PyramidScan Project correct?" James asked.

"Sure, we have been looking at adopting some of that technology, but it is very new, and I'm not convinced it will be as helpful as they are thinking," said Nicole.

"You would be wrong," James said.

Nicole cocked her head and furrowed her eyebrows. "What are you saying?"

"This info is for this room only."

James pulled out the manila envelope and unfolded the graphs and charts. They all studied it for a few minutes.

"This is a load of BS. Right? This is all fabricated," said Matt.

"Yeah, Matt, the boss is trying to pull your leg. This is obviously fabricated. Right, boss?" Manuel asked.

James waited ten heartbeats. "This is the real deal, guys. There is far more going on in Khufu than anyone thought."

The project proceeded in the same way every other site was mapped. The first step was to set up a grid pattern on the ground near the suspected opening. Once that was done, Nicole was tasked with spending a full day flying the drone all around Khufu. The data from the flyovers was then translated, and then the ground crew would go in with their specialized equipment to pinpoint and scan any anomalies recorded by the drone.

Nicole was in the middle of completing another pass when Chris stuck his head out of the window and waved James over.

"You guys have those Black Sand's assholes running around like chickens with their heads cut off. As soon as the drone started its survey, they were all out of their offices, pointing and looking over here. I don't think they know exactly what to do," Chris said.

"I know they've been trying to get a permit to do exactly what we're doing right now for years. The fact that they have a base set up where it is tells me they're on the verge of getting approval. They're going to be pissed if we find anything. We'll have to work at light speed to get this done," said James.

"Keep your radio handy. I'll let you know the moment they start mobilizing their people to shut you down," Chris replied.

"How is it coming with the surveillance? Do you need more time to get an idea of an extraction plan?"

Chris responded, "It looks like they're not fully manned yet. There are six security and eight civilians. Of course, we haven't seen any sign of Dr. Abdel, but they are likely keeping him in their main office."

"If I were able to create some sort of distraction and get most of the security and civilians out of their camp, could you make that work?"

"Yeah, I think I could. If I had my preferences, though, I'd prefer to do it at night," said Chris.

"Okay, I'll try to make that happen. Chris, be ready. I'll radio you when I think we have an opportunity."

"Will do. We'll hold tight and wait for your signal."

James walked over to his crew and explained that they would have to cause a distraction to draw out the Black Sands' security.

"Nicky, how long until you can get that data processed? I don't want to wait a second longer than we have to."

"I'm on it, Jim. Give me half an hour, and I will be able to give you some answers."

It was the longest half hour James could remember. He was chomping at the bit to get the crew moving. They were all standing over Nicole's shoulder, watching the information being processed, with the 3D details being populated on the screen in real time. All at once, there were gasps in the room.

"Holy shit, is that what I think it is?" Matt said.

"Definitely a void here. We'll need to get the ground-based gear up there to be sure what we are looking at, but I think we've found a previously unknown room or tunnel structure below the surface," said Nicole.

"And you are sure this is not part of one of the other previously discovered tunnels?" James said.

"Absolutely. We're nowhere near any of those previous finds," said Nicole.

James's heart was racing. This was the culmination of his life's work. From his early childhood following around his mother on archeological sites, to finishing second in the International Science and Engineering Fair, then with his work on electromagnetic energy and the pyramids, and later with the B1 dig site's strange pre-Egyptian language at Caracol, and the dozens of projects between, this was going to happen.

He was going to get some answers.

CHAPTER THIRTY-ONE

The Problem with Religion

1151 BC

J ames felt he was in limbo. There was so much to do and to plan. He knew it was only a matter of time before Black Sands or some other group found the secret to what he called the Chamber of Time in Khufu. The problem was that he didn't know where to start. One option would be to place guards around the exit of the Chamber of Time year-round, but for how long? Forever? They would likely be heavily armed with modern rifles if they did come. What could a few soldiers do, let alone a few hundred, against a Special Forces team? Probably get themselves killed.

There were still big questions about how the pyramid even functioned. Was it a two-way door? Could James or anyone else walk in right now and activate the device to send them to the future? What if they were sent farther back in time? James had to start answering some of these questions if he was going to keep his new home safe. One thing was for sure: step one would be to learn as much as he could, as quickly as he could, about the Chamber of Time.

Something at the back of his mind was bothering him. He realized the danger from the rebel cultists should be handled as soon as possible. Otherwise, he would have Osiris's minions attacking his back while he was focused on Black Sands in front of him. Perhaps it was time to do something immediately about those threatening him and his wife. It was time for the Osiris Cult to be routed, but he wasn't sure Ramesses would be on board for a direct assault. He needed a plan.

James spent the next few days with Ptomak and the other priests who had journeyed from Khemenu-Ka. He asked them to seek out anything they could find about the workings of the Osiris Cult and their dealings. They scoured the documents, looking for anything James could point out to help Ramesses understand the danger of this treasonous cult. James sent a message to Pharaoh asking for an audience.

In the opulent chambers of Pharaoh Ramesses IV, where the walls were adorned with tales of gods and pharaohs, James Tiberius stood before the ruler, a man whose word was law and whose will shaped the destiny of nations. Yet James saw in Ramesses a man who could be swayed by reason and the thirst for truth.

"Ramesses," James began, his voice steady, "there is a matter of great importance we must discuss. It concerns not only the governance of Egypt, but the very soul of your reign."

Ramesses, intrigued yet wary, nodded for James to continue. James presented scrolls and artifacts he had gathered with the help of his loyal scribes and priests.

"These," he said, unrolling the papyrus, "are not only records of religious rites, but also of political manipulation."

He pointed to entries detailing how certain priests had amassed wealth and power, not through divine favor, but by controlling access to the netjeru.

"They've maintained your rule through the fear of divine wrath while enriching themselves."

James walked with Ramesses to the temple's base at the Altar of Osiris.

"I'm curious, Ramesses. Why do the priests not sacrifice people?"

Ramesses had a horrified look on his face. "People are unclean due to their sins, of course. The priest will only do a blood sacrifice of the purest breeds of cattle, sheep, or goats. Pigs are not even allowed."

"Hmm, isn't it interesting that for this netjer to be happy, your best food must be given to the priests for their purposes."

James took Ramesses by the shoulder and led him to the back of the temple. Lines of booths were set up here. Priests were sitting back, overseeing their acolytes. They were busy butchering the now bloodless, holy beasts with long, shiny knives. There were signs posted that stated 'holy meat was sold here' to feed the masses. The prices reflected the holiness of the product. They were outrageous, but nevertheless, people were lined up around the court to partake of the meat. There were also signs that promised long life and fertility.

"It would appear the reason Osiris wants perfect cattle as a sacrifice is to line the priesthood's pockets with gold," said James.

James shared stories from his own time about how religion had often been used as a tool for control in many civilizations.

"Your Majesty, the netjeru you honor do not demand such tributes of fear and control," he argued. "Your ancestors built a civilization on the balance of ma'at, on truth and justice."

James went on to explain how the priests had monopolized education, knowledge, and prophecy.

"The priesthood decides who can read, what they can read, what they can write, which prophecies are holy, and which are heretical. The priests keep both you and your family in a gilded cage of sorts, and you let them - even thank them for it."

James went on to challenge Ramesses on a philosophical level.

"Do you believe that if these all-powerful netjeru are righteous and just, they would place these corrupt, power-hungry priests to lord over you? I submit to you that the priests manipulate your population with the fear of their very souls being tormented for eternity. All this for their own power and glory. If your netjeru are real, I can't believe they would be fine with their names being used and corrupted like this."

Ramesses walked and listened to James, quietly reflecting on what he said. He then invited James to walk with him through the serene gardens, a place where he often came to ponder matters of state.

"James, my friend, you come from a time when Pharaoh is not seen as netjer, but here in our time and place, in Egypt, Pharaoh is the bridge between the heavens and Earth."

Ramesses went on as they strolled past the pools reflecting the starlit sky.

"The people need to believe in something greater than themselves. They look to me, not as a ruler but as a deity, a protector ordained by the netjeru. You know you are, like me, selected to be the protector of the people."

Ramesses paused, looking out into the distance in contemplation.

James went on, "I believe you to be an exceptional leader and a great pharaoh, but we both know you do not have the power of a netjer. You may have the essence or spirit of netjer in you, but you are not one."

Ramesses stopped and looked into James's eyes.

"James Tiberius, what you have said, if voiced by any other than you, would have been a death sentence. I know you understand many things, and your observations about the priesthood are true. But I think you may be overlooking some of the good things that come from our religion. We feel that the netjeru watch over us at night, and we tell our children that Amun-Ra is protecting them. Hapi, the netjer of the Nile, is prayed to in order to bring forth the yearly flood to enrich the soil. In every corner of our land, the people pray to their netjeru. Each village and city has its patron netjer."

Ramesses paused to reflect. "It is true, Jim, I am only a man, mortal like everyone else. Yet, I feel I must wear this divinity as a mask to show strength, conviction, and a righteous path. If I were to lose my faith and show my humanity, my fears, and later my death, that would invite chaos and destruction to what my forefathers have built. I must show the people I am a force of nature - eternal and unyielding against the tides of time."

Ramesses gestured toward the Karnak Temple.

"The temples, pyramids, and tombs are places of worship. They are meant to last for eternity, as I will as Pharaoh. The Osiris Cult believes that when my mortal body dies, my spiritual body becomes one with Osiris, and if judged worthy, I will become Osiris. That is why they are now afraid. They want me to be judged unworthy so that they will escape judgment. We will deal with them in time, but we must do it in a way that exalts Osiris, while judging the priesthood immoral."

"I understand, Ramesses, baby steps."

Ramesses's head fell back in laughter. "Yes, Jim, like you say, baby steps."

Their reflections in the sacred lake shimmered as they looked at each other. Ramesses saw a man of a different time and place. A person of great conviction and strength of mind who would always speak the truth, even to supreme power. James saw his friend in a new light. In revealing his own mortality, Ramesses had shown James what it was to be a pharaoh. He embodied an ideal to give his people something to believe in when all the powers around them vied for their very souls.

CHAPTER THIRTY-TWO

Dreams Really Do Come True

2016 AD

James and his crew could barely contain themselves as they hustled to the location of the possible void. Matt and Manuel set up the ground-based GPR and began to scan while watching the readout in real time. Manuel's new technology promised to revolutionize the ability to pinpoint anomalies underground.

Matt went on to describe the readout as they surveyed.

"Okay, walk about three meters to your right. It looks like we're close. Another three meters and...Stop right there. Now, back two meters. Mark it. People, I think we have marked an X on our treasure map."

James walked over and looked at the screen.

"Are you seeing this, Manuel? Do you agree? Is this our spot?"

"Uh, yeah, there's definitely something down there that is completely different from the surrounding material."

James went on, "Okay, what's the likelihood of an actual void here? Keep in mind that if we move a few stones to get a look, we are committing a felony."

"Sheesh, when you put it like that, uh, let me take another look. Yeah, well, I have narrowed it down to one of three possibilities. One, there is a solid piece of metal nearly four feet by four feet behind these stones. Two, there is a large pocket of water. Or three, this is a void that looks like it goes deeper into the pyramid.

"OK, we're going dark. I want all the lights off. No headlamps, no flames, and put your cell phone away. We came here at night for a reason. If Black Sands sees us, they'll come for us. Hopefully, it'll be them and not the Egyptian police. We need to be very careful here."

"James, are we going to do this? Are we going to excavate a section of the Great Pyramid of Giza?" Nicole said with an air of fear.

"From this point on, everything we're doing is voluntary. You all know our mission. We could end up in prison or worse. Nicky, if things start looking like they could go bad, I want you out of here. We may need you to get the lawyers and bail us out of jail."

"Thanks for that, Jim. I was worried about the optics if the CEO of Grit is caught up in this. It would be bad enough for our reputation as it is. And I don't want to go to jail," she said with an impish smile.

They all laughed, and Manuel said, "We don't want you to go to jail either."

"I guess we are doing this, guys. Matt, Manuel, see how this stone here looks like it was placed as an afterthought? All of these stones are jumbled. There is no way they were part of the original construction. They were placed here at a later date to cover this void. It's not cut with nearly as precise measurements, and there's a stone above it that spans the two lower stones. This isn't the first time it's been moved either. Let's get out our pry bars and move some of these stones back."

Once they removed the smaller stones, they revealed a single large slab blocking the way.

"If we can slide this slab back enough, maybe we can at least get a good look inside. I want to place those Teflon slides along the bottom. If we can tilt it back a few millimeters and fit them underneath, we may be able to slide the block back on top of the Teflon runners."

"Great idea, that should work," said Manuel.

"I have had a lot of time to think about how I would search the pyramids if I ever got the chance," said James.

Working under the light of the ancient moon and stars. They were able to drive two large pry bars on either side of the stone and tilt its front edge up a few centimeters. Nicole jumped to her knees and began feeding the Teflon strips underneath the stone. This provided the smallest opening at the back of the stone to insert the large pry bars. James and Manuel were the largest in the group and used the weight of their bodies to leverage the pry bars. The stone refused to budge.

"We know the stone's loose, or we couldn't have lifted the front edge. We can't use any power tools or heavy equipment, so we will have to use our bodies, like the original builders had to. We need more leverage."

"These are the longest pry bars that we have here on-site. Should we get some larger ones and try again tomorrow?" Matt said.

"We can figure this out. The Egyptians did it thousands of years ago. I think we can put our heads together and come up with something," said James, searching for some clue or tool that could help.

"I see something we can try," said Nicole. "Someone, grab two of those scaffold tubes down at the base."

"I like what you're thinking, Nicky. That could work," James said as he jogged down the steps and grabbed two long scaffold tubes.

James and Manuel placed the two pry bars in the proper locations.

Nicole took the lead. "Okay, let's slide the tubes over the pry bars. That will give us three times the leverage. Matt, you use your weight with Manuel, and I will work with James. On three. One, two ..." With one big push, the stone slid forward six inches.

"That's it. Great work, Nicky. Okay, we need another six inches. Let's reposition and give it another shove."

"That's what she said," Matt said in a deadpan voice.

"Yes, very funny, Matt. Let's focus," Nicole said while James and Manuel snickered.

With two more heaves, the stone slid forward about ten inches.

"OK, I need to get a look. Y'all hold up that tarp so I can turn on my flashlight," said James.

The three of them held up the tarp in an effort to block any light. They weren't about to let Black Sands know what they were up to. Not yet, anyway.

James poked his head through the hole. "It smells rotten and dusty here, but I'm not getting any sense that there are bad gases. Nicky, did you bring the multi-gas sniffer?"

"Of course, boss, I know how you are about that. Here it is." She handed the meter to James, who lowered it on its lanyard into the dark hole.

"It looks safe at the moment. I'm going in," said James.

"Hold up, are you sure? Once you drop into that hole, there is no coming back. They are going to arrest us for sure," said Manuel.

"Like I said earlier, this part is voluntary. I won't ask you to stay, and I won't ask you to leave. It's up to you, but I have waited my entire life for this. I'm going in."

James wormed his big body through the narrow hole. The excitement of the moment pushed away the blackness of his claustrophobia.

"What do you see, Jim?" said Nicole. "Speak up. We're dying out here."

"I'm in a small room. It seems to have many artifacts strewn about the floor. These are old. I can't tell you how old, but none of this is modern. I'm seeing what looks like small carved statues lying about, and even some wrapped bundles of some sort of plant. I'm going on. I don't want to disturb any of this."

James snapped a few pictures and continued.

"Guys, there's a steep ramp here leading down into the pyramid. I'm going to pin the sniffer to my vest and proceed down. My God, the walls are covered with hieroglyphics."

Shadows and light from the flashlight made the characters dance on the walls.

"If I'm reading this correctly, these drawings are some of the oldest I've seen. They're at least fourth dynasty and likely older. Oh, there's a ledge here. It looks like it had a wooden ladder at one point, but it's long since deteriorated. I'm going to need you to pass me the telescoping ladder." He made his way back to the entrance.

Manuel handed the ladder through the hole. James walked down the ramp and opened the ladder to drop into the abyss. James turned and tried to snap pictures of every inch of the walls and ceiling. He knew it was a matter of time before they were discovered, so he had to get everything he needed now. James climbed down the ladder and realized another steep ramp was diving farther down into the pyramid. The ramp was very long, and James wondered if he was getting close to the center.

As he walked, he recorded everything. The drawings were everywhere, and he didn't want to miss anything. He was shuffling along sideways as his left foot landed on open air. James fell over but was able to brace himself and not fall down the next ledge.

James pressed the button on his lapel radio and said, "Crap, I'm at another ledge. Looks like it's about ten feet. The ladder I have is not long enough to get me down. Do we have a longer ladder at the camp?"

"We do, but it's not going to fit in that hole. We'll have to pull the stone all the way out to get it in there," said Manuel.

James moved his flashlight around, amazed at all the drawings that hadn't been seen by a human in thousands of years.

"Guys, I can't give up now. I've got a crazy idea, and I'll need Manuel and Matt in here. Nicky, you stand as hole watch."

Manuel and Matt had been dying for a chance to jump into the hole. Nicole, on the other hand, was more suited for GPR duties on the outside and would never go into small places.

"We're on our way," Matt said as he jumped into the hole. Manuel followed.

They were in awe of what they were seeing as they followed the ramp down to the first ladder.

"When you are both down, bring the ladder with you," James said.

The two showed up carrying the already-extended ladder.

"Like you said, this ladder's way too small. If we drop down that ledge, it's three feet short of the top. I don't know how we can scale that," Manuel said.

"It's not going to be we; it's going to be me. I'm going to drop down. You two can lower the ladder with the rope. Once I'm done here, I can climb to the top, and you two can pull me out. Then we can pull the ladder out with the rope to use it on the other ledge. How does that sound?"

"Well, it sounds a bit crazy and definitely not how we normally do things, but hell yeah, it'll work," Manuel replied.

Jim held the ledge, lowered himself as far as he could with outstretched arms, then dropped the last two or three feet.

"I'm going on. I think I can see the end, and it looks like I'm near the center. I'm going to video all of this. These hieroglyphics are different. I haven't seen many of these words used... Hold up. What the hell is that?"

"What is it?" yelled Matt.

"Guys, the tunnel ends here, but you are not going to believe what I am seeing right now."

"Jim, come on!" Nicole said over the radio.

"I think this could be a door or something, and it's covered from top to bottom in carvings. I have to take some more pictures. Yeah, these symbols are from the pre-Egyptian culture. These are similar to the ones we found at Caracol and Alexandria. What in the hell is this place?"

Nicole gasped over the radio. Manuel said, "What? You're shitting me."

James could hardly contain his excitement. He began to study the markings, feeling them with his fingers.

"I feel like there is something more here. I am sure this must be a door." He pushed with his hands and then with his shoulder.

"It's not budging," said James.

"Jim, are you reading me?"

"Yeah, go ahead, Chris."

"I think you guys need to wrap this up. We are picking up movement. I think they may have spotted you."

"Damn... Understood, prepare for phase two," said James.

"Phase two, understood," said Chris.

"Nicky, you know the drill. I want you to turn on all the job site lights, and then you high-tail it back to the camp. Before you leave, I want to hand you the camera. We can't let them have it. In fact, Nicky, why don't you head back to Cairo right away? I don't want you involved in this."

"Right, understood," said Nicole.

James made his way to the ladder and climbed up to the top. He was able to get his hands over the top, and Matt and Manuel grabbed him and pulled him up.

"Damn, how much do you weigh? You're killing me," Matt said with a groan.

"Yeah, funny, let's get moving."

They pulled up the ladder and made their way to the next ledge. They were able to scale the ledge easily and then exit the structure through the hole. James handed the camera to Nicole, who soundlessly began her way off the pyramid.

"Nicky, take that ladder. I don't want them to know we made it all the way in," James said, and with a quick nod, she was gone.

"Do you think there is any chance we can replace this stone before anyone gets here?" asked James.

Manuel replied, "We might be able to, but they are going to see us now with all of these lights on, so I don't think it will matter."

"True, but if we can get it back in place before the authorities arrive, Black Sands will still have to wait for approval to get a permit to go in. They won't bother with a permit if we leave it like this."

"Got it. Let's do it," said Manuel.

The block slid back into place much more easily than it had moved out. Once it was back, they tilted it and pulled out the Teflon runners.

"Matt, I want you to go ahead on down and take these pry bars with you. I'm going to sit here and wait for them to arrive."

"You mean, we're waiting," said Manuel.

CHAPTER THIRTY-THREE

The Voyage Home

1151 BC

James knew his time in Karnak was coming to an end. It was imperative that he begin studying the Pyramid. He felt he had to find a way to either prevent it from functioning or at least try to understand it as much as possible. James charged his entourage to begin preparing for the barge journey back to Khemenu-Ka. He had to protect this past, his home, from what he knew would be coming.

James brought the subject up at one of their weekly meetings, where all the priests and court members would sit at a large table and discuss current happenings. These meetings usually ended with a flurry of questions for James, to which he was more than happy to respond. When the conversation was again brought back to James and his "afterlife," he pivoted the conversation to discuss what he considered the impending invasion from the future. No one in the chamber seemed to take it seriously. Only Ramesses seemed to grasp the concept and possible consequences.

"These people, who I believe are coming, can, with only a few men, completely conquer the whole of Upper and Lower Egypt. They have weapons that can decimate entire cities," James said.

"Yes, Yemhotep, I understand your concerns, but I hardly think it is so dangerous that we need to post an entire army at the base of the pyramid indefinitely," said the tjaty Nebamun.

"It will not be forever, but we must, at least until I have found a way to ensure they cannot come," said James.

"Do you have any idea of the cost Pharaoh will have to incur to station an entire army at Khufu? The logistics alone are staggering. We would need to build an entire new city to house and feed them," said General Djehuty.

"You don't seem to understand me," James said. "It's not a matter of if they will come. It is a matter of when, unless I can figure a way to stop it. Egypt will inevitably fall."

This got all of their attention.

"Surely not," said Djehuty.

"That's preposterous," exclaimed Nebamun.

Ramesses rose. "Stop! All of you. You have heard the words of Yemhotep, yet you question him with such disrespect. Have I not said Yemhotep is a Netjer of Egypt? Yemhotep understands the afterlife that we can only imagine. If he believes we will be attacked by these netjeru, with weapons we cannot stop, we have no choice but to provide him with whatever he needs. I proclaim that Yemhotep be given any resource he believes necessary to protect this kingdom. We will prepare to receive these invaders and create a new fortified city, Per-hotep, in honor of Yemhotep."

James translated the name as "house of peace and contentment" and didn't know how to respond. He simply smiled and said, "Thank you, Great Pharaoh. It is an honor."

With that proclamation, the discussion was over, and Egypt was fully on board with James's mission. He went on to instruct Djehuty as to how many troops would be needed and where they would be building a new fortification.

James decided he could not wait for his entire assembly to mobilize. He had to leave now, in order to begin his study of Khufu and prepare for whatever came next. Neferu was excited to be heading home. It was a rare occasion that she would leave her town, much less travel from one end of Egypt to the other. She had been preparing for several days and had nearly half of the barge filled with furnishings and other items that were scarce in their village. Pharaoh decided to make sure James was outfitted with everything he needed, not only for security purposes but also to take advantage of the trappings of his station as a netjer of Egypt. Pharaoh couldn't have James living like a commoner. It was imperative that he look the part.

While the barge on the voyage to Waset was nearly empty, this barge was loaded to capacity. Any space not taken up by Neferu's trade goods was occupied by all of the builders and architects, who were tasked with planning the new fort. More workers and building materials would follow in the next few days. Soldiers wouldn't be arriving for at least a month, in order to get the first few barracks up. Ramesses went a step further and ordered a new palace to be built in the newly named Per-hotep. He also suspended all government building projects with orders for all resources to be put at James's disposal. Pharaoh's command had mobilized the entire nation.

The trip back was uneventful. They were traveling with the current on this trip, but it would still be around a two-week journey. James wanted nothing more than to sit back and watch the countryside roll past, taking in all the sights and sounds he could only have imagined a year ago. But he was far too busy sorting and reading the dozens of chests of scrolls that he had removed from several temples prior to leaving Karnak. The priests were furious and tried to bar the removal of the chests. James had expected this and had come with a warrant from Pharaoh himself. A dozen soldiers pushed the priests back as James's entourage collected the scrolls.

"These scrolls are sacred texts. Only priests of the purest of soul are even allowed to read them, much less remove them from the sanctuary," said the head priest.

"You are lucky then," said Ptahhote. "Who better than Yemhotep, Netjer of Egypt, to study them?"

Ptahhote winked at James, who returned the gesture with a smile.

"I imagine you are anxious to get back to your wife and children, back to governing your town," said James.

"Yes, James, I am anxious to get back to my kids," Ptahhote said, glancing at James with a side-eye.

"What? Trouble at home? The great Ptahhote is afraid of his wife?" James said with a laugh.

"I am no more afraid of my wife than you are of yours."

"I am not sure about all of that. My wife can scare the hell out of me sometimes," James said as they both laughed.

"I am concerned she will be angry that I have been gone so long."

"You can tell her it is my fault. You had no other options."

"Yes, that is what I'll do. I will blame you, and then you can deal with her," Ptahhote said, with a straight face, and then they both busted out laughing.

"Yemhotep, have you given any thought to my position?"

"What exactly are you referring to?" James asked.

"It seems now that Per-hotep is to be built into a city that will support much of the armies of Egypt, my position as Imi-r niwt is no longer needed.

Surely you will be appointing a Haty-a to that position. I would like to know how I am to support you and your mission," said Ptahhote.

"You have been with me from the very start. You were one of the first people I laid my eyes on in this time, and you have been competent, steadfast, and loyal. I see no reason why I would not raise you as Haty-a."

"Haty-a? Yemhotep, I would be honored. Are you sure I am up for the responsibility?"

"My mother had a saying. She always told me when starting a new job or project to 'fake it until you make it,' using the English idiom. "You should step up to the challenge with confidence and do your very best to succeed. If you do that, you may fail at times, but in the end, after all the work, you will have grown into the position."

"Very wise words from the mother of a netjer," Ptahhote said.

James went back to sit next to his wife. He put his arm around her and pulled her close. She sank into his arms and laid her head on his chest. After taking a deep breath, she let it out with a long sigh of contentment. They both knew this journey was a brief respite from their mission. The real work would start when they reached home.

They would again exit the barge at Men-nefer and continue on land to the Giza Plateau. Men-nefer had already been notified of the mobilization of the workforce, and caravans of workers were leaving each day to make the trek to Per-hotep. James gave Ptahmose, the high priest of Ptah and Haty-a, leave to return to his duties. Ptahmose had been a quiet addition to James's entourage but had always been there with sound advice when needed. Ptahmose bowed low to James and pressed his face to the ground.

"Great Yemhotep, I have followed you since you graced my villa with your presence. I have heard you speak and witnessed many miracles. I must apologize. When I first heard word you were the returned Ka, I believed that to be untrue. I believed you to be a charlatan, much like the Osiris Cult. For this, I beg your forgiveness. You have maintained that you are not the Ka of a pharaoh and that you do not come from heaven. I hear your words and tell you today that you are no charlatan. I believe you are a netjer who simply does not recognize his own divinity. I am now and will continue to be your servant."

James motioned for Ptahmose to rise to his feet and grasped his forearm in friendship.

"Thank you for your confidence, my friend. I may need to call on you someday when the fate of the entire kingdom is at stake. It is good to know I have you here watching my back. Sometimes, I feel I have half of the priests in the kingdom ready to kill me, and I am sure requisitioning some of their ancient texts did not help." James gave a curt nod and walked toward the waiting caravan.

It took only a day to travel on the road to their final destination. As the caravan approached, James could already see much progress in the construction of the encampment. Neferu was the first to notice the increase in population. To James, this seemed like something out of the gold rush days, where a tent city housing thousands of people would pop up near gold deposits. Starting nearly half a mile before the village, tents were beginning to line the road. Workers and carts were traveling back and forth, minding their daily business. Things in the once-sleepy village had changed.

Neferu saw servants running at full speed ahead of them. Some children were running and playing next to the road. One of them pointed at James.

"It's them!" she said, and the children ran before them.

They entered the village, and as they turned the corner toward home, they saw masses of people lining the streets. Each citizen held aloft a palm branch and waved to them. Nearly the entire town was there to greet them as cheers rose from the crowd.

Ptahhote stood atop his mount and yelled to the crowd, saying, "All hail the Great Netjer James, who is named Yemhotep, Netjer to the citizens of Egypt."

The crowd went wild. "Yemhotep, Yemhotep!" they roared.

James noticed the same young orphan girl who had stolen his Rolex sitting on a roof watching the procession. As soon as she saw that James recognized her, her eyes went from excitement to terror, and she was gone.

As they arrived at the villa, James climbed down from his camel and had the camel drop to aid Neferu in dismounting. The entire household, including the brick factory workers, lined the way to the front courtyard. At the very head of the line, Bibi waited with a huge smile, and as James and Neferu approached, the entire household knelt with their faces to the ground.

"No, no, please stand," James said. "You all know what I think about all of this bowing." He pulled Bibi to his feet. To Bibi's amazement, James went on to shake his hand.

"Bibi, how are the little ones? Everyone is healthy, I presume."

"Yes, Lord, thanks to you," Bibi said as Neferu approached.

"Your factory is strong and still growing, My Lady."

"You have done well, Bibi, and you will be rewarded," said Neferu, who turned to the crowd and, in a loud voice, said, "Now, my husband and I would like to settle in. We have much to do in the coming weeks."

The party was over, and everyone went about their business.

"You are welcome, my James. If I had not told them to go home, you would have felt obligated to stand here and answer questions for the rest of the day. Shall we retire to our rooms and get cleaned up?" she said with a wink. He needed no further encouragement.

James realized that while this was the end of one journey, it was also the beginning of a new one.

CHAPTER THIRTY-FOUR

Just a Peak

2016 AD

James knew there was trouble when he noticed it was not only Black Sands people, but Egyptian police that were heading toward them.

"It looks like we may have poked the beehive," Manuel said while watching the procession approach.

James looked over at Manuel.

"It looks to me like their entire camp has been mobilized to see what we're up to."

The first to arrive were the same Black Sands goons who had come to their camp earlier, but this time McDermott was with them, and of all people, Dr. Geist tugged at his heels. James seethed, watching the two of them walk toward him. Four Egyptian policemen followed them.

"You people think you can do whatever you want out here, don't you? You think the rules don't apply to you. We've been watching you all day and know you've disturbed some of the stones. Admit it," McDermott said, his face red with anger.

"I don't have a clue what you are talking about. We have a legal right to survey this area, signed by Dr. Muhammed."

"I would be interested to see this document," Geist said as he approached. "Mr. Jones, it's been a while."

"Officers, please arrest this man," said James, pointing to McDermott. "This man has been interfering with our legal project and should be removed."

McDermott was barely able to control himself.

"Do you know who I am, asshole? Do you have any idea who you are screwing with here?" said McDermott.

"Oh, I have a pretty good idea what kind of person you are. You're the cowardly piece of shit who pays off politicians in order to steal other people's hard work and hires thugs to attack and harass his competition," James said.

"I am Lance McDermott. I want you to remember that name you... you nobody. You're another fanboy archeologist with no clue what you are dealing with. Officers, you need to arrest these two."

"What exactly are you alleging they are doing that is illegal?" said the officer.

"Do you really believe they have a permit to be here? I know for a fact that Dr. Abdel could never have signed this permit," cried McDermott.

"That's interesting. How, may I ask, do you know for a fact that Dr. Abdel didn't sign this permit?" Asked Manuel.

"Because I tal ... Because he's ..."

"Since Mr. McDermott here can't seem to explain how he has first-hand knowledge, may I suggest he is the one who does not have the proper authority to be here. Mr. McDermott, would you mind showing the nice officers here your legal permit for access to Khufu?" said James.

"You know as well as I do that we don't have full approval yet. You are trying to confuse things," said Geist.

"I am not sure exactly what to believe here," said the officer. "I don't know if I trust either of you. I am going to shut this whole thing down for now. We will let the Ministry of Antiquities decide who has the legal right to proceed here."

"Perfectly reasonable, officer. Thank you. I agree that this is something the ministry should figure out. We'll be packing up and leaving directly," James said as he began collecting his gear.

"You can't let them leave. You need to arrest them," McDermott yelled.

James caught McDermott's eye and motioned back to their camp.

"I wonder. Would it be helpful if I could bring Dr. Abdel here, Lance? You don't mind me calling you Lance, do you? I'm sure he could solve this once and for all. Lance, where do you suppose that Suburban is going over there? They seem to be in a hurry, Lance."

Chris, Frank, and Ivan peeked out from behind a stone fence likely built over three thousand years ago. This history was lost on them, as all they saw was cover for their incursion into the Black Sands camp. The three were decked out in their desert camo, and all were heavily armed. Chris was wary about carrying all of the firepower. He was afraid it could escalate into a shooting battle, but he decided that if that were to happen, he would rather it was the other guys who were under-armed.

They watched the group at the pyramid grow until they were convinced that all but one security guard had gone and that the only people left were scientists and field workers. They made their way to the first trailer. They all knew this one would be full of offices for the scientists. They wrapped around the building and silently made their way to the main office. They had one goal: the rescue of Dr. Muhammad Abdel. They knew he had been taken against his will, so deadly force could be necessary.

Chris had been watching this encampment for days. He was aware of exactly where each security camera was placed. They had decided to go in with masks since they weren't sure what the repercussions of this little adventure would be. They didn't see any reason why Black Sands should know who it was that rescued the doctor.

They made it to the front door. It was unlocked, which made Chris a little nervous. They were either confident in their security or lazy. All three men burst through the door with guns drawn. The guard sitting at the desk was caught completely by surprise and was quickly cuffed and gagged. They grabbed his key ring and walked to the back, where they believed Dr. Abdel was being held. Chris tried the knob. It was also unlocked. Alarm bells began ringing in Chris's head. Something was seriously wrong.

Chris was the first to enter. He swept his rifle to the left as Ivan followed, sweeping right, and Frank followed after.

"Clear," they each said after entering.

"I have Dr. Abdel. Doctor, are you alright?"

Dr. Abdel had been sitting at a desk reading when they burst in. He was startled and didn't seem to grasp what was going on.

"Ivan, Tank, I'm not liking this. Keep your heads on a swivel," Chris said.

"Dr. Abdel. My name is Chris, and we're here to extricate you."

"Uh, what? Wait, no, you can't take me," he said frantically.

"Doctor, this is our one shot to get you out of here. Please come with us now."

"No, you don't understand. I can't go. They've threatened my granddaughter. They said bad things will happen if I don't find a way to approve their applications."

"Doctor Abdel, James Jones sent us to extract you. He was talking with you before you were abducted," said Chris.

"Oh! I see James is here to help me. I understand now why they told me that Grit had an approved application to survey Khufu. I never gave him that authority!"

"No, Doctor, you are not understanding. That was all a distraction so that we could rescue you. We have no time. Will you come with us?"

"You must tell James I'm sorry. I can't leave. They have promised that if I do this for them, my granddaughter will be safe, and they'll put me in charge of this operation," said Dr. Abdel.

"Doctor, you know you cannot trust anything they say. They'll turn this around and work against you as soon as they have a reason," said Chris.

"That may be true, but for the time being, I think I have no option but to stay. My granddaughter ..."

Chris wasn't sure what he could do, so he pulled out the professor's phone and opened it using the facial recognition. If they couldn't rescue the doctor, at least they could get the info off his phone.

With that, Chris turned around and walked out. John Westing was waiting for them in a black Suburban. They jumped in, and the first thing Chris did as they sped off was text James.

The color slowly faded from McDermott's face as he realized what had happened. He instantly got on his phone and made a call. James continued to collect his gear with a smug grin as a text came through. James watched as McDermott's face went from a look of shock to a sly, cruel smile. At the same time, after reading the text, James's smile turned into a frown.

"Officer, before you go, I want to put someone on the phone for you." McDermott handed his phone to the officer.

"Yes, hello, Dr. Abdel, I see. And you did not grant them any permits at all for work here? You think it was all a misunderstanding? I see, thank you very much, sir."

The officer spun Jim around and pushed him hard against the stones and cuffed him. Manuel was next.

"James Jones, you and your partner are under arrest."

CHAPTER THIRTY-FIVE

The Time Is Coming

1150 BC

The entire area was bustling with activity as Pharaoh's edict had brought in tens of thousands of workers. That caused the need for everything to increase, from more housing and food to latrine facilities. James was tired of the constant sewer stink and the diseases that could follow, and decided they would do things differently for his city. James felt like he was being torn in so many different directions. Something had to give, but public sanitation, while dirty and unpopular, was an area James was sure would be a good place to start.

He grabbed a few papyri and called in his top people, Ptahhote, Bibi, and two engineers sent from Ramesses. They were using the factory's meeting area as a command post. James pulled out a scroll showing a diagram of the entire town, including the burgeoning military base right next to it. James began drawing grid lines along the streets. These lines connected and culminated about a quarter mile downhill from the town.

Ptahhote said, "Yemhotep, these lines remind me of the way a trickle turns into a stream and runs off a mountain to a river and on to the ocean."

"Very perceptive," James said. "What you are looking at is our new wastewater removal system. We will be digging channels down the streets, as I have shown with these lines. They will all eventually come together and empty into this large pit outside the city. From there, the solid waste will collect, and the water will spill over into this next pit and again into a third pit. By the time the water exits the third pit, it should be clean enough to spill out onto the sand."

"Will we not have the same problem with the wastewater, as you call it, stagnating and pooling in the streets?" Asked one of the engineers. "Yes, I see what you are saying. This plan, while very interesting, is not viable. We have to do these projects the same way we always have. That is the safest option."

James chuckled. "I don't think you understand. I was not asking you for your opinion or permission. I was showing you this so you could facilitate its construction. I have far too many other things to work on."

"But, Yemhotep, you can't ..." started the engineer.

James cut him off. "Bibi, that's why I brought you into this conversation."

"Netjer James, I am not worthy to address these people, much less lead them. They are my betters. I am a simple foreman."

"Not anymore, Bibi. You are now in charge of this project," said James.

Both engineers were disgusted. "Surely you are jesting. This peasant has neither formal training nor practical experience," the lead said.

Ptahhote stood back with a smirk. He had already witnessed James when he was starting a project like this, and it was best to sit back and watch.

"Bibi is simply the only man for this job, and I will tell you why." James unrolled a new scroll that had drawings and diagrams of how to build clay pipes. These pipes had a large enough diameter to carry any wastewater, or even rain runoff, out of the city.

"Bibi will construct these pipes. We will be creating hundreds, if not thousands, of these. You will need to hire many more workers. It will be the job of the royal engineers and architects to provide Bibi with any support he needs."

The two engineers looked at each other and said, "Your will be done, Yemhotep."

"Bibi, once we have those trenches dug, we will be running your clay pipe and then burying it. We will need a junction at every block in order to tie in public latrines." He looked at the engineers. "We will need at least one latrine every one hundred cubits or so. I don't want people to have to walk far to use the bathroom, or they will dump their waste in the streets again. In fact, once this is finished, I think I will ban the practice of throwing waste in any public area. It is unhealthy. If private residents want to run pipes into their homes, they can do so at their own expense. Do you have any questions?"

They all raised their hands.

"How about this? You all get started. You see where the grid is set up? Survey the areas and make sure the pipes are all heading down. I don't want any waste flowing in the wrong direction or pooling in a low area. I think you engineers are capable of that, aren't you?"

They both nodded.

"Great, now get started," James said as he looked back to see Neferu at the top of the stairs.

"Wait, there is something else I want done. There will be no slaves working on any project that is being paid for by Pharaoh. If people are using slaves in their own households, I don't have the authority to stop that, but if they are working on any of the Pharaoh's projects, they will be free men. Do you understand?"

"Excuse me, Great Lord, this is highly irregular. I plead with you to reconsider this. It will make this project much more expensive," said the lead engineer.

"You have your directions. Now get started."

Bibi and the two engineers left.

"Now you see why I have you here, Ptahhote. I cannot be everything to everyone. I need you to be my right hand. I know you to be a competent person and need you to manage all of this." James gestured toward all of the work going on. "Can you do that?"

"I am at your disposal and will do everything in my power to facilitate your vision, as Pharaoh has ordered."

"So you are doing this for Pharaoh then?"

"I started on this journey with you in order to satisfy my duty to Pharaoh. I continue now with you because I believe in your vision."

James grasped his arm, and Ptahhote walked away with his work in front of him. It was time to start.

Neferu casually walked down the stairs.

"How did that go, Nef? Did I come on too strong? Do you think they are up to the task?"

"Yes, my James, you did very well. I believe they understand your vision."

"I hope they do. I can't be split apart to handle every detail. I need to be studying the scrolls and the pyramid. I fear we are running out of time."

James decided his first task in understanding the pyramid would be physically exploring the structures he knew about. He was very familiar with some aspects of the pyramid that were common knowledge in his time, and some that were not. He got out his pencils and drafting tools and began to diagram the pyramid as he knew it.

There was an entrance near the base that opened to a descending passage down in the rock, near the center of the pyramid. James estimated that this subterranean chamber was likely below the Chamber of Time that he had discovered. About a third of the way down that passage was an ascending passage, which opened to the Grand Gallery, an enormous, sloped hallway with very high ceilings. Entering the gallery, you could opt for another passage that led to what was called the Queen's Chamber. Continuing up the Grand Gallery ramp, the end was at the King's Chamber. The PyramidScan Project had revealed a few other larger voids inside the pyramid, as well as the tunnel James had discovered to the Chamber of Time.

As James was finishing his drawing, Ptomak arrived.

With a bow, he said, "You summoned me, Yemhotep?"

"Yes, Ptomak, have a look at this. Does this look like what you were expecting from Khufu?"

"No, I'm sorry to tell you, but it is forbidden for the priesthood to create or possess any diagrams or maps of burial chambers."

"Oh, I see. That makes sense, and that is why we have never found anything like that in my time. So you know nothing about the interior?"

"No, nothing at all, great Yemhotep."

"Well, you are about to find out. I want you to meet me with a Sem priest at the main entrance. We are going to see if we can see what is inside."

"The priests will not be happy about this. You know the Sem priests are followers of Osiris. They may protest you entering the great tomb."

"Ptomak, I have no time for their complaining and protests. Let them know this is my direct command. This is far too important to let their superstitions slow us down. The very existence of Egypt is threatened. They must understand that."

"I believe they will comply, but this will surely create malcontent."

"Just have them meet us at the entrance and begin their ceremony," said James.

He had packed his satchel with all he thought he would need for the day's exploration when Neferu came down. She had taken to wearing the very beautiful and expensive clothing of her station lately, but this time she came in a simple kalisaris, and her hair was tied up in a bun.

"I am coming with you, my James." It was not a question.

James smiled, nodded, grabbed her hand, and headed toward the pyramid. His two faithful guards, who had been part of his entourage since the day he emerged from the tomb, followed closely behind.

At this time, the main entrance had a grand stairway to access the platform in front of it. At some point in the future, all of this would be dismantled, and the entrance would be hidden.

Ptomak walked up with the Sem priest and two of his acolytes in tow. Upon arriving, he noticed that two of the workers who were ordered to aid them were at the main entrance.

"Have you found something?" James yelled up at the workers.

They instantly dropped their stick and prostrated themselves.

"Please forgive us, Yemhotep. We were curious."

James climbed to the top of the platform and said, "Rest easy. How could I condemn someone for simple curiosity?"

"It's not you, great Yemhotep. It's them." He pointed to the approaching Sem priest. "They have warned us not to touch the casing stones."

"Fine. Priests, come up here and prepare the tomb to be opened," James said.

"You don't understand, Yemhotep. The Wepet-Ur ceremony is of absolute importance and cannot be rushed," said Sebekhotep with an air of contempt.

The obese priest was barely catching his breath after climbing the stairs.

"Okay, fine, continue," said James.

"I will do as you say, but be wary. Osiris is watching you and will judge."

"Get to it. I am not interested in what Osiris is thinking or watching. I have dealt with your cult before. I am more concerned with you doing as I ask," said James.

The priest smirked, knelt, said a few words under his breath, and then lit a bushel of wheat on fire with his flint.

Once he saw the flames on the wheat, James didn't wait for the priest's permission. He said, "Okay, let's start by removing these four stones."

The priest scowled, then sat on a stone with a mug of beer to watch.

The stones were removed, revealing an open area. There were massive blocks in the shape of a chevron, which James knew to be part of the main entrance. James walked up and touched the large stone in the middle, blocking the entrance.

"Let's move this stone first. That should reveal the locking mechanism for the entrance."

Once the stone was removed, James could see down the first passage.

James looked back at Ptomak and Neferu.

"This is very strange. In my time, there are many slabs of rock at different points blocking access to the different chambers, many of which can only be accessed from inside. It seems that some of those are not in place. Either these chambers are currently set up to be accessed, or this tomb has been robbed."

Ptomak gasped, "My Netjeru, no, I cannot imagine what the people will say if they find out that Khufu's chamber has been pilfered."

"We don't know anything yet, but don't you think it is strange that none of the walls or ceiling in these passages are covered in drawings like every other tomb?"

"Yes, that is strange. We spend years drawing the stories of their achievements, titles and deeds reflecting the status of their lives."

"Yes, Ptomak, I think this pyramid was built to be more than a tomb."

James reached back to grab Neferu's hand. "Are you coming?"

She held his hand and smiled. "A year ago, I would have run away if such a thing were mentioned. Today, I cannot wait to see what is inside."

James lit a torch and handed it to her. "Okay, now both of you need to listen. We are going to explore these passages. Many are steep, so watch your step. Also, there could be deadly gases that have built up over time. If either of you smells anything strange, especially the smell of a rotten egg, tell me."

"I do not know what you mean by gases. You expect to find rotten eggs in here?" said Ptomak, confused.

"No, the deadly, uh, *air* that I am concerned about smells like rotten eggs."

Ptomak nodded, and they went on.

They first headed up the ascending passage to the Grand Gallery. From there, they made their way to the Queen's Chamber. To everyone's surprise, the chamber was immaculate, swept clean even. They made their way back to the Grand Gallery and ascended to the King's Chamber. There was a sarcophagus with the top askew. There were no carvings or drawings at all, and the sarcophagus was empty.

"My Netjeru," said Ptomak, "they have stolen Khufu."

"Hold on, Ptomak. Look around. What do you notice?"

"This tomb is empty. It is swept clean, like the last chamber. This room was never meant to be the final resting place for a pharaoh," Neferu said.

"Yes, that is exactly what I'm thinking, Nef. This pyramid is not a tomb at all. It is something completely different."

"If this was never meant to be a tomb, Yemhotep, what is its purpose?"

"That is exactly why we are here. I think we should keep all of this information to ourselves. I have no idea what the Osiris Cult will do with this information. It is best that they do not hear about it. We will tell them that everything is in order and replace the stones. That might keep them satisfied for now."

As they were leaving, James ordered all of the stones to be replaced in exactly the same positions as they had been. Without anyone noticing, James placed a small stick across two of the stones. If anyone were to disturb them, he would know.

CHAPTER THIRTY-SIX

Jailbird Jim

2017 AD

As the fluorescent lights flickered above, James sat on his bunk. The heat was stifling. He had lived in Texas most of his life, so he was used to a bit of heat, but what he was subjected to in prison was different. James felt he could hardly breathe at times. He hadn't felt a cool outdoor breeze in six months. The only time James could cool down was when the nights turned frigid. James would stay fully clothed while shivering underneath a blanket so thin it would probably be called a sheet in any other sleeping situation.

James was told the authorities were planning on charging him with criminal trespass and willful destruction of antiquities. No charges had been filed at this point, and Dr. Abdel had been lobbying the judge to drop the charges. His lawyer contacted Dr. Abdel after James mentioned he might be willing to help. Without any real contact with the outside, James had no idea how his case was proceeding. For all James knew, Manuel could have been in the next cell over for the last few months.

James's world had shrunk to a ten by fifteen foot coffin made of brick, the air so thick with heat and the sour reek of unwashed bodies, that each breath felt like swallowing mud. The cell, packed with eight men, where only four should've fit, was a cauldron of impending violence. Every night, the groans of the restless turned to snarls while fists slammed against flesh over a scrap of bread or a corner of a blanket. James had learned fast to sleep with one eye open, his back pressed to the wall, after a wiry inmate with a scar-twisted sneer had tried to shank him with a splintered spoon on his third day.

The man had hissed, "Foreigners got no place here." James wrestled him down, earning a bruised jaw and grudging peace. The guards didn't care. Half the time, they'd watch through the bars, betting on who'd bleed first. Their laughter was a jagged echo in the dim light.

Despair gnawed deeper than the hunger pangs or the lice that burrowed into his scalp. James's only lifeline had been a single visit from his lawyer, which had dissolved into a haze of vague promises, leaving him adrift with no word from Manuel, Nicole, or anyone associated with Grit. He'd pace the cell's cracked floor, tracing the same six steps, imagining Black Sands seizing his scrolls, his life's work crumbling to dust while he rotted.

One night, a gaunt prisoner coughed blood onto the bunk beside him, a wet, rattling sound that lasted hours until dawn revealed a corpse. Thoughts of his mom's last minutes were at the forefront of his mind. The corpse was left to stiffen until midday, until the guards bothered to drag it out like refuse.

Could be me next, James thought, the realization sinking cold and heavy, his toothbrush clutched like a talisman against the creeping mind rot. Claustrophobia tightened its grip, the walls seeming to pulse inward, whispering that freedom was a mirage he'd never touch again.

The lowest point came during a midnight scuffle when a hulking brute named Tariq, reeking of stale beer smuggled past the guards, pinned James's arm and held a jagged fork an inch from his throat.

"Give me your shoes, American," Tariq growled, his spittle flecking James's face, "or I'll gut you and take 'em."

James's heart hammered, his free hand reaching back for leverage as the others watched, some jeering, some too broken to care. He drove his knee into Tariq's balls. A desperate gasp escaped as the blade nicked James's neck, a thin trickle of blood staining his collar. The brute stumbled back, temporarily defeated and cursing, but the threat did not end there. James knew sleep would be a gamble now, each night a roll of the dice against a shank or a chokehold.

"I'm not dying here," he vowed, despair clawing at his resolve, yet a flicker of defiance burned on, fueled by the hope that Nicole's voice might still cut through this hell.

A guard approached the cell. "James Tiberius?"

"That's me," James said.

"Grab your shit. You're coming with me."

James's "shit" consisted of a pair of slip-on shoes and a small bag with a toothbrush. The guard led him to a waiting room. Inside, he was relieved to see his lawyer and Nicole.

"Tell me you have some good news," he said.

"Yeah, good news, James. You're getting out of here."

"Hell, yes." He looked over at the lawyer. "Thank you so much."

"You don't need to thank me. Nicole here has been browbeating the prosecutors since you got in here. Between her encouragement and Dr. Abdel's insistence that you meant no harm, they have agreed to release you."

"That's great. Thanks, Nicole, you are a lifesaver."

"Don't thank me yet. We had to agree to a few special conditions," said Nicole.

"Such as?"

"First, you are banned from all Egyptian archaeological sites."

"That was expected. For how long?"

"For life. They said if you are ever seen again near an antiquity in Egypt, they will revisit the charges. They want you out of the country and don't want you to come back."

"They can't do that. I have Egyptian citizenship," said James.

"Maybe they can't, but they did. I think you should call this a win and get back to the US," said the lawyer.

"Nicole, does this affect the work Grit is doing here in Egypt?"

"We were able to keep Grit completely out of the crosshairs. They held you personally responsible," said Nicole.

"I guess that's for the best, banned forever. When can I get out of here?"

"They are processing you out now, and we have you on a flight home in a couple of hours. In the meantime, I thought you might like to get some lunch and go over what you have missed in the last six months," said Nicole.

"How is Manuel?"

Nicole laughed and said, "Manuel has been back in the States. They only held him for two days."

"Damn, lucky bastard. This place was hell. Do me a favor, Nicole, next time I have the bright idea to pull some stupid crap like that, knock me over the head and put me out of my misery."

"Will do, Jim."

They grabbed a bite on the way to the airport, and within a few hours, James was on the plane and heading home. After a few long flights and a couple of short layovers, they arrived at Houston International. Nicole had a car waiting.

"Where are we going?" James asked.

"I figured you would be exhausted after everything, so I am going to take you home."

"Wait, shouldn't we stop at Grit? It's on the way. We should get everyone together and have a meeting. I need to go over everything."

"Relax. You have been locked in an Egyptian prison for six months, and there's no way you're already recovered from seventeen hours of traveling. Let's get you home, and you can come into the office in the morning, mkay?" Nicole pulled out her best southern belle accent. She found men were more apt to do as they were told when she used it.

James nodded in acceptance, and they made the two-hour car ride with him nodding off in the back seat. James's head popped up as they came to a stop in his driveway.

"What the hell? Why are all of these cars at my house?"

Nicole shrugged and shook her head.

"I've been gone for seven months, and this is what I come home to? Who the hell are all of these people?"

James jumped out of his seat, marched to the door, and swung it open.

"What the hell is …."

James looked around at a room full of smiling faces holding champagne glasses.

"Surprise? I guess," said Khalid with a big hug.

"Kal! What the hell? What are you doing here?"

"Came by fer the party. Been spendin' more time with yer crew these last few months."

Matt interrupted the conversation. "Hey, boss. Damn, you look like crap. Have a seat."

"It's nice to see you too, Matt," James said.

The living room was fully decorated with white and black balloons. There was a huge welcome-back sign that looked like each letter had been printed on a piece of office paper and then taped together. There were probably about fifteen people in all, and half of them were dressed in black-and-white striped clothing.

"We were all supposed to wear black and white stripes," Nicole said as she stared at Manuel strolling up in a Hawaiian shirt.

"Jimbo, you made it out. Wow, you look like crap. Did Nicole not feed you on the flight home?" Manuel said with a hug.

Nicole eyed Manuel. "That's about enough, you ass," Nicole said as she punched Manuel in the shoulder.

"Ow, damn, that really hurt," said Manuel as he pulled her in for a kiss.

"Well, that's new," said James as Nicole winked at him.

With "Free Bird" by Lynyrd Skynyrd playing in the background, each person at the party came up and gave James a hug and congratulations. The party went on for a few hours, and James was about four single malts deep when Nicole spoke up.

"Here's to Jim, who has returned to us after navigating through a challenge that surely tested his resilience and strength. Cheers to you, your freedom, and all of the bright days ahead."

The crowd all cheered. "Now, as your boss, I feel it is my duty to tell you to get your butts home. Tomorrow is a new day, and I am not buying any of your excuses for a sick day."

"You're no fun," said Matt as he tried in vain to stand. He had been sinking into the couch for the last hour.

"You stay put, Matt. I'll be driving you home. Now, Manuel, Khalid, I think we need to sit down with Jim and fill him in on what we've been doing," she said.

Manuel and Khalid looked at each other, then at James.

"What is it? What's going on?" said James.

"I'd include Matt, but I don't think he's moving off that couch. Let's have a seat at the table," Nicole said as she dropped a thick folder on the dining room table.

James was confused. *What was this all about? Things must have soured here when I was gone,* he thought.

Manuel flopped down in his seat, looked at his phone, then slid it over to James.

James looked at the phone, cocked his head, and furrowed his eyebrows. He glanced at Manuel as both Nicole and Khalid took a seat.

"What am I looking at? Wait, I've seen this before, I think. Oh, this is the photo from Muhammed's phone. How'd you get this?"

"Funny story, Chris grabbed his face ID when they tried to rescue the doctor. It turns out that Black Sands had him wrapped up so tight with threats to his family that he was fully cooperating with them."

"I see why my plan fell through. I hadn't considered that."

"Ya can't win 'em all. It was a good plan, Jim," said Khalid.

"That's another thing. Since when are you working with Grit?"

"I'm still workin' fer Black Sands, like ya asked me all 'em years ago. Soon as ya were in prison, I was tryin' everything I could ta keep 'em from knowin' who ya are. I was falsifyin' some records they were gettin' from the 'Gyptians, so they still think yer name is James Jones. Since, I've been frozin' out of meetins', an' they won't tell me crap. They know I'm up ta somethin'."

"So is this photo what I think it is?"

"Jim, we've been studying this picture since you left."

Nicole pulled out some large pages with the image from the phone blown up.

"What we're looking at is your so-called pre-Egyptian script. You'll notice that it's much newer than we were thinking. The scroll that this photo was taken from was created sometime around the founding of the Library of Alexandria. We are putting it around 240 BC."

"But the script on my three scrolls was, what, like 2200 BC? What do you make of that?"James stopped to study the photo. "Oh, this is Greek, right alongside the pre-Egyptian script. Could this be a translation of an older scroll? That's it, isn't it? This is a picture showing a Greek translation of the pre-Egyptian. This could be our Rosetta Stone," James said.

Nicole looked at Manuel. "He's pretty quick." She looked back at James. "It took us two months to put all of this together. We considered opening your safe and working out the translations ourselves, but I was afraid that would be overstepping. This is your project. How do you want to continue?"

James stood. "My mind is reeling right now, and all I want to do is run to my office and start working on the translations, but it's already late. There are two bedrooms available if you want to stay. I can't tell you what kind of condition they're in, as I've been a little busy lately. It looks like Matt is good on the couch."

Nicole grabbed Manuel's hand and headed to the first room, while Khalid gave James a quick hug.

"I haven't seen you in forever, Kal. I was kind of wondering if you may have gone over to the dark side."

"Ya don't need ta worry 'bout me. Yer dad was my best bud fer twenny years. I've been collectin' a big check from Black Sands fer years now, but I'm not one of 'em. I've been sendin' info ta Nicole since ya were arrested. The things I've seen this company do'd turn yer stomach. They're a den of snakes, and we gotta stop 'em."

"That's what I was hoping you'd say," James replied. "Now let's get some sleep. It looks like we have a big day tomorrow, and Nicole is going to be a taskmaster."

CHAPTER THIRTY-SEVEN

Kite

1150 BC

James wasn't exactly sure what to make of his discovery. He had assumed the rooms in the pyramid were not created to be a burial chamber. He had read accounts of various pharaohs being entombed in the pyramids over the years. The last being the Great Pyramid's namesake, Pharaoh Khufu. As far as James could tell, he was the last pharaoh to have been entombed at the Great Pyramid. Where was the mummy?

Where were all the trappings of his wealth that were buried with him? Why did this structure not have hieroglyphics and drawings all over the walls and ceilings, like every other tomb he had seen? He knew the answer was here to be found. The scrolls he had interpreted back at his home got him this far, but he had to know more. If he was able to activate the time travel mechanism and end up here in 1153 BC, someone else would follow. If it were Black Sands, they wouldn't be coming in peace. They would be here to conquer.

James woke early and left the house before breakfast was prepared. He needed to walk and clear his head without all of the guards following him around. He was sure he didn't need security here. This was his home, and these people loved him. He didn't have anything to fear. He decided to walk around the base of the pyramid, stopping at the ledge where he had initially arrived in Egypt.

There had been a sarcophagus in the Chamber of Time, but there was no mummy and there were no trappings that would have been placed inside. The locals had believed it to be a tomb and had been delivering offerings for many years.

After considering this, James climbed the stairs to the main entrance. The stick had been moved. It was lying at his feet. James inspected the stones, and it was clear that someone had removed them during the night. James assumed they had seen what he had, the absence of anything that would have shown this to be a tomb. He could think of only one possible suspect: The Osiris Cult was back.

Ramesses was confident he had rooted out all the bad actors, but that was the only explanation. It must be a splinter group that left with Amenemhet after the Abydos incident. That would mean he and Neferu were not safe; in fact, there were only a few he could fully trust.

As he descended the tower, James went over, in his head, who the possible traitor could be. They would have to be zealots to disobey the will of Pharaoh. It was definitely an Osiris cultist, and the only one James could think of was Sebekhotep; he had inconveniently killed the prisoner during the interrogation and was not at all happy about entering the pyramid. He was there when James was brought out of the tomb all those months ago. James decided he should be the one to keep an eye on. He left the pyramid and headed back to the villa. By now, they would have noticed he was not at home and might become concerned.

He then realized he probably should have told someone where he was going. He made it to the edge of town and strolled through the market as merchants set out their goods. He noticed the waif, who had stolen his watch, eyeing him, ready for a hasty retreat if confronted. Each merchant made a point of bowing down on both knees when he passed. *How am I going to keep people from doing that?* he thought.

James turned a corner to walk through an alley, as a shortcut home, when everything went dark.

He woke up with a bag over his head. He could tell he was moving and was inside a cart of straw. His hands and feet were bound, and he tried to speak but found he had been gagged as well. James was already not a fan of tight places, but being tied up, hooded, and gagged brought him back to his days in the Egyptian prison.

All he could do was struggle against his bonds and try to scream out, but it didn't help. Thrashing about, he was able to remove the hood partially and instantly had a face full of straw and dirt. The motion stopped, and James heard someone approaching. He could tell it was Sebekhotep. The priest went on to replace the hood and then beat James with a wooden club.

"The blasphemer keeps his mouth shut. The impostor stays quiet in the cart, or he will be beaten." The priest delivered one more hit to James's head before walking away, and shortly, the cart moved again.

James was able to wiggle enough to lower the hood to look at his watch.

When I returned from the pyramid, it was about 7 a.m.; it is 5 p.m. now, so I have been traveling for about ten hours.

He guessed the average speed would have been approximately two mph.

Ten hours at two miles per hour puts us somewhere as much as twenty miles from home.

He thought about Neferu and was sad she would be upset and frantic to find him.

At this point, I would expect the entire town to be in an uproar. With that many people concerned for him, surely they would be able to put two and two together to figure out what had happened. *Damn, I should have left a note.*

Finally, the cart came to a stop. James quickly replaced the hood. Two men grabbed him by the feet and pulled him backward out of the cart, hitting his head on the ground on the way down.

"We will be staying here tonight. You keep watch, and I want you to cook a meal."

There are three of them. If I can get free, I think I can take them.

"Should I make enough for the great Yemhotep?" laughed one of the men.

"I hear a netjer can live for eternity and not need food. Let him starve," said Sebekhotep.

"Mmmm." James struggled to speak through the gag.

Sebekhotep leaned over and removed the hood and gag. "I guess we don't need these. There is no one within miles of here."

"Why are you doing this? You were there. You helped me come out of that tomb."

"Yes, I was there. I don't know how you were able to pull it off. I have decided you are a grave robber who was trapped there and double-crossed by his own people. I saw you in that tomb, all charred and injured. You are no netjer."

"For the record, I never said I was a netjer."

"Yes, I know you always claim not to be a netjer while going around all of Egypt acting like one. That ends today. Today, you become a slave to Amenemhet, the true and rightful pharaoh."

Sebekhotep replaced the hood and gag, then shoved him up against a stone wall and tied him there. They had done a thorough job. James was going nowhere.

A few hours later, they had all fallen asleep. James could hear three distinct people snoring. This could be his only chance to get away, but his wrists and ankles were tied too well. James settled back, but there was no way he was going to sleep. These nuts were probably taking him to be sacrificed on an altar.

Suddenly, James heard the rustling of leaves behind the rock wall. A moment later, his hood was pulled back, and to his astonishment, he saw a young girl looking back at him. She motioned for him to be quiet and pulled out the gag.

"Thank you," James whispered. "I know you. You are the girl who stole my watch," he said with a grin.

The young girl looked abashed. "You take that back. I did not steal. I am not a thief," the girl proclaimed a bit louder than James was comfortable with.

"Fine, you are not a thief," he said quietly.

That seemed to calm her down.

"Aren't you that fellow they call Yamahoto? You know, the Netjer," she said as she chewed the food she had "borrowed" from the priests.

"Ramesses, the Pharaoh, calls me Yemhotep and says I'm a netjer."

"So this guy Rama ... Ramm."

"Ramesses," said James.

"Right, so this guy Ramesses says you are a netjer, and that makes you a netjer?"

"Something like that," James whispered.

"Can he make anybody a netjer? Maybe he would make me a netjer. I would love that. Netjeru can eat as much as they want."

"I wonder if you wouldn't mind untying me," said James.

"Why are you tied up? Seems like maybe they would have a good reason to tie you up if they are going through all this bother. Are you a murderer or something?"

"No, that one there thinks I am not a netjer."

James pointed to Sebekhotep.

"That seems about right, but why all the bother? Didn't you tell them that Romm…"

"Ramesses," James said

"Right, didn't you tell them that Ramesses said you are a netjer?"

"I did, but they don't seem to care. They want to take me back to their temple and sacrifice me. Would you mind untying me?" James asked again.

"They are going to do what? Sacrifice you? You mean like what they do to the goats at the temple?"

"Yeah, I think that's the plan. Would you mind untying me?"

She eyed James. "You're not going to murder me, right? You promise?"

"Yes, I promise."

James held out his hands, and the young girl swallowed the rest of her bread, then knelt down to work on the ropes. She struggled with them for a few minutes with no success.

"Yamahopet, these ropes are too tight. I can't get them off."

"Call me Jim, and could you maybe search for a tool or a stick to help?"

"I don't see anything around here," she said quietly, while looking around the ground.

"Oh, wait." She pulled an eight-inch bronze dagger covered in ornate engravings from her tunic. "Will this work?"

"Where did you find that?"

"I traded that fat priest for it."

"You traded for it? What did you trade?"

"I shoved a bunch of those red rocks into his bag. I figure that if those rocks are important to you, they must be very valuable," she said with a wink.

"Great thinking," James said. "Now, can you go ahead and cut this rope?"

The girl worked at sawing through the cords. After the first was cut, the rest basically fell off. James reached to take the knife from the girl, and she turned and bolted off. James was able to work loose the knots and was free within a few moments. He stood and stretched. He felt that he had two options.

One, sneak over and try to kill all three men while they slept.

They do deserve it, he thought, but after everything, he was tired and not in the mood for violence.

Two, he could get up and walk home. They weren't likely to follow him and try their luck again, being far too concerned about capture. The decision was made, and James walked down the road in the opposite direction from where they were taking him.

James had walked for about an hour when he came to a divide in the road. He had no idea which way to walk, so he chose a path and began. In the distance behind him, he heard a voice call out.

"You're going the wrong way."

James looked around and didn't see the source of the voice. A moment later, the young girl stepped out from behind a palm tree.

"You're going the wrong way, Yama ... Uh, Jim. This is the road home." She pointed to the path not taken.

"Oh, thank you. I am a bit confused, since they had a hood over my head."

"That makes sense," she said.

"Why did you run off earlier? I am not going to hurt you."

"You tried to take my new knife. I traded for it fair and square."

"Sorry, I wasn't trying to steal it. I wanted to use it to cut the ropes."

"Sure, you were," she said with a side glance.

"Will you walk home with me?" James said.

"No, I won't walk with you, but I'm going this way toward home. If you want to follow, it's up to you."

"I will follow you. What's your name?"

"Why do you want to know my name? Nobody asks my name."

"I'm not nobody. I'm a netjer, remember," James said with a chuckle.

"I don't remember my name, but the people in the market call me Kite."

James knew that a kite was the smallest unit of currency.

"Why do they call you Kite?"

"The old ladies say I'm almost worthless, like a kite."

"I think Kite is actually a pretty cool name," said James, using the English word.

Kite glared at him and shook her head.

They walked along for another hour before James was tired of the silence and hoped to get some answers from the girl.

"So, how did you know to find me with those priests?"

Kite laughed, "I saw them smack you over the head with that club. That must have hurt."

"You followed them that whole way?"

"Of course I followed them! I had red rocks I knew you would want, and you are my best customer," she said in a very serious voice.

They walked for a few more minutes.

"I have barely seen you around since you returned my watch and ran out of my house last year."

Kite stopped in her tracks. "I told you I didn't return your watch because I didn't steal your watch. I traded it for painting the face of your wife, and the red rocks, of course."

"Oh, I see. Isn't it customary for people to agree on a price before trading?"

"Well, I don't know anything about that. I do know I am not a thief. I would never steal anything. Well, almost anything." She looked at the ground in shame. "Sometimes, I find food sitting out, and I take it, but I don't think it's stealing, because if I don't take it, some dog or a bird or something will get it. It's not stealing."

"Thank you for returning my watch, anyway."

"I only traded it back to you for those delicious honey cakes that were on the table in the kitchen. That was one of my best trades. Are there honey cakes in the afterlife? I have always thought that if there aren't honey cakes, I ain't going."

James laughed to himself and followed Kite home.

CHAPTER THIRTY-EIGHT

A Letter from the Gods

2017 AD

When James finally woke, the sun was already high in the sky. He rose and rifled through his drawers to find some clothes. Everything seemed to be how he had left it. He walked out and saw Khalid, Matt, and Manuel finishing breakfast. Nicole was slaving away in the kitchen, doing dishes.

"Glad you could join us. I wasn't sure if we would see you at all today," said Matt.

"Matt, leave Jim alone. He was in an Egyptian prison for six months. I think he is due for some extra sleep. I wasn't sure we would see you today either, after you passed out on the couch before the party was even over," said Nicole.

"No thanks to Khalid. He kept wanting to play Egyptian drinking games with tequila shots. How are you not hungover?" asked Matt.

"Boy, I've been drinkin' the devil's cactus juice since 'fore ya were born."

"Jim, sit. I have some eggs and bacon ready for you," said Nicole.

"Aren't you the boss, or am I missing something? How did they get you to cook breakfast and do the dishes?" asked James.

"What? Am I supposed to sit there and watch them screw up breakfast? You'd have to be a moron to screw up eggs and bacon."

"That's not fair. The bacon was only burnt because you distracted me, and eggs are supposed to be hard. No one likes all that nasty runny yolk," Manuel piped in from the background.

Nicole looked over at James and shook her head. "Why do I do this to myself? Stuck here with all of you bachelors. Why don't one of you go find a girl or something?"

Manuel yelled back, "I found one." He blew a kiss to Nicole.

"I haven't seen Chris or any of his guys around. Are they out on a project?"

"No, Jim, they were getting bored here. They didn't have you and your projects to watch over, so they took a new contract. Chris said that whenever you need him to give him a call," said Manuel.

James scarfed down his meal. He was in a hurry to start working on the translations. He got up and walked to his office in the hope of getting some answers. He unplugged the ethernet cable from his high-end gaming PC, which masqueraded as a work computer, and pulled up the pictures they got from Dr. Abdel's phone.

He pulled up the first high-definition images of his three scrolls alongside what he was calling the decryption scroll. He went through each vertical line to find pre-Egyptian symbols that matched the symbols on the decryption scroll. After about twenty minutes of searching, he saw a symbol that was very similar, if not the same, so he looked at what he assumed was the corresponding translation into Greek. The Greek word was "lithos". He realized this would take a while, maybe weeks or months to decipher. James jumped when he heard a cough behind him.

"What in the... Are you guys going to be breathing down my neck for the next few months?" James asked everyone standing behind him. "At least shut the door. I need to keep the humidity constant in here. Matt, are you eating a cookie? You're getting crumbs all over the floor. This needs to be a clean space. Alright! Everyone out of my office. Now!"

Matt looked at the others. "I guess the boss is back." He turned to James. "I liked you better in prison."

James picked up his mouse pad and hurled it at Matt as he ran out of the room.

"Guys, listen. It's going to take me some time to make use of this. I can already tell that these pictures will be a game-changer, but there will still be a bunch of holes that I'll need to fill. I'll probably be at this for a couple of months."

"Does that mean we're not going to see you for a while? Last time, you were AWOL for nearly a year studying this stuff," said Manuel.

"You're going to have to get out of the house once in a while, Jim. It's not healthy to lock yourself in your office for months at a time. You spent six months in jail. You need to get out and have some fun," said Nicole.

"I can't have any fun until I get some answers. This is all I have been thinking about for the last six months. You guys don't get it. My mom died for this crap. I need answers."

"I'm going to be sending you food. I know you're not going to feed yourself properly, and when we come by to check on you, you need to answer the door," Nicole insisted.

"Not that again. I told you I thought it was a salesman trying to get me to have my roof inspected."

"That's what you said, but we were worried. Promise you won't completely disengage like you did last time," said Nicole.

"Fine, mom. Thank you so much for taking care of me," James said, as he mentally prepared to disengage from society.

Nicole smacked him on the back of the head and walked away. "We're leaving now. You need to keep us up to date. Okay?"

He spent the next forty days creating a database correlating the ancient text with words or ideas in Greek, and then he would translate it into English. James knew this would not be a perfect translation. It may not even be a good translation, but it was all he had to work with. The actual meaning of any word could be completely wrong. Many of the concepts represented in this new script had no Greek equivalent. The language was definitely more advanced than any ancient language James knew of. Vastly more advanced.

Certain phrases and sentences began to become familiar, and after about three months, James had been able to create very rough translations of the three scrolls. He had spent the last two weeks in a bit of a trance, methodically translating as dispassionately as a machine would. There had been a few occasions when he would be working and suddenly realize he had been staring at nothing and hadn't written a word because his mind was racing.

James had promised to keep everyone informed about his progress, but did not when he started to understand what he was reading. He felt he had a poor understanding of the scrolls, but what he had learned was almost too much for him. He decided it was time to re-engage and tell someone.

Over the past few years, Grit had grown into the premier GPR company in the world. He knew most of that growth had been in spite of him, rather than due to his leadership. He had only taken over the business to assist his obsession with Black Sands and the pyramids. James sent out an email to all of the top Grit staff. It was time to have that meeting he had been promising for months and share his findings.

They were all to meet at Grit headquarters in Conroe. James was the last one to arrive. Khalid, Nicole, Manuel, and Matt were already seated at the enormous walnut table. The room was surrounded by thick soundproof glass walls.

"I took the liberty of inviting Kal. There's so much information, and I want to have a good roundtable discussion," James said.

No one said a word. They all sat eagerly, wide-eyed in anticipation.

"First, I want to get some housekeeping out of the way. I want to thank all of you here. Without each of you doing what you do, there's no way that we could be here today. I know my projects haven't brought anything significant to the company's bottom line. I have always viewed Grit as a means to an end, enabling us to access all these different sites and the ability to temper Black Sands's acquisition, as well as subsequent censoring and removal of any instance of the Anunnakish language."

"The what? Anunnakish?" said Matt.

James had named this pre-Egyptian language Anunnakish.

"I'll get to that in a sec. First, I wanted to tell you that I've instructed my CPA to figure out the best way to transfer ownership and control of Grit to you three," he said, looking at Nicole, Matt, and Manuel.

"I've been mostly absent for a couple of years working on my own project, and you all are what makes Grit work. I have set aside twenty percent of the shares to Nicole and fifteen percent to both Matt and Manuel. I am going to keep fifty percent because it was all my money."

"Jim, that's so generous. It was always your vision and expertise that we relied on, but I'm not going to say no to twenty percent," Nicole said with a huge grin.

"Wow, fifteen percent? Am I like a millionaire or something? Can I give myself a raise?" Matt asked as Manuel smacked him in the back of the head.

"Just because you own part of the company doesn't make you the boss, dumb ass. Jim, this is over and above. Thank you," said Manuel.

"Now that's out of the way, I'm guessing you'd like to hear what I've found. Let me preface this by saying I don't know how much of this is true or reliable, but what I have found is incredible." They all nodded and smiled.

"The scrolls tell of a people who lived long before what we currently know of Ancient Egypt. These people knew of things like advanced flying machines, motorized boats, and I am confident they even referenced space travel."

"Are you being serious right now?" Manuel asked.

"This could be completely wrong. I don't think it is wrong, but it could be. This race of people actually came from the stars and weren't native to Earth. When they arrived, they found a primitive population."

"Any idea how long ago that was?" asked Khalid.

"I'll get to that. We were barely able to tie a flint rock to the end of a spear at that point, surviving as hunters and gatherers. I believe the travelers called themselves something like, Anunnaki. At least that's what I pieced together phonetically."

"Are these the same 'gods' that the Sumerians reference?" asked Nicole.

"Yes, I believe these are the same race of people who interacted with the Sumerian and Babylonian cultures. The humans saw these aliens and believed them to be gods. The aliens were so far advanced that they effectively were gods. Their people had long lives, and it doesn't seem from the writings that there was such a thing as old age. Many of those who came here were already thousands of years old."

"I think they must have crashed their ship beyond repair because they spoke of returning home and couldn't. I also have the impression that they were being chased or were escaping from something."

"Could these be the same gods they reference in Mesoamerica?" Matt asked.

"I think so. I assume their craft must've landed somewhere near Egypt or Mesopotamia, only because they seem to spread out from there all over the world. They built cities in Africa, Asia, and North and South America. I have no idea how many came, but it seems that they were unable to grow as a people. Something about Earth didn't allow them to reproduce. No one came and went for a few hundred years."

"Later, when they realized they would be here for the long haul, they began interacting with the indigenous peoples. I believe the aliens in Egypt began to view the population almost like pets. They taught them about everything from agriculture to basic metallurgy and organized them into cities. There was an Anunnaki in each city that governed the people. They had large palaces built and would rarely venture outside. When they did meet with humans, they adorned themselves with headdresses that looked like various animals. I can only assume why they did that. Perhaps to hide some alien physical features or to simply increase their mystique."

"So what happened to all the cities? Why don't we see them today?" Nicole wondered.

"Most of the cities they had built were on the coast, and I believe these cities were swallowed by the rising sea levels due to the melting of glacial ice sheets that covered most of North America and Europe at the end of the last Ice Age. I am not exactly sure when they first arrived, but if it were somewhere around 8000 BC, the ocean was nearly 100 feet lower at that time than it is today. I think their cities were slowly consumed, constantly pushing them further inland and destroying evidence of their presence."

"So where did they all go? Did they die off?" asked Matt.

"At some point, a group of these Anunnaki decided they were tired of living on a planet so primitive. They wanted to reconnect with their people, so they began the construction of the pyramids. They told their human subjects that they must build these great structures to collect what they called the "breath of the gods." The scrolls didn't specify exactly what technologies they used to build the pyramids or how they would collect energy to function as some sort of door or portal to another place and time. Still, it mentions massive structures underneath the pyramids that store the energy."

"You're saying the pyramids are some sort of space travel devices," replied Manuel.

"I think the pyramids were made to allow travel through space and time. I wrote a paper suggesting this years ago. I can see in the record when the Anunnaki began leaving Egypt. They didn't all go at once, but a few dozen would go every few years. There are nearly a thousand years between when the first aliens left, and the last had gone."

"I'm convinced this is exactly why pharaohs insisted on being buried with all of their possessions. They were made to believe that once they perished, if they were placed in the king's room of the largest of the three pyramids, they would be taken away to the place of the gods and be resurrected to spend eternity with them."

"This is true in all the records up to the Pharaoh Khufu. For some reason, Khufu was the last pharaoh entombed in the Great Pyramid. However, that didn't stop future pharaohs from building pyramids and tombs for themselves with the expectation of traveling to the afterlife. This would also explain why the Egyptians would look to one of these animal-headed gods to answer prayers for thousands of years."

"One real problem is that the scrolls barely talk about how the pyramids function. I do know there's a sort of control room that is activated using your mind. I am confident the Anunnaki were able to simply think of the time and place where they wanted to go, and it would happen. Everything inside the pyramid structure was sent along as well."

"Are you saying that if we find this control room, we may be able to use it to travel to the stars?" Matt asked.

"I don't think it's that easy. It's likely the pyramid is no longer functioning. I think it's been something like four or five thousand years since it has been used."

The group sat stunned, looking at one another.

"How much of that do you really believe, Jim?" said Nicole.

"I don't know, but I can tell you that most of this has some factual basis. This didn't read like a story. At least one of the scrolls was written by the hand of an Anunnaki."

"Any idea where they could've come from or gone to?" Manuel asked.

"No idea. If I could get back into our tunnel discovery at Khufu or even Caracol, I think I might be able to get some questions answered."

"I don't see Black Sands letting you anywhere near the Caracol site, and you're completely banned from Egypt, so I don't see that happening soon," said Manuel.

"Now you see my problem. I have all of these puzzle pieces neatly stacked and ready to put together, but someone has thrown away the box with the original picture on it. I have no way of getting the information I need to be able to publish these findings."

"Hold on, publish yer findin's? Are ya crazy? Ya can't publish that. Them Black Sands ass'oles won't hesitate ta disappear ya, me, an' all the research if they think yer steppin' on their golden goose," said Khalid.

"So what was this all about then, Kal? What are we doing here if we are not bringing light to this? My mom died trying to find these answers, and here's what I've never told any of you. I have evidence that it was McDermott who sabotaged the shoring that collapsed and killed her. She was going to expose the whole thing. I think Geist might have been in on it as well."

Kalid jumped to his feet. "Jim, are ya bein' straight with me? I know ya wouldn't joke 'bout this!"

"McDermott was the last person in the tunnels before the shoring collapsed. Those clamps were tight when both Hank and I checked. This information, once verified and studied, will rock the very foundation of our world. Why do you think Black Sands is so militant about it? Everything about them is for power and profit. What do you think they are after?"

"It's obvious they want this pyramid tech. If they can find a way to travel through space and time, they could use that information to create loads of influence and wealth. They want to be the ones in control," said Nicole.

CHAPTER THIRTY-NINE

The Waiting Game

1150 BC

K ite was not used to people acknowledging her. It was strange when they took notice and asked questions like, "Are you hungry or cold?" She was used to living in the shadows, out of sight and mind. She didn't mind telling them though, because if they cared to ask, there must be a good reason for it.

Kite's new friend Jim introduced her to Neferu after they had returned from the abduction. Neferu grabbed her by the arm and dragged her to a tub of water. At first, Kite was afraid that Neferu was going to drown her, but instead, she had her strip off all of her clothes and climb into the tub. The water was so warm and relaxing, she could have fallen asleep if it wasn't for that big girl Meryt, who decided to start scrubbing her with a rough sea sponge, of all things. Kite had seen this type of sponge hanging in the market, but couldn't fathom what they were used for. She tried taking a bite out of one she found in a trash bin once, but quickly realized it was not food. Now she knew. After the scrubbing, they told her to get dressed.

She would have been less happy about getting out of the tub, except the water had turned cold.

When she went to find her clothes, they were not where she had left them. A white kalisaris of her size was draped over the stool. This new kalisaris was much finer than the clothes she had been collecting since she was a child, and it didn't smell bad. It actually smelled like flowers, so she decided to try it on.

Meryt took her downstairs and directed her to a room where she could sleep, and it was indoors. She was to share a room with Meryt, probably so they could keep an eye on her. No matter, the room had windows, so she could sneak out and be gone in a heartbeat if needed. She couldn't remember the last time she slept indoors—no, she could remember. It was last year when she was sick, and these same people took her in and nursed her back to health.

She thought maybe she could trust these people, but then decided she could count on no one. In the end, she could only rely on herself, but that netjer did seem very nice to her.

He must want something from me.

She figured maybe he wanted whatever the priests wanted from the older girls at the temple, but he never asked for anything. She had planned on taking him back to his villa and then head back to her alley to catch some sleep, but as soon as they arrived, everyone was so excited to see this god, Yama-something, that they threw a big party.

She was about to leave when Jim called her over and said he would trade her some of the honey cakes if she wouldn't mind sticking around and teaching him about Egypt. Neferu seemed a little nervous about it, but it seemed like a good trade, especially considering she had finished the last of her food cache, and the recent rain would have ruined anything in the garbage piles.

So this was her new job. She was moving up in the world. Yesterday, she was a street rat no one cared about. Today, she was the new guard for the most important man in town.

Did he say guide or guard? She couldn't remember, but she still had her bronze dagger if there was any danger, and didn't know the difference between a guide or guard, anyway.

Kite decided to take her new job very seriously and had something to say about everything. Neferu, perched on a stool with a ledger of brick orders, had dubbed her "our tiny overseer of mischief" after catching her "borrowing" a fig from the kitchen stash.

"She's quicker than a jackal and twice as sneaky," Neferu laughed.

James, sprawled nearby on cushions, reading a half-finished scroll, chuckled, "Sneaky? She's like a sandstorm. My sandals went missing again, and I'm betting they're funding her next 'trade'!"

Kite began with the water filters, those brick marvels James had rigged to banish the wasting. She'd appointed herself their guardian, patrolling with her prized bronze dagger like a miniature sentinel.

"No one's fouling up Jim's water magic on my watch!" she'd proclaim, brandishing the blade at imaginary foes.

Neferu, hauling a basket of linens, caught her mid-strut and said, "Keep that dagger sharp, little warrior. Someone's got to scare off the flies, and James is too busy napping!"

James shot back, rolling off his bench, "Napping? I'm trying to save the world. Nef, Kite's here to steal my figs and call it guard duty!"

Kite, munching, shrugged and said, "I like figs. Guarding's hungry work, Netjer-man, pay me in cakes, and I'll save your scrolls too!"

James worked with Kite daily on her English and numbers. Neferu would sit in when she had time. James could see the same brilliance in Kite that he had in Neferu. She was perhaps the smartest person he had met.

By midweek, Kite had wormed her way into Neferu's daily rounds, darting ahead to shoo loitering servants. "Move it, you lazy Nile slugs. Great Neferu's got bricks to count!"

Neferu, suppressing a grin, handed her a reed pen one evening.

"Here, you menace, mark the tally since James thinks he's too divine for paperwork, and use the new numbers he taught us."

James, peering over a copper pot he was fiddling with, snorted, "Divine? I'm trying to keep this household from collapsing under your reign of terror. Kite, did you 'trade' my pen for that dagger polish?"

Kite, twirling the blade like a scepter, said, "Pens are boring. Shiny blades scare the priests!" Neferu doubled over laughing, nearly spilling her tea.

"She's got you there. Our little Kite is sharper than your pen!"

"Maybe, but the pen is mightier than the sword. You can quote me on that if you want."

"Jim, no way you just made that up."

Jim shrugged and chuckled.

Their villa rang with such banter. Kite went about her chores with passion. James grumbled through his grins, and Neferu steered all the madness with dry wit. One morning, as James puzzled over a hieroglyph, Kite plopped down beside him.

"So if you're a netjer, why is Neferu always bossing you around?" she teased, dodging his scroll as he half-heartedly tried to smack her with it.

"Because, you sticky-fingered brat, even a netjer needs a queen to keep the chaos in check," he said, ruffling her hair.

Neferu, sweeping in with a tray of bread, added, "And queens need a Kite to keep the netjer from losing his sandals." Their laughter bounced off the stone walls, a bright thread in the tapestry of their home.

As the months went by, James studied while the new city, Per-Hotep, rose around them. He spent hours in the Chamber of Time trying to work out the Anunnakish script on the walls and the sarcophagus. He was disappointed that he didn't have all the notes from the decryption scroll he had used to enter the chamber in the first place, but he had stashed enough of the notes in his satchel, along with his mom's notebook, to help some.

Kite, who had been at James's side since their first day back, asked why he was so interested in an old box. James went on to explain to her where he had come from and why he was concerned about more people from the future coming back to their time.

"So if you are so sure someone is going to use the big shiny box to come here and kill everyone, why not break it?" Kite said.

James looked around for a moment, then looked at Kite. "Why not break it? Huh," he said.

"Well, I don't know. That actually makes a lot of sense. If I completely demolish this thing, would that stop someone from coming here?"

"I mean, if you break it now, won't that mean it will be broken in the future when they go to use it?" said Kite.

"That is a very smart thing to say, and normally I would agree, but what you don't understand is that I believe the future I came from is not the same one we are creating. Does that make sense?"

"I guess I understand, and if it were the same future, and we were to break the big box now, then it would be broken in the future, and you could have never come here in the first place," she said.

James looked around, half hoping his guards, or Neferu, were hearing their conversation.

"So if you came here in the first place, everything starts over fresh from there. Hmm, so doesn't it mean the bad men are gone or were never born and could not come here?" said Kite.

"That would be true, but when I first traveled here, the pyramid created what I call a wormhole. It is like a tunnel from the future to the past. It intertwined that future with this one. As long as that wormhole is still entangled, we can theoretically go back and forth from that future, which no longer exists, to now. I think the people in that future are experiencing the same passing of time we are here."

"You seem to understand this better than anyone else here in Egypt. Kite, I need you to help me. You are smarter than I am, and I need you to always question me like this, okay?"

"Sure, you paid for the honey cakes fair and square. So, how does it work? Do you climb in the box and pray about where you want to go?"

"Um, I think the pyramid collects energy over time, and once it is fully charged, you must press these symbols while holding in your mind's eye where you want to go. That is how I came here anyway."

"So this thing can read your thoughts?"

"Yeah, I think it can," said James.

Kite shook her head, sat back against the wall, and pulled a fig out of her pocket for a snack.

James saw Kite's fig and decided it was a good time to head back for dinner. They walked together and talked while James's two guards followed quietly behind, back to the villa.

Neferu was there to greet them when they arrived.

She reached over and mussed up Kite's hair, saying, "Hapi has a big pot of fish stew ready, if you are hungry."

Kite was off in a flash. She was always hungry.

"Any luck today?" Neferu said.

"No, not really. If I only had all of my notes, I feel I would have a much better idea of exactly how it works. I think it charges over time, and once used, it needs to recharge to work again. I believe that's why it took so long for the Anunnaki to go through it and off to wherever they went. I may have used up all the energy coming here."

"Something seems odd to me, my James. If you used this device over three thousand years from now, didn't you use the power it had saved up to that point to get here? Are you sure you also used up the power it has been saving up for the last one thousand years?"

James shook his head. "I don't know that for sure. For all I know, I could walk up to it right now and activate it to go back to the future. To be honest, I am afraid that if I test it, I'll end up stuck in a dark tomb in some unknown time. I'm not in a hurry to test that. Enough about my day. You came out to greet me, so you must have some news."

Neferu had a huge smile. "The palace is complete. We can move in."

"That is great news. Should I start bringing down the furniture? I am sure you want your own bed there for the first night in a new place."

"Husband, you are joking with me, aren't you? You know I have already had the servants move all the clothing and furnishings we need. Anyway, the furnishings I bought in Waset have been arriving for the last few weeks and will already be moved in. The indoor toilet is installed exactly like the drawings you made. I have seen it. It's marvelous! All you have to do is have a servant empty a small bucket of water into the tank above the toilet, then once you are done, you can pull the little rope, and *swoosh*, everything is gone."

"I can't wait to see it, but that raises another question. Have you talked to Bibi about the factory? Now that he is making the sewer pipes, I am sure he is running ragged. And since he is the only one who knows how to make my new toilets, he will get even busier."

"I have not spoken with him, but I agree. Now that we are moving to the palace, it is time. Meryt, can you please go grab Bibi and have him join us in the meeting room?"

They walked into the room and had a seat. A few seconds later, Bibi came barreling in.

"What's wrong? What happened?" he asked.

"Oh, nothing is wrong. We wanted to have a chat with you," said Neferu.

"Okay? I have some new buyers coming in today. Is this going to take long?"

"You have been doing such a great job this last year, Neferu and I have decided it is time for you to take full control of the factory," said James.

Bibi had a stern look on his face. "This is what you want, mistress?"

"Yes, Bibi, this is what I want. Yemhotep and I have decided to reward you with half of the factory's profits," said Neferu.

Bibi's eyes grew large. "One half of the... Neferu, I am a simple peasant. I am not worthy. That will make me a rich man."

"That is not the end of it. We have decided to give you the villa. It will be a place of your own where you can grow and raise your family. We do not have need of it any longer, and you deserve it," said Neferu.

There were tears in the big man's eyes. "Can I go now and tell my wife?"

"Please do and give those kids of yours a big hug from both of us," said James, waving as he left.

Neferu sheepishly looked away for a moment, nervously trying to decide if this was the right time to broach a different subject.

"James, there is something else that we need to discuss," said Neferu, with glistening eyes.

"What is it, my love? Whatever it is, I'm sure we can fix it before we move in."

"Move in? Oh no, it's not that. I'm ... uhm ... I'm going to have a baby."

His eyes grew wide. "I didn't think ... I mean, I didn't know if ... Oh my God, Nef, that is amazing!" James grabbed her and gave her a huge hug.

Neferu had tears in her eyes. "I didn't know how you would respond. We have never really talked about it."

"Are you joking? This is perfect, and I love you so much. We are moving into our palace, and now we have a baby on the way."

James purposely avoided the palace's construction. He was sure these people knew far more about their construction techniques than he did.

He had provided drawings for the bathrooms. Each toilet was designed and built at the factory. He knew the moment any of the high priests or nobility saw them, they would all be coming to him and Bibi for new toilets of their own. He also ran piping for a shower and tub, and had a giant cistern placed on the palace roof to accommodate their water needs.

For the time being, the cistern would be filled by workers carrying buckets, but James would figure out how to bring fresh water to every home. Above the bathroom, he designed a room that would provide hot water. A large kettle would be heated, and the water would be gravity-fed to the shower and tub. It was a workaround for modern indoor plumbing, but James was confident it would work. The palace was designed to house his entire entourage. Ptahhote would remain with his wife in the much smaller palace in the town.

James and Neferu were barely settled in when Meryt came in to announce they had a visitor. Djehuty was arriving to give James an update on the progress of their fortification. James and Neferu reclined at the large new dining table as Djehuty walked in.

"Greetings, great Yemhotep, I trust your new palace is to your approval?"

"Yes, thank you for asking. How are you faring with the construction of the new fort and barracks?" asked James.

"The fortifications are complete, and I am happy to say that by the end of the week we will have a full retinue of our best soldiers posted here. We will consider this the main posting for the bulk of Pharaoh's armies."

"I think that is a wise precaution," said James.

"Have you been able to find out any more about how the pyramid functions?"

"I am convinced it takes time for the pyramid to collect enough energy to work. I still have no idea if it is currently charged or was depleted when I arrived. I believe it will take a while for the people in my time to figure out how to power and operate the Chamber of Time."

"That is good to know. From what you have told us about them, I'm not sure even Pharaoh's host can stop them," said Djehuty.

"I really don't know, but I have been designing new weapons for you that will allow you to defeat them in time. If we have even a year, I might be able to give us a good chance."

"And if we don't have a year?"

"If we don't have that long, it will take an act of netjer to keep this kingdom together," said James.

"It is a good thing we have a netjer on our side, then," said Neferu with a wink.

James shook his head. It was all so much pressure.

"I have news from Lpet-sut," Djehuty said. "The Great Pharaoh Ramesses IV has been informed of your progress here and your amazing inventions. He has decided to join you here at your palace."

"Please say that again, Djehuty. I thought I heard you say that Pharaoh is coming here to visit," Neferu said as her face turned white.

Neferu started breathing hard, and James put his hand on her leg to calm her. "Did the Great Ramesses happen to mention when he would be arriving?" Neferu asked.

"Yes, of course. Ramesses will arrive via barge and is expected at Men-nefer within a week.

Neferu quickly stood, ran out of the room, and began barking orders.

"You said he will be arriving in Men-nefer? Would you join my entourage as we caravan to meet him? I suspect Neferu has other duties to deal with."

"Yes, Yemhotep. Everything is coming along well here with the fort. I will join you," said Djehuty.

CHAPTER FORTY

Snap, Crackle, and Pop

2018 AD

J ames had, once again, fallen into a funk. With no new information, he was unable to progress any further with his theories. He had studied the scrolls ad nauseam and could tell he was getting nowhere. Nicole tried to get Grit some contracts in areas where it was thought Anunnaki artifacts could be found, but it seemed Black Sands was always there first. They didn't say outright that they were blackballing Grit, but it was obvious that they were.

Who could blame them after the Khufu Pyramid debacle? The mission was the opposite of subtle. That probably wasn't my best decision.

He spent a few days working as a grunt on a dig site in Belize, then helped Matt do initial drone scans on a promising new find in China. These things didn't fulfill him. He always had the ancient script on his mind. He eventually retreated to his office, where he could continue the studies of the Anunnaki and their interactions with nearly every early civilization from 2,000-8,000 BC. He documented every instance he could find that detailed anything resembling interactions with gods or otherworldly beings.

Now that he had a better understanding of who they were, these instances had become obvious. He considered that maybe his best option would be to write a book detailing his findings, but he knew it would be overlooked or ridiculed unless he had definitive proof and not just loosely translated scrolls that were thousands of years old.

There had to be more to find. James once again pulled back from his friends and stuck his head into his studies.

James's cell phone rang.

"Hello?"

"Jim, Kal. They're goin' in today."

"Got it. Thanks, Kal."

Khalid had returned to his work at Black Sands after his last meeting with James. The theories James had put forward were always at the forefront of his thoughts. The Egyptians had virtually locked down Khufu for a year after James's ill-fated excursion. It took Black Sands over a year to buy enough bureaucrats and politicians in the Egyptian government to obtain a permit to work. They knew James had removed a few stones to reveal a new tunnel system, then later replaced them.

Dr. Abdel was on hand to supervise Black Sands's work, but everyone knew they had something on him and could get away with pushing boundaries. Lance McDermott was tired of waiting. He believed many of the answers they sought would be found in the new passage.

Khalid had requested the foreman position on this excavation, and thanks to his longevity with the company, he was given that opportunity.

They worked the first day to build a platform outside the entrance to facilitate the extra workers they needed to slide the large block of stone out.

To Dr. Geist's annoyance, McDermott decided to be the first to access this new tunnel leading to the heart of the Great Pyramid in thousands of years. He opted for fashionable khaki pants and a jacket, instead of his normal suit. He was going to be a real explorer on this one. He clipped his multi-gas sniffer to his shirt and walked down the corridor. Dr. Geist and his student archaeologists followed behind him with video cameras to document the entire process. He didn't invite well-known archaeologists with him on this one, as he feared they would try to share credit. This was to be Black Sands's greatest find. It would be impossible to keep the ancient scripts out of the media after an epic discovery like this.

McDermott came to a ledge and saw a drop-off, and the passage went on as far as the light would reach. He called for a ladder, and within minutes, it was set in place and tied off. He cautiously climbed down the ladder and the steep ramp, clutching at the stones on the side to keep from slipping. He came to another drop-off and fell on his butt before sliding off the edge.

"Be careful. This is extremely dangerous. If any of you want to go back, I won't hold it against you."

The grad students ignored him and took photos of the walls and ceiling.

Geist spoke to one of the students.

"Go back and tell them that we need another ladder. There is a 3.3-meter drop-off."

The student scurried back up the passage. The ladder was brought in, dropped, and tied off. Once at the bottom, he walked a few meters further and came to a dead end.

"Someone get Khalid and Dr. Abdel down here. I have made a profound discovery," said McDermott.

"*We* have made a discovery," said Geist, glaring at McDermott.

A few minutes later, Dr. Abdel and Khalid climbed down the ladder.

McDermott pointed to the door of the Chamber of Time.

"You see here and here." He pointed to a few specific characters. "These are the same characters we found in Caracol and Alexandria. This is irrefutable evidence that we have found the original pyramid builders. I want all of this photographed and documented. It is finally time for me to publish my findings and present the world with this new information that will change our basic knowledge of ancient history. This, my friends, will put my name alongside people like Sir Arthur Evans, who helped define the Minoan civilization, or Howard Carter, who discovered the tomb of Tutankhamen."

"Sir, I'm not sure if ya seen this," said Khalid as he held out his phone.

"Whatever it is, it doesn't matter. What I have discovered here will go down in—"

"Sir, I think ya might wanna see this," Khalid interrupted.

McDermott snatched the phone from Khalid.

"What could be so important?" he asked as he scanned the pictures.

"These are pictures of this very door. No one had my permission to post these." He yelled back up the passage, "Whoever posted these pics, I hope you have a good lawyer. You have all signed NDA's."

"I don't think yer understandin', sir. These weren't posted by anyone workin' for Black Sands. These photos were posted by James Jones on the archaeological forums," said Khalid.

"That's preposterous. We would have found it and removed it. I am the first person to enter this passage in a millennium."

"I don't think so, Mr. McDermott. These were posted nearly an hour 'go and are dated from the day James Jones was arrested."

"Are you telling me he accessed this area more than a year ago and kept it to himself?"

"Perhaps he didn't have time to post anything, seeing he was...in jail," said Dr. Abdel.

"That man has been a constant thorn in my side. I have largely ignored him to this point, but no longer. I'll see that man arrested," said McDermott

"Ya already had 'im arrested, sir. He's out now," said Khalid.

"Are you trying to be funny, Khalid? Because if you are, you can pack your shit and—"

"Oh no, sir, I was concerned that if ya have 'im arrested, he won't be able ta come here ta translate the script. He says he's made great strides in translatin'. I know Dr. Geist and yer people have been workin' on it fer years."

"James Jones here, working for me? First, I don't believe he would come, given our history. Isn't he banned from accessing the pyramid anyway? I doubt he understands half as much as he is letting on."

"Sir, if you've any hope ta discover the meanings of the script 'ritten on this wall, you'll need ta have James Jones examine 'em. He says he believes this wall's a door ta a much larger chamber. I'm sure 'tween ya and Dr. Abdel, he can get a temporary reprieve ta allow access ta this passage. Or I guess, re-access the passage."

They had come to his house without even a phone call. Two large black SUVs loaded with six big operator types. To James, it seemed like something out of a Tom Clancy book. After the huge, muscly dudes climbed out of the vehicles, a small, thin man with glasses slid out of the back seat.

He was blond and blue-eyed, gazing at James as if trying to size up the man. He wore black slacks with a black blazer and white button-up dress shirt. The top three buttons were undone, exposing a large medallion on a gold chain that he was obviously very proud of.

"James!" It was a statement, not a question. "I am very happy to have found you."

James recognized the CEO of Black Sands Corp., who had him thrown in prison a few years before.

With a slightly tilted head and confused expression, James said, "What in the world could you possibly be doing here?"

"That, my friend, is an excellent question. I know we have had our differences in the past, but do you perhaps have a place where we could sit and discuss a few things?"

James pulled a double-barrel shotgun from under his dad's Cracker Barrel rocking chair and set it on his lap.

"Y'all realize you're in Texas, and this is my homestead. I suggest you six ugly assholes stay put. McDermott, if you want to talk, there's a seat here."

He nodded and approached as James motioned for him to have a seat.

"I'd offer you some lemonade or sweet tea, but I won't because I don't like you."

"Now, now, Mr. Jones, let's not start this off like that. I am here to talk."

"Okay, then talk."

"Listen, I think we got off on the wrong foot. I don't wish you any ill will, Jim. Can I call you Jim?"

"No."

"Mr. Jones, then, fine. I am simply coming to you as a fellow scientist who wants some answers."

"Scientist? You're no scientist, just a hack corporate suit."

"Regardless, you seem to be the only one who has been able to decipher even the tiniest bit of this new language."

"Anunnakish."

"Come again?"

"I have named the language Anunnakish."

"I see, so you feel these are the writings of the same gods who visited the Sumerians and Babylonians?"

"And Asia and North and South America," said James.

"I see, Mr. Jones. I came to the right person. What will it take to get you to come back with me to Egypt?"

"I'm not going anywhere with you, especially to Egypt. Thanks to you, if I set foot in that country, they will throw me back in prison."

"No, Ji ... Mr. Jones, you don't need to worry about that. The Egyptian government has seen fit to commute your sentence. You are no longer banned."

James's heart skipped a beat. *They had somehow done it. I might actually get a second chance at Khufu.*

"So how much did that cost you?" James said with a smirk.

"I have no idea what you are talking about," McDermott said in his best innocent voice.

Bile rose from James's stomach as he contemplated working with the monster who had conspired to murder his mother. He knew that the only way to accomplish his mother's final wishes would be to play nice ... for now.

"Against my better judgment, you got me. There is no way I am going with you, though. I'll see you in Cairo."

"Very well, Mr. Jones. I look forward to our next chat."

As suddenly as they came, McDermott and his crew were gone.

James called his main crew from Grit and filled them in. They were all very hesitant for James to go through with it, suggesting it would likely end badly, but James was resigned to this path, and he would see it through.

This time, James would be ready. He arranged for his house and property to be cared for. It turned out that Chris was between projects and was happy to move in and care for things temporarily. James called his lawyer and filled her in, just in case. He also called the trust that his parents had set up for him. He had turned thirty and would finally be responsible for making the major decisions about his sizable portfolio.

He packed his gear, and as he drove away from his home, he wondered if he was making the right decision. He felt his mom and dad's presence and knew he was on the right path.

James once again stood on the stones outside the passage. It had been a calm, sunny day, but dark clouds were rolling in. It hadn't rained in months, but these definitely looked like rain clouds. James had his satchel with him, which included many notes, including his mom's notebook, that he would need to translate the Anunnakish writings. He could access anything he didn't have with him on his phone. He looked back to see the Black Sands encampment some distance off.

How the hell did I get myself into working with these assholes?

The laborers had started sitting down and unpacking their lunches. They were mostly Americans. Apparently, Black Sands had decided not to use local labor on this project.

The rain had begun to fall as James entered the passages for the second time. Khalid was there following behind to "keep an eye on 'im."

Geist and two grad students followed behind to document the progress. James went through the now-familiar passage and down the two separate ladders to his destination, the only place he wanted to be in the world. It took him only a few minutes to recognize the word for "portal." The marking was recessed a little and seemed strangely out of place. He pressed in on the symbol, and it popped out of the wall. James looked at Khalid as if to say, "Are you seeing this?" With a slight tug, the door opened to a gush of wind and dust. The door had been airtight and sealed.

Crack, boom. James and Khalid both jumped. It was enough to scare the two grad students away.

"Thunder," said Khalid.

James nodded, and Khalid checked his multi-gas meter and nodded for James to proceed.

He had agreed with McDermott that if he could decipher the script on the door, he would immediately call it in.

"That's far enough, Mr. Jones. We agreed to let you translate the glyphs, not enter the chamber," said Geist.

James turned to look at Geist for an instant and stared into his eyes. "I know what kind of person you are, Geist. You're a coward. You going to stop me?" James turned back and entered the chamber.

"Stop! Stop now, I said. Mr. Khalid, you must stop him."

"Ya don't pay me ta be a security guard. Ya want 'im stopped, have at it," said Khalid.

Entering the chamber, James saw that it was about twenty feet long and ten feet wide. The walls sloped in, toward the ceiling, which was around twenty feet high itself. James set his lamp on the sarcophagus, stood back, and took in the room. Everything he saw was covered in gold. The walls, the ceiling, and the sarcophagus were all ornately carved and beautiful. He knew he was running out of time, so he started snapping pictures of everything. The sarcophagus was especially interesting. Somehow, it seemed to be calling to him.

Vivid images of his mother popped into his mind's eye. He knew how excited she would've been if she were there with him. While reminiscing about the trip with his parents to Ramesses IV's tomb in the Valley of Kings, he reached out to touch an unfamiliar symbol on the sarcophagus and was gone.

CHAPTER FORTY-ONE

Distant Thunder

1150 BC

Dark clouds began rolling in as Djehuty and James arrived in Men-nefer with their entourage. They had taken their time preparing and traveling, as they weren't expecting Ramesses for a couple more days. As they rode up to the gate, a messenger was waiting for them. The message was from Ptahmose and read, "Great Yemhotep, I was made aware of your plans to travel to Men-nefer to greet our Great Pharaoh Ramesses IV. I had hoped to meet you at the gate upon your arrival, but more urgent business has come to my attention. I humbly ask you to attend a celebratory feast at my villa."

James looked at Djehuty. "Do you have any plans?"

Djehuty smiled and shook his head. Once they neared the village, they were greeted by stewards who directed the retinue to their quarters. Two beautiful, scantily dressed servants grabbed their hands and led them to the picturesque atrium on the bank of the Nile.

As they walked through the door, James had a strange feeling that something was amiss. His hand instinctively went into his satchel to prepare for the unknown. James first saw Tentopet and realized what was happening. He looked around and saw Ramesses speaking with Nebamun at the other end of the room.

When James and Djehuty were announced, Ramesses, with a huge smile, turned to see his friend and compatriot and went to welcome him. Ramesses walked over as Djehuty went to his knee. James looked over at Djehuty and considered if he, too, should show this respect. As he prepared to kneel, Pharaoh grabbed his forearm and held him to his feet.

"Yemhotep, you kneel for no one."

James considered what Ramesses said and couldn't help but feel that Ramesses was more like an older brother to him than some pharaoh from a long-dead civilization.

James pulled Pharaoh in, gave him a hug, and said, "I have missed you, my friend."

Ramesses was not expecting physical touch and was a bit rigid. Normally, touching Pharaoh without his express consent was a death sentence, but in this case, he returned the hug and said, "It is good to see you, too."

James then went over to Tentopet and gave her a curt bow.

"I am happy to see you here, Tentopet. Neferu was not sure if she should expect you."

"I have been hearing about this new palace of yours, Yemhotep. I have to see it for myself."

"Neferu will be honored to give you a tour," James said.

They all lounged around a table discussing the recent developments surrounding the construction at Per-hotep. James described his new wastewater system, including the new hot shower and working toilets. Ramesses and Tentopet were eager to see them. An unseasonal light rain began to fall as the sky darkened. Growing up in Texas, James knew the smell of an approaching thunderstorm. There was a bright flash, then a *crack, boom!* Tentopet jumped to her feet as the walls of the villa trembled.

Ptahmose had a worried look on his face. "This storm is concerning. This is not the time of year we would expect one like this."

James had a questioning look on his face, which turned to concern.

"Ptahmose, to be clear, how often does a storm like this happen?"

"It is very rare. We had a similar storm more than a year ago, but it was also strange and went away as fast as it came," said Ptahmose.

"Yemhotep, the last time we had a storm like this was right before you were found in the tomb," said Ptomak.

"Damn!" James looked over at Ptomak, then to Ramesses. "We have to go."

"But, Yemhotep, you just arrived. Surely you will stay here for the night. Anything important can wait until tomorrow," said Ptahmose.

"It cannot wait. Ramesses, I am concerned this storm is the harbinger of an attack from the pyramid."

"But I thought you were confident we had time to prepare. Surely this is just a storm," said Ramesses.

"I feel I am right, Great Pharaoh, and I ask for your leave and the fastest horse in Men-nefer."

"Yes, of course, Yemhotep. Ptahmose, have the two fastest horses prepared. I am coming too. We will ride together, Jim. Djehuty, I know you would prefer to come with us now, but I need you to prepare as many of the city guards as possible to fit on horses and ride as fast as possible. Yemhotep and I will be leaving now."

Ramesses donned the gilded leather armor with bronze scales that his servants always carried for him. He was mounting his horse when a servant ran out.

"My master requests you wear his best armor, great Yemhotep," the man said, as he knelt before James.

"Tell him I gratefully accept his offer". The servants helped him into it. Ptahmose's armor was a bit small, but he was the only one even close to James's size.

They galloped off at top speed. Ramesses figured it would take around an hour and a half to reach Per-hotep.

Neferu was busy at the palace, directing the servants to make-up rooms and preparing for a feast when she heard a loud boom. The thunder had subsided, and the clouds had begun to dissipate, so she wondered what it could be. There were a few loud bangs, then a few more, then many more.

James had warned Neferu about what she should expect if they were under attack, and this sounded like what he described as gunfire. She ran to the second-story balcony and looked toward Khufu. It was nearing evening, and the sun was low in the sky. She saw a couple of flashes of light coming from the same entrance to the pyramid where James had appeared all those months before. After she saw the lights, she heard *boom, boom, boom*. Neferu stood there looking stunned as Kite came running in.

"There are strangers coming out of the pyramid. I have seen them shoot lightning from their staffs," Kite said.

"This is what James has prepared us for. Quickly, come with me, Kite. Meryt, send word to Sekhmet, wife of Ptahhote. We must prepare now," said Neferu.

Neferu had drilled all of her servants on what to do in case they were attacked, but they were only barely prepared because they had just moved into the palace. She realized this was the absolute worst-case scenario, and James wasn't there to lead them. She waited for a few minutes for Sekhmet and her maids to arrive, then entered the safe room.

The safe room was a hidden room that was stocked with enough food and water for a dozen people for a week. There were enough sleeping mats and blankets available for everyone. As Sekhmet and her maids hurried into the safe room, Neferu turned to the small group huddled within. Both servants and royalty clutched their wide-eyed children, their breaths uneven with fear. Social constructs that would have divided the groups were gone. Neferu stood at the door and pulled the lever to activate the locking system. Before the large stone slab slid into place, Kite ran past Neferu and out of the room.

"Kite, wait, come back," Neferu yelled after her.

"I have to warn Jim. If he comes back and doesn't know they're here, they'll kill him," she said and ran toward the front entrance. Neferu tried to go after her, but it was too late. The locking mechanism was already in motion. A huge slab of stone slid down into place, blocking the way. From the outside, it would look like just another bare wall.

Neferu leaned back against the wall. "Go warn him, Kite," she quietly said to herself.

She knelt beside a trembling girl, no older than Kite, whose hands gripped a tattered doll.

"Listen to me, little one," Neferu said softly, brushing a lock of hair from the child's face. "This room is our shield, built by Yemhotep's wisdom and blessed by the netjeru. We are safe here, and I will stay with you until the storm passes."

Her voice, steady and warm, seemed to quiet the room, and the girl managed a small nod, then clutched Neferu's hand as if it were a lifeline.

Neferu rose, her gaze sweeping over the women, some whispering prayers, others stifling sobs.

"I know you hear the thunder and the strange fire staffs outside," she said, her tone firm, yet kind. "But we are stronger than this terror. You've built our home with your hands, fed our people with your care, and now we protect each other. Tell me your fears, and we'll face them together."

A young mother, cradling an infant, spoke of the lightning staff, her voice quaking. Neferu squeezed her shoulder, offering a faint smile.

"Yemhotep has faced worse and returned to us. So will we."

That sparked a flicker of courage, binding them closer in the dim light.

When James and Ramesses grew near the outer walls of Per-hotep, they dismounted. The streets were empty, and everything was too quiet. They both knew something was terribly wrong.

"They are in the palace," a little voice spoke up behind them.

James and Ramesses spun around to see Kite sitting on a rock wall behind them.

"Is everyone okay?" said James.

"Your lady turned the handle, and the rock slid down. It slammed to the floor like you said it would. The bad guys saw it too. They tried to grab me, but I was too quick. Oh, I forgot, I guess everyone is not okay. They used their lightning, and many soldiers are not getting up."

"You were supposed to be inside with Neferu, Kite."

"I had to warn you, and I wanted to see Pharaoh. Did you see him?"

"Kite, I want you to meet my good friend Pharaoh Ramesses IV."

"You are Pharaoh? Oh, I brought you something." Kite pulled a partially smashed honey cake from her pocket. "I heard Jim's lady say it is good to have a gift for visitors."

Ramesses took the honey cake and thanked Kite.

Kite was eyeing a particularly shiny gold medallion hanging from Ramesses's tunic when she looked over at James, who was glaring at her and shaking his head. She was not very excited about giving away a honey cake with no compensation.

James looked at Ramesses and shook his head. "Damn! Too soon. We are not ready."

"What do we do, Jim?" Ramesses asked.

The first thing we do is retake the palace. Then we need to destroy the Chamber of Time.

"James, if we destroy the chamber, are you confident it will stop the travelers?"

"No, but I am sure these men are only the first to come. Many more will follow, but if we can damage it enough, I do not believe they can use it."

James instructed Kite to go to the tunnel entrance, then report back to him how many people were there. James and Ramesses walked around the outside wall of the town toward the nearly completed barracks. It would house as many as ten thousand troops in time, but was only manned by about one hundred at this point. When they were close enough, James pointed to two figures dressed in desert camo standing in front of nearly one hundred soldiers who were lying face down with their hands on the back of their heads.

"Why are they not fighting?" Ramesses said in shock. "Only those two men are guarding them?"

James pointed to the gate, where a dozen soldiers were dead.

"Ramesses, do you remember the time in Abydos when I used the lightning to distract those men? The weapons they have are far deadlier than that. Your men have no chance. We are going to have to take them in a different way."

Kite came running up.

"Kite, be careful. Don't let them see you."

"Do not worry. I'm fast and don't think they are scared of me, but they should be," she said as she pulled the jeweled dagger from her sleeve.

"Stay out of sight, Kite. Let Ramesses and I take care of these men," James said. Kite responded with a shrug.

"There are two men at the passage entrance," said Kite, "and I saw only two men in the palace."

"With these two, that makes six heavily armed soldiers. I think we should try to kill those two men guarding our troops. If I can get their weapons, we have a much better chance. Kite, I need you to do something important for me. Find Bibi and tell him what is happening. Then, I want you to stay with him and protect his children. Can you do that?"

"Yes, Jim, you can trust me," Kite said, wide-eyed.

"I know I can."

CHAPTER FORTY-TWO

A Tricky Situation

1150 BC

The sun was setting behind a bright red sky. James watched two Black Sands goons pointing at some men arguing.

"They are not sure what to do. They did not expect this many people near the pyramid," said James. "If we can get close enough, without them seeing us, I think we have a good chance. Ramesses, I need to warn you. These men are nearly as deadly with their hands as they are with their weapons. If they get hold of you, they can kill you."

"I understand. I will be right behind you."

There were two men arguing loudly, which allowed James and Ramesses get within six feet of them behind a stacked rock wall.

One of their radios chirped. "Are you two still guarding those soldiers? We don't have time for that. You should grab the saw and wipe them out. Over."

"Boss, you really want us to waste the whole bunch of them? Over."

"I already told you we don't have the resources available to hold them. Kill them all. Beta team should be coming through in thirty, and I need the rest of the town secured before the science geeks get here. Over."

"Fine, I'll walk back to the passage and get the automatic. You stay put here," he said to one of the guards.

James eyed Ramesses and mouthed, "We have to do it now. Follow my lead."

The men were covered in body armor that would probably not stop a rifle round but would surely stop an arrow. James stuck his knife to the back of the guard's neck.

"I would recommend you stay still," James said in a very calm voice.

The soldier froze in place, but James could see him flip the safety off on his rifle.

"That will be enough of that. Put your hands up."

"I think you'd better back off, bud. I don't think you realize who you are dealing with. Oh, shit, you must be the asshole scientist who disappeared. James, isn't it?"

"Keep your mouth shut," he said in English before turning to his friend. "Ramesses, take his rifle from him."

Ramesses's soldiers noticed what James and their pharaoh were doing. The man James was covering suddenly spun around and disarmed James, knocking his knife a good ten feet away, then slammed his fist in James's face. James staggered back in time to see the man's head fall from his body. Ramesses was standing there with his long curved khopesh sword over him. The soldier who was walking back to the passage heard the commotion and turned in time to see his friend's head fall. He went to raise his rifle when twenty Egyptians jumped up to grab him. He was barely able to swing his M4 around before he was swarmed. He was beaten to death within a minute. James pulled the sidearm from the dead soldier's holster and handed it to Ramesses, then briefly explained its operation and picked up the M4 with a few magazines.

Ramesses noticed one of his soldiers walking toward him with the other M4 in hand.

"Intohep, it is good you are here," said Ramesses.

James walked up and greeted the approaching captain of the guard. "I was not aware you were in Per-hotep."

Intohep knelt before them.

"I sent him here in advance of my arrival this morning," said Ramesses.

"Intohep, I am going to show you how to use this new weapon. Ramesses, if we go now to the palace and surround it, we will not be able to remove them in time, but I have a plan.

The radio buzzed. "I haven't heard any shots, so I am assuming you two are still screwing around with those soldiers. Get it done, now! Over."

James held the device. "Copy that. Over," he said.

Ramesses stood in the courtyard in his bright armor and yelled out. "You creatures from the future who have come to my kingdom to kill and pillage, your time here is at an end."

The two men in the palace looked at each other, then walked to the palace's entrance. "What the hell is that freak saying over there?"

"I have no idea, but he looks serious." They both laughed hysterically.

Ramesses raised and then lowered his arm. Fifty arrows were loosed.

"Oh shit," said one of the Black Sands thugs as an arrow stuck him in the arm, and three others stuck in his chest armor. The other man had two in his chest as well.

They quickly raised their rifles and stepped through the door as they began firing at Ramesses and his soldiers. Two of Ramesses men went down instantly. Ramesses jumped behind a wagon as wood splintered around him. There were two quick three-round bursts of fire and then two more. James and Intohep had been on either side of the entrance, waiting for their opportunity to shoot. Intohep's first rounds flew past the men, but James was able to hit both men with three rounds each. They were moaning in pain as Ramesses walked up and finished them off with the pistol.

"We should release the women from your safe room, James," said Ramesses.

"They are safe now, Ramesses. I would like to keep them that way until this is over. We can send a messenger with word that we are okay."

"A wise decision. What is our next move?"

"We have cleared them out of the city and the barracks. According to Kite, that leaves the two guarding the passage. They said another group would be coming. We need to get to the passage and destroy the chamber before the next group arrives," said James. "We will have to lure them out like we did at the palace. This time we have four rifles. Would you please do me a favor and not stand out in the open like that? They may not care what you are saying and shoot you next time."

Ramesses' face turned red. "Wise advice. That was very close earlier. I had no idea how fast they could use those...rifles."

They approached the base of the pyramid as quietly as they could. Nearly all of Ramesses's men had their bows, and it was dark enough that they were able to get within fifty yards of the entrance without being noticed.

One of the guards reached for his radio. "Boss, is that you approaching? We are seeing movement in the ruins below us."

"Negative, it's probably just some goats. Over," said James.

"Goats? Chief, is that you? Over."

"Affirmative," James said, as he took aim.

Boom! The shot rang out, followed by one hundred arrows flying through the darkness.

The first man dropped, and the second was hit with a few arrows.

Brrrap, Brrrap. James looked over as Imhotep unloaded his entire magazine on full auto without even aiming.

James motioned for Imhotep to stop as he stealthily approached the entrance with his gun drawn. The first man was clearly dead, but there was no sign of the second. James went ahead through the entrance and motioned for Imhotep and the others to stay back.

Neferu had been waiting patiently in the safe room for what seemed like hours. Many of the women knelt together and prayed. Others held their children close. James had said it could be days before they would be able to repel any attackers. Sekhemet's youngest daughter came and sat on her lap. She was trembling, and her eyes were heavy with terror. Neferu stroked her hair and sang.

Hush little lotus, close your eyes
The Nile's sweet waters flow tonight
The reeds will sway beneath the moon

Sleep little darling, dawn comes soon
The jackle guards your dreams at night
The falcon watches while he's in flight
The stars of Nut shine in the sky
Wonderful dreams you cannot deny
Hush little lotus, close your eyes
The Nile's sweet waters flow tonight
The reeds will sway beneath the moon
Sleep little darling, dawn comes soon
With courage and bravery, you will sleep
Dawn will come soon, so do not you weep
In morning, Ra will light the sky
Quiet, little one, and sleep tonight

The young child was nearly asleep, and Neferu cradled her and handed her to Meryt when three loud explosions startled her. She nearly dropped the child on the floor. Near the palace's entrance came more of the "gunfire" that James spoke of. This time, it was very near, and there were screams of pain and then silence. A few minutes later, a voice came through the talking hole drilled through the stone.

"I was ordered in the name of Yemhotep to come to you and tell you that they have killed most of the invaders. The Great Ramesses IV and Yemhotep are now attacking the entrance to the Chamber of Time. They will drive these invaders from the afterlife back to face Ammit, who will devour their souls. He asks you to stay here and be safe," said Ptahhote.

Gasps and cheers came from all of the women who were present.

"It is Ptahhote. He is alive," Sekhmet wailed out in an uncharacteristic show of emotions.

Neferu decided she would listen to her husband this time. But...he was still out there fighting and could still be in danger. She sat quietly, nervously tapping her feet for another ten minutes.

"It has been long since we have heard any thunder. I cannot stay here any longer."

Neferu motioned for some servants to help her manipulate the release that would trigger the counterweight, which hauled up the large stone door slab. Once the counterweight dropped, the door slowly rose.

Neferu motioned for everyone to stay behind.

"If you see any of those men, you must turn the lever and close the room once again."

"My Lady, you must not leave. Yemhotep commanded we stay here until he returns," said Sekhemet. Neferu walked out to a grisly scene. There were bloodied dead soldiers and broken clay pottery strewn about. James had been right about the carnage these invaders would bring. She frantically went between soldiers, looking at their faces and praying they were not familiar.

A few moments later, she heard the *brrrap, brrrap* of a thunderstick. Neferu stepped out of the front door. Her linen kalisaris swayed in the breeze.

She could see some motion in the distance at Khufu. *It has to be James,* she thought. She decided she was done waiting and reached down to grab the first sword she could find, then ran toward the noise.

James felt he had a better chance going in by himself than with three completely untrained Egyptian soldiers with submachine guns. James cautiously walked into the first chamber, clearing the room. He quietly walked ahead, climbing down the first ledge where they had constructed a ladder a few weeks before. In the distance, he could hear a man breathing hard and wheezing. James peered over the second ledge, and two shots whizzed past him, barely missing his head.

"Hey, you're quite a ways from home, soldier," James said.

"You speak English?" the man said.

"Yeah, I'm from Texas. How about you?"

"Oklahoma," he said.

"See, we are basically neighbors. Why don't you drop that pistol, and we will see about getting you home?"

"You must be James Jones. Been here all this time, have you?"

"Yep, this is my home now. I don't appreciate y'all coming in and killin' my people."

"Whatever. McDermott says this is not the same timeline we're from, so no one who is alive here matters."

"They may not matter to you, but they matter to me."

"So what, you come here, and because you were here first it belongs to you? I call bullshit on that. We have every right to take advantage of this place, like you are."

"Maybe you do, but I don't give a rat's ass about you or what I have a right to. This is my home, and it will be defended. Drop your weapons and walk with me to the chamber. We can figure out how to get you back. It looks like you have a punctured lung. You stay here, and you won't make it. You head home, and you will be out of the hospital by morning."

"Screw you, Jones. In a few minutes, this place will be packed with Black Sands security. You think you and your merry band of spear chuckers are going to stand up to 'em? Ha!"

Neferu approached the entrance to the tunnel. There must have been one hundred of Pharoah's soldiers, all with bows at ready. Ramesses was standing next to Intohep at the entrance to the tunnel. Neferu pushed past the soldiers, who started stepping aside and opening a path for her as she approached Pharaoh.

Neferu knelt before Pharaoh. "Great Ramesses, please tell me of the fate of Yemhotep."

"Oh, please stand, Neferu. James asked us to stay behind while he checks the tunnel. He went in after an intruder who was wounded."

Kite, who was always around but rarely seen, bolted past Ramesses and Neferu, down the tunnel. Neferu tried to grab her, then started to run after her as Intohep grabbed her arm. "It is not safe, My Lady," he said.

"We have to get Kite and find Yemhotep," she said as she struggled to free herself.

"Neferu, please stay here. Yemhotep had a reason for us all to wait. You know he has a plan," said Ramesses.

Neferu was not going to stop until she heard James yell from the tunnel, "The guard is down. I'm going to keep going in."

James didn't have a plan and knew he was running out of time. He looked around to see a fairly large metal case behind him. He picked it up, and it must have weighed thirty pounds. He didn't know what was in it and didn't care. He threw the case with all of his strength down the ledge and tried to slide down the ladder after it.

As he neared the bottom, his foot got stuck on a rung, and he flailed backward, landing on his butt, and the ladder fell and smashed into several pieces. James's aim was spot on. The case had hit the soldier in the head. He was out cold, and the case was cracked open.

James yelled back through the tunnel, "The guard is down. I'm going to keep going down."

He stopped for an instant, noticing light coming from the case. According to James's theories about the operation of the pyramid, electronics should have been burned out from electromagnetic radiation. This case must have been protected from an EMP. When he opened it, his heart sank. The case was loaded with plastic explosives, and there was a timer counting down.

Crack! Hot lead slammed into his back and through his chest. The pain was unimaginable. He couldn't breathe, and his vision started closing in.

"Well, shit, the timer has been activated," said the guard as he winced in pain. "You shouldn't have touched the case, dumbass. Now we are both dead."

"You're calling me the dumbass? Who brought the big-ass bomb in the first place?" James groaned.

He noticed some movement up on the ledge. It was Kite, and she had her dagger out. James tried to yell out to her to run, but he couldn't speak. His eyes opened wide as she held her jeweled dagger and jumped down, jamming the blade completely through the body armor and through the man's heart.

Kite scrambled over and held James's head. He could barely talk. "Kite you have to get out of here. This whole place will be destroyed in a few seconds."

Then he looked back at the broken ladder and the ledge. There was no way she was getting out in time. James settled back, holding her hand, and looked into her eyes.

"Kite, I don't think either of us is making it out of this one."

Neferu waited for what seemed like hours but was actually only a couple of minutes. Her heart was beating out of her chest. She wouldn't be able to rest until she saw the love of her life, the father of her unborn child, Netjer of Egypt, standing safely in front of her.

Intohep knelt in front of Pharaoh. "Great Pharaoh, I would ask permission to disobey the orders of Yemhotep. It has been too long. I would ask you to allow me to go after him."

Ramesses was worried about his friend and agreed with Intohep.

"Yes, go now and report back to me."

Intohep turned and was only a few feet down the corridor when light, sound, and fire rolled out of the tunnels.

He was blown to nothingness while the entire host was knocked to their backs. The explosion's energy was directed straight out of the tunnel. Everyone around the entrance was knocked unconscious. Djehuty, standing with his soldiers, came running up with his men to find Pharaoh and Neferu, who were slightly injured but fine.

Neferu came to her senses. She sat on the same ledge where she had first met her love. Tears came to her soot-covered face as she screamed out for James.

Kite sat next to a bloodied, dying James. "Can they fix your chest in your future?"

"Uhm, maybe they could, but we don't have what we need here to ..."

Kite started pulling James toward the chamber.

"Kite, what are you doing? Oh, yeah, great idea." James did his best to half-crawl while Kite dragged him to the chamber. He settled right next to it. "I don't know if this will work, but here goes nothing."

James thought of his loyal friends who would do anything for him at Grit, and he touched the same symbol he had all that time ago.

Epilogue

2021 AD

J ames realized he was conscious before opening his eyes. He was lying in a bed and felt drugged. He tried to collect his thoughts. He remembered lying next to the sarcophagus and pressing the symbol with Kite. Where was she?

He quickly opened his eyes and started to sit up. The pain in his chest was incredible. He looked around and saw a young girl sitting asleep in a chair next to his bed. It was Kite. She wasn't wearing her normal linen kalisaris that Neferu had made for her. She was wearing a T-shirt and jeans and had a cup of vanilla pudding nearly spilling out onto her shirt. James looked over at her and laughed. She opened her eyes, caught his glance, and smiled.

"You have been sleeping for many heru. They had to do something called surgery on you," she said.

"I remember little after the Chamber of Time," he said.

"There is not much to tell. You were asleep on the floor when we appeared in a room full of people. They were all confused about seeing us, but one of them recognized you. Some big men dressed like those who shot you pulled you out of the pyramid. They did not know who I was, but I would not let them take you without me. Some other people came, and then they put us in a cart that made a loud *woowoo woowoo* that brought us to a giant bird. I fell asleep, and when I woke we were on another one of those loud carts, faster than a horse. One of the kind ladies here brought me these clothes and showed me how to put them on."

"Have you been able to talk to them?" James asked.

"I have been trying to use my English that you taught me, but they are speaking so fast and saying words I have never heard. One man spoke Egyptian, but I laughed at him, because he sounded like a baby."

"Kite, thank you for saving me. If you had not thought of going through the pyramid, we would not have lived. You saved me, and I want you to know I will be here for you. You are in a strange place, and I am sure you are afraid. We are in this together. Understand?"

Kite sat and nodded with tears running down her face.

Nicole and Matt walked in. "Boss, you're here. You're back. You just disappeared."

"Khalid called us a few days ago and told us that you simply appeared back in the same room that you disappeared from. Where have you been?" asked Matt.

Nicole had tears in her eyes. "I can't believe it's really you. We were going to have a funeral," she chuckled.

"I have a story to tell you all, but it will have to wait. I don't want to have to tell it fifty times."

He looked over at Kite. "I want you both to meet Kite. She's ... my daughter."

Kite recognized the word and had a huge smile.

Nicole and Matt looked at each other. "How long were you gone?" Matt said.

"It's some kind of miracle that you were able to get out of Egypt. Once you reappeared, Black Sands wanted the police to hold you there and put you back in prison."

"I'm not in Egypt? Where are we?"

"Back in the good ol' US of A, thanks to Khalid. He liberated a Black Sands Gulf Stream and flew you directly to Houston. You're at Houston Methodist," said Matt.

James let out a sigh of relief. "How were you able to get Kite past immigration?"

"The ambulance met the plane, and I doubted anyone would bother to check," said Nicole.

"Khalid said she wouldn't leave your side and tried to stab some of the Black Sands' people when they tried to separate you," said Nicole.

"Sounds about right," James said with a wink to Kite.

"After you disappeared, they worked for months trying to figure out what happened. I don't think they have any clue how you were able to do it," said Nicole.

"Oh, they know. I ran into a squad of their thugs on the other side. That's how I ended up here," said James. "What I can't figure out is how they were able to power the pyramid. Everything I have learned suggests it takes years to build up enough energy to open a portal."

"Open a portal? You have to start spilling the beans. I'm freaking out," said Matt.

Two police officers and two goons started to enter the room. James heard some commotion and saw Chris and Frank barring their entrance.

James could hear McDermott screaming in the background, "I want him arrested, you hear me. He stole an airplane and trespassed on our duly and properly permitted worksite."

James yelled, "Chris, let the police and McDermott in. The goons can stay out."

Chris peeked in and waved to James. "Nice to see you up." He let the three enter.

"Sir, I'm Deputy Rogers with the Texas Rangers."

"Pleasure, James Tiberius," said James.

"Tiberius? No, he's lying, trying to pull some kind of scam again. His name is James Jones. And I demand, Mr. Jones, to know exactly what you did to my portal. It stopped responding," said McDermott.

"Your people blew up the other end with their bomb. That's what happened."

"Do you have any sort of identification?" said Deputy Rogers.

James didn't have his license or any identification whatsoever.

"I'm afraid all my identification has been lost, Officer."

Nicole stepped up. "I can help." She pulled a passport from her purse and handed it to the officer.

"Says here his name is James Tiberius. Are you sure you have the right guy, McDermott?"

"Yes, I have the right guy. I hired him myself."

"Mr. Tiberius, did you happen to steal a Gulfstream jet?" said the deputy.

"No, sir, I have been unconscious for days now. In fact, I only woke up an hour ago or so."

Khalid and Manuel walked in.

"Wow, it's a party," said James.

"There he is, Officer. That man is the one who stole the plane," said McDermott.

"I'm confused, Mr. McDermott. You said this James Jones fella stole the plane, then James Tiberius, now this guy. What's the story?"

James looked at Khalid, who motioned for James to continue.

"No one has stolen anything. My employee recognized that I needed immediate care and made an emergency flight to Houston on a company plane."

"There, you see? He admits it," said McDermott.

"What Mr. McDermott doesn't understand is that he no longer works for Black Sands Corp."

"What are you talking about? Are you delusional? I am the CEO of Black Sands and have been for five years."

"You were the CEO right up until this morning. I don't think you've recognized my last name. Does Tiberius sound familiar?"

"What? Why would I care about your name? James Jones or James Tiberius makes no diff—Uh. Tiberius? As in Hank Tiberius, the founder of Black Sands? He has been dead and buried for something like ten years."

"Yes, he has, and he left me all of his stock in Black Sands Corp. held in a trust. He was hoping that by the time I turned thirty, I would be ready to take back the reins. Khalid has been collaborating with my lawyers for the last few days, and as of this morning, we have officially taken over. Perhaps you should answer your phone when members of your board of director's call."

"But I thought they were going to chastise me for the pyramid debacle," said McDermott, who seemed to be in shock.

"Hank built this company. All you did was destroy his good name, and I know you and Geist are responsible for my mother's death."

McDermott's eyes bulged out. "You ... Your mother was ..."

"Yeah, my mother was Sara, the woman you had murdered in Giza."

James looked at the Texas Ranger. "No, I can't prove it, but look at him and tell me you don't believe me."

"I'm sorry for all of the confusion, sir. Would you mind me showing Lance here, and his associates, the way out?" said the ranger.

McDermott turned and strode out the door while pulling out his phone. "Geist, it's all gone to hell. We need to start the backup plan."

They were glad to see him leave, even if what he said was ominous.

"How did you coordinate this with Khalid? Weren't you passed out?" said Nicole.

"Oh, I was, but Kal had a doctor on the flight. I woke up a couple of times, and we were able to contact my trust and get things moving. I'm very lucky, actually. I was nearly reported as legally dead. That would have been a nightmare to figure out."

"I want everyone to come in and hear me out. Nicky, Matt, Kal, Chris, Frank. Um, where's Manuel?"

"He is at home watching the baby," said Nicole with a grin.

"Baby? Congrats, Nicky. That's incredible. Boy or girl?"

"It's a boy. We named him James. James Tiberius Franco."

"James Tiberius Franco. It has a nice ring to it," James said, beaming.

Kite jumped up on the bed and sat next to James.

"Now, it's time to start. I need all of you. We need to begin auditing all of the Black Sands projects. Let's put off any current project that could interfere, because I need all hands on deck. We have to find some way to get me back to the past and my home."

The Texas sun was dipping low, casting long shadows across the Tiberius homestead's porch, when a familiar white pickup rumbled up the drive. James squinted, recognizing the dust-caked vehicle as Khalid's. Kite, perched on the porch rail with a half-eaten apple, perked up, her eyes darting between James and the approaching figure. Khalid stepped out, his weathered face breaking into a grin as he tipped his cap.

"Thought I'd drop by, see how the new boss is holdin' up," he said, while motioning to Kite, his voice carrying that steady warmth James had come to rely on.

James waved him over, patting the new rocking chair beside him. He had decided that his dad's old chair needed company with Kite hanging around, and bought a new one for her at Cracker Barrel.

"Kal, you're a sight for sore eyes. Been a whirlwind since we got back."

He settled in, his gaze turned as he watched Kite scamper off to chase a stray cat.

"She's a spitfire, that one," he said, then turned to James, his tone shifting to something quieter, more serious.

"Yer plans for dealin' with McDermott and Geist are in full swing," Khalid said with a wink. "Yer doin' good, kid, but I see that weight in yer eyes. Yer carryin' more than this ranch now. Egypt's still gotta hold on ya, don't it?"

James nodded, his fingers tracing the armrest, the memory of Neferu's laughter flickering like a ghost in his mind's eye. Khalid leaned forward, resting his elbows on his knees, his voice dropping to a fatherly note.

"Listen, James, I've seen men break under less than what ya faced. Tombs, time jumps, corporate snakes; ya got grit, but don't let 'em grind ya down. That trust, this family, Kite, they're yer anchor now. Ya don't gotta figure it all out t'day. Take it slow, like back in the tunnels, one step at ah time. You've lost ah lot, but gained somethin' too." He clapped James's shoulder, firm but gentle.

"And hell, if ya need ta chase that pyramid 'gain, ya know I'm in. But don't forget ta breathe, son, yer home."

James met Khalid's eyes, feeling a knot loosen in his chest.

"Thanks, Kal. I needed that more than I realized, but you have to know this isn't home anymore."

Khalid chuckled, pulling a folded map from his pocket and an old survey with notes from Khufu, and placed them on the table.

"I came 'cross somethin' I thought might interest ya. I know ya had expected it ta take a few years fer the pyramid ta charge enough ta send the Black Sands crew. I noticed they were makin' lots of calls ta Maui, ya know, the scientists running the DKIST," said Khalid.

"That array monitors the sun for solar storms and possible solar flares. Are you telling me it's that simple? They were able to predict a large solar flare and were able to power the pyramid? Damn, that makes sense. Ramesses called it 'Netjer's Breath,' but that must be it. Kal, you know what this means? I might be able to do the same to get home."

"But ya said the time chamber was destroyed."

"Yeah, it was, but that doesn't mean I can't find another way."

"Thought ya might say that, but let's bring things back ta now and talk 'bout somethin' lighter. Kite's been askin' me 'bout video games. Maybe we can slay some Nazi zombies t'night?" said Khalid.

James smiled, the first real one in days, and nodded. With Khalid's steady presence beside him, the future felt a little less daunting.

End of Book 1 – The Pyramids of Time

Glossary

Terms

Akh - Restless Spirit

Ba - Soul of a Spirit

Deken - Ten Days (Week)

Desher - Sulfur

Haty-a - District Governor

Hem-netjer - High Priest

Heru - Day

Imi-r Mesha - Highest General

Imy-r niwt - Village Leader or Mayor

Ka - Spirit within a Tomb

Kalisaris - Dress

Ke-nee-oo - Palanquin

Kite - Unit of Weight, often Currency

Kohl - Dark Eye Makeup

Lah - Moon

Ma'at - Truth and Justice

M'u - Water

Netjer - God

Netjeru - Gods

Ra - Sun

Renpet - Year

Seba - Stars

Sem - Funeral Priest

Shendyt - Kilt-Type Clothing

Ta - Earth

Tjaty - Vizier

Wen-ku - Slave or Peasant Garb

Wepet-ur - Opening of the Tomb Ceremony

Wesekh - Beaded Ornamental Collar

Places

Khemenu-Ka - Town at Giza, later Per-hotep

Lpet-resyt - Luxor Temple

Lpet-sut - Karnak Temple

Men-maat-te HwtSeti I - Temple at Abydos

Men-nefer - Memphis

Per-hotep - Fictional City Built by Yemhotep

Waset - Luxor City

Afterword

I have always wanted to author a book, but could never seem to get motivated to actually start typing. I wrote this story after waking from an amazing dream, one of those dreams that comes to you when you are exhausted but can't fully fall asleep. When you are not completely conscious and your mind is running one hundred miles an hour and you can direct the flow of your mind's eye.

I have always loved stories about time travel that incorporate aspects of real science with a whole lot of imagination and mythology mixed in. This book has been a labor of love, as they say. I hope you enjoyed reading it as much as I did writing it.

This is the first book in a series that I hope to write for years to come. For more information, you can find me on social media as D.C. Bond or my website at www.bond-007.com.

Exploring Theories of Quantum Entanglement

Quantum entanglement happens when a few pairs or groups of particles become intertwined (entangled) and interact with each other in a way that the real quantum state of the matching particles cannot be shown or described as being independent of the state of each other, even when great distances separate them.

Albert Einstein famously referred to this activity as "spooky action at a distance." Later experiments were performed in which physicists measured one entangled particle, which instantaneously affected its partner, no matter how far apart the two particles were. This effect confused Einstein, as it seemed to defy his understanding of classical physics, where nothing, including information, can travel faster than light. Entanglement suggests a strange relationship between particles that transcends physical space and time.

Throughout my life, I have always been aware of certain perceived mystical powers and their associations with objects, specifically pyramids. Many "New Age" beliefs state pyramids can concentrate and focus electromagnetic energy from the Earth and the cosmos. While I may not buy into all these theories, they are fun to explore in science fiction.

Today, some people use items shaped like pyramids for meditation and healing, believing that their geometry enhances healing through cosmic energies that are entangled with human consciousness. These theories have extraordinarily little or no empirical evidence to support their claims. However, I can think of many things that make sense and have little evidence or data to support them. Perhaps, someday, physical science will catch up to Quantum Theory and give us some explanations other than hyperbole. Until then, let us use our imagination.

Various civilizations have built pyramids all over the globe. There are dozens, if not hundreds, built throughout Mesoamerican civilizations. Many more have been discovered throughout Asia and Africa. Let's apply some of our newfound quantum theory to the Great Pyramid of Khufu. We don't know when the pyramids were originally constructed, nor do we know exactly why they were built. It is strange that ancient peoples used construction techniques that are completely unknown to us and built these mega structures without using our modern technology. Even with our current machinery, the construction of the Pyramids of Giza would be a huge undertaking.

Three of these pyramids were constructed in a pattern that seems to align with the stars in Orion's belt. The Great Pyramid of Khufu, the largest of the three, stands approximately 481 feet tall today. It was originally taller, but erosion has reduced its height. It is one of the last "Seven Wonders of the World" that still exists.

When we apply quantum entanglement to Khufu, we can theorize some possible explanations for its existence. If it was built using technology we are unaware of, perhaps that technology extended far beyond the mere construction techniques and architecture. What if it could collect and store electromagnetic energy, harnessing its power?

Electromagnetic energy travels through space or matter in the form of waves and particles. They are created by the oscillation of electric and magnetic fields. Electromagnetic energy spans a wide spectrum, including radio waves, microwaves, infrared, visible light, ultraviolet (UV), X-rays, and gamma rays. The type of electromagnetic energy depends on its wavelength and frequency. Shorter wavelengths correspond to higher frequencies and higher energy.

When we talk about electromagnetic energy from the Sun, we're primarily referring to the solar radiation it emits, which includes infrared (heat), visible light, and a smaller portion of ultraviolet light. This energy results from nuclear fusion in the Sun's core, where hydrogen atoms combine to form helium, releasing vast amounts of energy in the process. This energy travels to Earth as electromagnetic waves and is the primary driver of life and climate. At certain times, the sun experiences periods of storms, increasing the release of electromagnetic radiation. These storms can produce large solar flares that expel so much radiation that they can destroy modern electronics.

Suppose the parts of the pyramid, or its specific location, were somehow entangled with other sites, structures, or cosmic events throughout time. A pyramid could be constructed with an understanding of quantum theory, far beyond what we know today. Perhaps a pyramid is a cosmic node in a network of similar structures.

If these theories are true, they would be capable of sending or receiving information from the past, present, and even the future. Could this explain the many great technological leaps that various civilizations have experienced? With enough power, it may be possible to use these nodes as a means to entangle more than just a few particles or information. With enough power, could actual matter be transferred between nodes? It would function like a wormhole, allowing matter transfer between the entangled nodes in space and time. Maybe someday we'll know.

Acknowledgements

I want to express my heartfelt gratitude to my incredible wife, whose unwavering support and meticulous editing brought this story to life. Her patience, sharp eye, and love for storytelling polished every page, turning my dream into a reality.

To my two daughters, your creativity and courage in speaking your minds are a source of inspiration. This book would never have been started without you. It is as much yours as it is mine, a testament to the love and strength we share as a family.

To Jason and Jayden, thanks for always being available and letting me bounce ideas off you.

I also want to thank those of you who read the early drafts and provided amazing feedback. Specifically, Sue, Pam, Bob, Aloisia and Tyler Lenz. You all had wonderful ideas to help the plot flow. I also need to thank Amber, Hannah, and Martha for that final proofreading push. I know you all have little ones to care for, and your time is valuable.

www.ingramcontent.com/pod-product-compliance
Lightning Source LLC
Chambersburg PA
CBHW070836260626

47170CB00007B/2387